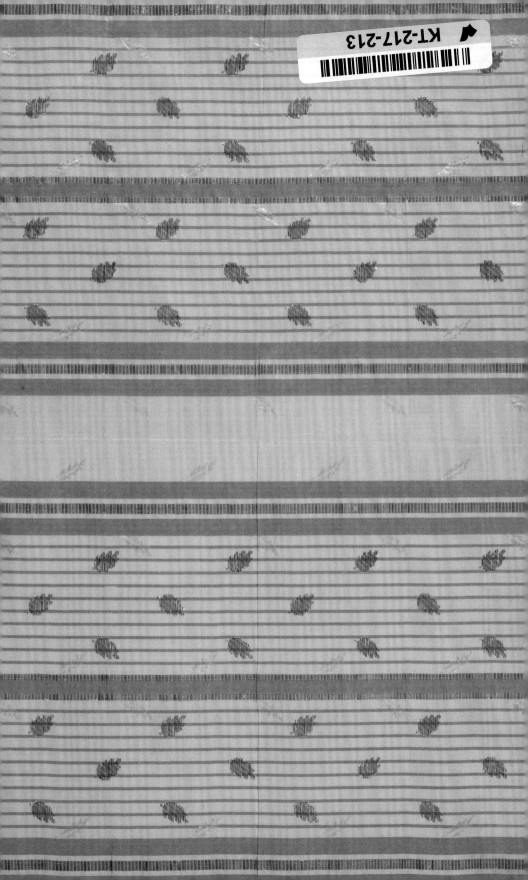

The Mermaid and Mrs. Hancock

The MERMAID *and* Mrs. HANCOCK

Written by

IMOGEN HERMES GOWAR

A History in THREE VOLUMES

LONDON:

Printed for Harvill Secker:

An Imprint of VINTAGE BOOKS, *20 Vauxhall Bridge Road.*

MM.XVIII.

HARVILL
Secker

3 5 7 9 10 8 6 4 2

Harvill Secker, an imprint of Vintage,
20 Vauxhall Bridge Road,
London SW1V 2SA

Harvill Secker is part of the Penguin Random House group of companies
whose addresses can be found at global.penguinrandomhouse.com

Penguin
Random House
UK

First published by Harvill Secker in 2018

penguin.co.uk/vintage

A CIP catalogue record for this book is available from the British Library

ISBN 9781911215721 (hardback)
ISBN 9781911215738 (trade paperback)

Typeset in 11.25/16.5 pt Adobe Caslon Pro by Jouve (UK), Milton Keynes
Printed and bound in Great Britain by Clays Ltd, St Ives PLC

Penguin Random House is committed to a sustainable future
for our business, our readers and our planet. This book is made
from Forest Stewardship Council® certified paper.

VOLUME I   1

VOLUME II   177

VOLUME III   317

EPILOGUE   481

VOLUME I.

ONE

September 1785

Jonah Hancock's counting-house is built wedge-shaped and cof-
fered like a ship's cabin, whitewashed walls and black skirting, beam
pegged snugly to beam. The wind sings down Union Street, rain-
drops burst against the windowpane, and Mr Hancock leans forward
on his elbows, cradling his brow in his hands. Rasping his fingers
over his scalp, he discovers a crest of coarse hair the barber has
missed, and idles over it with mild curiosity but no irritation. In
private, Mr Hancock is not much concerned with his appearance; in
society, he wears a wig.

He is a portly gentleman of forty-five, dressed in worsted and
fustian and linen, honest familiar textures to match his threadbare
scalp, the silverish fuzz of his jowls, the scuffed and stained skin of
his fingertips. He is not a handsome man, nor ever was one (and as
he perches on his stool his great belly and skinny legs give him the
look of a rat up a post), but his meaty face is amiable, and his small
eyes with their pale lashes are clear and trusting. He is a man
well designed for his station in the world: a merchant son of a merchant's son – a son of Deptford – whose place is not to express
surprise or delight at the rare things that pass through his rough
hands, but only to assess their worth, scratch down their names and
numbers, and send them on to the bright and exuberant city across

the river. The ships he sends out into the world – the *Eagle*, the *Calliope*, the *Lorenzo* – cross and re-cross the globe, but Jonah Hancock himself, the stillest of men, falls asleep each night in the room in which he first drew breath.

The light in the office has a murky cast to it, full of storms. The rain comes down in sheets. Mr Hancock's ledgers are spread out before him, creeping with insect words and figures, but his mind is not on his work, and he is grateful for the distraction of a scuffling outside the office.

Ah, thinks Mr Hancock, *that will be Henry*, but when he turns around from his desk it is only the cat. She is almost upside down at the foot of the stairs, with her rear in the air, her hind paws splayed wide on the bottom step, and her forepaws pinning a squirming mouse to the hall floorboards. Her little mouth is open, teeth flashing in triumph, but her position is precarious. To right herself, he calculates, she must let go of her quarry.

'Whisht!' says Mr Hancock. 'Begone!' but she catches the mouse up in her jaws and prances across the hall. She is out of his sight, but he hears the thrum of her dancing paws and the dampish thud of the mouse's body hitting the floorboards as she flips it into the air again and again. He has watched her play this game many times, and always finds her enquiring, open-throated cry unpleasantly human.

He turns back to his desk, shaking his head. He could have sworn it was Henry coming down the stairs. In his mind's eye the scene has already taken place: his tall thin son, with white stockings and brown curls, pausing to grin into the office while all about him the dust motes sparkle. Such visions do not come to him very often, but when they do they always disturb him, for Henry Hancock died at birth.

Mr Hancock is not a whimsical man but he has never been able to shake the notion that, the moment his wife laid her head back on

4

her childbed pillow and sighed her last wretched breath, his life diverged from its proper course. It seems to him that the one he ought to have had continues very nearby, with only a thin bit of air and chance separating him from it, and every now and then he catches a glimpse of it as if a curtain has momentarily fluttered aside. In the first year of his viduity, for example, he once felt a warm human pressure against his knee during a card game, and looked down in fond expectation of a stout little child hauling itself to its feet beside his chair. Why was he so appalled to discover instead the left hand of Moll Rennie creeping along his thigh? On another occasion, a brightly painted toy drum caught his eye at a fair, and he had carried it nearly halfway home before he remembered that no small boy was there to receive it. Fifteen years have now passed, but in rare unguarded moments Mr Hancock might hear a voice carried in from the street, or feel some tugging at his clothes, and his immediate thought is *Henry,* as if he had had a son all along.

He is never visited by his wife Mary in this way, although she was a great blessing to him. She was thirty-three when she died, a placid woman who had seen much of this world and was amply prepared for the next: Mr Hancock does not doubt where she has gone, or the possibility that he might one day join her there, and for him this is enough. He only mourns their child, who passed so swiftly from birth to death, exchanging one oblivion for another like a sleeper rolling over.

From upstairs comes the voice of his sister Hester Lippard, who visits every first Thursday to fossick through his larder and laundry and linen press, and exclaim at what she discovers there. A wifeless brother is a troublesome inheritance, but one by which her children may one day profit: if Mrs Lippard does him the charity of removing her youngest from school to serve as his housekeeper, it is in reasonable expectation of reward.

5

'Now you see the sheets have taken mildew,' she is saying. 'If you had stored them as I advised you ... did you note it all in your pocketbook?'

The faintest of mumbles in response.

'Well, did you? This is not for my benefit, Susanna, but for your own.'

A silence, in which he pictures poor Sukie with her head hanging, her cheeks livid.

'I declare, you make more trouble than you save me! So where is your red thread? Where? Is't lost again? And who will pay for more, do you think?'

He sighs and scratches. Where is the fruitful family to fill the rooms of this house, which his grandfather built and his father made fine? The dead are here, without a doubt. He feels their touch everywhere in its pitched floorboards and staircase spine, and in the voices of the church bells, St Paul's at the front door, St Nicholas's at the back. The hands of the shipwrights are alive here in the long curves of its beams, which recall the bellies of great ships; its lintels carved with birds and flowers, angels and swords, testament for ever to the labour and visions of men long dead.

There are no children here to marvel in their turn at the skill of Deptford woodcarvers, unmatched in all the world; nor to grow up to the rhythm of ships leaving the docks gleaming and laden, returning battered and ragged. Jonah Hancock's children would know, as Jonah Hancock knows, what it is to load one's faith and fortune on board a ship and push it off into the unknown. They would know how a man who awaits a ship, as Mr Hancock now does, is distracted by day and wakeful by night, prone to fidgeting, with a bitter taste rising in the back of his throat. He is snappish with his family or else overly sentimental; he hunches over his desk scratching out the same calculations over and over again. He bites his nails.

What knowledge is all this if it dies with Jonah Hancock? What good his joys and sorrows if there is nobody to share in them; what purpose to his face and voice if they are only to be assigned to dust; what value to his fortune if it withers on the vine with no sons to pluck it down?

And yet sometimes there is something more.

All voyages start the same, when men in coffee-houses gather about, and scratch their chins, and weigh risk against obligation.

'I'll go in on that,' says one,

'And I,'

'And I,'

for in this world there is no achieving anything all alone. Cast in thy lot and share the purse. And this is why a prudent man does no business with drunks, with rakes, with gamblers, with thieves, or anybody with whom God might have cause to deal severely. You cast in your lot and you share his sin. And it is so easy for a little craft to be dashed against the rocks. So easy for cargo to settle five fathoms deep in the dark. Sailors' lungs may brine and their fingers may pickle; all that protects them is God's cupped hand.

What does God say to Mr Hancock? Where is the Calliope, *whose captain has sent no word in eighteen months? The summer trails away. Every day the mercury drops. If she does not return soon she will not return, and the blame may well lie with him. What has he done, that might demand such punishment? Who will throw in their lot with his if they suspect him ill-favoured?*

Somewhere a tide is turning. In that place where no land can be seen, where horizon to horizon is spanned by shifting twinkling faithless water, *a wave humps its back and turns over with a sigh, and sends its salted whispering to Mr Hancock's ear.*

This voyage is special, the whisper says, a strange fluttering in his heart.

It will change everything.

And all of a sudden, in his silent counting-house, this faded man with his brow cupped in his hands is gripped by a great childish glee of anticipation.

The rain eases. The cat crunches on the skull of the mouse. And as she slaps her tongue about her muzzle, Mr Hancock permits himself to hope.

TWO

Owing to the rain it is unlikely that many birds are abroad, but perhaps a crow has just crept from the rafters of Mr Hancock's house, and now fans out its bombazine feathers and tips its head to one side to view the world with one pale and peevish eye. This crow, if it spreads its wings, will find them full of the still-damp breeze gusting up from the streets below: hot tar, river mud, the ammoniac reek of the tannery. And if it hops from its ledge and rises above the rooftops of Union Street it will come first and swiftly to the docks, the cradles of ships-to-be, which even in their infancy rear above all the buildings. Some, polished and tarred, flags a-flutter and figurehead winking, strain to be launched; others, mere ribs of fresh-stripped wood with only air between them, lie in dry-dock vast and pale and naked as the skeletons of whales.

If, from here, this crow steers itself north-west following the turn of the river, and if it flies for six miles without pause . . . well, is this likely, for a crow? What are their habits? What is the range of their territory? *If* it were to do this, coasting across the sky as the clouds recede, it would approach the city of London, the river crenelated on each bank with docks large and small, some built tall from yellow stone, some of sagging black wood.

The wharves and bridges pen the water in tight, but after the storm it squirms and heaves. The white-sailed ships strain upon it, and the watermen have gathered their bravado to steer their little crafts away from the bank and race across the current. As the sun creeps out, this conjectured crow will fly over the winking glass of the Southwark melon farms; the customs house, the tiered spire of St Bride's, the milling square of Seven Dials, and eventually come upon Soho. As it alights on a Dean Street gutter, its shadow will briefly cross the first-floor window of one particular house, stealing the daylight from the room within so that the face of Angelica Neal is momentarily lost in darkness.

She sits at her dressing table as cool and fragrant as a rosewater custard, picking at a bowl of hothouse fruit while her friend – Mrs Eliza Frost – tweaks the last scorched curl-paper from her hair. She has been laced back into her stays and half-draped in a powdering robe, but there is a flush of the bedroom in her cheeks, and her eyes are dragged irresistibly back to her own dimpling reflection as if to the face of a lover. A canary skips and whistles in its cage, mirrors twinkle all about, and her table is strewn with ribbons and earrings and tiny glass bottles. Each afternoon they carry it from the dark dressing room into the sunny parlour so as to spare their candles, 'But these measures will soon be unnecessary,' says Angelica, as a little storm of hair powder flies up around her. 'When the season begins, and there are more places to be seen – more people to see me – our living will be far easier.' On the floor the crushed triangles of curl-paper are dense with Wesleyan homily, snipped as they are from pious tracts passed out daily to the whores of Dean Street.

'Humph,' says Mrs Frost, who now clutches a hank of her friend's yellow hair and is busy teasing it all into a great soft heap on top of her head. She has to remove the pins nipped between her lips before she can reply properly. 'I hope you are right.'

They have been in these rooms for a fortnight, paying with notes peeled off a wedge which, although jealously protected by Mrs Frost, is swiftly diminishing.

'How you do worry,' says Angelica.

'I don't like it. Money coming in spits and spots. Not knowing one day to the next . . .'

''Tis not *my* fault.' Angelica opens her eyes very wide. Her chemise slips an inch down her bosom. It is not Angelica's fault: until a month previous she was in the keeping of a middle-aged duke, who doted upon her for the three years they lived together, but in his will forgot her.

'And you reduced to letting any man make free with you,' says Mrs Frost. The sunlight flashes off the back of the brush. Mrs Frost is tall and narrow, the skin of her face unpainted and very smooth and taut, like kidskin. It is difficult to age her, for her person is like her dress, neat and plain, sponged lightly clean each night, kept carefully from the world.

'Any man who can afford it, which keeps the numbers down. Listen, my dove, I do know your opinion but since I pay your way I am not obliged to hear it.'

'You are compromising yourself.'

'How else am I to keep us in stockings? You answer me that, you who are so conscientious in your bookkeeping. And don't you draw in your breath, for I know what you will say. You would lecture me on my extravagance, but no man hands banknotes to a drab who looks as if a sixpence would content her. I have my appearance to consider.'

'You have nothing to do with the accounts,' says Mrs Frost. 'You cannot imagine how this complicates my life.'

A little flash of electricity whisks through Angelica's body. She grips the arms of her chair and stamps her feet on the floorboards, so the curl-papers leap reanimated, and scratch their printed wings together. 'My life is very complicated, Eliza!'

'Keep your temper.' Another vigorous burst of powder.

'Leave off!' Angelica swats her hands about her head. 'You will cover up all its colour.' Angelica is protective of her heavy gold hair, for it was once the making of her. In her tenderest youth she found herself assistant and model to an Italian hairdresser, and (according to legend) it was from him that little fat Angelica learned not only the art of grooming but also the art of love.

The women are silent. At moments of impasse, they know better than to talk it out: they retreat resentfully back into their own heads, as pugilists to their corners. Mrs Frost shakes an armful of paper into the fire, and Angelica turns back to the fruit bowl, popping grapes off their stems one by one, gathering them into her fist. She licks their juice off the heel of her hand. The sunlight slanting through the window is warm on the down of her cheek. She is twenty-seven and still beautiful, which owes something to luck and something to circumstance and something to good sense. Her bright blue eyes and voluptuous smile are gifts of Nature; her body and mind are unmarked by the toils she might have known as a wife; her skin is clear, her grot fragrant, and her nose still whole thanks to the little pouches of sheep gut she keeps in her cabinet, tied with green ribbons and carefully rinsed after each use.

'Dying was the best thing he could have done,' she says to Mrs Frost, as a peace offering. 'And just in time for the season.'

Her companion remains silent.

Angelica is not to be deterred. 'I am entirely independent now.'

'That is what troubles me.' Mrs Frost is tight-lipped still but she advances again on Angelica's hair.

'What fun I shall have, indebted to nobody!'

'Supported by nobody.'

'Oh, Eliza.' Angelica can feel her friend's cool fingers upon her scalp; she pulls free and twists in the chair to look up into her face.

'Three years I have seen nobody! No society, no parties, no fun. *Kept*, in a dull little parlour.'

'He kept you very generously.'

'And I am not ungrateful. But I made sacrifices, you know: that artist who put my picture in the Academy. He would have painted me a hundred times if the duke had not forbidden him. May I not now enjoy a little wildness?'

'Hold still or I shall never be done.'

Angelica leans back in her chair. 'I have been in more precarious positions than this. I have been all alone in the world since I was only fourteen.'

'Yes, yes.' Mrs Frost – before she was Mrs Frost – had swept the grates at Mrs Elizabeth Chappell's celebrated Temple of Venus, while Angelica Neal – before she was Angelica Neal – danced naked.

'Well, don't it follow? If one man can settle on me, so will others. But now is the time to be out in society; I must place myself in the right circles; show my face everywhere until it is well known again, for really that is what is vital. None of the very great courtesans are especially beautiful, you know, or not many of them. I *am* beautiful, am I not?'

'You are.'

'Well, then,' Angelica says. 'I will be a success.' She sinks her teeth into a peach and sits back to watch her reflection chew and swallow.

'I only wonder—'

'I do believe that men find me more attractive than ever,' Angelica plunges on. 'I need not be a mercenary, fawning over any body who will have me. I am in a position to make my own choice.'

'But will you not—'

'I think the blue ribbon for my hair.'

Outside on the street there is a great commotion. Bouncing

along the cobbles comes a sky-blue landau emblazoned on each side with a bare-breasted golden sphinx. Angelica jumps up. 'She is here! Take off your apron. No, put it back on. I won't have you mistaken for one of the party.' She flies to the window, divesting herself of her powdering robe's smocky folds as she goes.

The sun is sinking, infusing the street below with a honeyish haze. In the landau, amongst a clutch of young ladies in white muslin, rides Mrs Chappell herself, the abbess of King's Place. She is built like an armchair, more upholstered than clothed, her bolster of a bosom heaving beneath cream taffeta and gold frogging. When the landau comes to a halt she staggers to her feet, arms outspread and rings a-twinkle. Two negroes in sky-blue livery hop from the footplates to help her descend.

'New servants again, poor dupes,' says Angelica, watching them each taking an elbow while the girls heave at the swags adorning her vast rump. 'They don't know yet that she pays them half what they are worth.' The landau is remarkable well sprung and Mrs Chappell lurches onto the cobbles in a flash of starched lace: several tiny dogs scamper forth; the girls spill after them; and all together they caper in the street, a festival of plumed tails and plumed hats as Mrs Chappell staggers in her footmen's grip. 'Canny of her, to employ those blacks so lately arrived from America that they mistake their own value. Imagine, Eliza! Delivered from bondage to *her* employ.'

These shining visitors to Dean Street do not go unmarked. A washerwoman with a bundle on her back hisses through her teeth, but her apprentice, hair scraped up under her cap, stands stock-still and stares. Four boys set up a whooping, and men raise their hats or lean on the handles of their barrows and grin. The girls dimple smugly, swishing their skirts this way and that, their fans in constant motion: they incline their necks and turn out the white skin of their forearms. Angelica hauls the window open and leans out, shading her eyes with one hand. 'My dear Mrs Chappell!' she calls, which sets the girls off fluttering ever more vigorously, and turns all heads up to the window. The sun blazes in Angelica's hair. 'How kind of you to visit me!'

'Polly!' barks Mrs Chappell. 'Kitty! Elinor!' and the girls stand to attention, fans waving, bright-eyed.

'Eliza,' hisses Angelica, 'we must move this table.' Mrs Frost starts heaping ribbons and jewels upon it.

'A flying visit,' calls Mrs Chappell, pressing her hand to her bosom with the effort of projection.

'Come up, come up!' cries Angelica, the attention of Dean Street pinned upon her. 'Have a saucer of tea.' She pulls back from the window. 'Christ, Eliza! Have we any tea?'

Mrs Frost whips from her bosom a twist of pink paper. 'We always have tea.'

'Oh, you are an angel. A darling. What would I do without you?' Angelica seizes one end of the table. Mrs Frost the other, and thusly they bear it between them, shuffling as if they were hobbled so as not to dislodge its slew of trinkets. The fruits in the bowl bounce and tremble, and the mirror rattles on its stand.

'You know what *she* is come for,' Angelica pants. 'And are we in accord?'

'I have made my opinion plain.' Mrs Frost attempts primness, but she is trotting backwards while carrying a laden table, and must keep flicking glances over her shoulder to avoid reversing into the wall.

'Give me time and I will set your mind at ease.' In the dressing room, they manoeuvre the table around Mrs Frost's hard little cot. 'Hurry, hurry! Put it anywhere, we shall have time to straighten up when they have gone. Now run, *run*, and let them in. Remember to wipe the saucers before you pass them around, Maria dusts like a slut.'

Mrs Frost vanishes swift as a will-o'-the-wisp, but Angelica lingers in the gloomy dressing room, pondering herself in the mirror. From a distance she looks well – small and elegant – and she goes closer, pressing her palm against the tabletop to lean in. The glass is cold and her breath makes a little fog which blooms and shrinks across her reflection. She watches her pupils expand and contract, studies the edges of her lips which are chafed pink from the business of the afternoon. The skin around her eyes is as white and unlined as the inside of an eggshell, but she has a tiny crease in each cheek like the indent of a fingernail, and one between her eyebrows which deepens when she frowns at it. She can hear the girls giggling in the corridor downstairs, and Mrs Chappell's admonishments: 'What giddiness! Such unruliness in the street – did I teach you to behave in such a way?'

'No, Mrs Chappell.'

Angelica cracks her knuckles. She goes back into the parlour and chooses a chair to recline on, spreading her skirts out carefully.

'And will you be proud of yourselves, when some clever soul puts it into print? When it's written up in *Town and Country* that Mrs Chappell's nuns, the cream of England's girlhood, play leapfrog in the street like a mob of brewers' daughters? Well, I never, *well*, I never. Come, Nell, I must lean on you, these stairs are beyond my powers today.'

Breathing stertorously she enters Angelica's apartment, supported by the red-headed Elinor Bewlay.

'Oh, dear Mrs Chappell!' Angelica cries. 'So glad – so pleased. What a pleasure to see you.' This is by no means untrue: Mrs Chappell is as near a thing to a parent as Angelica knows, and it should not be supposed that their line of trade diminishes their affection. Bawds are not, after all, the only mothers to profit by their daughters.

'Sit me down, girls, sit me down,' snorts Mrs Chappell, and she labours towards a tiny japanned chair, with Angelica and Miss Bewlay clutching at her arms like girls struggling with a marquee in a high wind.

'Not that one!' gasps Mrs Frost, her eyes darting in horror between the chair's spindly legs and Mrs Chappell's bulk.

'Over here!' squeaks dark-eyed Polly, the quadroon, dragging an armchair from the corner and sliding it into Mrs Chappell's path at the last possible moment. The bawd, although sizeable, enhances her natural bulk with a vast cork bum beneath her petticoats, which emits a cloud of dust and a hollow thud as it hits the seat. She subsides with a long wheeze. Winded, she flaps her hands at her left foot, and Polly lifts it gently to rest on a stool.

'My *dear*,' huffs Mrs Chappell when she has found her breath. Her lips are mauve. 'My Angelica. We are just returned from Bath. I cut our stay short – I had to satisfy myself that you were well settled. I did not sleep for worrying, is that not so, girls? You cannot imagine my distress at the lodgings I heard you took.'

'For a very brief time,' objects Angelica. 'There was a financial misunderstanding.' She glances over at the girls, who perch together on the sopha, watching the conversation with their heads cocked. Their skin is free from blemish, and their little bodies neat as mannequins beneath their spotless Perdita gowns, delivered from nakedness by a whisper of white muslin and the slenderest of drawstrings.

'I have not introduced you to my Kitty,' says Mrs Chappell. She stretches out her hands to the smallest of the girls. 'Stand up, you.'

Kitty makes a studied curtsey. She is a spindly dazed-looking creature, with a long neck and large pale eyes, greyish like the rim on skimmed milk, her eyebrows dabbed on a shade too dark.

'Thin,' says Angelica.

'But an elegant frame,' says Mrs Chappell. 'We are feeding her up. I found her down at Billingsgate, covered in fish scales and reeking like low tide, ain't that right, girl? Turn around, then. Let Mrs Neal look at you.'

The girl's skirt makes a hushing sound: the scent of petitgrain rises up from its folds. She moves slowly and carefully. In the corner, Mrs Frost pours the tea, a musical arc, and Polly and Elinor pass out the bowls as their abbess talks in laboured snatches. She breathes as if she were singing an opera, exhaling through each phrase before sucking in another desperate lungful and plunging onwards. 'They told me she'd had smallpox. Very small pox indeed, says I, there's not a mark on her. Quality, this one. See how she holds herself. I did not teach her that: 'tis her natural bearing. Show her your ankles, Kitty.'

Kitty lifts her hem. Her feet are small and narrow, in little silver slippers.

'Does she speak?' asks Angelica.

'That is our next task,' grunts Mrs Chappell. 'She's a mouth like low tide too. She'll not open it again until I give her leave.'

They fall quiet in their assessment of the child; or at least they leave off speaking, for Mrs Chappell wheezes like a set of bagpipes even in repose.

'She will be a deal of work,' remarks Angelica.

'I like them this way. The middling girls are the ones as cause me trouble. Been sent off to a dame school. Taught the pianoforte. Got their own ideas about what delicate manners are. Give me street urchin over tradesman's daughter, every time. Save me undoing somebody else's work.'

'*I* was a tradesman's daughter.'

'And look at you! Not one thing nor another. You chase every fancy that comes upon you. I can hardly bear to discover what has become of you from one week to the next; if you're set to be married, or running a few good visitors. Or you are reduced to a street-walker –' she is breathless for a moment, fixing Angelica sternly with a pouchy wet eye – 'which is not what I trained you for.'

'I never did such a thing,' protests Angelica.

'I hear what I hear.'

'I may on occasion have happened to *walk* in the *street*. But which of us has not been driven to that?'

'Not my girls. Do you consider how your reputation reflects on mine?' She clears her throat and moves on to business. 'Here, Mrs Neal, I know that your misfortune is through no fault of your own, and that you are thought well of by many of our best gentlemen. Ever since your bereavement they have been asking after you. "Where is our favourite little blonde?" they say. "Where is our dear playmate with the beautiful voice?" What can I tell them?' She presses Angelica's hand to her crêped bosom.

'You can tell them my address,' says Angelica. 'You see that I am well set up here. And so near the square, 'tis terrible genteel.'

'Oh, Angelica, but you all alone! It grieves my heart to see you unprotected. My dear girl, we have room for you in the nunnery – we will always have room. Will you not consider returning to us?'

The girls Polly, Elinor and Kitty have been exposed to a level of training more rigorous and exclusive than near any in the world, but when they feel themselves free from scrutiny they retreat into child-hood, and now they bounce gently on the sopha, buoyed by one another's fidgeting. They are impressed by Angelica's glamour, and want her as an elder sister, to sing duets with them and teach them new ways with their hair. Late at night, when the men are at last stupefied, perhaps she will pass out cups of chocolate and tell tales of her own scandalous girlhood. They watch as Mrs Chappell leans forward to put a hand on Angelica's. 'It would be a weight off my mind to have you under my roof once more.'

'And a weight in your purse, to advertise my services,' Angelica says, smiling her finest.

Mrs Chappell is an expert in frank conversation, but usually on her own terms. 'Certainly not,' she splutters. 'Certainly that is not my first concern. And what of it? 'Tis protection I offer you, first and foremost. Think of it, dear. A dedicated physician; a steady flow of the right sort of men; the wrong sort gain no admission. No bills. No bailiffs.' She is watching Angelica carefully, intent as a she-cat at hunt. 'It is a dangerous city we live in.' She pats Angelica's hand once more and continues jovially, 'And when you find a new protector – well, say no more. You will be released from my service in a moment.'

In the corner, Mrs Frost's face is a picture of desperation. She is trying to catch Angelica's eye, but Angelica cannot look at her. She thinks, *I am not so young as these girls. I have only a few seasons left to show myself at my best.*

At length, she says, 'I knew you would ask me back. And, madam, I am grateful for your remembrance of me. You are a true friend.'

'I mean only to help you, my pet.'

Angelica swallows. 'Then may I direct your help to where it is most needed?'

This is a request not many mothers are receptive to. Mrs Chappell hems.

'As a prudent businesswoman,' says Angelica, 'I trust you have carefully considered where my value lies. Is it in my continued presence in your house? Or is it in my rising in the world?'

She pauses. She watches the pulse quivering in Mrs Chappell's jowls. The girls look on, complacently fed and clothed. Mrs Frost has taken her seat on the little stool by the door. Now Angelica sees her press her hand to her bosom, in fact to the hidden pocket in her stomacher, where she keeps her dwindling pad of banknotes.

'I propose a middle way,' she says. Nobody speaks. The next leap is a great one for her, but she waits three, four seconds before continuing slowly. 'I mean to trade on my own bottom. 'Tis the right moment for me, surely you see that.'

Mrs Chappell considers. Her tongue – surprisingly pink, surprisingly wet – flicks briefly across her grey lips. She says nothing.

'As a *friend*,' Angelica continues, 'I will do you the favour of appearing at your house. You may have it known that you can send a chair for me any time it pleases the company, but in return I want my liberty. I trust that the next few years of my life may be very fruitful: I have proved myself a good mistress, and for the right gentleman I can be so again, if I am free to receive him.'

'You think you are able to make your way alone?'

'Not all alone. Madam, I shall need your help. But you launched me in this world; would you not have me press on? And to what would I owe my success, if not your methods?'

The abbess's smile is slow in coming, but when it does she fairly beams. Her gums are pale and expansive, her teeth as yellow and oblong and all-of-a-type as the keys of a harpsichord.

'I have trained you well,' she crows. 'You are no mere whore – you are a woman of substance, as I always hope my girls will be, as fine a little frigate as ever I launched on London town. Kitty, Elinor, Polly – especially you, Polly – mark this. You have the opportunity to ascend, girls, and ascend you must. Ambition! Always ambition! No streetwalkers, mine.'

Angelica's heart pounds under her stays. For a moment the world swims around her: she has never dared talk back before. After Mrs Chappell and her girls have left, waving and calling out endearments, she flings herself down on the sopha in jubilation.

'This proves it,' she says to Mrs Frost, who is clearing away the tea things in quick, jerky movements, her head down. 'She cannot afford to make an enemy of me. She gives me my way.'

'You should not have rejected her,' says Mrs Frost. Her lips are tight, her words little.

'Eliza?' Angelica sits up. She tries to peer into her friend's face, but she will have none. 'Oh, Eliza, you are angry with me.'

'You might have considered our security,' spits Mrs Frost.

'We *are* secure. Or we will be. If I did not believe so before, I do now; Mother Chappell has an instinct for success.' She does not like her friend's brand of cold, tense rage: she rises and follows her across the room, beseeching, 'My dear, my dove, sit down here with me. Come, come.' She takes Mrs Frost by the shoulders and tries to steer her to the couch, but she is rigid as a Dutch doll under her cotton and calamanco. 'I swear to you I will keep us safe. We are on the up, you and I.'

It is as if she is a ghost, her voice unheard, her touch unfelt, while Mrs Frost ties her apron a little tighter around her waist, picks up the tray of the whores' leavings, and removes from the room.

'Oh no, no,' says Angelica. 'Do not leave me in this manner. Have pity.' But she hears Mrs Frost's steps retreating without so much as a pause, and reminds herself, *she will be enjoying this.* I, *begging* her. *What nonsense.* Out loud she spits, 'Suit yourself!' and then, going to the head of the stairs, shouts down, 'You are a foolish, stubborn woman! Surely you are.'

But Mrs Frost is long gone.

THREE

In the evening, Mr Hancock stays in by the fire with his niece Sukie as he has all week.

'Would you not go to an alehouse?' asks Sukie, and she can hardly be blamed, for he is not restful company. He cannot remain in his chair three minutes before rising as if a wasp has crept under his seat, to pace the parlour opening and closing boxes whose contents he has made himself familiar with five times over already; he leans upon the mantel and opens a book but its pages are gibberage to him and he lays it down again. Twice he goes to stand on the landing and has Bridget the maid hammer at the front door from without to satisfy him that no caller could possibly go unmarked. 'A few hours will not hurt,' Sukie pursues, thinking wistfully of her own plans for the evening, viz.: to make free with his tea caddy and skim spoonfuls of cream off the milk basin in the larder.

'But if there is news of the *Calliope*, and they cannot find me . . . ?'

'I should like to meet the man who ever succeeded in hiding in this town.'

'Hmm.' He sits down, his chin on his fist. Then he stands up again. 'Perhaps I had done better to have remained in the city. In the coffee-house, they will have the most reliable news.'

'Uncle, what difference does it make?' says Sukie. 'If word comes tonight, what can be done before the morning?' She is shrewd, like her mother; she quirks her eyebrow in the same way.

'I will know,' he says. 'I cannot be easy until I know.'

'And you are making certain that nobody else can be either. Sir, we may hear nothing for a good long time ...'

'No. It will be soon. I am certain.' And yes, he is quite certain. Every nerve of his body hums like a strung viol. He advances upon the window and looks out onto the darkening street.

'Your ceaseless mooning!' she exclaims, a phrase straight from her mother Hester's mouth, and his muscles go tight, for her white cap and pursed lips have melted forty years from the room as if she were his great sister and he a little boy. But Sukie sparkles with mischief. 'Aren't I just playing?' she says, and he is so relieved to breathe again that he lets out a guffaw.

'You saucy miss,' he says. 'What if I were to tell her how you ape her?'

'Then I might tell her of all the time you spend in taverns.'

'You never would.'

He acknowledges that it does him good to have a young person in his household. It gladdens him to hear her and Bridget's shrieks as they chase one another down the stairs, and to see them stroll out together on errands, arm in arm. He will even tolerate an apple-pie bed every now and then, for what else is to be expected of a girl of fourteen? In all other particulars Sukie is, after all, an excellent housekeeper, and infinitely preferable to the surly hirelings who came before her. If she were his own daughter he would have had her cast her sharp little mind over his ledgers, but he must assume that what she knows her mother must shortly know too. He has taken the precaution of buying her a fine silk day dress and allowing her to wear it about the house so that, by its constant rustling, he will know her presence.

Sukie, meanwhile, is secretly pleased to have been sent to her uncle: of all the situations that might have called for a spare daughter, this is the best by far. She dreads the day her brother will get another child on his fat wife and she, Sukie, will be called to Erith to scrub the nursery and mop drool. Here she has her own room, and she and Bridget find themselves often at their leisure, for a modest old man makes little work.

'Will I read to you, then?' she sighs. 'The evening will not pass itself.'

'Very well. Pope's essays, if you please.'

'Oh, yawn! Uncle, it don't please me even one bit. No. Choose something else.'

He sighs. 'I think you have something in mind.'

Indeed, she wastes no time in whipping from behind her chair a handsome little volume of the sort sold all down Fleet Street.

'This is a good one,' she says, bending close to the firelight to riffle through its pages. 'I am halfway through so you will have to guess at what adventures came before.'

'So many novels,' he wonders. 'Such a mob of Emilias and Matildas and Selinas: I had not thought the exploits of young ladies could take up so much print.

'I am addicted to them,' she says happily.

'*I* am not.' (But this is untruthful: he is a sentimentalist, and furthermore he enjoys Sukie's reading aloud. She has a high bright voice, and bobs her head with narrative energy.)

'You will like this one, Uncle! 'Tis full of excitement. And highly instructional.'

'Your mother is right, I allow you too much pin money. Your library is larger than my own.' Mr Hancock's books number eighteen in total, excluding his bible which may be classified as an artefact. Then, because he enjoys her company more than he does Alexander Pope's, he says, 'Well? Will you read it or no?'

She wriggles in her seat to get comfortable, and clears her throat: '*Heh-eh-eh-hem.*'

This is the moment there comes a great thundering at the door. Mr Hancock scrambles with his pipe, spilling tobacco over his shoes in his haste to rise.

'Sit down, Uncle!' says Sukie, who is on her feet too.

'It sounds important.'

'Even so, 'tis not proper for a gentleman to answer his own front door. You want to hire a man,' she says, and while he is stammering and grappling with the question of whether he is or is not a gentleman, and furthermore the cost of a liveried footman, and furthermore the absurdity of it, the hammering starts again.

'Don't go,' Sukie warns him, adding in her mother's voice, 'Bridget must see to it, that is what she is for,' but she cannot help kicking off her slippers and creeping across the room in her stockings. She nudges the door ajar with her toe and presses her face into the gap: she will have a clear view across the landing to the front door at the foot of the stairs.

'What do you see?' he asks.

'Nothing,' she says. 'Bridget!' she hisses into the darkness.

When the door sounds again it is with a true pounding: the panels tremble and the iron bars across the fanlight set up a high resonant hum.

'Open up, sir!' calls a voice from outside. ''Tis Tysoe Jones!'

'He himself! He has not sent a boy. Confound it. Something is amiss,' says Mr Hancock, and he barges past Sukie and down the stairs. It is dark as doomsday but he has run up and down these stairs since he first learned use of his feet, and there is a flutter of light behind him as his niece comes forth with a taper to light the sconces.

'He must not find our house unlit and we sitting only with the fire,' she is muttering.

Mr Hancock is down the stairs with a scuffle and a clatter, his lungs juddering in his chest as he repeats, 'Something is amiss. This is not the usual way of things,' and thinks, *what will we do now? If the ship is lost, and the cargo with it, ah! that will be a blow.* Is it one he can absorb? And what of his investors? Many men stand to be disappointed on his initiative. He is ticking over the figures in his head even as he reaches the hall and comes to the front door. *God be praised,* he thinks, *for bricks and mortar: if it comes to it I may sell my tenanted houses – this one too, but God forbid, God forbid, that I be the one to sell my father's house.*

He unlocks the door with palsied hands, the big key from his bunch first, followed by bolts top and bottom. The metal is heavy and uncooperative in his fingers: he wrenches once, twice, at the top bolt that always sticks – 'Oil, Sukie, fetch me oil for the door –' until it shoots home too fast, nipping the side of his palm so he curses. Outside, he can hear Captain Tysoe Jones stamping and swearing on the step.

'I am here!' Mr Hancock calls, clasping his injured hand.

As he opens the door, there is a little crescendo of light as Sukie puts the taper to the last of the candles, and here is Captain Tysoe Jones, ruggedly lit. He is in his sea clothes still, a jacket so faded by salt and sun that it appears dove-grey except for wedges of its old blue preserved under the lapels and the cuffs. His person is equally stained and faded: his face brick-coloured and tough as the soles of feet, with white creases about his eyes and mouth. The stubble on his cheeks twinkles as if a light frost has settled there. He clutches a canvas sack and looks mightily irritated.

'No time like the present,' he says.

'Forgive me. I could not – I was unable to –' Mr Hancock gestures at the door helplessly.

'Let me come in. I have walked from Limehouse.' His arms are crooked up to his chest, and he holds the sack as one holds a sleeping infant. 'I wish to stand no longer.'

'Did you come home on the *Calliope*?'

'No.' Captain Jones steps past him into the house. 'My letter explained everything.'

'I received no letter. I have had no word from you since you left London in January last. Nothing!'

Captain Jones removes his hat. He holds his bundle easily: it is neither heavy nor cumbersome. 'Good evening, young lady,' he says to Sukie.

Her curtsey is perfunctory, not her most elegant although she practises it often enough in the bubbled mirror that hangs above the fire. She has lost her composure and is dumb as a child, mouth firm shut and eyes wide. 'You must have tea,' she says at last.

'Ale,' says Mr Hancock, feeling cruel for correcting her. 'And have Bridget bring out the blade of beef.'

Sukie scuttles into the kitchen, her head ducked. He thinks, *if the ship is lost, her father has lost the five hundred pounds he invested.* What will Hester say?

He waves Captain Jones into the counting-house, remembering too late that the candles within are extinguished. He wishes to be a good host but in the thick-wadded darkness the words burst from his mouth: 'Where is my ship?'

'Hanged if I know. Might we have a little light?'

His hands tremble as he lights the candles on the great desk. 'And what of its cargo?'

'I took no cargo,' says Captain Jones, seating himself with a long groan of relief. 'I sent you a letter.'

But there has been no letter! He is stupefied within, and he must appear stupefied without, for Captain Jones prompts him: 'A letter.

I sent it with the *Rosalie,* which departed Macao shortly after I arrived.'

'The *Rosalie* was lost with all hands. I received no letter.'

'Ah. And so you will not know.' They sit in silence. Captain Jones fills his pipe. Its feeble light magnifies his frown of concentration as he draws upon it, darkness creeping into every crease and wrinkle. There is the suck and smack of his lips on the pipe stem, and the tock of the clock, and the tiny creaks and ticks of the old wooden house easing itself into a more comfortable position. The canvas bag sits on Captain Jones's lap all the while. 'I sold your ship, sir,' he says.

Mr Hancock's innards seem to liquefy. Sweat cools his palms. He reminds himself, *I trust this man. He is my agent; my fortunes are his. He will act only in my interest.*

'It was for good reason,' Captain Jones says. 'I found an extraordinary thing, but it cost more than I had. You always gave me leave to make whatever choices I see fit.'

'Aye, within the bounds of sensible cargo! A bolt of fabric, some novelty to try in the market; when one thing cannot be got, to substitute it with something of no greater risk ... To have lost my ship – that is my income.'

'And mine too.' Captain Jones is at his ease; he has had a long voyage to make himself comfortable with this new situation, and besides he has always had an eye for extravagances. He sits forward in his chair, and starts to grin. 'But I assure you, we shall recoup it numberless times! You never saw the like of what I have found for you. *Nobody* saw the like.'

'What is it?' He thinks, *some idiot thing I will not be able to sell. A kitten with two heads, or a new type of poison, or a set of obscene etchings that will put me in jail.*

'Where is the girl? Have her come in here.'

'Do not make a spectacle of this foolishness,' he sighs.

'This spectacle wants witnesses! Bring in your entire household. Light all the lamps.'

Mr Hancock is too rattled to stand up for himself any further. He stumps out to the hall but there is no need to shout out for Sukie. She and Bridget – this one bleary with sleep, her cap askew, she must have nodded off in the scullery again – are hovering by the door already, the tray of ale set down on the floorboards to keep it from rattling. In the darkness their faces are pale echoes of one another, two ovals turning to him in enquiry.

'You heard,' he says. 'Light the lamps.'

'Yes, sir,' says Bridget. He can hear the quiver in her voice: excitement has made her breath knot up in her throat. The pewter mugs on the tray clink and splosh as she picks it up, but her steps on the floorboards make no noise.

'Put your shoes on,' he says. 'Any body might think you had been eavesdropping.'

He brings the tray in himself and after scuffling for their slippers the girls follow him. Captain Jones has put the bag on the desk. By the way the cloth falls, Mr Hancock thinks there is no softness to the thing it conceals. Light as a bird and small enough to carry in the crook of a man's arm; how can it be worth a tall ship and all its promised cargo?

Behind him, Mr Hancock feels the girls shift closer together, for they are always touching, these girls, pressing against one another as kittens do when their mother leaves them. He hears the tentative movement that will be Bridget closing her hand around Sukie's elbow, and squares his shoulders. He is sorry that he has no kindly friend to touch his arm.

'On my voyages,' says Captain Jones, 'I have seen many strange things. Things that you cannot begin to imagine, ladies. I have seen cows with necks as tall as trees. I have seen ordinary-sized Chinean women with feet no bigger than hot cross buns. And I have—'

'Out with it,' Mr Hancock interrupts.

'Is it in the bag?' asks Sukie.

'You are a young lady of striking perspicacity.' Captain Jones observes the faces of his audience and sighs. 'Very well. Let us get this over with. Perhaps once you see the marvel I have brought to you, you will be more enthusiastic.'

Captain Jones eases the canvas away, and at first they cannot think what it is they see. For it is brown and wizened like an apple forgotten at the bottom of the barrel, or like the long-dead rats Mr Hancock once found bricked up in the kitchen wall, parched and cured by the elements, skin that cracked under the pressure of a thumb.

It is the size of an infant, and like an infant its ribcage is delicate and pathetic beneath its parchment skin, and its head is large, and its fists are drawn up to its face. But this is as far as the comparison may be extended.

For no infant has such fearful claws, and no infant such a snarl, with such sharp fangs in it. And no infant's torso ends in the tail of a fish.

'I bought it from a Dutchman I met in Macao,' says Tysoe Jones. 'And he from some Japanese fishermen, who captured it alive. I am sorry it has not survived.'

'A vicious thing,' says Sukie.

'You don't know that.'

'I know how it looks.' By the time she goes to her bed tonight, she will have forgotten that it is dead: in her imagination it already quivers with rage, clawing to escape a fishbowl, lashing the water in the face of its impotence. As surely as if she had seen it with her own eyes, she knows that the water around Java teems with thousands of little creatures just like it: she hears their hoarse cries and feels their fury.

'It can't harm you now,' says Captain Jones, but she stares at him. He spreads his hands. 'Didn't I bring it all the way across the ocean? And it did not sink me, as they say mermaids do, and it did not bite me, as I *know* that apes do.' He chuckles, but she is not reassured. 'Come closer. You must take a better look.'

They crowd in. There is a little squeak in the girls' breathing. They want to peer at it, inspect it, but at the same time they cannot but recoil. It is so perfectly dead.

'I don't see a single stitch on it,' says Mr Hancock, at length. 'No glue, no paint. How is it done?'

'*Done?* You think it is *done?*' Captain Jones is aggrieved. 'Like a conjuring trick? No, this is not *done*! It simply *is*. If it were done by any hand, 'twere God's alone.' He warms to his theme. 'After all the trouble I have taken! After I crossed half the earth twice! Which is, in a practical sense, the entirety of the earth. When, sir, have I ever brought you counterfeit?'

'No, never, never. Of course not. But you must appreciate that a mermaid – well, it is quite impossible.'

'Not so much as a blade of grass in all the tea I've ever borne safely to your warehouse,' Captain Jones laments.

'No, no, no. I did not mean to imply—'

'This is not a *toy*,' says Captain Jones. 'This is not a – a – a *bauble*. You cannot buy it at a fair. This is a genuine mermaid.'

'I do see that.'

'Take it in your hands, sir. Inspect it at your leisure. I assure you, you will not be disappointed.'

It lies on the table, desiccated and furious, its mouth open in an eternal apish scream. Mr Hancock cannot help checking its little breast for the twitch of a pulse.

'Go ahead. It is your mermaid. Pick it up.'

And so he must. He takes its tail in his two hands, and its scales rustle in his palms. It is so dry and so frail he suddenly has a peculiar urge to dash it to the ground, but he does nothing. 'Complete even to its fingernails,' he whispers. There are wisps of silky black hair on its head. He cannot think what to feel: surely this thing was a living being once.

'But what am I to do with it?' he ventures. 'This is not what I ordered. I shall have to disappoint a great many people.'

'They must expect disappointment every now and then. That's the nature of our business.'

'But this is unprecedented! My ship is sold voluntarily by its captain, who uses the proceeds to buy – on my account – the most dismaying oddity? Who will sympathise with that? Who will invest in my ventures again if I cannot assure them my ship is in safe hands?'

Captain Jones rubs the back of his neck. 'I did not think of that.'

Exasperation fizzes. 'Tysoe, Tysoe! A year and a half you have had to think on it! You abandon these knotty points to me, as you always have.' The tap of Sukie biting her nail recalls to him that she and the maid still linger. Mr Hancock does not mind discussing business in front of Bridget, who has neither the reason nor the interest to note it, but as for Sukie . . . 'Out, girls,' he says, setting the mermaid down gently on the desk.

'But may we not—'

'This is talk for men. You've your own duties to see to, have you not? Go, go.' He ushers them out protesting anon; after bolting the door he turns back to Captain Jones. '*Why* would you think this a cargo I would be glad to receive? I have no expertise—'

'What expertise?' Captain Jones says sharply. 'There is no expert in the world on this topic. It is a genuine mermaid, it'll want no extra work on your behalf. Only a fool could lose money on a mermaid.' He rakes his fingers through his hair. 'Only a fool could be angry to get one!'

'But what am I to do with it?'

'Why, exhibit it!'

'I am not a showman,' says Mr Hancock primly. 'I shall notify the Royal Society. This must be an important development for science, and I am not a scientific man either.'

Captain Jones waves his hand in disgust. 'And then how will you recoup your costs? Listen, 'tis common sense. Find a coffee-house, charge a shilling per view, and say three hundred view it in a day – I am being conservative – why that is ninety pounds in a week.' Seeing Mr Hancock shake his head, he hastens on. 'You might tour the country with it. Take it to fairs. The provinces' appetite for such things has never been quenched.'

'Ninety a week, though?' wonders Mr Hancock. He rents out each of the houses on Hancock Row – his modest empire of six dwellings on Butt Lane – for thirty-five shillings a month and thinks himself rich.

'Four thousand a year. Again, I am being conservative.'

This figure takes his breath away. That such an insignificant thing might hold such riches. 'And 'tis mine?' he croaks. He looks at the mermaid where it lies, tiny and frail; reaches to pick it up; mistrusts his hands and retreats once more.

''Tis yours. Not your partners', not your investors'. Only yours.' He has nobody to consult with. His partner, Greaves, with whom he shares offices and sometimes ventures, has taken the *Lorenzo* to what now designs itself the United States. There is old business to salvage there, new opportunities to seize, but Mr Hancock himself has no stomach for the America trade. Since the war such defection feels personal, and painful, and so his business with Greaves diverges evermore. Even if he were here, what could his advice be?

Hester, then. What will *she* say to his acquiring such a freak? 'The Hancocks have never run a circus,' her voice intrudes as if she were there at her elbow. 'We are reputable merchants of the finest wares; we do not deal in novelties. You will make us a laughing-stock.' Mr Hancock stares at it.

'What did you spend on the damn thing?' he asks at length.

'Twelve hundred. Now, now, do not look so – it was cheap at the price.'

'And you sold the ship for . . . ?'

'Six thousand.' To his credit Captain Jones betrays some fear. 'I had no choice! As God is my witness, you would have approved had you been there.'

Mr Hancock feels numbed, as if ice-water filled his veins. 'The *Calliope* was worth eight thousand,' he says softly, 'with her new mainmast.'

The captain hangs his head. 'I know it. She was a fine girl; I was sorry to part with her.'

Mr Hancock puts his hand to his face. 'So why did you?'

The captain takes a bill from his breast pocket and smooths it out carefully, holding it up to the light, his eyes conciliatory. 'There's a strongbox for you with four thousand eight hundred in't, all accounted for after I paid off the crew. I am an honest man.' He raises a hand to halt Mr Hancock's indrawn breath, and continues with insistent cheer, 'That will reimburse all your partners' investments on this voyage. You'll not lose face.'

'But you have lost me two thousand, and another two thousand in goods as ought to have come back with you. And you have lost me my ship.'

'Hancock, I swear. The mermaid . . . 'tis not a bag of magic beans, you know. There is real worth in this venture, if you will only take a chance on it.'

Mr Hancock sighs. 'I do not like chance. I try to be a steady man.'

'Well, 'tis out of your hands now.' Mr Hancock could strike him, the man is so provoking in his optimism as he declares, 'Providence has taken your ship, and given you a mermaid instead.'

'*You* did that.' He rises. 'Time you took your leave, I think.' He unbolts the door and passes ahead of his friend into the hall, where he finds the girls engaged in a level of industry unlike them even in broad daylight, and certainly at such an hour: Bridget dusts the banister with vigour and Sukie counts and re-counts the candles in their sconces.

'Come, Hancock,' Captain Jones pursues undeterred. 'Why not try it? Just for some little time? Recoup the cost of the ship – recoup it *double* – and then sell the little wretch on. It won't take no time.'

'Will you stay to eat?' pipes Sukie, making up for her earlier dumbness. 'Or sleep here tonight? I can have a bed made up.' The guest bed is always made up, as she well knows: it only wants for Bridget to sprinkle the stale sheets with lavender water.

'No, thank you. I am anxious to return to my wife.' Captain Jones's smile is fond and sad. 'I have not seen the smallest of my children since it was five weeks old, and now I hear he is a hearty little fellow, and can kick a ball, and count to eighteen. I shall push on to Woolwich tonight if it makes no odds to you.' His hand is on the latch; he steps out into the night. 'Now, Hancock, think about what I have said.'

Mr Hancock turns his face away. 'Aye,' he mumbles, 'I'll think on it.'

'We must celebrate this!' Jones grins confidingly. 'I've a mind to show my face in London again. All through this voyage I was sustained by the memory of a happy few hours I spent at a bathhouse on Long Acre. Is not a bagnio the perfect place to celebrate a mermaid?'

'Hush you, there are girls indoors.'

'Goodnight, sir. Goodnight!'

Mr Hancock locks the door carefully. In the counting-house he finds Sukie and Bridget squashed into his great chair at the desk, resting their chins on their arms as they stare at the mermaid. Bridget is yawning mightily, but Sukie's frown is alert.

'Begone,' he says. 'You are about my feet too much. 'Tis time you were a-bed.'

'What is a bagnio?' asks Sukie, stretching her legs out before her.

'A place where gentlemen go to get cupped.' He shepherds them away from the desk. 'And bled, and bathed – and suchlike. Healthful.'

'I see.' She is taking the snuffer to the candles while Bridget extinguishes those in the hall. He, nightlight in hand, bolts the shutters. 'And the mermaid,' she continues, 'will it make our fortune?'

'We do make our own fortunes.'

'The sea-captain said a great deal of money.'

'Well, what does it signify? You are just a little girl of this house; if you are keeping the bills in order and timely it is of no importance to you how much or little else there is in the pot.'

'Mother says 'tis a dreadful discourtesy to keep women out of the accounts. For if they are to be ruined they've a right to know about it.'

'Nobody is to be ruined,' he grunts. 'And you are to tell your mother nothing of this.'

'It is *all* of our concern. My papa's investment—'

'His investment is safe; if it is not he may take it up with me himself. Now I'll hear no more of it.'

She turns as she stands at the very last candle, half her face lit up and her hair floating in illuminated wisps. Her eyes flick to the dark desk where the mermaid's crooked fingers are silhouetted. 'And do we just leave it in here all night?'

'Why, 'tis not going anywhere.'

She shudders, and brings the snuffer down on the flame.

He makes his habitual nightly round of the house, candle aloft: through the kitchen to bolt the doors and shutters there, while Bridget makes ready her cot in the corner; then up the stairs with Sukie's skirts rustling at his heels to see that all is secure. They do not speak as they damp down the fire in the parlour and make fast the door leading to the attic so no thief picking his way along the rooftops may opportune himself.

When all is tight and dark, Mr Hancock repairs to his room on the second floor and draws the bolt to. He hangs his breeches and stockings on the chair as the building relaxes into silence: the grunt and sigh of its joists; the blunder of the wind in its chimneys. He is parting the curtains of his bed when he hears the stairs creak. He stops, and strains to listen. They creak again; closer; at the turn of the stair before the first floor, he judges, where the banister rail rattles in its fitting. From the locked and lightless rooms below, something approaches.

With his shirt hanging about his knees, he goes to the door and listens. Somewhere below him, a tap, a scratch, a fingertip on wood.

Through the floorboards he hears Sukie whimper; she has heard it too. Now she is moving across her own bedroom floor. The nape of his neck prickles. Surely she will not investigate. He is charged with protecting her, and yet even as her latch clicks he is rooted to the spot.

A whisper below: 'I am so glad you are awake!' It is Bridget. Of course – who else would it be, what other souls wander the house at this hour?

'You scared the wits out of me,' Sukie hisses.

'Aye, well. Think how I feel. I'll not sleep a wink, with that thing so nearby.'

'Ain't it peculiar?'

'It's not Christian, any body can see. Now, Sukie, what if it comes for us?'

'Bunk in with me. We'll take turns sleeping while the other sits watch. Now hush, hush, don't wake Uncle.'

And the latch clicks closed. Below he hears them whispering yet, excited sibilances that dissolve into silence. Closing his eyes to his candle he seeks the sense of young Henry, some friendly companion to stand with him in the dark, but nothing comes. He takes to his bed alone.

FOUR

'Eliza!'

It is noon and Angelica is awake. After Mrs Frost left her she entertained a group of gentlemen with much merriment until three in the morning; she sits up in bed hot and cross, and desirous of a saucer of tea. 'Eliza!' she calls again.

There is no answer.

She rises, her chemise wrinkled and bunched about her thighs, and trots into the dressing room. The table is still skewed in the middle of the floor, and Mrs Frost's cot is cold and empty, the counterpane pulled up smooth to the bolster.

'Now surely she cannot have stayed out all night,' mutters Angelica, 'for where would she go?' She does not allow herself to think, *perhaps she does not mean to come back*, but the notion nevertheless flutters behind her ribs. She walks into the parlour – which is disordered from the night's doings, the cushions tumbled on the sopha and scattered glasses sticky with ratafia – and even into the scullery, sighing, 'Eliza, Eliza,' for she already knows her search will be fruitless. This has never happened before, nor anything at all like it. She stands in the middle of her large room and tugs at her fingers until the joints go pop: her old friend Bel Fortescue will call for her soon, and the eyes of old friends are the keenest of all. Furthermore, while

Angelica's aristocratic keeper is reduced to worm-fodder, Bel's is vital and prospering, and cherishes her as passionately now as the day he first met her. 'I'll not be her sorry friend,' mutters Angelica. 'I am every bit as good as her.' And yet she has been abandoned to manage her appearance all alone.

Her curls are still fresh and want only a fluffing, which is hardly beyond her powers. And she casts about for what she can wear that might be donned without Mrs Frost's helpful hands and careful eyes. What a boon, then, is her own Perdita gown, for once she has pressed her waist into the faithful clasp of her pink silk stays, she effects the gathers of white muslin with only little trouble, and conceals her mistakes with a wide blue sash. Lesser women might take fright at so scant and humble a gown, but Angelica, lovely in both face and figure, requires no embellishment of dress. She is easy as a nymph in her soft drapery.

'And so 'twas more easily done than I feared,' she congratulates herself as she crouches before her displaced dressing table, tapping rouge into her cheeks. And she is well satisfied with herself, and misses her companion not one bit.

Bel Fortescue, when Angelica climbs into her carriage, surveys her gauzy dress with only a flicker of humour. 'What nakedness, Jellie,' she murmurs, for she is naturally soulful even in amusement. She is a small little woman with treacle-brown eyes, a comrade in the Cyprian corps for ten years or more. Her face is round and her chin is pointed; she has a little flat nose like a child's and her hands are childlike too, small and tidy. Men have wept for her grave sweetness, but if any have come to her in the hope that she will be like a child in all respects, they have been disappointed. For even as a girl of sixteen Bel was a queen of self-possession; as a grown woman she is untouchable. Her clever earl, although he has furnished her home and filled her library, dares not beg entry to her bed.

'What, this?' Angelica plucks at her muslin, kept upon her body by such slim strings. 'I think it the most practical thing I ever came upon. So simple, so light.'

'So simple and light,' says Bel, ''tis hardly there at all.'

'I have worn less.'

'Not on the Mall.'

Angelica puts her nose in the air.

'Oh, dear heart,' says Bel Fortescue warmly. 'I am glad to see you so much yourself.' In the depths of her dispossession, Angelica once allowed herself to weep sincerely in her friend's presence; this was a mistake, for Bel now searches her face for sorrow with a great intensity, and puts a hand on her arm. 'You *are* well, are you not?'

'Oh, most robustly!' The carriage is built so as to be smooth in its movements and almost silent; done up in pink silk so they nestle like pearls in an oyster shell. Its windows are small and curtained, but Angelica peeps out as they roll past the great things of Piccadilly. 'Now, Bel, who is about? You must tell me. There are a great many old friends I am anxious to restore my connection with.'

''Tis very quiet, as yet. Parliament ain't yet convened; nobody of remark is returned for the season. You could afford to stay a little longer in seclusion, if your nerves . . . ?' Bel's solicitude is too much.

'I am here, am I not? Perhaps it were better I arrived before the rush; I do not like to be the last person into a room.'

'Nobody would have blamed you,' Bel persists, 'if you had remained in the countryside. We understand.'

'Ugh! I had died if I had stayed there one moment longer! I do not like the countryside, Bel; there are too many animals and the light is not flattering.'

'But you know that you—'

'And how low the ceilings are there! Why, I am *glad* to be back in the midst of things. Where are we going?'

43

'Berkeley Square.' Bel's eyes shine. 'I am taking you to Negri's to feed you sweetmeats.'

'Oh, Bel!' Angelica clasps her hands.

'I know what you like – jellies, syllabubs, biscuits. I daresay there are few enough of those in the countryside. Here, has Mrs Chappell visited you lately?'

'Ah! Now we get to the heart of it. And what is it to you?'

'I am interested. Were I still a gambling woman, I'd hedge that she would get her claws back into you, once you were at liberty.'

Angelica sighs. 'She came yesterday.'

'And you told her . . . ?'

'I refused to go back to her.'

Mrs Fortescue is entirely too polite a person to laugh or grin immoderately, but she straightens the flounce at Angelica's shoulder. 'Good.'

Angelica, for the first time, catches her amusement. 'Bel, think what it would be like!' she exclaims. 'At my age! Being as I am!'

'A poor choice,' nods Bel soberly. 'A most diminishing choice.'

'She will let me set my own prices and I'll dine at her table, and we'll be best of friends . . .'

'. . . and then she'll invoice you sixpence for the bowl of oranges she put in your room!'

'Yes, indeed, and as a kindness she'll have her woman get a stain out of my dress . . .'

'. . . so that'll be half a crown on your account.'

'And every time I take a glass of sherry she'll make a note.'

'The fresh bedclothes! Oh, do you remember?'

'Clean sheets every day!' It has been a long time since Angelica last had the opportunity to air her grievances, and she snatches joyfully at her friend's hand. 'She would keep me her slave by the laundry bills alone. If my duke had not bought me out the last time,

I cannot think I would ever have got away. Bel, I cannot do it again; I cannot be so servile. Am I wrong? Is this my most prudent choice?'

'No, no. If we had wanted to be so closeted we would have stayed at home in our villages, ain't that so? Besides –' she glances quickly at Angelica – 'I begin to suspect Mother Chappell is losing her touch.'

This is too far for Angelica to follow her. 'Oh no,' she says, shaking her head. 'No, I do not think that can be so. Mrs Chappell is the premier abbess in all of London.'

'She was,' says Bel. 'She is an old woman now. She cannot fathom the desires of the world as she could twenty years ago. There are younger madams coming up, while *she* depends on her old faithfuls.' Thought animates her little person as she speaks: now her eyebrows lower in a frown; now she spreads her palms as if to gauge the balance of her argument. 'Of course she has as fine an eye for beauty as ever she did, but lately I see she also has an eye for girls who will do as they are taught and no more. They do not transcend her the way they used to – the way they *ought* to. They are the most cultivated and educated whores in London, but a whore is a whore is a whore, ain't that so?'

'I daresay,' says Angelica. 'Why does she want *me*, then?'

'*You*,' says Bel, 'have a genius that cannot be taught.'

Angelica wriggles in her seat. 'I do?'

'Yes. 'Tis what makes you a courtesan and not a jade.' She leans forward in her seat. 'Mother Chappell no longer dares take on girls with that genius, for she is afraid she cannot mould them. She hopes your attachment to her will make you biddable; that is precisely why you must not return to her.'

'Oh.' She thinks for a moment. 'Eliza says I ought.'

A shadow of disdain touches Bel's face. 'You still keep *her* with you?'

'She has nobody else.' Angelica does not mention Mrs Frost's defection; she does not wish even to think of it.

'She is a fearful woman,' hisses Bel, seizing her wrist. 'She seeks to make you less than what you could be. As Mrs Chappell does. This is the problem with women. *Men* are not fearful; they build one another to greatness. Women believe their only power is in tearing one another down.'

'Quite! Quite! So I need your help. If I am to remain independent from Mrs Chappell I had better start making independent connections.'

'I know a gentleman. Not your sort,' Bel adds hastily. 'But he admires you and you might favour him with a few hours' company. The playhouses are opening again, are they not? Well, *he* has a box at Drury Lane.'

'A *good* box?' Angelica asks suspiciously. 'One fit for me to be seen in?'

'You never wonder whether *you* are fit to be seen in *it.*'

'Fool; I know I am. I am fit to be seen in the box of the Prince of Wales himself if he would only extend me the invitation.'

'Mr Jennings will have you, I know,' says Bel. 'He is a rogue – but not *so* much of a rogue – if your object is merely to broadcast your return, he will suit you very well. I shall write and have him keep a seat for you tonight.'

Angelica squeaks. 'Oh, Bel! Thank you!'

'Only behave yourself, and do not give me cause to regret it.' The carriage grumbles to a stop in the shade of Berkeley Square, and Bel's face clears like rainclouds chased away. 'And ah, we are arrived! What will you have? My man can run in for the order.'

'What, and lose the pleasure of browsing?' Berkeley Square is a parade ground waiting for Angelica's feet. 'I want to go in there myself.'

'Oh, please, do not make me. I cannot bear to be looked upon any more.'

'Come, Bel!'

'Why can we not take it away and eat it in the carriage?'

'Because that is not why we are here.' Angelica's mouth takes a stubborn set; Bel affects not to see, but she cannot ignore her friend's hand tightening on her wrist. Angelica takes a breath. 'I have been away so long, Bel,' she says, and now she breaks her gaze. 'I need this.'

'Oh, Jellie ...'

As they descend, people turn to look at them; genteel girls nudge one another, and wives touch their husband's shoulders.

'Do you mark that?' whispers Angelica. 'We are retreated from the world and yet still we are not forgot. Don't it please you?'

'Not particularly,' says Mrs Fortescue. 'They have left off abusing me as a Jezebel; I suppose that is something.'

'*I* like it,' says Angelica, shifting her hips so the soft froth of her dress swirls around her legs, which are entirely naked save for her stockings and slip and two layers of muslin. What a thing it is, to be walking once again in London, furthermore in the company of the most gossiped-of lady in town, and looked at, looked at, looked at!

The bubbled-glass window of the confectioner's is lined with tall jars filled with sugarplums of all kinds, all lacquered and sunrise-tinted, and a multitude of sugar sculptures that shimmer like ice, and a palace cast from jelly, glass-clear, with tiny air bubbles frozen about the redcurrants and apricots and grapes suspended within.

Inside, it is a veritable temple to sugar which betrays nothing of the heat and toil – the boiling and skimming and coaxing and measuring – that must go into its making: everything here is cool and sparkling, with knots of gentle women and men chattering cordially at the marble tables. The back wall is lined with bottled liqueurs and syrups of all colours and all flavours – bergamot, muscadine, cinnabar, rose – and frothy-headed syllabubs are lined up on slabs of chilly marble, and from the back room comes an endless processions of fine things. Striped jellies are borne forth to the chattering diners beyond; sparkling sherbets, little frozen *bombes* and mice and lions and turrets. On the counter, glass salvers are piled with cakes and fancies: tiny amber caramels and tarts of translucent custard, and leathery fruit-paste jumbals contrived in true-love knots. Angelica's favourites are the millefruits, crisp clouds fragrant with orange-water, their surfaces rugged with cochineal and gold leaf and almonds and angelico.

'Like jewels,' she sighs. 'Delicious little carbuncles. I shall take some home with me.' She knows from the air of the room that she is being watched and listened to; the conversation is not the same busy lapping it was when first she entered it, and as she moves towards the fruit display she hears the rustle of sleeves and cravats as their owners shift to keep their view. The confectioners, although their real talent lies in marrying fruit to alcohol, sugar, cream, are wise enough to present the finest offerings from London's gardens and hothouses in their most virgin state: peaches and plums ripe to bursting; tangles of redcurrants; polished strawberries; melons breathing their musk out in great waves, pineapples wound about most artfully with vines. 'Oh! Pineapples!' Angelica cries. 'Bel, I want one.'

'Now is your chance.'

Angelica colours, charming in any woman let alone one of such beguiling embonpoint, and lowers her voice to a plaintive whisper. 'Eliza will not be pleased.'

'That woman is not your keeper,' hisses Bel. 'Buy a pineapple.'

'She says such things make trouble.'

'Well, that is what pays her way; if you did not need an attendant she would be sewing sheets in a garret.'

'Oh, but she is a tyrant with the purse-strings. She says in our –' and now she only mouths the words – '*current situation* we must forgo luxuries.'

'Then she's a fool. Even if you have nothing else, you must have luxuries. What, would she have the world see you eking out pease porridge for your meals?' She sighs. 'Well, so be it. There is one way left to get it.'

Angelica's lips twitch up at the corners. 'Really! You think it will work after so long?'

'Of course.'

Angelica looks about herself to gauge the attention of the room. And yes, the eyes of the customers flick discreetly over her; not only the women peeping over their almond biscuits, but the men too, and some of them, she sees, are of the first water. She draws a deep breath. 'Pineapples,' she says with a penetrating coquettery, 'are my *favourite*.' Bel's eyes are shining, and she continues with renewed enthusiasm, 'To my mind they are the finest of all fruit. I wish I had one, that I might enjoy it at my leisure.'

'Come away, Mrs Neal,' cries Bel with a shudder. 'I cannot stand the sight of the horrid things. I will not have one in my carriage.'

'Would you deprive me of my pleasure?'

'Aye! Madam, I would. You will go without today.' They turn away, and Mrs Fortescue raises an eyebrow. 'Well played,' she whispers.

'You think it will work?'

'Wait and see.'

FIVE

Mr Hancock has been in and out of the coffee-houses around the Exchange for thirty years; it does not take him long to light upon one in which to show his mermaid. It was once a favourite of his father's, and to those with long memories and moderate imagination has a reputation as the place to overhear great discourse on biology. The level of debate therein is not now what it once was, it serving mainly middle-aged merchants who flatter themselves on their scientific bent, and what man of some means is not now-a-days a man of science? It is known as the Pineapple, 'so called,' says its proprietor Mr Murray, 'for this was the first place in all of London where such a fruit could be tasted of. And since then we have displayed all sorts of wonders to the satisfaction of all. Miss Jermy, patched black and white like a cow, she was one of ours. And the little lad with feet for hands and hands for feet, the Lord rest him; and the African mask with the terrible curse on't; and that little white fox. Destroyed the wainscoting,' he adds regretfully. 'I shall be wanting a deposit from ye, in case of damage.'

'I cannot imagine it will cause you any trouble of that sort.'

'Humph. I have heard that before. What of its diet? And how large is its tank?'

'Why, it is not *alive*,' says Mr Hancock. He has swaddled it in an

Indian shawl as once belonged to his mother, and in the office of the coffee-house he unwraps it with some ceremony. He expects surprise from Mr Murray, but he betrays none as he inspects it. He looks at it as if it were no less ordinary than a bushel of apples, although he has the courtesy to wipe his hands upon his breeches before picking it up.

'I see,' he says. 'More of a sea-goblin, ain't it? That's what I'd call it.'

'Its appearance is unlovely. Do you think it will draw any crowd?'

'Why would it not? A marvel's a marvel.' He taps his nose wisely. 'To my mind, its ugliness adds to its appeal. Folks don't mind being scared when they know there's a pie and gossip to be had downstairs.'

'And so you would have it?'

'Aye, why not? We'll call it a mermaid, draw 'em in. And I get twenty per cent.'

SIX

Mrs Fortescue chooses a jelly, rosolio pink. At their table she traces the rim of her spoon against its surface before piercing it with slow purpose. She puts a morsel to her mouth, and meditates on it. Angelica, delving into the sweet wine under her syllabub, is silent too. She would have liked to sit further into the middle of the room, where she might be admired from more angles, but Bel's patience for spectacle has been exhausted already.

'I have something to tell you,' she says. 'Shh, now do not make anything of it. I do not want these people's attention.'

'Well?'

Mrs Fortescue bounces her spoon against the taut jelly. 'I may get married.'

'Oh!'

'Hush! Hush! Don't raise your voice.'

Angelica looks about her furtively and leans forward to whisper, 'To Lord—'

'Do not say his name here!' Bel draws herself up; her eyes blaze warning. 'I cannot stand to be the subject of any more gossip.' Her voice is gentler as she continues, glancing about herself. 'Of course to His Lordship. I have not been in the keeping of anybody else these last three years, have I? And the countess died this spring, so really there is no obstacle.'

'*I* see obstacles,' growls Angelica. 'I see what he is and what you are.'

'I will be whatever I choose to make myself. Have I not come this far?'

'But, *Bel*!' She puts down her spoon. '*You!*'

'What do you mean by that?'

'You do not remember what you used to say? "Never shall I be a wife, Jellie –"' she affects a stern little frown and wags her finger, although her voice trembles unaccountably – '"for that is a life of servitude, and servitude I do *denounce*."'

Bel gives a little sigh, and taps her bottom lip with the bowl of her spoon. 'I denounced it, but it did not denounce me. I have all my life sought freedom for myself, but now I think – the world being what it is – that freedom cannot be got. More expedient, do you not think, to choose its best imitator?'

'But you are already well set,' says Angelica. 'A fine house all of your own, and a carriage to drive where you will. He has even let you keep your friends.'

'Aye, indeed, and I read as I wish, and he is not afraid for me to meet men if I find them interesting or useful to my learning.'

'So how can it be better? What would you wish changed?'

Bel knits her chocolate-brown eyebrows. ''Tis not secure.'

'Money is its own security.'

'And how am I to come upon *that* when I grow old and ugly, and he casts me off? I've nothing in my own name. Have *you* any savings put aside?'

'Not a penny!'

'And so what d'you suppose will happen? We cannot be novelties all our lives.' She spreads her hands beseechingly. 'Jellie, he *asked*.'

'And *you* said yes.' Angelica is stung, although she cannot say quite why. It is as if Bel has laughed off a vow that Angelica imagined they both took with equal solemnity. She looks about the confectioner's nervously, for in her surprise she has forgotten to modulate her expressions and her movements. She would not like to be observed as uncomfortable.

'Dear heart. Dear Jellie.' Bel sighs. 'I have tried all other kinds of prostitution, why not this? 'Tis simply the best contract I ever saw drawn up, and its terms are for life.'

'His life or yours?' Angelica scowls into the curds of her syllabub.

'That's not for me to guess.'

''Twill be yours if he gets a baby on you,' says Angelica. 'Those little hips weren't built to bear much.'

'Well, so be it. It cannot be said I passed my life idle, nor unexamined.'

'Can we leave this place? I want some air.'

'Of course, of course. A turn around the square?' Bel's voice is kind and coaxing. 'A peek in the jewellers' windows, what say you?'

'Oh, very well.'

They depart with their arms linked. 'I have missed your company, Jellie,' whispers Bel. 'Truly, although your tempers are hot and never what you claim them to be.'

She returns to her apartment to find a great pineapple waiting for her outside its door, with a card bearing the regards of Mr Such-and-Such who *begs her forgiveness but . . . happened to observe this afternoon . . . extends this gift as a token of his warmest friendship . . . &c &c &c . . .* but still no Mrs Frost. The living room is still in disarray, its curtains still drawn and its crockery still soiled and scattered; observing this, and feeling the sting of a double abandonment, Angelica comes close to weeping.

'This is worrisome,' she says aloud. 'Perhaps she has been hurt. Or drugged. Perhaps she don't realise I have need of her. Surely there is some way I might send for her.' But they are so very rarely apart this eventuality has never arisen before, and besides, Angelica has never so much as wondered where her companion might go when she is not by her side. As an hour passes she begins to fret. 'For I am to be seen at the theatre tonight,' she laments, 'and I cannot very well dress myself for *that*.'

She paces the room, wringing her hands, until the girls trading on the ground floor protest at her ill-use of the floorboards by banging up with a broom handle. Then she strips off her gauzy smock and her silk slip as smooth as skin, and lets them fall under her feet since there is nobody present to collect them up. She sets about lacing up her hefty court stays with much tugging and panting, but first they are skewed to one side and then to the other; then the tape snaps in her hand and she shrieks with rage.

There is a little tap on the door.

'Eliza?' she calls hopefully, but it is only Maria their maid, who sleeps in the scullery and eats their crusts. 'Where is Mrs Frost?' demands Angelica.

'Sent me, mum.'

'I see that. Did she tell you where she would be?'

'Not my business.'

''Tis *my* business. You might tell me.' Angelica presses a sixpence meaningfully into Maria's hand, but after briefly inspecting it the girl pockets it and says not another word. 'Christ almighty,' says Angelica. 'If I were your mother I'd have drowned you at birth. *You* had better lace me in, then. Wash your hands first – my word, at least wipe them – this silk costs more than your year's wages.'

Since Maria is too stupid to help carry the table, they must prepare Angelica in the cramped dressing room. 'Now smooth it in,' says Angelica, opening the jar of pomade, 'just a little at a time. Is that within your powers?'

But it is not. Maria is confounded by every item she comes across: she showers the room with hair powder and boxes Angelica's ear with the bellows. Her attempts to heap and pin Angelica's hair into place gives her the appearance of a haystack in a gale; she spears her thumb with a jewelled pin and blots the blood on Angelica's best kid gloves.

'This will not do!' says Angelica. She feels the tears coming and chooses rage instead: 'Useless, unhelpful girl!' Maria upturns a bottle of rouge onto the rug. 'I cannot bear this! Why, you are fit for nothing! I am better off by myself.'

'Or with another assistant,' says Mrs Frost, who stands in the doorway of the dressing room shaking out her shawl.

'Oh, Eliza, Eliza, at last you are here. What am I to do?' rattles Angelica. 'Bel has arranged for me to go to the theatre, and I am a state! You must help me.' By the sour look of her friend's face, she is not yet forgiven, *but I will let her have her temper*, thinks Angelica, *since it don't inconvenience me.*

'Out,' says Mrs Frost to Maria, who retreats at pace. 'We can save this,' she continues, and sets about tousling the powder through Angelica's abused hair with quick deft hands. And she paints her friend's face, and pins and hooks and stitches her into her layers of petticoats and skirts. She must stoop before the transformed Angelica to secure the jacket of her gaudy striped redingote; she grasps her at the waist and runs pin after pin through the silk and into her stays.

'You came back,' says Angelica, and Mrs Frost sticks her again, right above where her soft navel must be, until she feels the shaft of the pin come up hard against whalebone.

'Did you think I would abandon you?'

56

'Oh – not for ever. But –' Angelica allows herself a laugh – 'I thought you meant to hurt me a little.'

'I would not do that.' Mrs Frost is still terse.

'You are a good friend. We may have our differences in opinion but—'

'One more thing.' Mrs Frost seizes the long ivory busk from the dressing table and rams it down Angelica's front with such briskness that she staggers. 'There. Now I am satisfied you are fit to be seen.'

Angelica sighs with pleasure at her reflection. 'Ah, Eliza. My love. You know I cannot be grand without you.'

And this provokes a little smile.

When Angelica returns it is almost dawn, and her link-boy so tired that he can barely run before the chair, but trudges alongside it, taking the weight of his guttering torch in both hands and upon his shoulder, so that it sizzles and spits alarmingly close to the too-large wig that swivels about on his head and every now and then slides down over his eyes. At her door she is overcome by charity for the poor child, and gives him a shilling. *I shall not account for* that *to Eliza*, she thinks with a little triumph. *How provoking she will find it, to have her books out of order by so small a sum.*

The ground-floor rooms of her lodgings present as a mantua-maker's, but down the passage a woman's moans are audible, and the squeaking of a bedframe rises in rapidity and vigour. *So somebody's work is soon to be done*, she thinks as she climbs the stairs, which idea she finds comforting, as if she were part of a great benevolent order. The whore's day ends as the baker's begins, and there is a time for every purpose under heaven.

This present moment's purpose is reconciliation, and she goes direct to the dressing room, where Eliza Frost sleeps flat on her back with her toes turned up and her arms at her sides: her plain white smock, ruffled at the neck and wrists, does not detract from her resemblance to a corpse freshly laid out. She does not groan or grope about when awakened. Her eyes flick open in silence and she turns her face calmly to the door.

'Good morning, slugabed,' Angelica hisses. 'Here I am, alone. Come and keep company with me.'

Mrs Frost follows her into the bedroom, and lights a candle while Angelica kicks her shoes under the wardrobe and sets about peeling her stockings off.

'Ay, me, what a night, what a night. I was grateful you did me up so marvellous fine, for Mr Jennings' box may be clearly viewed from all parts of the theatre. One might have believed that *I* was the sole entertainment.' Mrs Frost helps her out of her striped gown while she chatters on. 'In fact, there was one woman spent the whole evening staring at my hair and clothing, and in the third act she took out her pocketbook right there in the theatre and made a little note to herself. Imagine! It was almost *too* flattering. I was not moved to make any notes myself, for I believe there was not one woman there better presented than I.'

'How was the play?' asks Mrs Frost. 'Did you take in even a line of it?'

'Oh! I regret I watched a great deal too much of it, knowing I was only invited there for one night. I should have looked more about myself; I believe I missed some gossip. I must find a gentleman who has a good box, Eliza, and who will let me sit in it every night; that way I need pay no mind to the play unless there is really nothing else to see.' She sighs mightily. 'I am at least satisfied that I myself received attention of the most *felicitous* sort. You may be sure that everybody knows I am in town, and I would not be surprised if I now receive a great flood of invitations. Hmm, then what?'

She wears only her white lawn chemise now, her body a shadow beneath it as she fills the basin from the ewer. Mrs Frost is shaking out the mantua and petticoats, checking them over for rips and stains before putting them aside to be sponged in the morning. 'Oh, then dancing, and then the men were playing at cards – I did not put any money down, you need not worry about *that*, I merely acted as Mr Jennings's luck, and he did very well by me. Mark you, I did well by him too.' She puts her foot up on a stool, and the candlelight glows in the filaments of fine hair on her thighs as she rinses her commodity. 'My pocket is on the chaise; I think you will be pleased by the sum you find in it.'

They slip under the sheets. Angelica curls up like a little creature, but Mrs Frost is wide awake. She rolls onto her side and says, as if there has been no break in conversation, 'You will not consider it?'

'What? Oh, not now, Eliza. Let me sleep.'

But Mrs Frost is set on it. 'You are fortunate that Mrs Chappell would still have you.'

'I'll not go back to a bawdy-house.'

'Not any bawdy-house,' Mrs Frost says pleadingly.

'All cats are grey with the candles out. It comes down to the same thing.' The relief of being in her own bed and wrapped in the arms of sleep makes her soft and affectionate; she wriggles close to her friend. 'I know you think it is the prudent thing to do,' she mumbles, 'but if I go back there, I may never get out again. At least not before I am old and raddled and poxed, and she discards me as so much trash.'

'You will command higher fees,' Mrs Frost perseveres as her friend throws an arm across her. 'You can earn your way out in a moment.'

'She will never allow that to happen.'

'Why not consider it?'

Angelica, cross, must surface again from her pillows. 'You make me sorry that I brought you in here. This is a delicate moment for me, which Mother Chappell apprehends quite as well as I do. I can return to a brothel, or I can seize my liberty. The doings of tonight make me surer than ever that I shall do well.'

''Tis the rent I worry about.'

Angelica's irritation gets the better of her. 'So go down onto the street and start earning it yourself. Go on. A clean-looking woman like you, well spoken, you might make two shillings before breakfast.'

Mrs Frost blanches. Angelica's eyes are wide again, enamel-blue. 'No?' she asks. 'You don't like that idea?'

'That is not the arrangement,' mutters Mrs Frost.

'No. This is the arrangement, isn't it? And if you don't like it . . .'

Mrs Frost hangs her head.

'Yes, dear. You can go back to your husband.' She narrows her eyes. 'Oh, forgive me. You would have to find him first.'

'I'll not stand for this.' Mrs Frost is out of the bed and making for the door.

'But you do,' Angelica mocks her. 'You always do. You purport to disdain this life and yet you always return to it. What am I to make of that?'

And then she is satisfied, and she falls asleep without another thought.

SEVEN

Mr Hancock takes out adverts in newspapers and pastes up bills about town. On Mr Murray's advice, he procures a tall glass dome, under which they balance the mermaid upright. 'So as to look its visitors in the eye,' Murray explains with relish. They set it up on a small table in a room just large enough for visitors to pass all the way about the creature, and satisfy themselves of its authenticity before leaving the way they came in. 'There need be no more adornment than this,' says Murray, but even so Mr Hancock commissions a nearby draughtsman to imagine the dramatic moment in which the Japanese fishermen caught the creature in their nets. The waves rear up and the fishermen wear triangular straw hats; in the background there are many pagodas. The mermaid, in this image, claws its fists to its mouth and seems to be chattering in the most menacing manner, while its brothers squirm to safety. Mr Hancock, well pleased with this rendering, pins a copy up on the wall, and sends for coloured prints to sell as souvenirs.

Thus, they are ready to open.

'No need for you to be here,' says Murray. "Tis all taken care of.' But Mr Hancock wishes to observe for himself the effect his strange protégé will have on the city, and besides, Sukie is wildly excited.

'You might let me accompany you,' she murmurs as she stands at his elbow for morning prayers; 'Your mermaid's first social engagement,' she persists as she brings in the day's loaf; 'We might make a day of it,' following him up to the turnpike as he departs to his business in the city. Even without her persistence he would have unbent to her: he likes the sherbet stand in Seven Dials as much as she does, and he is glad to have her find his business interesting, even glamorous.

He gives her leave to walk to her eldest sister's house in Wapping, and there spend three nights pillaging Rebbie's wardrobes for a suitable mermaid-launching costume and catching up on what mysteries whispering sisters miss when they are kept apart from one another. He therefore may blame nobody but himself when he rises on the morning of the mermaid's debut to the smell of burning cloves, and finds an unfamiliar woman leaning over the parlour mirror blacking her eyebrows with some alacrity.

'Christ's teeth, Sukie, what are you about?'

She turns with a grin on her painted mouth, and although she looks mightily pleased with herself he cannot tell why. He had expected her to seize upon a gaudy yellow taffeta, or a painted silk, something showy and indulgent, with all manner of ruching and scalloping such as might appeal to a bright-eyed young girl. In fact she has chosen an ensemble that unsettles him in its refinement and simplicity: a little jacket of white quilted cotton, printed with small black sprigs. Its tight sleeves have not so much as a ruffle upon them, and the body of it ends at her waist with a single flounce and nothing more, as if it were a practical riding jacket. He cannot even complain about how much of her bosom it exposes as she has tucked a fichu of sheer muslin about her shoulders.

'Well?' she asks, holding out the edges of her good blue skirt, which to him looks dreadful flat without hoops beneath it.

'You need not have restrained yourself so,' he says. 'I would have paid for something finer.'

Her lacquered eyebrows lower and he knows he has said the wrong thing. 'This is the *finest*,' she says. 'We cut up Rebbie's bedspread for't. *I* know how to dress for an occasion.' She is frowning at his somewhat threadbare stuff jacket.

'Very well. I would not have the first idea, of course.'

But sitting in the carriage, she still huffing, he keeps catching a glimpse out of the corner of his eye of some slim, neat, fashionable lady. And it is a shock, time and again, to turn his head and be sure it is only his little niece, wearing a smart jacket and with a vast plumed hat on her head, her eyelashes lowered and her nose tucked into a novel. He likes it less when they arrive on the corner of the Exchange, for once in London there is no arguing: she is certainly *à la mode*. He fears he might lose her amongst the grown ladies who are admired as they stroll the pavements, each in their figured white gowns or their glove-tight redingotes and white stocks at their throats. On an impulse, he seizes her hand and holds it tightly.

'You are a good girl to accompany me,' he says. 'And you look very fine.'

'Ah, you are a sentimental old man,' she says, taking his arm, her feathers bobbing over their heads. They walk together and she gazes about her, for the passers-by are of great interest to a visitor, comprising of ringletted Portugal Jews, and Mohammedan Turks in strange draperies and turbans, not to mention the gaudy gibbering Italians and the haughty French all there for reasons of trade or genteel asylum. She stares too at the passing ladies; their array of bright chintzes, their hats and their jewels and their blowsy wigs.

'Do you think they are all here to see our mermaid?' Sukie whispers, tightening her grip on his arm.

'Since they are walking in the opposite direction to it, we must assume they are not.' He is steering her towards the Pineapple coffee-house on the corner when a hawker, an old woman with a wart on her upper lip, thrusts a rush basket of scraggled flowers, plucked from the ditches of Stepney, into his path.

'A nosegay for the lady?' she croaks.

'Thank you, no.' He bats her aside.

'Ah, now, don't she deserve it? Flowers for your sweetheart? Pretty girl like her, she deserves something for her troubles.'

Sukie is peering back over her shoulder at a sumptuous merchant's wife borne past in a chair painted with roses; she seems not to have heard, but Mr Hancock is disturbed.

'What can you be thinking!' he snaps. 'She is a child!' and he drags Sukie onward, all his joviality evaporated.

'A change is coming,' the woman calls after them, and he feels the muscles clench about his spine where, if he were a dog, his hackles would have risen.

'What?'

'I believe something unlooked-for has already come to you, ain't that so? You have been surprised of late.'

He strides on, not betraying his perturbation, but Sukie tugs him. 'Your mermaid!' she whispers. 'How does she *know*?'

'Who in this city has not received some windfall?' he snaps.

'A change in your station! A change in your fortune!' the hag persists, and she totters after them, her flowers lolling on their stems. Her shortgown is much patched; her arms poke from its flapping sleeves, broomstick-thin. 'I have the sight,' she calls, 'and the spirits whisper news of you to me. If you would know more it will only cost you—'

'Begone!' He turns to flap his hands at her. A cold perspiration has settled upon the back of his neck. He drags Sukie down the next alley, and she squeals as she steps into some unnameable sludge, slithers, stumbles.

'A change in your fortune,' she gabbles even so. 'Did you hear that, Uncle? An unlooked-for change. I think today will be auspicious indeed.' They emerge into the light, and she turns her ankle one way and then the other to inspect her ruined shoe. Muck has sprayed also up the back of her stocking. 'Ugh.' She curls her lip; then, looking up, 'Is this it?'

'Yes.' For they are indeed arrived at the Pineapple coffee-house. There is a bill advertising his mermaid posted to one window, but otherwise it appears as it ever did, and Sukie's face grows all the sourer.

'But it is so quiet,' she says. 'There are no crowds. No lines of people.'

'Is that what you expected?'

She straightens her absurd hat. 'It may be better inside.'

When he holds the door open for her, a few middle-aged middle-sort men in sober felt jackets look up from their broadsheets, but they do not appear to be a-buzz at the prospect of witnessing a marvel. The most animation they collectively display are those groups who gather along the benches, muttering together: 'What do you make of this tip?'; 'Has the *Richard* passed Kent yet?'; 'And what of your own stock, hmm, or do you mean to take our news and refuse to share your own?' But even they are barely moving their lips.

This being territory that Mr Hancock likes and feels easy in, it is little wonder that young Sukie is disappointed. The air is coffee-toasted and fragrant, cosy and quiet, and nobody obliged to spend anything in order to exchange gossip and speculation in comfortable masculine quietude. Mr Murray has sense to dabble in freaks; the money is not in coffee.

'Nobody is here,' says Sukie, lowering her very black eyebrows.

'Come, that's not true. See all these gentlemen?'

Those at his favourite table – plain and honest and solid like himself – are waving and beckoning. 'Hancock!' they call, and he joins their group although he feels the mortification of Sukie behind him. 'Hancock, what is this we hear about a mermaid?'

'I own one,' he says.

'You're short a ship, though, ain't that true?'

'No ship.' He buttons his lip. 'No ship, but a mermaid.'

'A courageous trade-off.'

He shrugs. 'That you may decide for yourself, for a shilling. 'Tis upstairs, ready to be viewed.'

'Oh! Mark this, gentlemen, he is already a true showman, no concessions for his old friends. And are you to run a circus now, Hancock? The business of honest trade too plodding for you?'

He laughs along with them but his palms are clammy and his stomach sour. On the landing outside the mermaid's chamber, 'Those men are jealous,' Sukie says, and he turns to her gratefully.

'Think you so?'

'Of course! Think of their disappointment when their next shipments come in and it is only miserable tapioca as usual, when Jonah Hancock was blessed with a mermaid.' She ruffles her skirts cheerfully. 'I know I am right.'

The landing is empty of people, save for Mr Murray's boy Daniel who has a cashbox to take payment and sits with his legs splayed before him, picking at his teeth with a little blade. He barely raises his eyes at their entrance. Equally deserted is the chamber in which the mermaid lies. Sukie puts open the door and walks all about it, her footsteps loud on the floorboards. 'Well,' she says, ''tis still early for the crowds. What shall we do now?'

They sit on the landing for over an hour. Nobody comes. The boy Daniel rolls up his jacket for a pillow and commences to doze; Mr Hancock bites his nails until he tweaks a hangnail and it begins to bleed. The pain is insistent. Sukie perches and reads her book, rising every now and then with a sigh to wander into the little room and look again upon the mermaid.

'Why do you keep going in there?' her uncle asks, blotting his bleeding thumb on his handkerchief. 'Nothing has changed.'

'How do you know? You have not been looking.'

At eleven on the clock, they hear scuffling downstairs, and voices. 'Up, up this way,' says a female. 'Careful on the stairs, my poppet.' And at last comes into view a well-dressed mama and her attendant nurse, each clutching the fist of a small child. These children – and one is really no more than an infant, quite bald beneath its little cap – scramble gingerly upward, stop-start, stop-start, their breathing loud and their tongues protruding as they exert themselves to place both feet on one step before pushing off to the next one.

'Our first customers,' whispers Sukie, clasping her hands, and in smiling silence she and Mr Hancock watch the slow and fumbling ascent of the children.

'Here for the mermaid?' asks Murray's boy, rousing himself.

'Most assuredly!' The women jiggle the children's hands to provoke their enthusiasm. 'A mermaid, Harry! Cassy! What do you think of that?' They turn their indulgent grins to Mr Hancock. 'They have spoke of nothing else, you know. We are very excited, are we not, little ones?' The children goggle in dumb confusion.

'Delightful,' Mr Hancock says. 'This is very pleasing to see.' He cannot help adding, 'For I am owner of this mermaid.'

'You own it!' The mama is thrilled. 'And did you catch it yourself? Did you see it alive?'

'It died very shortly,' he says. 'Poor creature.'

'Well! We are fascinated to see it. Shall we go in, little ones? Shall we go and take a peep at the mermaid? Yes, you would like that!' They drop their coins in the tray and lead the babes into the dimmed room, closing the door behind them.

At first there is silence. Then a querying upnote from one of the ladies; then a lusty howl. The bellowing of the children reverberates through the stud wall, and the party bursts forth in short course, the children clutched in the ladies' arms, scarlet-faced and inconsolable.

'You monster!' cries the mama, her infant's fat tears splashing on the floorboards, and snot flowing over its top lip.

'To upset innocent children in such a way!' berates the nurse, and they descend the stairs at a far greater speed than they got up them, the children weeping all the way and the women broadcasting their own disgust and disappointment: 'A horrid little imp!' 'The day quite ruined!'

Mr Hancock attempts to pursue them, calling out, 'Ladies, how can I apologise? May we not settle this?' but they turn up their noses and affect not to hear him. On the street beyond he can hear them resume their shrill narrative of terror to passers-by.

'Scared the babies out of their wits! A horrid thing, it was, a menace and a disgrace.'

He retreats up the stairs, where Sukie is standing with her palm clapped over her mouth in horror. He sits and, taking off his wig, rubs the palms of his hands over his prickled scalp. 'Oh, my girl!' he mumbles, elbows about his face. 'We are finished before we began.' She plumps down next to him, lacing her fingers together in her lap, and they sit sombrely.

'Perhaps 'tis not so bad,' she ventures. 'They are only two people.'

'But they have gone forth from here to tell the entire city. Damn Jones! His taste for frivolities will ruin us yet. And I am no better, for I am so credulous.'

She says no more, although she is a little embarrassed at her uncle's despair under the dispassionate gaze of Mr Murray's boy, who rattles his tray – empty but for two shillings – most provokingly.

EIGHT

Presently Mr Hancock gathers himself. Catastrophe as it may be – that he has forfeited a year's profits, that his reputation has lost a great deal of its gravity – is it not fortuitous that although he has overstepped himself in this folly, there are more terrible ways to lose what he has lost? No ships have been sunk, for one thing; not a single life lost, and if his pride is not quite what it was, he reminds himself that pride is a sin.

But poor Sukie, who looks now upon his shame with calm and childish eyes, has suffered most by this, although she does not yet guess it, and it is her dowry that gnaws at his spirit. He has witnessed more than once the way in which all the ardour in a young man's eyes is extinguished by a single column of figures, and a host of terrible scenes flock his head: Sukie at her first dance, bashful excitement fading to shame as the beaux glance at her but do not approach, as her own peers whisper behind their fans; Sukie, grown older and thinner, sitting at the parlour window still, watching for the approach of a lover who has forgotten his promises; Sukie, alone in her querulous marriage bed, watching the damp spread across the wall while her infants cry for hunger and her husband drinks his cares away. Oh, dear Sukie, what depths his folly might bring her to!

'Let this be a lesson to us,' he says bravely. 'I will buy us a rabbit pie for our dinner – what do you think to that?'

'Oh, we are not leaving now,' says Sukie. 'You mean to let one single misfortune turn you back from your path?'

'I—'

'We have a ship to earn back!' she snaps. 'And a creature people will pay to view. Only a fool would not hold fast.'

'Nobody wishes to view it,' he says sadly.

They are interrupted by voices below: 'This way to the mermaid?'

'Dear Lord.' He closes his eyes in forbearance. 'I cannot endure this again.' He makes to rise, but Sukie pulls him back.

'Where do you mean to go?' she asks. 'Will you hide behind the curtains until they have left? Stay here with me, sir, see how it unfolds. Not long,' she adds more gently, 'but we must *try*.'

A pair of young clerks comes up, scrubbed and keen. Mr Hancock watches with dull terror as they pay their money and pass into the room where the creature awaits. But there are no screams. There is some silence, and then, as he strains his ears to hear, laughter, betraying – could it be? – real pleasure. The men emerge at their leisure, grinning ear to ear.

'I never saw such a thing! And real, is it?'

'The genuine article,' says Mr Hancock.

'Extraordinary! I do not know what to make of it.' The pink-faced clerk is shaking his hand now. 'You are a lucky man! This is the oddest thing in the city, I am sure of it.'

'Thank you,' he says quietly. Then, gaining confidence, 'Do spread the word. Tell your friends.'

'I shall speak of nothing else! To think I was first to see this.' And the men retreat incredulous, and all a-bubble with the spectacle.

Shortly thereafter comes the stampede. Old maids and rich

70

gents, pie-men and flower-girls and clerks and foreigners, their boots clatter up and down the stairs and their voices fill the air in increasing excitement. They demand to see the creature that made the children cry; that made their mama faint dead away; that put a Jesuit priest into a fit which (it is said) he is yet to come out of. In the afternoon, chairs draw up to deliver fine gentlemen and their ladies; a corpulent old woman is fairly carried up the stairs by her posse of white-clad daughters so great is her desire to observe the creature, and in the evening lovers come clutching hands, the girls squealing and the men preening their scientific minds. They queue out into the street, until Mr Murray distributes bone tokens amongst them and bids them avail themselves of his victuals in the downstairs room, an exercise that disgruntles the regular customers but intrigues their visiting ladies, who have harboured dark suspicions about the places their men spend their time.

The whole day passes and still the people crush into the little room so that they can only shuffle around the mermaid, peering and shrieking at its goblin glare. Another draughtsman arrives with his pencils and sketchpad and sets about making a series of studies to be printed up post-haste; he is joined in short order by one more, on the business of a scientific society, who send their warmest greetings to Mr Hancock and hope he will be agreeable to a lecture series on his extraordinary creature. Hawkers arrive – first one, then all in a swarm – to pass oranges and hot pies and small beer about the coffee-house and up and down the staircase, and although the cashbox fills up at remarkable speed, Sukie will suffer nobody to touch it but herself, scowling at Master Daniel Murray as she heaves the takings into Mr Hancock's own strongbox. Mr Murray scrawls tickets dated days in advance. 'Could you not have ordered more mermaids?' he asks Mr Hancock. 'The one is hardly enough to share around.'

The end of the evening finds merchant and niece sore of foot for constant pacing, and sore of cheek from constant smiling. They can hardly credit the reversal in their fortune; the morning might be forty years distant, it has so little to do with their present situation. It is ten of the clock and the queue has not much abated.

'What will we do?' asks Sukie. 'Turn them away until tomorrow?'

'I durst not,' says Mr Murray, who betrays a grain of admiration now. 'They will riot for certain. As long as there are those as wants to see it tonight, I shall let them in.' The thought of his twenty per cent pushes his own tiredness from his head. 'You go on home, if it pleases you. The girl is ready to drop.'

Mr Hancock turns to Sukie. 'Are you?'

She is rubbing her eyes. 'A little. Only let me count up our takings.' This gives him a little pang, since she is now intimately acquainted with his financial doings: if she reports back this aberration to her mother ... but then her mother will hear of this, he accepts with a chill; perhaps she has already heard. He decides Sukie is far enough stepped into this business that it will do no harm for her to continue, and so he helps her carry their strongbox down to Mr Murray's office. All day she has scribbled shillings and pence down in columns on a large leaf of paper; now she sets about matching the coin to the figures.

'You will need a new ledger devoted to the mermaid,' she says. 'Daily takings and outgoings; and a separate book to account for every coin as you receive it. And you want a day-book, separate again, to record particular doings and correspondence, and a file to contain all that is written about it, and finally a large book to copy all the other books into.'

'You have given this some thought,' he says. He is impressed.

'Common sense.' She is stacking wobbly clipped farthings into towers and does not look up.

'No, you are an accomplished girl. One day you will be a wife of rare talent.'

'Like as not.' Sukie's secret ambition is to marry a gentleman in possession of a good trade but poor health, who will die very shortly after the children are born and leave her be. In such circumstances no body could blame her for entering into business herself, and thus thriving. 'Here,' she says, frowning, 'I need you to count this again. I am distracted, I daresay; my total does not seem right.'

He scoops the coins towards him and begins again while she rises and paces the room, her palms in the small of her back. Rebbie's borrowed stays pinch, and do not hold her in the way she is accustomed. The coins chink against one another, and his lips move silently. At last he sits back in his chair.

'Well?' she asks.

'What did you come to?' He looks a little stunned.

'Thirty-eight pounds, four shillings and sixpence.'

'Then you were correct. At least by my count, this is the sum we took today.' She gives a little yelp, and he rises to embrace her. 'Dear niece, all may yet be well! What a venture!'

She nearly skips for joy. 'More than your sea-captain had supposed!'

'If we go on this way, we shall be . . .' Shall be what? He can hardly imagine. 'No. Best see it as one remarkable day.'

'So let us bow out while luck favours us.' She yawns.

'Ah, there is your good sense again.'

We fill their minds even when we are far away. They fancy they see us even when they do not. They tell one another stories about us.

The stories are of men who, walking on the shore, hear sweet voices far away, see a soft white back turned to them, and – heedless of looming clouds and creaking winds – forget their children's hands and the click of their wives' needles, all for the sake of the half-seen face behind a tumble of gale-tossed greenish hair. They cast themselves into the water, sometimes, their shirts gone to air about their bodies, or wade ungainly across the shallows, stumbling on weed-slick rocks, the gooseflesh standing out on their calves. And sometimes they never return.

Those that do, how can they explain themselves? What can they say? They felt largeness beyond words; they heard in the visitor's lovely song something so unknowably perfect, pristine as mountain ice, that they would cast everything precious aside to hear more of it. These females from the other side of the world's mirror pursue their own lust with impunity, never thinking to wait meekly to be approached, but complacent in their own beauty, calling out, I want you; I want you; come to me.

The stories are of brave men who turn their faces away, who remain resolute on the shore despite the ringing in their ears and the thunder of their hearts. And then what? The stories are of mermaids spurned who burn down churches, who strike men dumb, who see to it that your cradle will remain for ever empty. Petulant and cruel, these females, and vengeful.

The stories are of the bravest of men, who crept so softly down that the lady, communing with the wind and tides, or raising her silver arms to wring out her wet hair, never heard his approach until he seized her up. The stories are that mermaids once subdued make fine and modest wives, as loving mothers as any, except that they have a peculiar sense of humour, and often laugh aloud at ordinary things, like an old man hoarding his coins, or a pail of milk gone sour in a thunderstorm, as if there were something foolish to it all.

And then of course there is no leaving a sea-wife unattended. She is restive, and paces as if she still heard that dreadful calling from the water; she will go to the shore and stand there as the sea foam races about her new-minted ankles, her face sheened with tears. Unwatched, she will seek out the scrap of mackerel skin that fell from her when first she was dragged from the water. Given the means to return to the sea, she will unhesitatingly cast off the bonds of motherhood, forget her uxorial vows. She will vanish for ever in the turn of a wave as if it had all meant naught to her. For mermaids are the most unnatural of creatures, and their hearts are empty of love.

NINE

It goes on in this way for ten days. Mr Hancock neglects his office to loiter in the coffee-house, marvelling at the crowds of people he has drawn there. The first arrive not long after dawn, and they continue to stream through the doors even after St Edmund's bells chime twelve; they would go all night if the door were not bolted against them. A group of Catholics come to pray about the creature and cast its demons out, but although they gibber on, the mermaid does not stir so much as a fin. Students arrive from Oxford already drunk, and liberate it from its glass bubble for a game of catch-as-catch-can. After that Mr Murray arms himself with a cosh. A man from the Royal Society comes to inspect the mermaid: he does not declare himself baffled, but his face speaks it plainly.

'Ah!' he cries in triumph after hours of increasingly frantic scrutiny. 'There are stitches on it! And here, evidence of a wire frame.'

'Well, how else were it to be preserved?' asks Mr Murray in exasperation. 'It is only mortal, after all – its body no less corruptible than any other low creature's – we are fortunate it has been stuffed with such care as to preserve its original appearance. If it were a mere manikin it would require no such intervention: what greater testament could there be to its legitimacy than the fact that it has degraded, decomposed? You accepted the kongouro, did you not, and that was brought back a mere tanned hide.'

'But that creature was witnessed alive,' persists the man from the Royal Society.

'And so was this, I daresay. There's not a fishing town in England that has not been visited by merfolk at one time or another.'

'Captain *Cook* saw the kongouro – a gentleman – his word is beyond question.'

'Ah, a word's a word. Any gentleman can tell a lie; any scoundrel can talk truth.'

'An *abundance* of eyewitnesses!' The gentleman's argument falters; there is real terror in his eyes.

'All of them on the same voyage,' Mr Murray muses, 'not an independent sighting amongst them.'

'Well, how could there be, when no other man has ever gone there before?'

'Convenient, that. Look, sir, it strikes me as contrary that you will accept the existence of a kongouro, which you never saw or heard of before, on such slim testimony, and yet how many tales have you heard of mermaids, and how many sailors report seeing them? In the annals –' he waves his hand to indicate the sweep of history – 'there is *centuries'* worth of evidence to satisfactorily account for the existence of sea-maidens, and yet none at all for what creatures may creep upon the plains of an entire body of land that nobody visits and, need I really remind you, bears no name at all but *Incognita.*'

The expert hesitates.

'Look at the thing!' Murray exhorts him. 'And consider whether such a beast could be *invented.*' He pats him on the shoulder. 'You know for yourself what is true, sir.'

The expert leaves, murmuring about the precision of the dorsal;

the impossibility that the spine could be so fused; the skill required to create such a creature exceeds, surely, the artfulness of Man. He has been caught out before, when he declared that infant lions arrive in the world as puffballs, and he is anxious of attracting any more derision to himself.

Every day, the takings amount to twenty pounds or more. Mr Hancock is gripped by a sort of exhilarated helplessness: events sweep him onward whether he wills it or no, and he gratefully abandons himself to Providence. He has not the requisite canniness to steer his situation, and it is with relief that he says to himself, *all this before me is uncharted.*

On the eleventh day, he is passing through the downstairs room of the Pineapple, when a tall and lovely mulatto girl of about seventeen approaches him, smiling. 'Are you the mermaid man?' she asks.

'I – you may call me that,' he says.

'You are the owner of the creature we observed upstairs?'

'That's so.' He is not much surprised by her complexion – she is by no means the strangest person to walk the Exchange – but he wonders what is her provenance. She is the pride of a city-trading freedman and his Kentish wife, perhaps, or a sailor's parting gift to Wapping, or the cherished bastard of a rich gentleman. By her peculiar gentility he knows that she was not amongst the poor wretches liberated from their shackles after the American war, no longer to starve in a Virginia slave cabin but in a glorious English garret. And if she ever was enchained herself, she does not wear that memory upon her person. Her white gown is very fine, for all its plainness (and what is this mania amongst the young for plain gowns? To his mind, a beautiful face is only enhanced by a beautiful ensemble, and where is the sense in a lady dressing as if she were a dairymaid?) and she has the healthy radiance of a girl who is fed properly and rested well. Her teeth are white and all her own, her hair powdered and frizzed, her eyes warm and clever. She looks upon him without timidity, as if she never doubted her fitness to approach him.

'My name is Polly,' she says, extending her hand with the confidence of a duchess. 'Miss Polly Campbell. I am sent to fetch you over, if you'll come.' She bobs her head in the direction of where, he now sees, a gouty old woman sits surrounded by young girls in white muslin, who are sipping little bowls of coffee and wincing with displeasure. They make a peculiar scene amongst the dusty and bewigged old gentlemen, who look askance at them with mingled irritation and intrigue, and clerks who leer, and young ladies with their chaperones, who look, and twitch their lips, and look again. 'We do not wish to impose upon your time,' says Miss Polly Campbell, 'but my mistress has something to discuss with you.'

'I have a few moments,' he says, deciding that his life cannot very well become any stranger.

'Good evening to you,' says the old woman as they approach. She is fastidiously turned out in green silk, which flashes with cold fire, and she wheezes with every breath so that the fabric strains over her tight-packed bosom. She has a great powdered thatch of a wig and no neck at all to speak of, although a large jewelled cross gleams in the crease of flesh where one might once have been. She extends a hand, encased in green knitted mittens, from which her fingers emerge strangely delicate, as the paws of a little rodent; pink and plumply tapered. It is possible that she might once have been beautiful. 'Please,' she says, 'sit.'

And he sits, mutely, watched by his dull comrades.

'Do you know who I am?' she asks.

'No,' he says, but while he has never seen her face before in his life, he has seen her sort, and could take a fair guess at what she is.

'Bet Chappell is my name. I run a – ah – an exclusive *club*, of sorts –' the rings on her right hand clink together as she traces the whorls of the tabletop – 'in St James's.' She watches his face closely. 'King's Place.'

'By the palace?'

'So near we string our washing line upon it.' She wheezes at her own quip. 'Before my present situation I owned a coffee-house for many years – not much like this one, I do concede – so you see I am in the business of entertaining people.' The girls nod, folding their hands in their laps. 'So, Mr Hancock, I've a proposal for you. Your mermaid – 'tis a marvel. Quite extraordinary. We were delighted, were we not, girls?'

'Oh yes,' they say, 'we never saw the like. Never did.'

'*But* –' she holds up a hand – 'it wants displaying to its best advantage. I notice that no effort has been made in that direction.'

He protests that it hardly needs displaying; that its qualities speak for themselves; but internally he agrees that he is disappointed his great discovery sits in a bare room at the top of an unadorned staircase. And if a beautiful woman wants a beautiful dress, why would not a marvellous creature want a marvellous setting?

'Look,' she says. 'I see your strategy, if it may be called that. You display it in a place like this, and you can be sure your mermaid will be seen by the greatest volume of people. And each of them pays their money, and so you become rich. Perhaps.'

He waits to hear what she says next. She has such an authority about her as is shared by his sister Hester, who has all the good sense of a man, but where Hester lacks a man's means, it is evident that Mrs Chappell is at no such disadvantage. And so she continues. 'But you do not control what *sort* of people, Mr Hancock, and as far as I can make out you have no particular plans for reaching them. You simply hope that word will spread and the public appetite for this thing will sustain itself. But how long will that last for, d'ye think?'

Captain Jones's words return to him: 'Four thousand a year. I am being conservative.' What had he expected? That this popularity would last for ever? He would not expect such a thing of his tea bowls, so why this? 'It is clear,' he says slowly, 'that if I wish this thing to remain popular I cannot leave it to its own devices.'

'There you have it! And I believe that the way to do this is not to court vast numbers of people, but a few people of *quality*. I shall be frank with you. I wish to hire your mermaid.'

'Ah.' He knows already that he will say yes.

'It is all very well to delight the masses,' Mrs Chappell continues, 'but why run yourself to the bone pursuing their favour? To say nothing of retaining it. A circle of much greater influence opens to you, if you would enter it, for I shall bring your mermaid not to the Many, but to the Great.'

He observes that this is not a speech that has sprung immediately into her head, but one that she has been working up for some time. So this is no whim. She has been watching and thinking since the day she first saw it. 'And what would be the benefit to you?' he asks.

She smiles. 'In my line of work,' she says, 'the competition is unparalleled. There must always be a novelty. And nobody else has a mermaid.'

This satisfies him. 'What is your proposal?'

She presses her fingertips together – her rings clacketing – and touches them to her lips as if she were thinking deeply.

'A week of festivities. Soirées, viewings, you know. Exclusive beyond your ken. All the great men will naturally come by. Royalty, probably. My parties are written up in all the magazines.' She speaks nonchalantly but her small eyes glitter in their pouches. 'On the first night there will be a specially devised performance by my own girls, in costumes designed by me for the occasion. I have not yet lit upon the details.'

'And you will, what, charge entry?'

She swats at the youngest of her girls, who has dared to scratch at the nape of her neck. 'No, no. Nothing of the sort. I am not *exhibiting* it; merely sharing it among friends. There will be a strict guest list. No tickets for sale.'

He is bewildered. 'But *I*—'

'Of course, of course.' She clasps her little rat-hands impatiently. 'You are not handing it over for nothing. I shall hire it from you.'

And now what? How will he know whether the sum she suggests is fair? In his daily work he has a nose for these dealings; the value of what he is selling is deep in the marrow of his bones, for has he not grown up all his life with it? Might it not reasonably be assumed that when his mother was heavy with him, and his father climbed into the bed beside her, his talk was of chinaware and investment, favourable winds and promising deals?

He never spoke of mermaids.

'Two hundred pounds,' she says. 'For a week. You may name your dates; I shall in any case require time to prepare.'

Silence.

'I have a question,' he says.

'Please.' She bares her teeth, yellow as old ivory; they want a good rub with lemon juice. 'Ask me.'

'Since it pays to be clear on these matters.' He drums his fingers on the table. 'You are a procuress.'

'Yes,' she says. She does not blink; she does not turn her face away. The girls are still as they ever were.

'And yours is what is called a house of ill repute.'

'Nobody calls *my* house that. I have an excellent reputation.'

He is thinking rapidly; he is so far from what he was a fortnight ago.

'Was that your question?' she asks.

'No. I have one more.' He narrows his eyes. He has heard of the equivocating ways of elves and witches, and this woman – although she is most decidedly of this world, for what other would have her? – strikes him as having the same talent to tempt men into unknowing bargains. 'Once your week is done,' he says, 'the mermaid is still mine, and you will lay no other claim to it?'

'That's so. Two hundred pounds.'

Since nobody else in London is likely to supply her with a mermaid, he does not hesitate. 'Three hundred,' he says.

It is difficult to tell whether her wheeze is one of surprise or the natural spasm of her troubled lungs. She presses her handkerchief to her mouth, her thin lips purpling. 'Three hundred pounds,' she says, 'very well. That is agreeable to me.'

'Ah, no,' he says sorrowfully. 'I work in guineas.'

Her eyes are very sharp upon his face before she begins to grin. 'We understand one another, you and I. We are cut from the same cloth.'

I sincerely believe we are not, he thinks. *You chose this. I am only following what Fate has thrown my way.* But he smiles and shakes her hand warmly.

TEN

After taking the girls for their daily ride around the park ('It is healthful, and it is instructive. If it proves also to be effective advertising, that is all to the good'), Mrs Chappell has made it her habit to drop in on Angelica and scrutinise her for poor decisions.

'No trouble,' she says as the girls lower her into her seat, 'it is practically on our way home.'

'If *practically* means *utterly out of your way*,' sniffs Angelica, resentfully up betimes. She was borne home from the Pantheon not five hours earlier, her feet bruised from dancing and her voice hoarse from laughing, and now lolling in her Turkish wrap turns her peevish attention to the *Tête-à-Tête* page of *Town and Country Magazine* On the table a china pot of chocolate keeps warm over its flame, and the dresser is loaded with vases of peonies and tulips: these heavy fragrances, the one earthy, the other airy, more or less conceal the sour hint of piss that emanates from a gilt cage of snow-white mice. They sleep all in a tussle, their raspberry-pip eyes closed, twitching and squeaking in their mouse-dreams. It is a day of great sunshine again. The shadows of pigeons flicker across the walls, and the open window lets in the hiss of the breeze through the trees in Soho Square.

Angelica, pale and creased, feels it all as an assault; the light too bright, the girls too ebullient. 'How can I make a success of myself when you do not allow me my rest?' She squints over her magazine. 'Oh, here is our Bel, look,' she says, shaking the creases from smudged likenesses of Mrs Fortescue and her noble lover. 'Heaven forfend we might be allowed to forget her for one moment. A wonder, ain't it, that the press are so disgusted by this to-do and yet continue to devote whole pages to it.'

'She has done well for herself,' Mrs Chappell nods.

'And so will I,' says Angelica, not without pugnacity. The blackest and hairiest and plumpest of the dogs, who had lain meekly with his nose between his paws, springs at once to his feet and utters a yip of warning.

'There, now, Fox does not like your tone,' says the abbess, hauling him onto her lap and tussling his tufty face. 'I meant nothing by it. In fact, I have a task for you on that score.'

The girls, who sleep eight hours a night and know better than to touch the Madeira they pour out for their visitors, are devoid of languor, rustling and nudging, whispering, 'Oh, tell her! Tell her! Tell her!'

Angelica stretches. The sunlight glows rosy through her fingertips. 'What have you to tell me?'

'I have secured for us the most remarkable spectacle in London. To be displayed for one week only at my house. The strangest freak of nature I ever saw.'

'And *you* bedded Chesterfield.'

'You must have heard about it,' says Polly. 'The veriest oddity. 'Tis in all the papers.'

'Oh! It must be the pig that can do sums.'

'The pig may be a marvel at reading minds, but until it achieves mastery over its own bowels I cannot allow it on my Carrara again,' says Mrs Chappell. 'We are all very disappointed.'

'Guess again,' trills Elinor.

'How should I know?' She groans and wedges her fists into her eyes, but the girls are gazing at her expectantly. 'Very well. I suppose it is some sort of creature.'

'It is!' they rejoice, and Kitty rocks in silent joy.

'Why must you make such noise?' She rolls over on the chaise and wedges her face into the cold cushions. 'Why cannot you be still and leave me be?'

'But you have almost discovered it,' says Elinor blithely: in her life before her fall she was a dogged smaller sister, and the habits come back to her with little prompting. 'Think of a creature. A *magical* creature.'

'A unicorn, then,' Angelica mumbles through satin.

'Nonsense,' snaps Mrs Chappell. 'A unicorn! As if a man would travel to the other side of the world for a creature native to our own land. You are not even ashamed of your ignorance.'

'*I* never saw one here,' says Angelica.

'Because they favour virgins, and there isn't a one of *those* left as far as Kent.'

Kitty cannot hold it in any more, although she is forbidden conversation: the exclamation pops from her like a cork. ''E's got a mermaid, miss!'

Mrs Chappell swipes her fan at her with such ferocity she might knock the nose off her face, but Kitty, a lifelong expert at dodging blows, has already darted away.

'A mermaid?' repeats Angelica.

'Yes!'

'A horrid mermaid!' crows Polly. 'We have seen it.'

'And it is nothing like what you expect a mermaid to be.'

'Well, it is only an infant.'

'An *ugly* infant,' Kitty adds, and claps her hand over her mouth under Mrs Chappell's glare.

86

'But so were you, Kitty, and we are assured you will blossom quite beautiful.'

'Sharp teeth like a kitten's.'

'And dried-up. Brown. Dead.'

'Dead!'

They hold their saucers sedately but their eyes are very bright, and they talk faster than their mouths can keep up, at one moment all in unison and the next vying against one another. The dogs catch their energy and emerge from their skirts, scampering round the chaise with their claws clattering on the floorboards.

'That is enough,' says Mrs Chappell. 'It is clear you are not fit to be taken visiting. In future I shall leave you at home for more of Madame Parmentier's lessons in walking.'

The girls subside.

'It don't sound like any mermaid I ever heard of before,' says Angelica. For she was once a little child in Portsea, and there was held on a warm lap while sailors, joyful in their homecoming, danced and sang. And this small Angelica was bright-eyed in the firelight, her thumb in her mouth and her finger hooked over her nose, as they raised their voices to tell of the fair pretty maid who lured good men into oblivion.

It was the very jauntiest of all their songs, but, 'Not that one,' had said the owner of the lap, her voice a-buzz against Angelica's infant cheek. 'Not on a night so rough as this. 'Tis bad luck.'

'Ah, love,' said the sailors, 'but aren't we home now? So what is there to fear?'

'There are other boats out there yet. There will be other voyages.'

The men fell silent, but in the days that followed the children of the town took up the tune. They trooped wind-whipped along the sea wall, clutching sticks and dolls in their cold-raw hands, and singing the forbidden song of the mermaid. The grey waves crashed below and they raised their voices to chant, 'And three times round went our gallant ship, and she sank to the bottom of the sea, the sea, the sea . . .'

But Angelica's recollections of her childhood are as slender as a vision, or a dream. They come to her in slivers, so prism-bright and peculiar as to make her shudder, for they seem to be from a life lived by somebody else.

Still, she says, 'I have always wanted to see a mermaid for myself.'

'And so you shall.' Mrs Chappell pats her shoulder. 'Its appearance is not what one might first expect, to be sure, but it is all the more convincing for that. We would not want Science confused with Art.'

'How did you secure such a thing?' asks Angelica.

'From some wretched merchant, some cit,' Elinor interrupts, 'who is showing it off in the most dismal manner one can imagine. He has not the first idea what he has got.'

'Oh, now, Nell, you mis-speak. He is not so bad.'

'Aye, I mis-speak, for he ain't even a cit. He is from *Deptford*, not a Londoner, and greener even than our Kitty here.'

'Kitty is a sly little bitch,' says Polly. '*This* gentleman is meek as a lamb – this newly-anointed gentleman, I may say, for is a veritable mushroom, sprung up overnight. He has a fortune now that he did not have this time last week and it increases by the day.'

Angelica sits up. 'And what do you mean to do with him?'

'Why, take him into hand,' says Mrs Chappell. 'He is an innocent in this world.' Her pup Fox turns three times about in her lap, and she rubs its ear between her thumb and forefinger. 'He is lucky to have met me.'

Angelica snorts. 'Poor man. It will not last. Somebody will arrive next week with a wild boy or a dog that can climb up ladders, and his little bauble will be all forgotten.'

'But when the sun shines, we will make hay,' says Mrs Chappell. 'I mean to hold a week of soirées and balls.'

'Unlike you. You have favoured a more sober, discreet approach of late.'

'Time to make a change.' Mrs Chappell snaps her fingers at Polly, who is feeding one of the lapdogs from her plate. 'We are a venerable establishment.'

Angelica is become quite jokeous: she remembers Bel's observation, 'Mrs Chappell is losing her touch,' and determines to investigate it. 'Venerable?' she asks boldly. 'Or *démodée?*' To the girls she mouths *moribund*, but here she gets above herself: it is a hard word and they only stare at her.

'Watch your mouth, madam.' The abbess heaves in her chair. 'When you have run a celebrated institution for thirty years, you may smirk all you like, but things being as they are, that nasty expression of yours does you no favours.' Mrs Chappell settles herself again, clasping her hands over her bosom. 'I know my business. It don't hurt to look out novelties.'

'Horrid competitive now-a-days.'

'And yet mine is the only place with a mermaid. Such gaieties will be had.'

'And what will this gentleman make of *your* sort of gaieties?' Ought Angelica to better conceal her scorn? Mrs Frost thinks so, and creaks her cane chair with urgency. But to Angelica's mind, the best way to achieve a thing is to behave as if it has already happened, and so she behaves as if she were queen of the Ton. She claps her hands and crows, 'Oh, Mother Chappell, I can see him now, poor lost thing, hunting about the place for a bit of ale or pease porridge while the fine people disport themselves. And pity the lady who must be his nursemaid for the evening!' She looks to the girls.

'Which one of you is it to be then? Which of you must hold his silly hand all night while the fun goes on elsewhere?'

'Mrs Neal,' says the abbess with perfect serenity, 'I require a particular favour of you.'

'Oh?' Understanding rises slow across Angelica's face. 'Oh no. Madam, not me.'

Mrs Chappell adopts her most coaxing tones. 'This gentleman, as I say, is new in the world. I wish you to pay a special attention to him, my dear heart, to put to use your great gift for hospitality. No body in my house is as expert as you are.'

Angelica crosses her arms. 'I'll not be pimped.'

'To be sure, to be sure. But you remember our agreement?'

'This is beneath me,' says Angelica. 'You cannot think so little of me.'

''Tis just for one night.'

'Even to be seen with a man like him for one hour will hurt my reputation. I am not a plaything for any drear arriviste to take his turn on.'

'No, dear, no. But I will remind you that all the quality come to my establishment, and not one of them comes *here*. I extend to you the opportunity to be seen at the most exclusive party of the season.'

'I ought to be your guest of honour,' scowls Angelica.

'No, dear. That is Mrs Fortescue.'

Angelica searches for more words, but finds none. Eliza Frost rises from her chair with a suddenness that might bespeak a woman about to quit the room – it is only with effort that Angelica restrains herself from seizing her friend's hand – but she is only going to shake cake crumbs into the cage of sleeping mice. Angelica turns sullenly back to Mrs Chappell. 'What if I found I was unable to accept your very generous invitation?'

'Well, then, we would find ourselves in a difficult position,' says Mrs Chappell, who looks in fact as if her own position were never more comfortable. 'I should think, given the situation, there would never be any more invitations extended to you.'

Mrs Frost straightens up. She closes the latch of the cage.

'We agreed,' says Mrs Chappell, 'that you would be available at my house when you were wanted there. I help you, do I not? I mention your name to my gentlemen; I host your meetings with them—'

'No need to recall it to me.'

'So you must help me in return.'

Angelica considers, watched by Mrs Frost (uneasily), Mrs Chappell (coolly) and the girls (enquiringly). The mice are stirring and piping to one another; the dogs perk their ears; the shadows waver on the walls. She musters the broadest smile she has shown all morning. 'I'll take a glass of wine with the gentleman, and gladly. I like mermaids and I like parties. For a mermaid party I'll tolerate far greater hardships than that.'

'Ah, there's my amenable girl. Much obliged to ye, Mrs Neal. You will go far, I never doubt it.'

ELEVEN

October 1785

It is a curious thing that while the mermaid has been so celebrated – both on the lips of citizens and in their broadsheets – Mrs Hester Lippard has been utterly silent. In his more hopeful hours Mr Hancock permits himself to believe that perhaps news of his strange cargo has bypassed her entirely; it is more likely that her opinions are too numerous and blistering to entrust to folded white paper. By the first Thursday of the month, the day of her accustomed visit, the absence of her correspondence is as tense as the air before a summer storm.

Dreading the conversation which must follow, he takes a hansom all the way from Clerkenwell, an expense that weighs heavy on his conscience despite his new wealth, and – the traffic on the Strand being as it is – takes very little time off the journey. He knots his fingers and drums his feet on the boards as the cab rattles down Butt Lane – Mr Hancock bouncing about in the carriage like a pea in a hatbox – through a vista of gentle green fields. The new-built houses here are marvellous genteel: they stand alone, or in terraces of two or three, with large windows and an aspect across pleasant orchards and market gardens to the haze of London on the far horizon. Mr Hancock, agitated as he is, must cluck with pleasure as he passes Hancock Row, now let out to comfortable sea-captains and shipwrights and even a dancing-master at very satisfactory profit. *There will be more of this sort now,* he thinks. *Hancock Street! The most exclusive address in Deptford.*

As they approach the dockyards, the houses become smaller and more densely built; low dwellings with clapboard fronts and papered windows. A mere fifty feet from Mr Hancock's own street, a group of shipbuilders idle at the crossing. Two are peeling off from their comrades, returning to their homes where there must be bread and bacon laid out on the table, and wives waiting to pour a draught of beer. But they linger even so, touching the brims of their hats laconically to the coachman while one finishes a story and all laugh together in their comradely circle.

The coachman makes to touch his whip to the horse's flank, but Mr Hancock raps on the roof and leans out of the window.

'Hold back so they may pass,' he calls.

'Why, they are not going anywhere,' says the driver. ''Tis my right of way.'

'Not here. They cross in their own time.' In Deptford, traffic makes way for shipbuilders just as they say in Hindoostan the cattle are permitted to wander and lie where they will, no matter the industry about them. 'The world depends on fine strong ships,' Mr Hancock says cheerfully as the horse stamps and snorts on its tight rein. 'The skill of those good men fills every belly in London.'

'I fill my own belly,' mutters the driver, but he waits as the good men now take their leave of one another, stopping in the middle of the road to raise a farewell hand.

'Obliged to ye,' they nod as they pass, betraying yet no urgency.

Mr Hancock, his elbow hooked over the window frame, catches the eye of their leader Jem Thorpe, whose masterpiece some twenty years back was the cabin of the lamented *Calliope*. His wig is flecked with sawdust, and he swings a string bag of the wood trimmings swept up from the workshop floor.

'Jem!' calls Mr Hancock. He cannot help himself; the thought of Hancock Street is too beguiling to keep a secret. 'Hallo there! Jem! How's trade?'

'Steady.' He holds his hat up to shade his eyes. 'For now.'

'Aye, there's a rare thing.' Mr Hancock does not like to leave Hester unsupervised in his house to stalk about his parlour, peering at his china and his tobacco and the spines of his books in her hawkish manner. She may by now have found her way into the counting-house and be running her finger down the entries in his ledger. He loathes her oversight of his house, but he dreads also being with her; he ought to hurry back, but a conversation such as this one – authoritative, masculine – may serve to bolster his pride before she sets about dismantling it. 'And the Admiralty are seeing you right?'

'Tsk! Worse than ever!' Jem steps up conspiratorially. 'Ever a-snibbeting over wages and perks and hours. The best shipbuilders in the world, we are; they cannot get a better job from anybody but they would not pay us what we are worth.'

'It was always the way,' Mr Hancock nods sagely.

'We should have downed tools ten years ago, when Woolwich did.'

Mr Hancock shudders. 'That was a bad time.' His neighbours' passionate unionising fills him with anxiety; perhaps, indeed, the order of things is not satisfactory, but order must nevertheless be maintained. If not, what is there?

'Aye,' says Jem, 'very bad, to crush citizens who speak their minds rather than pay them any heed.' He spits into the dirt at his feet. 'It's not only those at the top who keep things as there are – power's a contract drawn up between all classes of men. There'll be trouble yet, you'll see.'

'Well.' Mr Hancock drums his fingers on the sill. 'Are you averse to bringing your work ashore?'

Mr Thorpe considers. 'House-building, is it? For you? I suppose you are speculating again.'

'Indeed! For I have come upon some money I did not expect.' He waits for Jem Thorpe to pursue this tantalising hint, but he only smiles, and inveigles his fingers under the edge of his wig to meet an itch. 'Building is the best investment in our modern times,' Mr Hancock blusters on. 'Unlike ships, you will always find houses in the same spot you left them. You ought to do it yourself.'

'I, a landlord? I shall have to think on that.' One of the horses snorts and tosses its head. Jem studies his nails. 'Very well, sir, when my work dries up you may expect me.'

'Whenever you are at your liberty.'

'And my team ...'

'I leave that to your discretion.' The shipwrights are a loyal tribe; one does not prosper without his brothers. This accounts for their Wesleyan tendencies.

'Good.' Mr Thorpe clears his throat. 'Thank you, Mr Hancock. This sets my mind a little easier.'

'Think nothing of it. God go with you, Jem Thorpe.'

'And with you, I'm sure. Good day.' Mr Thorpe turns off down the lane, striding firmly over the rutted mud and greasy puddles, swinging his wood chips to steady himself.

'Now drive,' says Mr Hancock, rapping his cane on the cab ceiling, 'for I am in a fearsome hurry. Buck up now, sir, for the love of Christ!'

And they draw up to Union Street, which was – until the arrival of the stucco palaces on Butt Lane – the very finest address in Deptford. Lintels carved with swirling foliage and precarious cherubs protrude one by one by one from uniform brick fronts in the most pleasing rhythm, but the driver remains undazzled. In London there are streets upon streets of such harmonious proportion; any common weaver or pickle-bottler might live in such a place.

'Two shillings sixpence,' snaps the driver.

'And worth every farthing. Allow me to . . .' He digs in his case and retrieves his tiny brass scales, true to a grain of sand and certainly to a clipped coin. 'Now just one moment . . .' He sits bolt upright in the back of the coach, furrowing his brow and willing his scales true with such fervency that his eyes start to cross.

'I'll take my chance on the coin,' says the driver.

''Tis as much for your own benefit as for mine,' says the merchant. 'You earned the full payment for your troubles, did you not?'

'I'd not argue with that.'

Eventually the balance is weighed and paid to the satisfaction of all parties, and Mr Hancock may at last quit the coach, and the coachman quit Deptford, vowing never to cross the river again in his life.

In the house, he hears his sister's voice before he sees her.

'A mermaid?' she barks. She stands at the turn of the staircase, her dress shrouded in a coarse linen work-apron, her hands on her hips. 'A mermaid! What were you thinking?'

'How did you find out?' he asks weakly.

'As if it could have passed me by! Mr Lippard saw it in the *Gazette* the very morning it came in. *Now did you know anything of this?* says he. *It cannot be,* says I, *for the Hancocks are respectable people . . .*'

'I know,' he sighs. 'Sister, it was hardly my choice.'

Sukie appears behind her, clutching her pencil and swollen pocketbook, her hair tucked under her cap and her shoulders slumped. He tries to catch her eye but she'll none of it, only turning the corners of her mouth down a little further.

'And *this* one,' snaps Hester, 'told me nothing of it, although she knows her own fortune depends entirely on this family's reputation.'

'She was ignorant of it,' says Mr Hancock. Sukie's eyes widen. 'I kept it from her entirely.'

'Lies! You had her selling tickets. There for anybody to see, as if she were no better than a carnival girl. Mrs Williams saw her with her own eyes; counting out money easy as anything, she told me, talking and laughing with any man that lined up.' Sukie's cheeks are scarlet. She drops her head. 'What will people think of her? Hmm? Do you think of her reputation?'

'No,' he says. 'No, I did not think.' Regretfully, he climbs the stairs towards them. Even now that they are both old his spirit flinches from Hester as his body flinched when he was a little child and she a great girl of sixteen: then, her grip was too tight on his wrist, her step too brisk to keep alongside, and she wiped his face but never kissed him, and taught him his prayers and letters with no satisfaction in his progress but only relief at her duty being done. She is now fifty-five, as straight and cool as a steel pin, with ten fine children to exert her will upon the world.

'You never think,' Hester goes on. 'You take no care at all. Those things that are said about a young lady are not easily forgot, but *you* do not care—'

'Come, take your ease,' he sighs.

'And *I*, who have devoted my life to this family, these children, for it to come to this?'

'Where is Bridget?' He squeezes past her and leads the way to the parlour. 'Have her bring us water for tea. You must be ready for some refreshment.'

Mrs Lippard objects to the practice of afternoon tea – perhaps rightly since its cornerstones are idleness, sugar and gossip – but nothing else is so conducive to a tête-à-tête, and she has a great deal to get off her mind. As all the rooms in the house, the parlour is small and narrow, its panelling stained a prudent tobacco colour to conceal the soot that the fireplace fails to draw. The tea-table is rackety and unfashionable, the service older than any Hancock now living, its thick off-white glaze daubed with blue intended to recall Chinese scenery. If it were ever a convincing counterfeit for the shell-thin luminous porcelain Mr Hancock now-a-days imports in quantity, its time has passed. A chip in the rim of the sugar bowl reveals coarse earthenware beneath.

Mr Hancock watches his sister's eyes sweep all before them. She has seen – he knows – the floss of cobweb on the wings of the seraph at the top of the stairs, which Bridget cannot reach without standing on the three-legged stool. She has seen the door to the kitchen left ajar and beyond it the door to the yard wide open for any stray dog or child to chance their luck. She has seen that the skirting was not scrubbed before its last painting, and so its surface is now for ever granular with trapped dust. She has seen things that he himself has not yet seen, and which he will discover with regret and agony after she has gone: she has seen, and he knows he has been found wanting.

Bridget trundles in with hot water in its pewter vessel, and Mr Hancock is proud of how well she remembers her place, for although she flicks a few appealing glances to her friend Sukie, she says nothing, and leaves dutifully.

'I want you to set up an order with the butcher,' Hester says. 'Meat to be delivered every week. Make a note, Sukie. Tuesdays: meat.'

'Oh no,' he says, 'I've no need for that. It makes needless trouble; 'tis only the three of us here, counting the girl, and I am out often enough. We buy it as we need it.'

'Spoken like a man!' snorts Hester. 'This is the sort of woeful disarray I cannot stand for. Not a thought for household economy; never knowing today what one will eat tomorrow. For shame, I never heard the like.'

'But who will eat it all?'

'I hardly care if it gets ate, or by whom,' says Hester firmly. 'Sukie needs to learn. And it will bring an orderliness of time that your lives are sadly wanting of at present.' She sighs. 'Sometimes I cannot judge which of you is the less grateful. You encourage one another in your lack of care. I know that the fault with Sukie is not in my rearing, for all her sisters are a credit to me, but *this* one . . . When I saw the state of her cuffs today . . .'

'Sorry,' says Mr Hancock immediately, although he can hardly be found accountable for such female concerns.

'Consider,' Hester says, 'that linens lie immediately upon the skin, and so what are people to think when they observe a cuff as filthy as hers were this morning?'

'That I had no time to change them after scrubbing the stairs,' growls Sukie, staring studiedly out of the window. 'That is what they are to think.'

'What were you about? Scrubbing the stairs with your good cuffs on, which cost three shillings at the last May Fair, and which you will certainly not see the like of again unless you can pay for them yourself?'

'Trying them out,' whispers Sukie.

'This is very regrettable,' says Mr Hancock helplessly.

'Regrettable is the least of it. I am ashamed to be associated with this household sometimes, I truly am, and sorely grieved to connect my husband Lippard's name with such slatternliness.'

Sukie twitches most briefly, as if nipped by a flea.

'And see what you have done now!' Hester remembers the

original reason for her exercised temper. 'You have gave up your finest ship for a folly, and you exhibit it around the city like a gypsy showman!'

'What would you have me do? I shall never own another mermaid,' he says weakly.

'Fie, for shame! I am glad that our poor father did not live to see this.'

He ought to raise his voice to her now, for she has no right. And yet he cannot treat her as what she is, a woman past her usefulness, yoked to another man's fortune and with many sons and daughters to attend to her interests before he should be prevailed upon. He cradles his tea bowl on his lap and watches her as she talks, transfixed as a hen by a serpent. Gold wire glints behind her teeth, and she talks on and on – 'uncommon misfortune'; 'an insult, when one thinks of it'; 'outraged' – only pausing each second sentence when her plate slips sideways across her palate and she adjusts it with a discreet smack of her chops. Then she concludes, 'And I'll wager you will not make even a penny by it.'

'I already have.'

'Pardon?'

'It has been extremely lucrative.'

She snorts and pours herself more tea with vigour disproportionate to the task. A few drops spatter the cloth, and he watches them soak slowly into it. 'It will never pay off your losses,' Hester says.

''Tis halfway to doing so already.'

Sukie nods. 'I have seen the books, Mama. 'Tis true.' *Or near enough*, her eyes admit to his across the table; Mrs Chappell's contribution is still the larger part of their takings.

'You have not had it three weeks!'

He taps his temple. 'I made the best of what I was delivered. You forget I am a canny businessman.'

'I merely hope you do not forget your duty to your kin,' sniffs Hester, taking another and sharper look at the quality of the floor-cloth, the clock, the marble-painted mantelpiece. 'Or perhaps in your good fortune you have decided the Hancock family numbers only *one*.'

'I know the size of my family,' he says wearily. A man without the immediate demands of wife and children finds himself called upon for a multitude of little wants elsewhere. He has three sisters living, each with more children than she can be expected to raise up on only her husband's fortune.

'A dowry for our Sukie,' he says, 'so she may better choose her husband. And did I not find Rachel's boy a place in our office, and settle a sum upon your Jonathan, to invest as he pleased, to be thus freer in choosing a wife?'

'Humph,' she says, and no more.

'And I am investing in land, and in property,' he continues smoothly, 'to better protect my earnings. The sea is a treacherous place for a fortune.'

'And yet our father managed it, and his father before him,' she says, with remarkable confidence for a woman who chose a brewer for her husband.

'I do not mean to be what our father was,' he says, and as he speaks he realises that he means it. 'I mean to be *better*. It is time to elevate ourselves; this is the moment for a man to climb.'

'Poppycock! Where do *you* mean to climb?'

'I hardly care.' The scales are falling from his eyes day by day, and he sees now that he has spent the greater part of his life at the periphery of things; an obscure planet through whose weak and inconstant orbit pass sisters and nieces and maids and housekeepers, before each is drawn away to her proper calling. This is no way for a man to be, whose natural place is as the axle to a wheel. 'I have lived an unexamined life,' he says. 'And I have now been shown a great thing. I would be a fool to want no more for myself.'

She is affronted, more than anything, that these words were said aloud. For Hester Lippard has toiled her whole life to be the sun at the centre of her life's orrery, the power that compels all others to move in their tight circuits about her. She has never detected this desire in her brother, and now she feels a shiver as if he has trod on the turf of her grave.

'A fool to seek beyond your place,' she says. 'Ambition is a dangerous thing.'

'We all must die one day. I ought not to leave the world just as I found it.'

'All the more reason to lead a prudent life, and protect those left behind.'

'I leave nobody behind,' he says. 'They are all before me still. I must advance.'

TWELVE

In their airy parlour in King's Place, Polly Campbell and Elinor Bewlay bend over their needlework. Mrs Chappell has retired to her apartment for an apnoeic doze, and her young charges are attended by her powder-blue footmen, who move without sound about the room and out again, seeing to their serene duties. At the window, little pale-eyed Kitty pores over her chapbook prompted by Madame Parmentier: 'Our f-ar-ther,' she intones, 'w-ho-o . . . who art in . . .'

'Do you think Mrs Neal is stooping?' Polly Campbell muses.

'Hmm?' Elinor licks a fresh thread for her needle.

'For she has not so much as *seen* the gentleman – if gentleman he may be called – and now she must escort him all evening? I had expected her not to capitulate so easy.'

Elinor shrugs. 'She is not so different from us.'

'Oh, she is. Utterly so. She can disoblige any body she chooses.'

'She's not so well set in the world as you think. She still needs Mrs Chappell's favour. And Mrs Chappell needs Mr Hancock's favour, so you see Mrs Neal is quite trapped.'

'Oh, Nell, but he is only a tradesman! Did you mark the patch of his wig that the moths had chewed through? And his horrid baggy jacket, with its patched elbows?'

'Money's money.'

'A woman in her position ought to be above that. *I* would not lower myself.' Polly is working on a little sampler, intricate with birds and creeping vines. In some other country, in the cool of the big house, her mother had her sewing fancy-work as soon as she could hold a needle. In the fields beyond the louvred shutters, women chanted as they worked, and Poll's mother hummed along without thinking. Her gold ring glinted and her needle plunged in and out of the canvas. This is what Polly remembers. 'I've an eye for the peerage,' she says now.

'Oh! They are all in debt! Gambling it away, the lot of them, drinking and stinking, and their wives are as bad. Devonshire borrows to clear his lady's debts and she borrows from Prinny to pay him back, although of course the money seldom reaches his pocket; they are all so mired in this horrid business they will never be free of it.'

'No!'

Elinor tucks her hair behind her ear and looks up from her work with the light of marvellous secrets in her eyes. 'I have the confidence of men who know,' she whispers, 'and I believe that silly couple owe about the region of sixty thou', all told.'

Polly lets out a low whistle, and Madame Parmentier's head swivels to her.

'I am surprised at such a coarse mannerism in you,' she snaps, and Polly presses her lips together before she smirks. 'Do not let me hear it again.'

The girls' eyes meet in mutual amusement. They are smug to have outgrown the jurisdiction of their old nursemaid, but even so they bend their heads over their work until they are sure she has returned her attention to Kitty's halting catechism.

'If they cannot even keep their wives, what hope is there for a mistress? I got into this line of work to *avoid* a spell in the Fleet.

Now guess how much debt – hum, let me see – Mr Moses Garrard has.'

'The *Jew*?'

'Well, that don't signify. For the sake of this question you might equally consider any modest tradesman who has done well. For they have no title, and were born to inherit no more land than we our-selves –' and at this Polly bites her tongue, for what does Elinor know how much land might be her birthright? – 'but what they do have is spotless credit, and you may trust they always will. The wealth of the peerage is a fairy glamour sustained by our banks, but a self-made man will have satisfied himself that every penny in his account is truly there.'

'It's a wonder you do not pursue this mermaid man yourself.'

'What! Me? Certainly not. He is a grotesque.'

'A grotesque of fortune and influence.'

'I am speaking generally. Once, you know, the whore and the Israelite passed their lives furtive and obscure; now the one may lie with a prince and the other ascend to a peerage.'

'In which case what might *I* attain?' This ought to be a private thought, but Polly says it aloud.

'You, the mulatto harlot? *Your* fate is unmapped.' Elinor Bewlay once thought herself monstrous for her red hair; beside the freakish Polly, with her brown skin and the hints of gold in her tight negro curls, she discovers herself a veritable mild-as-milk Madonna.

'Perhaps,' says Polly. She thinks for a little longer. 'I would gladly take up with a Portugal Jew. I find them admirable courteous.'

'I suppose you put them in mind of Moorish ladies,' says Elinor, 'who they must miss.'

'Whom,' interjects Kitty from across the room, and sits back well pleased with herself.

'As if they ever met a Moorish lady on Threadneedle Street,' scoffs Polly. 'As if you *know* what a Moorish lady looks like. You are horrid ignorant sometimes, Elinor Bewlay.'

'And you are merely horrid.' Elinor may appear as placid as a little red cow, but she has lived a year with Polly and knows how to provoke her. 'As if it matters whether you are really a Moorish lady; you are an object of indulgence, you will be whatever they think you to be.' She is not malicious, merely bored, and she conceals her delight as Polly's dusky cheek grows red, and her eyes begin to shine.

The argument is spinning faster in Pol's head than it is in the room, where all are mighty unconcerned. 'My father was a *Scotsman*,' she spits, as Mrs Chappell returns from her rest, 'and yet nobody once prevailed upon me to dance a reel. But *you* –' flinging down her sewing and wheeling round on the startled abbess – 'would have me play a houri one night and a hottentot the next.'

'I endeavour to appeal to all tastes,' soothes Mrs Chappell, unruffled, 'but in all my years no man has yet asked for a reel. When the time comes, I shall be sure to recommend you, dear Pol.'

Elinor gurgles with laughter and young Kitty smirks along with her, her mouth prudently closed. 'Scotch or African, what does it signify?' asks Elinor. 'So you've hill savages on both sides, what's there to be proud of in *that*?'

Polly seizes her furled fan and lunges to strike her across the cheek with it – 'I will have satisfaction!' – and Elinor is convulsed, quite weeping with mirth, her eyes scrunched tight and her fists clutching sheaves of her skirt.

'Oh, my!' she gasps, 'Oh, my, what a caper. What a *reel*.'

'That is enough,' says Mrs Chappell. 'The devil is in you girls today.' She turns to Madame Parmentier. 'Is this the week they all bleed?' Of the girls she asks, 'What is going on here?'

'She would disdain a man of trade,' says Elinor.

'She would deny my dignity,' snaps Polly.

'Upon the soul of the Magdalene, you are the silliest girls I ever took charge of. Forget your dignity. You can discover it again when you have made your fortune. As for disdain, there's no place for it here. This world elevates the industrious man, and if you are canny it will elevate you. Disdain! Dignity! I never heard of such squabbles. Now, are you able to put this aside?'

The girls are silent as a pair of mules.

'Yes? For I had come to bring you good news. Our mermaid is arrived.'

Kitty, at this, pushes back her chair and bounds over, a pantomime of mute excitement.

'Simeon!' barks Mrs Chappell, and in clips the taller of her two footmen, bearing on a cushion the grim little corpse. The girls twitter and crowd, but in their clean safe home it looks more an oddity than a thing of fear. Polly flicks its nose with an impertinent finger, and they all reel back chortling. She does not look Simeon in the eye, for he inspires in her an irritation she can barely express in words.

'I mean to put it in the little room off my great salon,' says Mrs Chappell. 'And to drape the place as if it were an underwater grotto, with sunken treasure and garlands of pearls. And all you girls will be decked out as sirens, and I shall have you seduce the assembly with your song.'

They are silent for a little moment. They look at the creature. 'Do you not think,' says Elinor, 'that it is – well, quite a *different* sort of mermaid? From the sort you would dress it up as?'

'Not the seductress sort,' adds Polly.

'I have eyes,' says Mrs Chappell.

'And so do our visitors. I think they will apprehend that it is a grotesque. A little imp.'

'Not like *us*.'

Mrs Chappell eyes them severely. 'None of you has yet offered me a seat,' she says. 'My suffering is never at the forefront of your mind. Attend to me, if you please.' They take her elbows and support her to the sopha. 'It don't signify what it looks like. What do people *want* of a mermaid?' she demands, spreading her shawl about her shoulders. 'A beautiful siren? Or a malevolent little beast?'

The girls say nothing.

'You know which. So which should we give them? The mermaid as it is or the mermaid as they would wish it to be?'

'But *look* at it,' says Polly.

Mrs Chappell takes from her waist a little tin of lavender comfits. She pops one in her mouth. 'Fan me,' she says. Young Kitty sets up an assiduous fluttering. 'They've their whole lives to stare ugliness in the face,' she says. 'I will not have them do so in my establishment. I mean this to be the most lavish and extraordinary event I have ever put on. Now, Polly, my little orator, will you recite me the last sonnet you got by heart?'

'In Latin or in English, madam? Or French?'

'English, English. I am bilious today, my stomach will tolerate nothing but the purest Shakespeare. And, Elinor, you might play awhile for me, at least until the tea is brought in. Kitty! Enough of your wafting. Rub my feet.'

Samuel, the second footman, appears in the door. 'Miss Polly,' he says. 'One waits for you below.'

'Ugh.' She rolls her eyes. 'Early again.' To the women: 'Am I presentable?'

'Here – come here,' beckons Mrs Chappell, spitting on her handkerchief; seizing Polly's chin she scrubs at a smut on her cheek. The girl bends to her as springy as a willow wand. 'Captain Tremaine, is it? Your usual Thursday afternoon? I would have him come sit with us for a while but I cannot trust you girls to maintain any conversational niceness today. Now, that plain cap won't do. Where is your turban?'

Polly's brow lowers. 'It is troublesome.'

'Well, you cannot be the Queen of Carthage without it. Now, make haste, upstairs. The robe laid out in the dressing room is the one I wish you to wear. And will you try – *try* – to have him gone by six; you will want time to dress again.'

'The sooner I go, the sooner 'tis done,' protests Polly, pulling away. As she rustles past the piano, Elinor cannot help whispering, 'Which are you, then? A beautiful siren or a malevolent little beast?' and Polly cannot help delivering a sharp nip to her persecutor's forearm.

'That is what I thought,' says Elinor.

THIRTEEN

'Where are you going?' asks Sukie, which surprises Mr Hancock. It is mid-afternoon, and he is busy in his counting-house, drawing on a pipe as he tots up the cost of his proposed new building works.

'Why, nowhere. I am busy.'

'But later. Bridget has your good cuffs all starched and pressed. You are going somewhere.'

He shifts his pipe stem from one side of his mouth to the other, and bends over his books. Tonight the mermaid will be revealed at Mrs Chappell's house, a place Sukie cannot even know of, much less visit. Indeed, he has told her nothing of its removal from Murray's keeping, but this makes it all the worse, for she is confused, and alert to clues. He regrets that it will not be displayed in a place whose grandeur equals its probity, where he could bring her to see the fine people, and be admired by them as the niece of the mermaid man. How breathlessly she would have reported on it to her mother and her sisters; how proud she would have been that she, and she alone, had been so favoured by fortune. Instead she scurries down the dark stairs of his house; eyes his dress and demeanour enquiringly; lingers outside his office door. 'I wish you would tell me,' she says, this girl of fourteen, with her hands on her hips. 'I was a help to you before, was I not? I could come with you again.'

'Who is master of this house?' he snaps.

She takes a little step back. 'Oh. I merely—'

He has never raised his voice to her before: her face is as stupefied as if he had raised his hand.

'You are prying,' he says. ''Tis not seemly. And what use would the knowledge be to you? My place is out there –' he waves his arms across to the window, the dockyard beyond – 'and yours is in here. I go out, you stay in. I do my duty, you do yours; then 'tis all harmonious. Do you understand?'

She has a thunderous scowl on her. *I have indulged her to a dangerous degree,* he realises. *She thinks too much of herself.* Aloud he says, 'Susanna, if you mean to keep a place in any household, do not overreach it. I'll have no more of your presuming.' Her bottom lip quivers. *Please God do not let her weep in front of me.* 'I am on my own business,' he says more gently. 'It's not for you.' Will she answer him back? His authority will not take much more challenging. 'Get you gone,' he says softly. 'Lay out my fine linens and brush my best jacket. I am wanted in London at nine tonight.'

For his own whoring, Mr Hancock naturally inclines towards the upstairs room of a genial tavern, where the passing girls are almost incidental to the gaming table, buxom and giddy, confident in their cups and at their cards. Even if he were to regularly frequent whorehouses – and he never has, not in the first dark years of his bereavement, and not now that they stretch before and behind him – Mrs Chappell's nunnery is like nothing he has known. It is in a narrow courtyard off King Street, and both outside and in is as grand as any ducal residence – indeed, it might be one, being in such proximity to Court – and the roads not only paved, but additionally so clean as to have been fairly scrubbed. The people he sees strolling or riding between park and palace are very grand – ladies in shimmering court dresses, and their men tall and modish in blue and buff – and walk without fear of abuse or soil. The women do not pick their skirts up to keep them from the filthy gutters; the men do not look nervously about them for bareheaded urchins who would pelt them with mud and worse. Mr Hancock, borne from the barber's in a chair to keep the marks of the city from his good clothes, feels a glorious relief.

He is not the first visitor to Mrs Chappell's nunnery this evening: the alley into King's Place is narrow in the extreme, so that a peevish crush of carriages must await entry in the street, horses wickering and coachmen squabbling, emblazoned all with crests identifiable to any observer as those of noble families. As Mr Hancock watches from his chair, a gentleman whose face he knows well from its regular appearance in print-shop windows leans out of a carriage and hails a passer-by by name.

'And in full view of the street,' he tuts. 'For anybody to see, as if they were proud of 't.' To the chair men he raps on the ceiling and says, 'We shall never get through the crush. Set me down here.'

He walks into the courtyard and up to a fine stuccoed house with torches blazing on either side of its steps and lights hung up all around in blown-glass bubbles. He feels as anxious as if he were sixteen years old and this his first visit upon Venus. *But this is merely the gentry's version of the same,* he reassures himself. *Underneath the show, 'tis an amusing evening with sympathetic women, and the end result will be no different.*

He is ushered in by a negro footman, of uncommon height and elegance. His powder-blue livery is almost angelic to gaze upon and when he says, 'This way, sir,' his voice is musical but modulated, soft yet penetrating. He is better spoken than Mr Hancock, and he smells of lilac-flowers. All at once Mr Hancock is acutely aware of the fraying cuff of his own good jacket, the gold threads on its pockets that have tarnished black. 'For who will be paying attention to me?' he had reasoned as he dressed at home, not bothering to light the candles for such a perfunctory undertaking. He sees now that this was a mistake. There is a splash of walnut ketchup on the calf of his stocking.

The marble floor of the atrium is polished as a frozen pond, its inlaid tables almost concealed beneath cornucopiae of flowers gaudy as jungle-birds: he could not name even one single specimen. There are a great many candles set about the place, and mirrors and chandeliers that double their light and double it again. Up above him, where the staircase spirals into darkness, he hears the whispers of girls, and the officious cloppeting of their cork-soled shoes on the parquet.

Mrs Chappell is there to greet him, a vast toad in white muslin, her stubby arms outstretched and her legs churning up her skirts as she paddles across the gleaming floor.

'Dear sir!' she says. 'Delighted, delighted.' He does not like procuresses – women debauched in their own youth who usher the next generation to the same fate – but he is relieved that his mermaid's entrée into high society has been overseen by an expert. She has launched numberless girls onto their glittering careers: she can be assumed to manage the same for his wizened freak.

'I believe you will approve of what we have done with the little thing,' she is saying now, patting his hand. ''Tis upstairs, in the salon. But first, a drink? We are having a little merrymaking in my private rooms. Just a cosy gathering, you know, but 'tis rarely now that all these luminaries are seen together in one place.'

'Does my mermaid please them?'

'Ah, they are addicted to novelty. This is the most uncommon sight since Mr Lunardi's balloon journey. And before that I daresay we've had nothing like it since Cook's return.'

'And so you would judge that I might make a true success of this creature?' he asks.

'Sir, if the Ton is enchanted by it, and London enchanted by it, the world will be enchanted too. 'Tis already settled: the mermaid is a sensation.'

He blinks. 'Much obliged,' is all he can think to say.

She claps him on the back with a phlegmy roar of mirth, revealing once again those yellow teeth arranged like a string of knucklebones. 'The gentleman is obliged! It is I who am obliged to *you*. But come with me, sir, do come this way. Take a glass –' for a tray has appeared from nowhere – 'take two.'

It is a relief to find Mrs Chappell's parlour so neat and proper, with a parquet floor and the walls papered with a green trellis design such as might meet the approval of any of his matron sisters. Tonight it fairly glows with richness, thanks in some part to its population. In the corner are a little brood of her younger girls, the red-haired one assiduously nodding over the harpsichord, the Creole (or mulatto, or whatever she might be, for this categorising age must have a name for every permutation) who first approached him, sullenly turning the pages. Mr Hancock has heard tales that the junior girls earn their keep by scrubbing the grates and making the beds themselves, in which case the faint clank and splash of buckets behind the jib door speaks for the narrow distinction between housemaid and whore.

His attention barely brushes across these girls, however, for here sits a group of women, splendidly dressed and languorous in the way of Olympian females, and lit warmly by shaded candles. They have been talking quietly together, but when they see him they fall quiet. They do not drop their eyes but look straight at him without abashment.

'Ladies,' says Mrs Chappell, and they rise without a moment's hesitation, elegantly and silently the way the sea gathers itself into a fresh wave, and in unison drop a curtsey with the same slow and elemental grace, and a long hissing of satin and lace. They smell of port and bitter almonds.

They watch him gravely, their fans fluttering, and he thinks they are not like any women he has seen in his life before. There are five of them, and each truly handsome, not with the clean prettiness of the younger girls he has seen thus far, but each with her own singularity. One is tall and slender, boyish and wistful; one bold and sleek as a kingfisher; one soft and fondly smiling like the perfect memory of an adored mother. Each of their faces is familiar to him, and yet each is entirely new, delightful and uncommon to look upon. He apprehends, perhaps for the first time, what taste and intellect the appreciation of true beauty entails, for these women are complex in their loveliness. Mrs Chappell speaks their names as he kisses their outstretched hands, but he knows them already: the first is a lady of the court who stooped to become a lady of the world; the second a comic actress; the third a one-time mistress of the Prince himself. The fourth is a keen little creature, with soft dark eyes and a russety glint in her coiffure. 'Mrs Fortescue,' says Mrs Chappell, and the ostrich feathers in her hair nod. And finally the fifth, whom he first observes is small and then observes is radiant: a buxom bright-cheeked froth of a woman, with hair falling over her shoulders and drifting around her face gold as sunset clouds.

'You,' he croaks, and a little crease appears at the top of her nose.

'Forgive me, I do not ... Have we met before?'

'No, no.' Heat rushes up his neck and suffuses into his ears and cheeks. He believes he recognises her – her face is somehow very familiar to him – but he cannot say from where.

'*I* know. You saw my picture in the Academy. It was very popular the year it was displayed.'

He does not go to the Academy. He does not like the jostle of it; he has no desire to crane to look upon a painted duchess he will never have call to recognise, or a landscape so unlike the vista of London that it must be fanciful; the history paintings are too huge for him, overpowering in their crammed, twisting bodies and urgent movement. But he knows where he has seen her: a yellowed print, curled at the corner and smeared by many fingers, tacked up in a coffee-house. *The Comic Muse*, it is titled, and a girl with Angelica's pointed chin smiles out, her robe falling from one plump shoulder, rippled chiffon only skimming her bosom. He had not thought it showed a real woman, only some tumbled mirthful fantasy, but yes. That woman is this woman.

'I have seen your portrait,' he says.

Her smile is like stars on water. 'So I am still recognised! And on the strength of *one single picture*. I have been out of the world for some little while, and yet I am not forgotten. Do you know my name?'

He looks at his shoes. She chortles, but he feels that she watches him more sharply than she might; he feels he is being weighed up, his worth gauged.

'Mrs Neal,' she says. 'And I know all about you: you are Mr Hancock, the mermaid man.'

With Mr Hancock's rusticity in mind, Angelica has dressed herself as a sort of courtly shepherdess: her creamy silk mantua is bordered with chenille flowers, which crowd around her wrists and neck like blooms along a country path. She has a healthy out-of-doors glow to her cheeks and her eyes. As the party resumes its seats, and he is encouraged into a wing-back armchair, she appears at his elbow with a glass of ratafia. It swirls viscous up the sides of the glass and burns his throat when he takes a sip. Angelica Neal pulls up a cane chair beside him.

'These are all my girls, or were once,' gusts Mrs Chappell, unwilling to leave off her introductory speech. 'I summoned them back to me for this important night – for your night – and without hesitation they came. They never cease to be my girls, you see, though they go all ways in the world.'

'Some ways more salubrious than others,' says the actress, and although a ripple of amusement passes through all the women, none seek to quip further.

'It takes a special sort to stay the course,' says Mrs Chappell. 'Although, as we were just raising a glass, our little Bel is leaving it ere long.'

'Don't say so,' says Bel Fortescue, resuming her seat. 'I am only getting married.'

The women are sleek as ever but the air prickles: Mr Hancock cannot guess what it is they communicate to one another but he knows when women are speaking through means other than words. Mrs Fortescue knows too; the corners of her lips twitch upward.

'Mr Hancock,' says the regal Whig mistress, louder and with more emphasis than is necessary in that small room, 'I have been desperate all night to congratulate you on your mermaid.'

'A wondrous creature,' the ladies chime in, turning to him like a clan of kind aunts.

'Oh, fabulous.'

'Of great value to science, I don't doubt.'

'How lucky we are!'

'Mr Hancock,' persists Mrs Fortescue, turning the intensity of her eyes and the sweetness of her smile upon him, 'do you agree that women are doomed to servility?'

The dazed smile remains on his face for some moments after his mind has begun to panic. He did not expect to be asked questions, and his head is very empty. In his general life, Mr Hancock sees no need or benefit in questioning how things are, and avoids the society of what he calls 'clever men' – that is, men who reflect on the *why* of things and who wish to discuss it. To now be confronted with a clever *woman* is beyond his preparation. He must grapple with what her meaning might be before he can even think to give her a reply.

'. . . servility?' he mouths.

'It is a philosophical question,' Mrs Fortescue says cheerfully, but if she means to soothe him her words have the opposite effect.

'You do not have to answer her,' snaps Angelica Neal, a waft of rose-otto at his side. 'She is too serious. Nobody wants her sort of debate here.' She places a hand on his sleeve.

'But we all are servile,' he blurts out. 'Men also.'

'Servile to what?' Bel Fortescue fixes him with her keen dark eyes as her questions press him into a smaller and smaller space. 'What are *you* servant to, sir? Do you, Mr Hancock, believe in the notion of free will?'

'Hold your tongue, Bel!' snaps Angelica. 'We are having a pleasant evening; why you cannot simply—'

'The woman is touched,' whispers the Whig, which sets all the women off a-muttering.

'. . . I have been saying it for years . . .'

'. . . altogether too absorbed in her own intellect . . .'

'. . . why is she still *invited* . . . ?'

'Money,' he says.

'Beg pardon?'

'Money. If you are asking, am I in command of all my doings, I say no. I am guided by money.' He does not know if this is his honest answer, only that, once he made sense of the question, it was the one that leapt from the top of his head. He thinks too late that the correct answer is 'God', and makes a note to pray more often.

'And does this trouble you?' asks Mrs Fortescue.

'No. This is how things are.'

'Yes,' nod the women vigorously. 'Yes, this is how things *are*.'

Bel Fortescue is still frowning, but Mrs Chappell stirs in her chair. 'And so we are all free,' she says with finality, 'free in this small little world of our own design.' She swings her head to Angelica Neal, who all of a sudden snatches up Mr Hancock's hand.

'I cannot wait one moment longer,' she cries. 'I want to see your mermaid! For can you believe it, I still have not had the opportunity. Will you accompany me?' She is dragging him away without waiting for an answer, her hair bouncing around her shoulders. Her hand is warm and slightly damp, but the sensation of being clasped by her delicate fingers is enough to set a slight kindling feeling in his breeches.

She leads him up to the first-floor landing, another vast space hung with red damask and the sweatier sort of history paintings – torn drapery, upraised cutlasses, and rearing, white-eyed horses: he cares for them as little as any others he has seen, but judges nonetheless that these are quality copies, done from the source and no doubt specially commissioned.

'That little vixen!' Angelica is saying. 'I never know what she is at.'

He does not know how to respond. 'You have known her a long time?'

'Aye. We were raised together in this house for some number of years. Of course, she was not called Bel then: her name is Harriet and she is quite flat-chested.'

There is a pair of closed double doors on the landing from where the sounds of a party emanate: there is a string quartet, laughter, the clinking of glasses. Another negro as cool and statuesque as the first swings these doors open, and ushers them within with a pair of spotless kid gloves. *This is a new kind of intimidation*, Mr Hancock thinks. No lantern-jawed bullies to keep the clients in their place, only handsome blackamoors to strike them into apologetic silence.

Angelica rattles on. 'Oh, she has ever talked this way, "indentured servitude" and "legal prostitution" and la-la-la – one wonders how she got to be where she is, for she is not so very beautiful ... ?' Inflecting this last phrase as a question, she looks back at him over her shoulder with her wide clear eyes. Her powdered cheek is apricot-soft, but his tongue is fat in his mouth, his mind too slow; he cannot say the words he wishes he could, and which she is waiting for: 'Not as beautiful as you.'

Whenever Mr Hancock feels overpowered by his situation, he turns his mercantile eye upon it. And so, on entering Mrs Chappell's great salon, he does not note the shards of rainbow-tipped light that bounce across the walls, but the rock-crystal pendants of the chandelier that scattered them, and he does not see the bare throats and bosoms of the girls but rather the gauzy muslin they are swathed in. He sees barley-sugar glass sconces and says to himself, *Murano*; he sees the pretty pink-and-green-painted porcelain vases and thinks, *Bow*; the fine silk upholstery ... he sniffs. French, without question. Smuggled. Now, is that not the measure of the woman? In his mind he strips the place down into its many precious parts – the swagged silk at the windows; the decanters of sack and port and shrub; the leopard-spotted heartwood tables – names them carefully and prices them up, as if by understanding the machinery he might also understand its effect. He marks the people, of course, but both sexes are a bafflement to him. They are not his sort, *although perhaps I must now try to be theirs*, he thinks to himself. Each of the women is dazzlingly turned out in fashions quite new to him, and he endeavours to commit to memory the particular ways they dress their hair and wear their gowns, so that he might describe it to Sukie later. She is always hungry to know the fashions of the city, but he has no eye for them: 'No, but what *kind* of train?' she demands, or, 'And you did not note whether she carried a fan?' and so he finds he has let her down once more.

'Mark that,' says Angelica, 'Parliament is in session *here* if not yet in the House.'

He looks, and yes, indeed, these men now filing in are all great men, their faces so well known to him that it feels as if he has stepped through flat paper into a moving version of the pamphlets passed around his coffee-house. He has furthermore seen some of them in person on occasion, when business sends him to the westerly end of Oxford Street or the fine leafy squares to its north, and sometimes in the reeking bellowing crowd at cockfights or exhibitions, but they are of a different water, he knows that, not to be touched or spoken to however close they pass him by.

'Are they all – are they here for me?' he asks weakly. 'For my mermaid?'

'Aye,' she says. 'It's the talk of the town.'

'All their important doings,' he says, 'and they set them by to come *here*?'

'To see your mermaid.'

He cannot credit it. Members of Parliament, titled men, with the most sharpened intellect and loftiest ambition, have been drawn to something he, Mr Hancock, brought before them. 'I had never expected such a thing,' he says, and she squeezes his hand as if he were a little child brought as a treat to the menagerie.

'You may expect this sort of thing now,' she says.

All this being said, to him they do not appear splendid. Their blue-and-buff costumes are too much of a muchness for him to tell one from another, although some of them are young and tall and others bent old men, or corpulent in their middle age. Furthermore they are neither clean nor tidy; they look as if they have not slept at all, and from their stained shirts and unfurled stocks comes the acrid smell of bodies so soused in liquor that it now emanates from their pores. He rasps his hand across his jaw; it is smoother, probably, than some of theirs, which straggle with three days' growth or more.

They mark him as he moves amongst them – he feels the twitching of their small eyes – but they cannot make sense of him. Is he a tradesman come stumbling in at the wrong door? A persistent drunk yearning after one of the acolytes of Venus? Or indeed, an angry father come to haul his daughter back to niceness? They cannot guess; they will not approach him, and they turn back into their conversations.

'Did 'oo *imagine*,' one drawls, 'that such a fing would come of it?'

'Hie could ey hev?' replies his friend. 'Ey never *titched* the girl before.'

Of course if Mr Hancock finds their speech peculiar it is only for his own lack of cultivation: if he cannot recognise their baby-talk and garbled vowels as the signallers of good breeding that they are, the loss is all his. Since he has spent two score years outside the society of genteel Whigs, he must be forgiven for hearing their speech as a cacophony of pantomime sneezes; they pronounce the first syllable with great energy, and trail off into a drawl as if between a word's first letter and its last they have lost all conviction in what they are saying. He is aware – and ashamed of – his dislike for them; he is a Tory through and through, as his father was before him. It is the logical, the patriotic, the honest choice. He has never until this moment felt in any means awkward about it.

At the far end of the room a crowd has gathered around another pair of double doors, and as he watches this crowd loosens and pulls back a step or two as a couple emerge, pink-faced and giddy.

'What is it like?' he hears the waiting people cry, but the gabble of the couple is inaudible at this distance: he only hears the girl's breathless giggle and sees her raise her fists to either side of her face

122

in mimicry of the mermaid's rigor. Some of the young men and women try to peep through the gap in the door.

'Oh, ho, no, you must wait your turn!' and in goes a trio of girls with their arms knotted around one another. Once within they let up a-shrieking, and barrel back out at once, clamouring their surprise and horror.

'All these people,' says Angelica Neal, 'come to see your mermaid. Come on your account.' She drags him through the crowd breathlessly, chattering over her shoulder. 'The girls are enthralled by it; they relish being so frightened. I believe you must have many extraordinary tales.'

Her eyes flick briefly to his mouth before she turns back to the door and raps her fist against it. 'Hurry up in there! We are more important than you!' She turns her back to the door so she can look up at him. 'I wonder does it reassure the men,' she says, 'the way Bel scorns the situation of women? They can feel easy that she has chose this life herself.'

Again he has nothing to add, save for a meek 'I daresay'.

'*I* chose it,' she says softly. She draws closer to him, a warm cloud of starch and flowers and her own ripe skin-scent. 'Do you know why?'

He shakes his head.

'Because I am never happier than in a man's embrace. There is no pleasure in the world that I like better.' Their bodies are very close; she presses her palms flat against the door on either side of her hips so that she is turned to face him square on. He tries not to gaze upon her bosom but it is always in his vision as he looks bashfully at her throat, her chin, her lips: it rises pale and soft as she breathes deeply, and the velvet flowers heave.

When the doors open behind her she falls flat on her back.

Three young navymen in plush indigo jackets and white breeches are coming out, and when she tumbles nearly straight into them they cannot disentangle their consternation from their mirth.

''Pon my soul,' says one, his black hair all awry, while the others – merry with wine – clutch their sides until tears squeeze from their eyes. ''Pon my soul, you dizzy maid, what were you about?'

Mr Hancock stands all dismayed; the collapse of his companion is one thing, but he has always felt wistful at the sight of young men in blue jackets; since his youth he cherished the ambition that a son of his would go to the navy, and it may yet be that young Henry carouses now on some foreign shore, a midshipman with ruffled curls just as these he sees before him.

When Mr Hancock makes no move to help her, the dark-haired lieutenant reaches down to take Angelica's hand. 'Do not trouble yourself,' she snaps, ruffled as a cat who has fallen off a fence.

'Forgive me,' says Mr Hancock, leaping belatedly to her assistance, but what with her great heavy skirts and her stays which prevent the necessary bending, she flounders there, and rises not at all. The men stand in a semicircle watching, one giggling helplessly, while she slumps on the floor, the merchant heaving on her arm with much perspiration.

After some minutes of this the lieutenant steps in again – 'You must permit me' – and he taking one of Angelica's arms and Mr Hancock the other, they hoist her to her feet in a moment.

'She is launched!' cries one of the men.

'I'll drink to that,' says another, and they rollick away with a great huzzah.

'Are you hurt?' says Mr Hancock, but Angelica, shaking out her skirts and fluffing out her hair, is only rageful.

'Close the door, for pity's sake,' she snaps. 'Do not make me any more of a spectacle.'

'Am I to stay?' he ventures, but she is too busy patting herself down to answer, grumbling.

'And who invited them, after all, such horrid tars? This vulgar sort of revelry would never have been tolerated in this establishment ten years back; the company is *not* what it was –' and at this moment she shoots him a look of such particular venom that he supposes he ought to leave her alone. Then again he is afraid to be out in that thronged room unescorted. Choosing to take his chances on a ruffled woman over a supercilious crowd, he shuts the door – bolts it for good measure – and they are alone in the mermaid's grotto.

In fact, it is very well done. Mrs Chappell has somehow contrived to bring in an array of great glass fish tanks, with gilt chasing, full of green water and pearly fish. There are green and blue shades on all the candles, so what little light there is has a queer underwater coolness to it, and the walls are swagged and draped with raw silk and strings of pearls. The mermaid itself is raised up on a plinth, surrounded by branches of red and white coral, and the flickering candlelight gives the impression of movement, as if the coral were fluttering and the infant mermaid squirming. Somewhere in the room, a little fountain is splashing.

And then there is the singing.

He sees no girls in the room but their voices weave around him in a high wordless melody, as if all the sirens had banded together to lure him to their shores. The noises of the party without melt into oblivion.

'Oh,' says Angelica. She has composed herself, and her eyes are upon the crooked little mermaid. 'So this is what they look like.' In the shifting light she is soft around the edges.

When she becomes aware of his gaze, she smiles as if she has never been put out in the first place. 'Do you like it?' she asks.

'I do,' he says, and she advances upon him across the room, her silks sighing.

'Come,' she says, 'I wish to look more closely,' and taking his hand leads him to stand before the creature. Although he affects a face of grave study, he has looked upon the mermaid far too many times to apprehend anything new about it, and his eyes rest upon it without seeing it at all. He cannot think, with her so close to him – and leaning in ever closer – of anything besides her. Every single nerve in his fingers aches and sings as she caresses them; she is so close that her arm presses against his, and the warmth of her body, the suggestion of her skin, is a shock to him. The invisible singing rises gently, and he thinks, *this is not the music of mermaids but of angels.* She puts her face up to his, very serious, so pretty that he wishes to press his lips to the little crease between her brows. But he does not move. Her lips are just parted; her eyes seek his.

With her body so near to him, he already feels he is about to die, but then she makes a little wriggle and her stays slip down her bosom. Either she is very expert in what she does, or there is an ingenuity to her clothes that is lacking in other women's, for she does it in a single swift movement and all the while looking perfectly at him. She only exposes another inch of herself, but her breasts strain against the band of chenille flowers, and the smell of vanilla and roses rises into the room, along with another smell, what he thinks must be that of her own body, something like that sharp and flowery scent that rises off the skin of orchard fruit – plums or peaches – a sun-warmed fragrance, a kind of promise. There is no slackness to what he sees of her breasts; they are full and pale, seamed with one or two pearly lines, quivering just fractionally in time with her pulse.

'Here,' she whispers and, lifting his hand, places it squarely upon her bosom. For a moment, his bare skin upon hers, he is lost. Her breasts are pressed together by her stays, faintly damp with her sweat, and they yield with a little spring to his fingertips. If he were bolder he would run hands over them, and press and squeeze and fill his palms with them, but he is quite simply petrified.

He stands stock-still, as if a small boy caught in the act of misdemeanour, but he cannot remove his hand from her body. She is as soft as – well, what is there to compare it to? She is not soft like velvet or silk, nor like lambswool. She is soft as human flesh, that is all, fair warm skin blanketed over a vale of womanly fat, and somewhere deep underneath it all are her tendons and muscles, her hot blood, her pumping heart.

'My soul!' he whispers, and there is a little falter in the singing, comparable to a giggle.

In the swimming green light she looks up into his face with a peculiar expression: mischief or adoration.

'What I wish you to do to me . . .' she whispers, and it is all he can do to control himself.

They press together a little longer. Her hair drifts around both their faces in the upgust from the candles. The mermaid hunches darkly under its glass dome, but neither one of them is thinking of it.

'But the night is very young,' Angelica is murmuring, interspersing her words with little wet kisses on his lips and his face. Her kisses are firm and delicate, like her mouth: he can feel the particular arch of her upper lip even as she presses it against him. 'We have already spent too long locked up together, when others are hammering to take their place in here.' She takes his hand again. 'Will you rejoin the party with me?'

He wants to pull her back to him: he puts his hands on her waist and cannot help then but to run them down her back and over her hips, up to her breasts; there is something compelling about the shape of her body, its symmetry, its dimensions, the very glide of her, that he thinks he could spend all day touching and never tire of.

'Come along,' she says again, tugging him towards her. He is hard as a yardstick.

'May I not ...?' he asks. 'Here, where it is private. I could be quick.'

'I daresay you could,' and there is a little flicker of he-knows-not-what in her eyes. Perhaps he has mis-spoke, but he has always had the impression they are grateful when a gentleman is quick. She pulls away, as if it is easy for her. 'Outside there is a party all for your sake. Mrs Chappell has laid on many splendid things that you have not yet seen – and I wish to dance.' She is unbolting the door but before she throws it wide she looks up at him one more time with those wide eyes of hers, and says, 'When you take your pleasure with me, sir, I mean to take my time about it.'

He sees a flash of white teeth upon her lower lip. Then she is all sunny mischief. 'Come!' she says. 'The entertainment begins.'

FOURTEEN

The first thing he notices as they return to the great chamber is that every member of the little orchestra has turned his face to the wall. They play on with their backs to the proceedings, their chins lowered, and even their leader has his toes a mere inch from the skirting, so that when he becomes too inspired in his conducting he raps his knuckles against the panelling.

'What is afoot?' asks Mr Hancock, his hand in Angelica's. All the party have moved off the floor, standing three or four men deep in a circle. Some lounge on couches, some even having their hair and lapels fondled by girls, but even they are strangely watchful, craning their necks to regard the room.

'The entertainment is about to begin,' says Angelica, and at that moment there is a little rustling of excitement, and Mrs Chappell, strident as a schoolmistress, announces:

'A dance! The sirens and the sailors.'

The footmen open the doors wide and first there enter eight boisterous young men, naked to the waist, wearing neckerchiefs and white broadcloth trousers that flap above their ankles. As the orchestra strikes up they execute a swift hornpipe, their neckerchiefs flying and their feet stamping. A little shine of sweat breaks out in the hollows of their backs, and above the stamping can be heard the careful rhythm of their breathing. They have scrubbed young faces, their jaws barely fuzzed, and their bodies are smooth and hairless.

'Those boys never went to sea!' scoffs Mr Hancock as the crowd applauds, but Angelica nudges him in the ribs.

The boys are still for a moment, their feet wide apart and their chests rising and falling in the glister of the chandeliers. Now the doors are opened again and the sound of high, liquid female singing floods the room. The crowd murmurs: the room seems to Mr Hancock to rise a degree or two in temperature, and is suddenly filled with eyes, all the men blinking and peering about, looking sharply here and there for what is coming. The light sits in many tiny stars on their moist lower lids.

Thus enter, singing, eight beautiful girls, the finest from Mrs Chappell's stables. Each holds a comb and a mirror, her hair falling over her shoulders and back, and each is as good as naked. They wear seed pearls around their necks, and their hair is sprigged with coral and laced with ropes of pearls, but they make no attempt to cover their breasts or their bellies. Skeins of sea-green chiffon hang from their wrists and float behind them, and around their waists they wear ingenious girdles of mother-of-pearl, a very many crescents strung together to suggest a row of scales, shimmering and clinking as the mermaids move their hips. A few slivers fall down fore and aft, rather in coyness than in true modesty, for he sees clear as day that all the hair upon their mounds of pleasure has, by some cunningness, been turned as green as the moss that fringes a seaside rock-pool.

'Ah! They are well done!' cries Angelica, breaking out into applause.

'If they set out to give themselves arsenic poisoning,' says Mr Hancock, but not so that it may be heard by anybody but himself. More loudly he adds, 'I never saw such a thing,' which is more diplomatic but no less sincere, for indeed he is nearly as astounded by these mermaids as he was by his own genuine article. He is also as little delighted. He recognises among the girls those he has seen before – the dusky one from downstairs, her nipples dark as raisins, her eyes closed as she begins a languid dance – and it does not feel quite easy to be looking upon those little misses, whom he still half-thinks of as errant housemaids or runaway daughters. He sees that their bodies are beautiful but he feels nothing but avuncular concern: to lay hand on such a child, at his age, seems both unseemly and distasteful.

'And yet who am I to say,' he reprimands himself. 'I do not make the tastes. That is for the great men in the room.'

The girls form themselves into a line, facing at two yards' distance the line of sailors, and as the musicians play on they sing a new song.

'Now the seduction begins,' whispers Angelica, and truly as the girls sing and beckon, the sailors begin slowly to advance upon them. The girls are coquettish behind their mirrors, stretching thick locks of their hair out from their heads with the combs, and letting the curls fall back over their shoulders all in perfect unison.

It is at this moment that Mr Hancock perceives that the sailors' enthusiasm for the sirens is not an act. In each of their broadcloth trousers there is an unmistakable heaving, which only grows more noticeable with each flick of the girls' hair, each lovely sway of their naked hips.

'What is happening?' he asks sharply. The mood in the room – that watchful eagerness he noticed even before the girls' entrance – has not dissipated. In fact it is building. The men are more alert than ever, and there is a steam of sweat amongst them, a strange tight breathlessness. Somebody lets out a small groan. The girls are dancing like true river-nymphs from an ancient fresco, their bosoms quivering upon their ribcages, sliding and yielding with their stretching muscles. And every man but Mr Hancock has his hand in his breeches.

'What is this?' he whispers. The man at his side is engaged in noisy wet kissing with one of the young ladies, and she is fumbling urgently at his belt buckle. The others watch the dance with terrible keenness, their wrists working vigorously, as the mermaids wilt into the arms of the sailors. And as the eight sailors' hands slide up the flanks of their eight mermaids in perfect unison, and eight bright nipples are rolled between eight sets of finger-and-thumb, these old men begin to disrobe themselves, shaking off their jackets and loosening their cravats. The mermaids seem almost to swim against their lovers, their bodies nudging and undulating in a way that is so perfectly, strictly dance-like but which is not a dance any longer.

The sailor partnered with the mulatto girl is the first to unbuckle his trousers, but the other seven follow in quick choreographed succession.

'I think they do not mean to stop,' says Mr Hancock.

Angelica is watching intently and critically, like a woman at a new play. 'Stop?' she says. 'Why, no. They are only just begun.'

Everywhere around the room, just at waist height, is a-flutter with movement. Men pleasure themselves as if in private, with their shirts falling open over their hairy bellies. Mr Hancock knows now how best each of eleven Members of Parliament likes to be touched. Some stand to watch the proceedings unfold; others have already retreated to couches, loosing the tapes of their ladies' white gowns so they fall away from their bodies like sea foam, and these lovely nymphs knead and flatter their flaccid lovers into enthusiasm.

The sailors drop their trousers. Their bowsprits are extended.

'Sheath up!' booms Mrs Chappell. 'If you did not purchase protection on the way in, you must avail yourself of it now. If I see any man going into the breach without armour, you may be sure he will never make another sally.' A maid, artfully draped, scuttles in with a vast marble dish of milk, in which the cundums have been soaked to perfect tenderness. Mrs Chappell shakes one dry and holds it aloft for the crowd to see. 'No excuses!'

The sailors grasp the mermaids' hips, the assembled worthies in the front row bring out their members to air, and Mr Hancock blunders for the door. He pushes through the men, crouched and lewd as baboons, without looking at them: he is even more anxious not to touch them, and he struggles through with his arms raised up to guard his face, using his forearms and elbows to force his path.

Angelica is pursuing him. 'Where are you going?' she asks, when she catches him up on the landing. He is sucking in deep breaths of the air, as a swimmer surfacing.

'I am leaving,' he says.

'Will you not . . . ?' She places a hand on his arm. 'Why not stay?' She is all honey and cherries. 'If this is not to your taste, we can take ourselves off. There are private rooms upstairs,' she adds in a sugared murmur.

'No. No, no.' He has no appetite for her now. Everything about her is sullied – her beauty too effusive, all there for any body to look upon. Nothing about her is secret or private: he sees that she is a bauble for old men's pleasure, nothing more. Her mouth is crest-fallen, and the little crease has taken up its place between her brows, but he cannot trouble himself with her expressions. 'I have made a mistake,' he says briefly.

'Come,' she coaxes in a high soft voice. 'Come sit down with me.'

'This is not a place for a man of my sort.'

'Come have a glass of something nice.'

'I must away.'

Before she can entreat him any further, he pulls his arm from her grasp and takes to the stairs. She watches him from the banister, as the footmen fetch him his hat and greatcoat. She leans over.

'My dear heart,' she calls, but he does not so much as look up; the only answer she receives is the hurried clatter of his footsteps on the marble as the top of his head passes beneath her and out of the door.

FIFTEEN

It may very well be that Angelica believes what she has said: that she finds no greater pleasure than in the arms of men. However, her believing it does not make it true. Angelica has endured many encounters that were not to her liking: some too brief, some too extended; some brutal, some tentative; some bizarre, some tedious. She has given pleasure to men made noisome by foul and boozy breath or foetid underarms or gallons of rancid eau de cologne, and she has indulged them to spend themselves all over – variously – her bosom, her belly, her feet, her bedsheets, her hair, and the small of her back, as well as inside nearly any orifice that pleases them. She has donned an admiral's tricorn, affected schoolgirl innocence, and she has nipped down the back stairs in her dishabille in search of a likely switch or whisk or carpet-beater when an evening demanded particular aggression of her. She has suffered deviants whose skill did not match their pride to work at her privates with their lips and tongues (and – God save her! – their teeth) for hours at a time, and she has applied her own mouth to things she would not inde-pendently have chose to.

Her career in coitus has not, in short, been a perfect round of pleasure on her part. But mark you, whatever small disappointment or boredom or terror she might experience during the act is more than eclipsed by all the attendant enjoyments of her profession. Whoredom appeals to Angelica's character in a great host of ways: she likes to live closely with other women and share her secrets with them; she likes to sing and drink and dance; she likes to be cosseted; she likes to be looked at.

What she likes best of all is to be desired.

It tickles her to see men grown stupid when they gaze upon her, all soft-eyed and slow in the head. In fact it inflames her. To find that her eyes and body and manner drive them out of their wits; to feel the humidity of their palms when they remove their gloves, or watch the involuntary twitch of their members when she moves close towards them; to discover that secret otherworld of commerce in which she is at least as powerful as they: all of this provokes in her the most exquisite excitement, and she goads them into ever greater passions of fever and fury. She likes to be pursued, but she does not feel she is ever captured, for it is only by her own decision that they lay hands on her.

And so she is perturbed. This eventuality had not occurred to her; she had no other plan for the evening, for how could this one go awry?

And he a wretched merchant, she thinks as she flounces back into the great and now orgiastic chamber. *I should have had him in an instant; he has no idea what he has given up, for in no other circumstances in the world will he ever be near me again.*

What should she do now? The shine has been taken off the proceedings, although there are a great many men here who might be ripe for cultivation, she having been dangled before them for three years, docile in the corner of the duke's country parlour with lace veiling her bosom and her hair unadorned. What red-blooded man does not desire his friend's mistress, after all, and what enterprising man does not step into the breach once this friend is no longer able to defend her? Now would be her moment to step back into the firmament; to flirt and charm and negotiate, for amongst these men who watched her for so long there must be a likely protector.

But she finds the will is no longer in her. *What so repelled Hancock that he could walk away so easily? Was it merely the scene, or was the fault in me? Is there something wanting in my manner or my countenance?*

Am I too old?

And she keeps to the shadows, and only smiles when hallooed by priapic admirers. She happens idly to think of the dark-haired naval officer: young, handsome; perhaps impressionable. Certainly the look that passed between them when he helped her up was not an ordinary one. There was no mistaking it; a communication passed between them at that moment, part greeting and part question. He must have felt it too.

But no, no. She will not look for him. If a paunchy cit has no time for her allures, a young rake must certainly laugh in her face.

She traipses instead to the private chambers upstairs, where the housemaids burst from the jib door with armfuls of linen, and Mrs Chappell hustles them about with breathless discretion: 'And the blue room occupied too? Well then, there is nothing for it, nothing for it. You will have to throw my own chamber open to use.'

Polly, her fish-scales rattling, her green dye smeared, is dancing on the spot with anxiety. 'And where am I to take the Admiral,' she demands, 'if *she –*' a glare at the equally smeared Elinor – 'removes to your chamber?'

'Christ! We are full to the gunwales.' Mrs Chappell presses her fists against her eyes for a moment, and then smooths down her gauzy apron with calm decision. 'Very well. Lucy and Clarinda, you will have to make up the servants' rooms for entertaining. The bedsprings are wanting and the stairs are steep, so do not take old men there, for once up there will be no getting them down again.'

'If only it were so!' snorts one of the girls, but Mrs Chappell waves her quip away as she rattles on:

'Then bring the couch from my room onto the landing, and that will serve for another meeting-place. As for *you* –' she turns to Angelica – 'if you come in search of a bed, Mr Hancock must be disappointed for the time being. There is not a corner of this house that is not given over to vice.'

'You need fear nothing from me.'

'Then what are you doing up here under my feet? Is anything amiss? Are you keeping the gentleman amused?'

'Oh yes – yes. Of course.'

'Because he must want for nothing. I shan't have you abandoning him, miss, this is his party and I wish him pleased. We need our mermaid.'

'He is mightily satisfied.'

Mrs Chappell narrows her eyes. 'Where is he?'

Angelica hesitates. But at this very moment the girls stagger out with the couch, and in their blind exertion topple a Japanese screen; the air is rent with a terrible crack and one lacquered panel shears in two. 'God's wounds!' exclaims Mrs Chappell. 'What have you done now, you fools?' The girls are white-faced; one begins immediately to weep. 'Get away,' Mrs Chappell snaps to Angelica. 'Whatever you wandered here for, I do not have the time for it. Make yourself useful; call them all to dinner. The old men have exerted themselves enough, I daresay; they are only cluttering the place up now in the hope of being fed. We may yet send them home by midnight.'

'And then the *real* party may begin,' says Elinor cheerfully, for she is parched for a glass of something strong, and may not indulge until her duties are done.

Casting one more glance around for the naval officer, Angelica trots back down the stairs and strikes the Chinese gong on the first-floor landing. 'Refreshments,' she announces to the great chamber, where some are straightening their garments and blinking about themselves. 'Downstairs, at your pleasure.'

A long table has been magicked into the vast ground-floor atrium, laid for fifty and spread with pies and tarts, roast fowl and jellies and ices. Mrs Fortescue alone is already seated. Her plate is empty but she has filled her glass generously.

'Ah,' says Angelica, taking a seat beside her as the guests drift down in various gradations of nakedness, 'the ghost at the feast.'

Bel's eyes move heavily over the scene. 'What happened to the mermaid man?' she asks.

'Gone.' There is a fortuitous tower of sweetmeats on the table, and Angelica pops one into her mouth. Its sugary crunch gives way to gushing syrup. She takes another and licks her fingers. 'He did not appreciate the lewdness,' she adds, her aplomb some way restored.

'No surprise.'

'I am sure *I* do not care.' Angelica speaks indistinctly, for her tongue is engaged in peeling the slick paste of a marron glacé from the roof of her mouth. 'I can do better than a stuffy old shopkeeper in a singed wig –' she swallows – 'and I mean to, tonight.'

Bel Fortescue is grave even in her gossip. 'Has someone caught your eye?' she whispers. 'Point him out.'

Up go their fans. Thus screened they survey the room. 'By the piano,' says Angelica, smiling so that, from a distance, she might appear to be exchanging some pleasantry. 'The navy man with the dark hair.'

'Talking to Mr Winstanley?' says Mrs Fortescue, looking amiably in the other direction. 'I know that man.'

Angelica is possessed by a little gust of excitement, but Mrs Fortescue straightens out her face and shakes her head infinitesimally. 'No,' she says. 'No money.'

'Well, that don't signify. I deserve some fun.'

'You are greedy and you have no self-control,' Mrs Fortescue admonishes her. 'Always snatching at the fattest bun on the plate. Dear, your situation—'

'Oh, my situation! Always my situation! And I must exercise good judgement, try to make prudent decisions for my future preservation. You sound just like Eliza, do you know that?' Her eyes are on the sweets again, seeking out a pretty lavender comfit. Her saliva is already running in anticipation: to feel it crumble and melt softly on her tongue. 'I want some fun, Bel. Do you remember fun? Pleasure – dissipation – I'll not be this young tomorrow.' She glances at the officer. 'What's his name?'

Bel sighs and raises her solemn eyes to heaven. 'Rockingham. George Rockingham.'

'Ah. A good family.'

'Much good as it does him; he is of a very sickly branch of it. I know his uncle, who is his guardian, and I assure you he is kept on a very straitened allowance, and he has no access to the rest of his fortune until he is twenty-five.' She leans to whisper in her friend's ear: 'He is younger than you.'

'Better than older,' snorts Angelica. 'I have not enjoyed a man of real vigour for far too long.' Seizing the opportunity of their intimacy in such a crowd, she says, 'Bel, will you not miss it?'

'Miss what? Vigour?'

'No, no. Everything. All of this. You are sacrificing a great deal in getting married, I think.'

Mrs Fortescue continues to watch the room. It is hard to tell from her sad, reflective little face what she might really be feeling: she is soulful even when she is rinsing out her stockings. 'I am quite done here,' she says.

'I see not *how*,' says Angelica, but Mrs Fortescue's words sink to the pit of her stomach like lead. She thinks of the earnest exertions of the little girls, and feels very weary.

'Do you not? I look at it all and I think –' she spreads her hands and widens her eyes as if in appeal – 'what a *farce*. Such empty mummings as I took part in for ten years, and thought myself *free*.'

'You were wrong to make a scene tonight,' says Angelica.

Mrs Fortescue laughs. 'Why? How can I smile these things away?'

'But you ought. *Some* of us are happy here.'

'Who? Name me one person.'

'Oh, 'tis all a glamour to you.' Angelica knows when to end a conversation. 'I am as free as I would like to be, and freer than any wife.'

'Of course you are.'

'I am! For now I depart to make my own free choice of what man to take my pleasure with, something no wife may do . . .'

'. . . although some have.'

'Without consequence? I think not. I am free as a bird.' She rises from her seat and it topples behind her, for her skirt is large and her sobriety compromised.

'Will there be no consequences for you?' Bel asks quietly, but her friend is already darting away.

Bright with excitement, Angelica glances once back. 'See how I go,' she says.

SIXTEEN

Virtuous people will not know that very particular pleasure two strangers feel when, without touching or speaking, they are agreed that they will end the night together. There is no pursuit, for Angelica and her George. They simply find one another. When Angelica bounces over and takes her seat amongst the group, they exchange salutation with their eyes but have no more to do with one another; she takes her time in clasping the hand of her old friend Lucy Chadwick, one-time lover of three princes of the realm, and honouring a few of the younger navy men with some light flirtation. Rockingham is similarly engaged with young Billingsgate Kitty, who will shortly be led away to her chaste bed, being not ripe enough for her own official debauchery although her time will soon come. He persists in the face of her dutiful muteness with what strikes Angelica as wondrous patience; she detects, she thinks, a glint of humour in his brown eyes but she does not seek to meet them. There will be time for all this yet. The group have just drawn out a die, an item of contraband since Mrs Chappell will have no gambling in her establishment.

'But surely even she would not object to an innocent game of hi-jinks,' urges one of the navy men. 'He who rolls lowest takes a drink,' and as the die is passed from hand to hand around the circle, and skitters dizzily across the tabletop, while the players hold their breath or shriek with mirth, Angelica and Rockingham are always aware of one another. When she laughs, his mouth opens in a grin without his bidding it, and when he claps his hands at their sport she might be observed to be clasping her own together. Put a die in these people's fists and of course they will be inclined irresistibly to make bets. They seize up morsels from the half-cleared table:

'I wager this walnut that Mrs Chadwick casts lowest.'

'A bunch of cherries on Carter rolling a four.'

They slap their palms on the table and slop liquor into one another's glasses with no regard for whether it matches what was there before. All social gatherings have a riptide moving through them – some revellers joining the party as others melt away, some retiring to a quiet room, others emerging refreshed – and it is this unseen, unsought tide that nudges Angelica and the lieutenant closer and closer together without their even trying. Little Kitty is swept away protesting; Lucy Chadwick judges herself to have graced the party with her presence long enough, and besides has two little children snuggled in the Hampstead countryside who will in a very few hours want her at breakfast, and so she makes for her carriage. She is replaced in short order by the erstwhile mermaids Elinor Bewlay and Polly Campbell, their hair freshly dressed and their modesty restored by matching silk wraps, giggling to embark on a night of outrage and intemperance now that Mrs Chappell is safely a-bed in clean sheets. Angelica is first five chairs away from Rockingham, then three, until when the clock chimes for a quarter after four, they find themselves side by side in the midst of the depleted group.

'Is it too late,' she says, 'to revise your first impression of me?'

His face splits into the most amiable of grins. 'But why? I liked it. A woman never fell at my feet before.'

'Be assured I never shall again,' she says.

'Rockingham,' he says, and he puts her hand briefly to his lips.

'Lieutenant Rockingham,' she nods, surveying his uniform.

'What, this?' he laughs, glances down at himself. 'No! I only wore it to come in here – a mermaid party, you know. I *was* in the navy once, only they would not tolerate my high spirits.' He rubs his hair roguishly and turns upon her the smile of a cherub. 'I am a student of law, for now.'

'Oh! So you shall be a lawyer, by and by,' but he looks at her so quizzically she fears for a moment that she has slipped unknowing into some low provincial dialect, as she was wont to as a girl, to her own mortification and her patrons' amusement.

'I should hope I'll *never* earn my living so. A gentleman wants a profession to keep the mind sharp, that's all, and perhaps to see him into Parliament.'

Ah, she thinks, *Bel was incorrect: of course he has means. God be praised, for he is so handsome.* She smiles as he goes on, 'One travels, of course, but it *wears* after a while; such an endless round of scenery and curios. I was glad to leave Naples by the end, I can tell you. Full only of sightseers, dilettantes, pleasure-seekers, not a one of them with a real appreciation for the place.'

'Oh, of course – of course.'

Their heads nod closer together until their fascination envelops them; they forget their friends and their old lovers, pains and anxieties as their worlds telescope into this one space where he is her best friend and she his.

'Mrs Neal,' their friends say, 'Angelica, 'tis your turn.' She is not listening; they have to prise her fingers open and press the die into her palm before she will drag her attention from her dark-haired friend.

'Must I?'

143

'Throw! Throw the die!'

'Very well, very well.' She turns away from the man with reluctance – *for I am yours really*, her manner tells him – but she is pleased for him to see her sportive side. She presses her lips together and closes her eyes as she warms the die between her hands, and flings it down on the table.

It leaps once, twice.

It stops just short of diving onto the floor, and balances on the table's inlaid edge, one single dot smiling up at the room. The company howls. The men's wigs are all askew, those that remain on their heads at all. It is strange to see these bloods reduced to tousled boys; their cropped heads are fascinating, touchable, this one a fuzz as close as a puppy's belly; this one a nest of coppery curls.

'Drink!' they call. 'Take a drink!'

'Oh no,' she says. 'I want no more of it.' She is comfortably drunk; she wishes to tinge her judgement no further, but her companions have no mercy.

'Rules are rules. Drink!'

'What was the game?' She turns appealingly to Rockingham.

'Hi-jinks!' roar her friends. 'And you could roll no lower. Drink! Drink!'

She utters an unwilling bleat. 'I cannot! Do not make me!'

'Drink!'

Rockingham, though not a lieutenant at all, remains gallantry personified. He puts a hand boldly upon her elbow and says, 'If the lady does not want a drink she should not be obliged to take one.'

His comrades boo, and she wafts her fan, for her face has become suddenly hot. The lieutenant lets go of her elbow. 'Rules are rules,' he continues. 'And we all agree that she who will not drink, must pay a forfeit.'

'A forfeit!' she gasps, and swats at him, which act of daring makes her giddy. 'What have you got me into?'

'What's it to be, boys? Ladies?'

Elinor Bewlay and Polly Campbell are whispering together, and squawk with joy. '*I* know,' says Elinor. 'She's to play *mermaid*.'

'I beg your pardon?'

'If we can do it, so can you,' says Polly. Her fingertips are still stained green. 'You must go outside . . .'

'. . . into the garden,' chimes in Elinor,

'. . . down to the fountain.'

'. . . and swim three times all the way around it.'

'Naked,' says Polly with satisfaction.

'Quite naked.'

'I shan't,' says Angelica. 'I can't. The fountain is barely two feet deep.'

'Mermaid!' the girls set up chanting. 'Mer-maid! Mer-maid!'

''Tis October,' protests Angelica, but they are up from the table and she is running with them, laughing now. 'You are absurd. I shall keep my chemise on.'

'Mermaids do not wear chemises,' says Polly as they burst out into the dark garden. The men are behind them, calling for lanterns; only Rockingham accompanies them, for he can be nowhere but at Angelica's side.

'Well, I am not a mermaid,' says Angelica. 'I'll go in the water but I'll not strip down to nothing.' In other circumstances she would have no such qualms. She loves to go naked before an admiring party: in her career she has danced on tables and rolled on petal-strewn couches wearing not even so much as a pair of garters, but now she hesitates. She does and does not wish to be naked before this man. Letting him glimpse her body in a moment during which he may not touch it or betray himself is tempting to her, but she had hoped to savour this unknowing a little longer. Tonight she would have flirted for hours more, and coaxed him into a dark corner to kiss her until they both trembled. She would have let him touch her first over her chemise, in the warm dark of her bedchamber, and then undress her or not as his passions dictated. It would take them a long time to discover one another. If he looks upon her now, half the fun is gone before they have begun. 'I think I shall not do it,' she announces.

He hands her a bottle of brandy. 'Go on,' he says. 'I'll close my eyes.'

The men are coming out with torches and lanterns, which dredge the little garden with yellow light. Their voices have a crispness that comes with cloudless nights, and bounce off the high walls. It is cool and fresh but not so cold the feat cannot be done.

Angelica takes off her slippers, and then her stockings. The flag-stones ice the soles of her feet, but she detects, perhaps, the last of the sun's warmth aching through. ''Tis not so bad,' she says. 'Help me, girls,' and they swarm over her to unpin her bodice and shuck her of skirts and petticoats which they trample carelessly underfoot as they tug at the knots of the bum-roll that girdles her hips. Elinor holds it aloft, a long satin pudding, and all are convulsed with laughter.

'Do not lose that,' Angelica says sternly, as the men toss it between one another, horrified and intrigued, 'nor abuse it; I had it made to my own measurements and there is not another like it. I said, *there is not another like it*; do not take such liberties; it does not go on your head.'

She has on only her stays over her chemise, and the girls' busy fingers are all over them, loosing their strings, easing them open to shake out the creases from the chemise beneath, the only thing now separating her skin from the air. It falls to just below her knees, its sleeves tight and plain, which makes her look as spotless as any of

Mrs Chappell's newest acquisitions. The girls fumble to denude her of this too, but she shrieks and slaps their hands away.

'Into the water with you,' says Captain Carter. 'They have you outnumbered!'

The fountain is fifteen feet across, a great shallow basin scalloped like a shell. The water cascades down from an acrobatic dolphin in its centre, churning the black pool up silver in the dark. At the bottom of the pool drift golden fish, dim ghosts in their sleep. Angelica scrambles onto the lip of the basin. Inside it is dead cold, and slippery with algae to the point of greasiness. 'Ugh! So I am going in, am I?'

'Yes!'

Her hair wafts about her. The water spatters her face and arms, and across her bosom so her nipples tighten as if a stitch had been tugged in them. ''Tis fearful cold.'

She swings her legs over the edge, and her feet are in the water, and her ankles and her calves. 'Ay, me!' she gasps. The marble ledge numbs her buttocks. Then she slides all the way in.

It is cold, cold, cold. Cold so her ribcage contracts and she gasps a quavering indrawn breath. Leaden cold on her commodity, the warmest part of any woman, and under the cusp of her breasts, and up the insides of her thighs, and gripping cold into her armpits and the crooks of her knees. She raises her hands up. 'I am in! Am I not in! I am your very mermaid!'

'Swim!' shout the party, bottles aloft. 'Three times round,' and this reminds them of a song, deliciously forbidden to any mariner, which they begin to sing lustily and in all tempos at once:

   'And three times round went our gallant ship
   And three times round went she
   And three times round went our gallant ship
   And she sank to the bottom of the sea, the sea, the sea.'

She feels her very organs are quaking. She cannot swim the shallow pool but walks it with her hands, grit under her nails and her palms slithering, her stomach grazing the gravel and her chemise floating like the skirts of a jellyfish. The fish are alarmed from their doze and dart about her, their cold bellies bumping her forearms. The falling water thunders about her and strikes her shoulders hard as pebbles, dragging her hair from its powder and pins. Her teeth begin to chatter, but she circles again, and rolls over onto her back, singing to the best of her quaking lungs' abilities:

'We there did espy a fair pretty maid
With a comb and a glass in her hand, her hand, her hand.'

Then, 'Where is my comb?' she demands, leaning over the rim of her great scallop shell. 'Where is my looking glass?' but by now she is fairly keening with the cold. 'Oh, I can take no more. Was it not bravely done?'

She reaches out for her handmaidens but they recoil.

'My silk,' cries Polly, pulling her splendid wrap about her. ''Twill stain, 'twill quite ruin.'

'There will be the devil to pay,' says Elinor. 'You know how it is.'

'I know, I know, you turn over three hundred a year and you do not own the gowns on your backs,' groans Angelica. 'A sorry state, when a woman of means may not spoil a dress or two.' Turning to the gentlemen she cries, 'Which of you is man enough to volunteer his arms to a siren?'

Which of them, of course, but Mr Rockingham, who is at her elbow before she has finished speaking, with a great linen towel and a twitch to his handsome eyebrow. He grips her forearm and lets her lean her wet hands against him as she scrambles onto dry land. 'Oof,' she gasps, as the gooseflesh erupts across her arms, but although he holds up the towel like a barricade to the company, he does not cover her up straight away. Her chemise is transparent and plastered to her body, with bubbles of air where it stretches between her breasts and the hollow between ribcage and belly. His eyes flutter across her without a word, and she feels no shame nor disappointment, only that this is the greatest caper she ever took a part in. A smile bursts across her face without her bidding it there, and she feels the tips of her ears grow hot. His smile mirrors hers, although he puts his chin down to hide it, and for a moment they stand together while webs of mirth and desire and joy stretch between them. Then he wraps her up and tussles the coarse linen over her shoulders and back.

'Come,' he says, 'I shall find you a cup of negus to warm you up. But then you have nothing to wear.'

'Not a stitch,' agrees Angelica. There are currently ten young ladies resident in Mrs Chappell's home, and a great wardrobe room laid on for them to choose from upwards of three times a day. This is, therefore, a barefaced lie.

'There is nothing for it. We shall have to take you to bed.'

'What a shame,' she whispers, the water pooling about her feet. 'I had been so enjoying myself.'

SEVENTEEN

The wool curtains are pulled flush around his bed, and if the dawn is approaching – and the great conversation of the birds suggests so – not one ray of it reaches him. He lies in his shirt, his breeches discarded and his cuffs flung into a corner, and keeps his eyes fast closed. Perhaps he is inclined to throw back his covers and pace the room, or take up a candle and a book. He might remove himself to his counting-house if he chose, or walk the dawning streets. He might but he does not dare: this is the hour for sleep, and so he dutifully adopts its attitudes.

And still he cannot help thinking.

I have made a terrible mistake. To put my greatest asset into such a den of iniquity; to associate my name with that level of barbarism.

He groans aloud. His eyes are closed, and at the corners of his vision clouds of colour roll. *But what am I to do? If I wish my mermaid to succeed, I must learn to conduct myself in these circles.* 'I have such losses to recoup,' he announces to his woollen chamber, and he lies thinking on that dreadful thought until the bells of St Nicholas's sound on one side of him and those of St Paul's sound to the other, and he knows it is time at last to rise. *And yet why must my mermaid succeed at all? Can I not put it away like so much old lumber, and forget this sorry episode?*

He raps on Sukie's door as he passes it: 'Up! Get up!' he calls, but he cares little whether she does or no. *Because of the money, of course. Because my sister is disgusted with me and my niece depends on me. I have nothing else of note in my life, and now that I am saddled with this freak I must profit by it.* And indeed he has profited, for one of England's most skilled priestesses of love, one of the very finest models of womanhood, was last night willing to take him to her bed. As if a man of his sort – a merchant, a son of Deptford – might have the opportunity to touch her! And like a fool he was appalled. *I rejected her and humiliated her. Is not that a judgement upon my own self rather than upon her? Is it merely that I lack the sophistication that comes naturally to another quality of man?*

Bridget is up, he knows by the cold air that nips past him as he comes down the stairs, for as usual she has left the yard door open while she goes to the pump. He has had words with her about this before but she will not change. 'Takes too long,' she replies, looking at her toes, and he thinks, *a woman of the house would know how to make her obedient.* She has not yet opened the shutters, and only a little daybreak slips through them: Mr Hancock has to lift his bunch of keys to within an inch of his nose to make it out at all, and as he peers and paws at it, a piece of the darkness unfurls from the skirting and wraps itself, velvet-soft and purposeful, around his calves.

'God's teeth!' he exclaims, picking up his feet like a stout old maid jumping rope. He wrenches open the front door: light floods in and the cat scampers out.

'What are you at?' Mr Hancock fumes, but he follows her onto the street and grinds the lock fast behind him. Overnight, Deptford's heady miasma had begun to settle, like silt in a puddle, but sunrise stirs it back up again and Mr Hancock stumps through that great rich stink of baking bread and rotten mud and old blood and fresh-sawn wood with the cat trotting on her tiptoes beside him.

What sort of a world can this be, he is fuming to himself, *in which a whore stoops to an honest man?* The end of the mortal world is heralded by signs of such disorder, a man yoked to the plough, a fox pursued by a hare. He has seen it etched on gravestones, too: a heart turned upside down.

He will not suffer a ferryman today, nor crush himself into the public coach that will bear him joltingly into the heart of the city. Nor does he desire to take the path along the stinking river, where every shipbuilder in every yard, and every waterman at every step, knows his name and his business. He chooses instead to walk the long way, spurning Southwark's crush and reek for a stride across open fields, and thus turns up Butt Lane, where the boys from the bakery run giddy on the flagstones, their shirts untucked and flapping. There is a heap of oranges outside one of the little shingle-clad shacks, all puckered and foxed, the saddest oranges in Christendom, their innards no doubt fibrous dry. They are by no means fit for sale but this makes no odds since they will never be sold. They are moral decoys, merely, for above them swings the sign of the jolly mariners, and within, the last raddled drab may yet be rinsing her shift before falling into her bed alone at last. Mr Hancock's lips twitch at the thought: he would like to spit on the threshold.

On the parcel of land next door, the shipwrights are at work, singing together as they haul up beams. *The world turned upside down indeed*, he thinks, *beginning with my own town.* For here the shipwrights take their work upon dry land, and amongst them there is not the usual hierarchy of kings and lords, but only that of skill, no class but what is ordained by one's work group. Here labourers prize their fine china and shelves of books; here wives are husbandless two seagoing years in three; here ship-masts tower over church steeples; here he is, sorry Jonah Hancock: a husband without a wife; a father without a son; paterfamilias of a she-house ruled by little maids, and whose years of faithful work have accrued no fortune to compare to what a freak goblin can bring him.

It is half a mile up to the New Cross turnpike, the road already moderate busy. A small boy bobs out of the whitewashed tollbooth to heave open the gate at the swift approach of the Dover stagecoach: behind it creeps a wagon laden with sacks and rope-lashed boxes, on top of which ride pale-faced newcomers to the city: an old man, with only a flour sack tied about his pitiful body, mumbling his toothless gums; a mother who draws her infant close beneath her shawl; two pretty country girls turning out their bundles in search of coins to pay their final stage. They look about themselves in bewilderment – 'Be we in London now?' – and pinch the blood into their cheeks and straighten their kerchiefs, 'For the fine ladies don't want maids as don't look healthy, don't look *decent*,' one says to the other as the wagon lurches onward.

To the west, towards the city, the fields are picked brown and bare, and the trees stand open-armed and stripped of fruit. Even the blackberries in the hedgerows are gone now, the coils of brambles that bore them sagging into wayside ditches full of grey water. Far away to the south the masts of ships are fewer on the river, and stand in tall huddles with their sails drawn close about them.

As he strides onward, another thought strikes him. Confound the rest of the situation. It is a fact that last night a pretty young woman – remarkable pretty, alive with her very prettiness – put her hand on his and gazed into his eyes. She kissed him on the lips, this buxom lovely girl. He might at this moment be basking in her embrace: her bedclothes tangled around them and her soft arm flung across his chest. She might lean above him so her golden hair streamed down around them, and the sunlight took fire in its strands. He had, in fact, the opportunity to lie skin upon skin and limb upon limb with another living body, to be the focus of another's touch and thought. This is what he turned down, last night. Not a whore, and not a prize, but a moment of contact between man and woman. 'Damn you!' he spits, kicking the dirt of the road, and alarming the old spinster sisters who have just toddled up from their cottage in the beetfield. 'Excuse me, ladies,' he says. 'I have a great fear of ants. A great and unreasonable fear.'

It is in this very fug of confusion and rage that he strides the leafy Kent road, where other men of his sort descend the steps of handsome brick houses to their waiting carriages. This new breed of man keeps his home in the countryside in preference to squashing his family into the apartments above his office: his children learn to paint and are sent away to school, and yet even after plucking up the courage to append an audacious 'Esq.' to his name, none of these men would stand for such behaviour as Mr Hancock witnessed last night. *For shame,* he thinks, *we live on a different scale of morality. And which is the correct one?* He regrets his solid provincial decency; he is sorry that the memory of the priapic sailors brings such a wave of horror to his soul; for those people are so much happier than he is.

Furthermore (he reflects as he comes upon Borough and the fields melt away to tight alleys and sunless yards, and the city begins to loom and to crowd, and thence with aching calves across London Bridge and into the mercantile crush of Lombard Street), furthermore, by whatever moral compass one chooses, his treatment of Angelica Neal – rebuffing her generosity at a function organised in his own honour – is reproachable. *I shall seek an audience with her,* he tells himself. *Apologise for my behaviour; she may be understanding of my confusion.* Yes, this seems to him a good plan. He tries not to think too hard about the other possibilities of being permitted into her lodgings: if in such privacy she will once again guide his hand across her body; if with the curtains drawn and her servants dismissed she will remember what business was left undone the night before.

It is, however, this thought that continues in his mind as he completes his morning circuit of the coffee-houses, an action he has methodically repeated for twenty years, checking off one by one the news-sheets he has read and the men he has whispered with until his routine is complete. A tiny alley behind Gray's Inn Fields leads him to the counting-house wherein the mercantile business of Mr Hancock and his partner Mr Greaves is gravely attended to by six clerks and their crook-backed overseer Scrimshaw.

The counting-house is a long red-brick building about a hundred years old, which might once have been imposing, but the city has crept up on it from all sides, and now it sits three storeys tall in its cramped court like a rhinoceros in a rabbit hutch. While the dwellings around it are better-built than those ramshackle edifices that grow up nearly overnight in the rookeries of St Martin's – and which are liable to topple over in a shower of brick-dust if any inhabitant turns over too heavy in their bed – they are hardly to be admired, being unornamented thin-walled places with mean lightless windows. They are home, however, to decent unassuming people: two sisters in crocheted mittens, erstwhile mistresses of a failed dame school; and a law stationer who has somehow contrived to fit his shop, wife, dog and seven children behind his narrow front door. Three of these children are in the yard as Mr Hancock approaches the offices: two boys and a little girl, who stand around a set of arcane chalk marks on the flagstones, and take turns to throw down small twigs and pebbles with some energy.

'Good day,' he says, and they tumble to bow to him.

'Good day, good day to you,' they chirrup, nice children in clean mended clothes, and he thinks without meaning to, *had I children of my own, I would bring them here.* He feels an airy rush about his coat-tails as if some little beings, buoyant with their play, were running to keep up with him. It is not merely a Henry who walks beside him today, but a whole gaggle of putative children, those who through his own inaction were never born. He mounts the steps of his building alone, and lets himself in.

The counting-house is habitually quiet and dry, never more so than with the departure of Mr Greaves and the removal of his wife to the country. The footsteps of the Greaves children are no longer audible from the lodgings above; the workday is not punctuated with domesticity – deliveries of cheese and milk and music teachers – the hall empty of visitors and of kitchen aromas. The counting-house now smells only of whitewash, parchment and sand, its only sounds the rustle of papers, the scratch of nibs, and the persistent sniffing of Oliver, the youngest clerk.

On the left of the entrance hall is a dining room, installed for the purpose of entertaining clients; its polished tabletop and empty candlesticks are peaceful in their abandonment. On the right is the counting-house where Scrimshaw the Beak hunches at his pedestal swathed in the black gown he had made up during the reign of a previous George, and the clerks balance on stools before him. Two are middle-aged, in the company through its permutations (for the Hancocks and the Greaveses, like all effective merchants, must be pliable in their ventures and their choice of business partners) since boyhood; the others are newer additions, steady young men with good prospects, among them always a Hancock nephew or two. He prefers not to take on any man with too evident an ambition, they being wont to make extra work, but he enjoys the satisfaction of watching faltering boys become confident men, training up a promising young clerk into a fine businessman on his own account.

The men all rise when he enters.

'Good morning, sir.'

'Good morning.'

They look at him expectantly. Although the arrival of the mermaid has little practical connection to the office – beyond the paperwork pertaining to the loss of the *Calliope* and its promised cargo – they have taken a keen interest in its fate. Now, they regard him in the polite but intense manner of well-trained dogs watching their master eat a plate of mutton chops.

'What news?' croaks Scrimshaw, fossicking drops of candle wax from his wig.

'Regarding?'

'Last night,' says Oliver.

'You went to King's Place, did you not?' says Jonathan, the nephew.

'I did.'

'And?' No other man in this room has ever seen within a King's Place nunnery, nor are likely to unless they are to ascend quite phenomenally in their lives. This is, however, the age of unlikely ascents. 'What was it like? How was it done? What of the *women*?'

He considers. ''Twas well done. The mermaid was greatly admired; they had displayed it in a manner theatrical and yet tasteful.'

The men nod in satisfaction. 'But what of the women?' The coals on the brazier shift and rattle.

'I ...' He thinks of Angelica, her back against the closed door, looking up at him. Nausea surges through him; he feels feverish, prickly. 'I found it a most immoral place.'

'Foul-mouthed, were they? Drunkards?'

'I cannot tolerate a woman who drinks,' nods the clerk his own age. '*That*'s the real evil. The lack of delicacy.'

'Nothing of the sort,' he says. 'They are good girls.'

'They always are, or start off that way,' says his clerk Brown, who took his wife the same year Mr Hancock married Mary, and who has twelve lusty children with her. 'I never met a doxy as started out wicked, but I have come upon a fair few who have become so. Stealing and such.' The other men murmur in agreement.

'What it is,' says Scrimshaw, 'is the bawds. *They* are the truly corrupt; spent their whole lives in the trade and now they will not save their sisters but draw them into greater sin.'

'Aye, 'tis the bawds who begin it all,' agrees Brown. 'Who makes the whores but they? A jade I'll forgive, she has her own reasons – but a madam?' He sucks his teeth. 'Never. She's out for her own profit. Profits by us, profits by them. Where's her punishment?'

'It was the luxury,' Mr Hancock says. 'I did not like it.' He feels the eyes of his employees upon him and adds grandly, 'There was something of the Fall of Rome about it. Such an excess of wine and naked women.'

'The rich!' grunts Mr Scrimshaw. 'The well-connected! *Politicians!* Idleness and excess curdles their brains. They live in a world of fantasy.'

'Yes,' he nods. 'Yes, that is it entirely.'

'No place for a man of sense,' says young Oliver wistfully.

'We are all best kept ignorant of it.'

'Yes,' Mr Hancock says, 'that is what I thought. I shall not call there again. Is my fire made up?'

'And burning merrily,' says Oliver, who sees to all the office comforts.

'Then I shall get to work. Good day, gentlemen,' he says.

As he passes into the adjoining partners' office and closes the door behind him, he hears the clerks burst into excited whispering, to dissect all he has said and cast their own opinions upon it.

Mr Hancock regrets that Greaves himself is in Boston, for the silence sits heavy with him today. He sits down at the desk, beneath the portrait of his father, and the portrait of his wife Mary's father, and under the gaze of a feathery miniature of his brother Philip who drowned in Deptford Creek while rollicking home one night. And he touches to his nose a handkerchief worked by dear Sukie and thinks, *this is a good honest place to be. And however wealthy I do become, I shall be no other sort than this.*

The morning's letters are on his desk, but he hesitates to read them. First he sharpens a new quill with unusual care; little coils of white shear away from it until he is satisfied that its mark will be both bold and firm. Then he lays out a sheet of fine white paper, and inks the following:

Dear Mrs Chappell,
It is with regret that I find I must withdraw my Exhibit from your Home. You and I navigate very different Worlds, Madam, and after last night's Proceedings I can no longer suffer my name to be associated with yours. I waive my right to the full balance of my fee and I will be pleased to have my Creature returned to me by to-morrow Morning and no later.

He looks over it a moment, then draws out another sheet to make a fair copy, minus the sentiment of 'regret' and with addition of the word 'demand'.

For class is a type of bubble, a membrane around one, and although one might grow within this membrane, and strain against it, it is impossible to break free from it. And a man of nobility is always such in his soul, however he may fall; and a man of humble sort is always such in his soul, however he may climb.

He signs his name with a hand so exuberant it sends a spray of ink across the page; sprinkles it with pounce to hasten the drying; blows upon it, shakes it clear, folds it and seals it. Then he rises.

'Oliver,' he says, stepping into the office, 'convey this to Mother Chappell.'

He retreats into his office before he can be prevailed upon to elaborate. He has set things right; that is all. He will be what he was before. He will not entertain baubles one moment longer. And he still cannot decide, as he sets about his books and slits the first of the day's letters, whether he is content with this, or tormented by it.

EIGHTEEN

And what a joy it is to bask a-bed with a man of one's own choosing! To have one's face cupped in his warm hands, to have him marvel at the dilation of one's pupils and linger over the rosy tenderness of one's lips, to have him chafe the warmth back into one's fingers and feet.

And what a joy it is, in turn, to observe the creasing about his eyes when he smiles, and to kiss the little margin of skin, pale and tender as a girl's, between the pink edge of his lips and the first of his carefully shaved bristles. And to discover the scar on his chin, which he received falling out of a tree when he was six; and the crook in his right little finger, which he received falling out of a club when he was nineteen. To learn these secrets about him.

They sleep at first at Mrs Chappell's house, in one of the bedrooms designed for receiving. The bed is so large it is almost a room in itself, and sprung with a buoyant ingenuity to which Mrs Chappell herself holds the patent. Angelica divests herself immediately of her wet chemise, slopping it onto the floorboards without a second thought. If the lieutenant glimpses her naked body before she burrows beneath the covers, it can only be for a moment; her desire to be warm trumps all thoughts of seduction. It is not, after all, as if any seduction is necessary, for this occurred all at first sight and now they are only eager to be closer together. The lieutenant strips as dawn breaks in King's Place, and Angelica watches out of one eye, already beginning to drowse. He is a lean and long-limbed person, with a furze of dark hair along his thighs, which curve like a taut bow.

When he slips into the bed she is already nearly asleep, and she nestles her spine up against his belly. They knot naked around one another, but nothing is done: they are delighted by the bliss of their bare skin, this is all, and his fingers tangle loosely in her thick hair and she glides her fingers along the back of his thigh. He puts his face by hers, his nose grazing her ear and his lips just upon her neck, until each of their breaths slows.

Thus they sleep and thus they wake. There ought to be little else said on the matter, for lovers are all the same, and only of interest to themselves, but on this count it is remarkable: *Angelica Neal has not felt this way before.*

Or if she has, she has forgot.

She who has made it her living to be touched thus, looked at thus, and rarely found it onerous, has forgot until now the joy of it. She feels as if she were made of glue – or magnets, or kindling ready to take the first spark that leapt on it – and is astounded by it as if this were an entirely new discovery. Later she will whisper that she will never want any other man again. Such is the drug which, dewed on the eyelids, makes yesterday inconsequential, and tomorrow certain, and today golden.

Angelica and George (for overnight they have dispensed with honorifics) sigh smugly together in the bed until mid-afternoon, hearing far away the clatter of the girls loaded into the carriage for their exercise, and the scamper of servants in the passages behind the wall as they set right what was made wrong during the night. They take of one another for the first time as a persistent little dog scratches and whines outside their door to be let in, and then doze before doing it again. Their only disturbance is by a maid who brings them chocolate and rolls, and retreats in haste.

'We should leave,' whispers Angelica, touching her fingertips to his as they lie face to face.

'Do not make me part with you,' says George.

'I have no intention of it,' she says, 'but I do not wish to be overlooked by Mother Chappell.' They are silent a moment. 'What are your engagements?' she asks. Their palms press flat against one another.

'None I cannot break, for the next two days.'

She grows brighter. 'Nor I. Come back with me.'

He draws her to him, his fingers finding their home in the small of her back, for truly every part of his body finds its correspondence in hers. 'Let us stay together as long as we can,' he says. 'I could not wish to be anywhere else.'

'I have an apartment,' she says. 'We'll not be disturbed.'

'A little longer here,' he says. 'A little longer.'

By the time they are dressed it is late in the afternoon, and the sun has gone from the courtyard. They emerge into the city as if they had been gone from it a long time; its customs unfamiliar and all but irrelevant to them, in their republic of two. They take a carriage and press close against one another within, and kiss and whisper as they watch the strange new world pass by outside.

NINETEEN

Not two hours after his message is sent to Mrs Chappell's, Mr Hancock is returned to the Exchange, and upon hearing his name called turns to see one of her beautiful footmen striding through the crowd towards him. His livery shines blue as the most virgin winter morning. His wig is white as angel's wings. His skin is brown and smooth.

'Mr Hancock,' he repeats. 'Sir.' The crowd parts as he advances. This man, whose name in fact is Simeon Stanley, is not the only black in the room, but he may be the very smartest. The most peculiar thing about him is his scent. He smells of starch. He also smells of lavender-water, tallow soap, damp wool (for the mist has left its dropples on the sleek shoulders of his greatcoat), and a sparing dab of middling-quality eau de cologne, but what he does not smell of, not one atom, is his own man's body. He is so miraculous clean it is as if he fell direct out of the blue sky: not even a whiff of armpit emanates from him, not a hint of onions on his breath, not a notion that he has traversed the streets in haste. His Adam-blue breeches must be fresh on, for a man's trousers become swiftly seasoned with the chafed, perspiring intricacies of their owner. Simeon Stanley may look like a man of flesh and blood, but for all his scent betrays it, from his crisply folded stock to the toes of his stockings, he might be made complete of feather-packed calico.

'I am sent by Mrs Chappell,' he says.

'She has received my letter then?'

'Aye, and is much troubled by its contents. She begs that you inform her what made you change your mind.'

Mr Hancock struggles what to say. 'You know the nature of that house yourself,' he says.

'Certainly I do, and I am proud to represent it,' says Simeon. 'Mrs Chappell has the ear of men who—'

'Aye, they are my betters,' Mr Hancock cuts him off. 'Mine and yours. I have heard it many times, only I find I have left off believing it. I am not less honourable than those men I saw in attitudes of the most appalling degradation.'

Mr Stanley clings to his original message. 'Do you feel you were misled? My mistress would be much grieved to think so. If there is something we can do – what would set this situation right, Mr Hancock? What will please you?'

'Nothing, but to have my mermaid returned to me.'

The black man turns his eyes up most earnest. 'Mrs Chappell is anxious that you are happy.'

'That is easily settled,' rejoins Mr Hancock. 'Now leave me be, for I am a busy man.'

Simeon clears his throat. He is not particularly heavyset, but he is tall, and now straightens his back so that his shoulders broaden. With perfect mildness he forms a fist – whose knuckles are notably scuffed and scarred for one so otherwise refined – and touches it into the pale palm of his other hand. There is the pat of skin upon skin. 'My mistress begs you recall the agreement you made with her,' he says quietly. 'The contract she signed to hire your mermaid for one week, and the sum of three hundred guineas she agreed to pay you in good faith.'

'Do not think to intimidate me,' Mr Hancock says, his eyes upon Simeon's clasped fist. 'I am a man of business, and I do not deal with bullies.'

This rankles. 'You call me a bully, sir?'

'What else were I to call you? You are employed by a madam to menace her clients. If you know of a better word, please, I should like to know it.'

'I am a professional,' Simeon says sulkily. 'A servant as good as any to be found in London's finest houses.'

'Right you are. So let us have no more of this thuggery. I am not in the habit of breaking my agreements, but needs must, do you not find? Sometimes for the sake of one's good standing 'tis better to break a contract than to honour it.'

'She will pay you more,' says Simeon promptly, for Mrs Chappell has briefed him thoroughly on what might tempt the merchant back into tractability. 'Another fifty pounds, what say you?'

'Guineas, she and I agreed . . .'

'Fifty guineas then.'

'. . . but that's a detail. I still refuse.'

'A hundred.'

Mr Hancock turns away; the footman watches him attentively for his next parry but none comes. He puts his head on one side; a smile of gentle bafflement splits his face.

'Surely, sir,' he says, 'that's acceptable to you?'

'I want my mermaid back,' says Mr Hancock, and turns to walk away, pushing out onto the street.

The footman follows with some effort, dodging amongst the convocation of businessmen and recalling to himself the next part of his script. 'If 'tis influence you want,' he pants, 'connections, why, she can help you . . .'

This gives Mr Hancock a moment's pause. He looks at Simeon with renewed interest. 'Say,' he clears his throat, 'you move about the town a great deal, one fine house to another, do you not?'

'I do.' Simeon wonders at this change of tack but determines to humour the gentleman.

'Then what would you say will be the next most fashionable neighbourhood? If a man were to build houses – if he had money, perhaps, but had never speculated in London before – where ought he to build?'

Simeon conceals a smile at this hobnail bumpkin with his threadbare wig, and endeavours to respond kindly. 'Perhaps Snow Hill, sir, or out on the Mile-End Road: a great many sea-captains and merchants in those parts are wanting great houses.

Mr Hancock shakes his head crossly. 'No, no no. I wish to build houses for fine people. No cits, no trade. Leisure.'

'Forgive me. A fashionable neighbourhood in town? I would say Mary-le-Bone, north-west of here. Fine clean air. Halfway into the country already.'

'That is where you would build?'

'I daren't think of such a thing.' Simeon puffs up his chest. 'But I shall have a tavern there some day, God willing. A fine pretty situation it is.'

'Mary-le-Bone,' repeats Mr Hancock. 'Much obliged to you. Much obliged. Mary-le-Bone.' Then he claps his hat back onto his head. 'As to the trouble with the mermaid, I regret you are wasting your time. I'll be wanting it back. Relay to your mistress—'

'Mrs Neal!' blurts Simeon. And this does stop Mr Hancock in his tracks.

'What of her?' He touches his unthinking fingers to his lower lip.

This is Simeon's last card, and he is sorely aware of it. Angelica's tools of persuasion are very different from his own, and may in this case achieve better results; either way, he will be glad to palm this trouble off. 'She desires to see you,' he says.

Mr Hancock shuffles his feet. 'She . . . ?' He shakes his head. 'No. No, I do not think so.'

'Aye, yes!' says Simeon. 'Very eagerly. Will you not visit her this evening?'

'I cannot.'

'Sir, do you know how often Mrs Neal requests the company of a gentleman? Almost never. *They* present themselves to *her*. But she waits upon you. You should go to her.'

Mr Hancock sighs. 'This is all part of your mistress's persuasions.'

Simeon shrugs. It is a fair hand; no need to overplay it. 'She waits upon you. Go or do not; here is where she may be found.' He takes from inside his jacket a card upon which is already written (in Mrs Chappell's own hand, although Mr Hancock does not know it) the address of Angelica's rooms. 'Take it.' He holds it out.

Mr Hancock eyes it. 'I have work to attend to.'

'Take it! Take it! What harm can it do? And then I shall leave you be.'

Truly, what choice does Mr Hancock have? With shaking hand and faltering heart, he reaches out and accepts Angelica Neal's summons.

TWENTY

Simeon, once he has watched Mr Hancock vanish amongst the crowd of his own sort, sets off apace. He is a figure of some interest, he knows, for his livery is the colour of heaven and he is half a head taller than most about him, but this – he observes – is due in part to their own slouching. *If they would take some pride in themselves,* he thinks, *they would not look so much at me.*

As it is, some jeer. 'Young prince! Young prince!' calls an apprentice. 'Mr Snowball, pick up your feet!' And yes, he must tread most scrupulously across the filth, wincing with disgust as he strides over the channel of effluvium that runs down the centre of the roadway. He passes the seafarers' hall, within whiff of the water, with alleys here and there that afford him a glimpse of great white sails. He passes the workshops of the cordwainers, the print shops at St Paul's, the fruit wagons of St Clement's, and everywhere he goes, with his quick, light step and his head held high, every pair of eyes in the great population of the streets sees that here is an important man; knows by his finery that he must be the most favoured messenger of an influential house. Simeon, swatting soot from one shoulder, strides onward.

He skirts the edge of St Giles, a low sort of a place where he might come by an accident at the wrong end of a blade. He hurries past an old Lascar begging on the street, who raises the leg of his pantaloon to show a great ulcer embedded like a yolk in the twiggy bone beneath. The man is naked beneath his jacket, and his dark skin slack and meagre over his ribcage. His eyeballs have a discoloured look to them, as if they had have been dipped in tea, and the corners of his lips are pale and scurfy. Simeon himself was never a sailor, but he perceives that this man will not join another crew. 'Brother,' calls the Lascar, holding out his bowl, 'brother, help me,' but Simeon wrinkles his nose. He thinks how he might describe this later to his friends, the footmen and grocers and cabinetmakers of his own race, with their elegant wool jackets and embroidered waistcoats and powdered hair. He puzzles over what words he might use, but he knows he will say nothing. For how can it be said? And what good will speaking it do? He strides away from the Lascar without looking back, but the memory of him will crouch in Simeon's belly for quite some time longer.

Do not imagine that he betrays any perturbation in his demeanour. He arrives at Dean Street cool as a china dog, and there is Mrs Frost's peevish face half lost in darkness behind the first-floor window. When she sees him, she raises it open and leans out at once.

'I've a message for Mrs Neal,' he says.

'Well then, you have wasted your journey, for she ain't returned from King's Place.'

'I am sent from there.' He gestures to his blue jacket, in case it has escaped her notice, but Mrs Frost's expression does not alter. 'Come down. I shall not shout it.'

She vanishes smartly, and in seconds emerges from the front door, like an automaton in a novelty clock. 'What is it then?' she snaps. She does not waste her courtesy on servants.

'Mrs Neal met with a gentleman last night,' says Simeon, 'and my mistress is anxious to persuade him of something. I bade him call here on her behalf, that Mrs Neal may flatter him as I may not.'

'So I must expect a gentleman?'

'Yes, and obstruct him by no means. He must be free to unburden himself; he is troubled by some business with my mistress.'

Mrs Frost harrumphs. 'Mrs Neal has her own interests to attend to. How many more favours does Mrs Chappell expect?'

''Tis all the one favour.'

'Well, it makes a great many demands on her time.'

He spreads his hands. 'Take it up with my mistress. Or with yours.'

'My mistress! Impudence! She is not my employer, she is my friend.'

Simeon looks her up and down. 'Much good it does you,' he says, and bestows upon her the most delightful of smiles.

Mr Hancock is a man of particular impressionability, this is true, but it takes him less than four hours to set his mind on visiting Angelica Neal that very evening. He knows not what he will say or do, *but she awaits me there*, he thinks, *I cannot do her the double dishonour of snubbing her invitation. Certainly I will not give way on the question of the mermaid, but is it not a fine pretext to see her again?* He has come to the conclusion that however disgraceful her circle, he must display courtesy beyond it. *For I, although not so socially elevated, am the better man. I would treat no girl that way; I would never disport myself so amongst my peers; I am cognisant, as those gentlemen are not, that all pleasures have their cost.*

He makes his way there as swiftly as he may, but all along the Strand the girls are coming out for their evening's work: they perch on doorsteps and window ledges, or stand in small groups, passing a bottle between them and flirting their brightly coloured skirts up to show their frilled petticoats beneath. There are some as stand on the edge of the pavement (if there be pavement at all), nervous and watchful, their eyes flicking from one man to the next as an animal's eyes will dart in search of safety. Every man who passes they try to meet his gaze; every gaze they meet their faces twitch into a smile. Mr Hancock strides with his head down but they approach him still, laying their hands on his sleeve as he passes.

'Walk me home?' one asks.

'I've something you want, sir,' confides another. The ones out in daylight have little besides the obvious to be ashamed of, their faces youthful and only lightly painted, the state of their dresses respectable at first glance if not at second. The ghastly ones – the toothless, the rotten, the old and the filthy – are not to be seen: they conceal themselves in their crooked alleys or wait until the small hours when they might conjure their lost charms with drink and darkness.

He is turning up Half Moon Street when a young one steps into his path. She is neither exceptional pretty nor exceptional plain; just a little brown-haired country girl of perhaps sixteen years, with a faded kerchief knotted about her neck and her stays all shiny with wear. She starts to trot alongside him, and although he picks up his pace she picks up hers too, her borrowed hoops rocking this way and that.

'Sir,' she says. 'You'll not stop a while?'

'Thank you, no,' he pants, for the exertion to escape her is more than he is accustomed to. Still she does not fall back.

'I know an alehouse near here,' she says. 'A decent place to pass an hour.' She twists her fingers wretchedly: she wears no gloves, and her hands are white and bony, with crescents of black under the nails. 'It has an upstairs room.'

'Be off with you,' he says. 'This won't do,' but the little jade pursues him still.

'Sixpence and a jug of wine, that's all I ask,' she says. 'I'll see you right.'

He stops, and she fairly trips over her feet: no wonder, for her shoes are too large and slither up and down her heel as she walks. He looks into her face. She is all unpainted, a spray of freckles over her nose.

'Who runs you?' he asks.

'Nobody,' she says.

'Is that the truth? No bully, no bawd?'

'No, sir, I do trade alone.'

He sighs, and rummages a shilling from his pocket. He holds it up for her to see. 'Enough to find somewhere warm and a bite to eat. Perhaps a candle. This is for nobody's spending but your own, d'ye mark me?'

She does not move. He has never seen anybody stare at a coin so intently.

'Go,' he says, holding it out to her. She looks at him stupidly. 'I want nothing of you, only that I shall not see you on the street again tonight.'

She holds out her palm, and when he drops the coin into it her fingers snap closed like a trap. She brings her fist close to her chest. 'Thank you, sir.'

She drops a curtsey, and hastens away, he hopes to a pie shop but perhaps back to the spot on the pavement where she began. *As if she will spend it on anything but gin,* he thinks to himself as she vanishes into the crowd. *As if a mere twelvepence could help the child. Where is her family and why does she not return to them? Confound it, a respectable man ought to be able to walk down the street without being accosted.*

And onward into Soho he goes, irritated by his own softening. All the way to Dean Street he finds women's hands on his cuff, their entreaties in his ears. It seems there is not one woman abroad who might not open her legs given the opportunity: the milliners' girls with their goods parcelled up whisper, 'I have time to tarry,' and the dressers who have been turned away superfluous from the theatres call, 'An unusual evening, that I am at my liberty! This chance will not come to you again.'

And yet all about them is industry. He sees printers' apprentices with their inky fingers, blacksmiths and pie-men and builders and lawyers. Doctors bustle the streets in their cauliflower wigs; apothecaries scoop from great majolica jars; furniture salesmen sit happy behind mullioned windows. But amongst all this brave order there are those who have fallen loose from it, as screws from a fine machine. In this city of a thousand trades, there is only one that the women return to as if they were called to it.

He comes to Dean Street; at Angelica's address the first-floor window is open and a narrow, tidy-looking woman sits within, leaning an elbow on its sill.

'Good day to you,' he calls up, raising his hat.

She does not look up immediately, preferring to finish whatever she is scribbling in her pocketbook, and then her irritable blink is something like Hester's when she has lost her spectacles, although she is much younger.

'May I help you?' she asks.

'I am after Mrs Neal,' he bellows. He is painful conscious of the other people in the street, the good washerwomen and tradesmen, the mantua-maker's seamstresses who are quick to gather at their window below Mrs Neal's as if it were a theatre box. It is unfortunate that he is unconscious of Angelica's giggling return to her rooms, not two hours earlier, wrapped in a wool blanket and with her soaked underclothes and Mr Rockingham in tow.

'This is the gentleman you met at Mrs Chappell's, I suppose,' had said Mrs Frost once they were alone in the dressing room.

174

'I don't see what it is to you,' Angelica retorted. 'Here, my gown must be left at Mrs Chappell's. What larks! You might send and see if it has been found.'

'But the gentleman—'

'Yes! For pity's sake, Eliza, yes, he is from Mrs Chappell's; I met him there yesterday and I shall keep him with me tonight. Does that satisfy you? Well, leave us be.'

Mrs Frost now raises the sash and leans further out, eyeing Mr Hancock carefully. 'And what are you wanting with her?' She is always judicious in her assessment of visitors. This man, his thumbs notched into his pockets, looks like neither a gentleman nor a bailiff, but if she had to choose she would lean to the latter.

'Why, I . . . I wished to see her. To talk, if I may. I met her last night.'

'That hardly sets you apart. Your name?'

'Hancock.' He removes his hat and turns it around in his hands. *The mermaid man*, he wants to add, but he bites it back as folly.

'Never heard of you.' She turns her head from the window. Within, although he cannot know, Angelica Neal is locked in her bedroom, cocooned in love. 'Well, she is not at liberty.'

'I met her last night,' he repeats. 'I did not treat her as I ought, and I—'

'Not today,' says Mrs Frost. 'She will see nobody.'

The girls in the mantua-maker's below seem to Mr Hancock remarkable short of occupation; they now push their own window as far open as it will go, and prop their elbows on the frame to watch the back-and-forth on the street. Mr Hancock, standing not two yards distant from their beady interest, shuffles his feet and endeavours to hasten his enquiries.

'But if you would perhaps tell her that I—'

'If I were to run every entreaty left with me for Mrs Neal, I would wear my feet to stumps,' snaps Mrs Frost. 'This is not your day, sir. Come by again, if you must.'

Then she pulls the window down, and leaves him confounded on the pavement.

'What now, sir?' asks one amongst his audience of seamstresses. 'Surely you'll not go home so insulted?'

He straightens his jacket and says nothing, but they lean out further to him.

'You'll not be refused entrance *here*,' one of the girls says.

'I beg your—'

'We'll give you a good price.'

'Come in, come in!' They jostle and whisper, and emit a great spray of laughter, and he retreats quite burning with shame and perplexion.

VOLUME II.

ONE

'You have lost me my mermaid!'

Mrs Chappell's chins quiver with rage as she slops across the marble floor in her wrap and her rabbit-fur slippers. She has forgone her wig for a starched and frilled cap, and wears spectacles very low down her nose: denuded of her rouge and jewels, she appears less imposing but far sterner. There is no weakness in her bare slackening skin or the furrow of her brow: in fact, she never looked more of a matriarch.

'Is this why you sent for me?' says Angelica, much put out. She had wavered, indeed, over responding to the abbess's summons, Mr Rockingham being so very much on her mind, *but I promised to oblige her, and there is always something in it for me,* she had told herself. Two days in the otherworld of his arms has made her ebullient, and proud of herself: she is in the mood to be amongst friends and revel in her own magnetism. If she had recalled that Mrs Chappell did no entertaining at all before two – that the first part of her day has ever been devoted to the driest of business – she might have prepared herself not to be greeted with perfect civility at King's Place, the site of such recent and dazzling triumphs. The house is rather unusually silent, as if the girls and dogs running about upstairs were not so lively today, and the footman who steps forward for her cloak lacks a certain sprightliness. 'And what are you talking about?' she asks. 'I have lost your mermaid? If I have, I am afraid I know nothing of it.'

Above, there is a rustling on the stairs, where Elinor begins to descend. 'Good morning,' Angelica calls, 'or has it yet struck noon?' but Mrs Chappell shoots the girl a look of dark warning, so that she turns tail and vanishes the way she came. 'That don't bode well,' quips Angelica, who has experience of that expression. Guilt now tweaks at her, and she thinks for the first time of Mr Hancock, the mermaid man, who was in her care and departed it – she now recalls – far from easy. Still, there is no reason to admit fault until it is proven beyond the possibility of denial.

'My room, if you please,' says Mrs Chappell stiffly.

'You are dreadful cross,' observes Angelica lightly, but she follows the abbess into the green-papered parlour without protestation.

The curtains are open and the fire is burning, but there is no tea laid out there, no Madeira or biscuits, and Mrs Chappell calls for none. 'You have lost me a mermaid,' she repeats.

'Will you permit me to sit down?'

The abbess harrumphs, and Angelica takes her place on the sopha, slumping over its arm. In this attitude she marks suddenly the ache in her commodity, and the rawness where her thighs touch. *Too much fun.* She cannot keep the smile from her face. Perhaps it is to the good that Rockingham has returned to his studies for a few days: although she is already drafting her first letter to him in her head, her body could not take much more of his ardour.

'Sit up straight,' snaps Mrs Chappell. 'And you can wipe off that saucy look too. I never was so vexed with you. Never so vexed with any of my girls.'

'I cannot bear the suspense! Madam, what have I done?'

Mrs Chappell extends a furious finger. '*You* have—'

'No, no, do not repeat it! I mis-spoke; you made yourself clear. I have lost you a mermaid. *How* did I effect such a thing?'

'Mr Hancock has removed it from exhibition in this house.'

She recalls his foolish panicked stagger away from her, and how he blundered through the crowd. 'You cannot blame that all on me,' she scowls. 'Any number of things may have displeased him. You orchestrated the entire night, after all; my role in it was very minor indeed.'

Mrs Chappell narrows her eyes. 'No more of your babble,' she says. 'Your pertness today is not at all to my taste. You did not take care of Mr Hancock, as I requested . . .'

'He did not like the show. What was I to do?'

'Set things right! If I had thought that nothing could upset his ease I'd have put him in the charge of our silly Kitty. I chose you because I trusted that whatever went awry, you would know how to bring things to his satisfaction.'

'But I—'

'No gentleman should leave this house disappointed,' says Mrs Chappell. 'You know that. But Mr Hancock was *sorely* disappointed. I directed him to you the next day, that you might put it right – and mark me, he was willing to go to you; that's half your job done for you. Why, you sent him away again!'

'I never did!'

'No?'

Angelica searches her memory, a blur of wine and bedsheets and sweat. 'I never so much as saw him,' she says firmly. 'Never heard him, had no notion he had called.'

'Eliza Frost was under the strictest instructions to let him in.'

'You spoke to her?'

'Simeon did.'

'Then the blame is on them! I knew nothing of it!'

Now is the moment to retreat graciously from the argument: 'A misunderstanding,' one or the other should say, 'a misfortune. It could happen to any body.' But the words stick in both their throats. Angelica cocks her head in invitation of an apology; Mrs Chappell looks in the other direction.

'You ought to run a tighter ship,' she snaps. ''Tis down to you to make sure these confusions do not occur.'

Angelica's judgement is swayed by her wounded pride. 'And you, madam!'

'*I* do not need *you* the way *you* need *me*,' says Mrs Chappell, and although her tone is measured, it demands to be heeded. 'I have been celebrated in this world since before you were born; since before even your mother was born I don't doubt; I have standing. *Your* reputation rests only on what I have sent your way. You would do well to please me.'

But Angelica is not heedful. 'You may believe that if you wish,' she says. 'But when I first returned to London, you and I were in accord that I was a valuable asset to you. And now that I am all about the town again, I'd reckon my value has only increased. Why, I could do as well as Bel Fortescue if I chose; so you had better not keep me down by assigning blame where there is none.' Will she relate this conversation to Georgie? She has not yet decided. It may indeed be indelicate to speak of such matters around him; she would not wish to seem a haggling street-wench. No, more graceful to say nothing of it, and let him see the new respect with which her old bawd must treat her. '*You* struck the deal,' she finishes with relish. '*You* hired the mermaid from the gentleman and *he* took it away again. That is not my lookout.'

Mrs Chappell claps her hands, less in real mirth than in the knowledge that it will goad her erstwhile protégée. 'Oh, you wish to equal Mrs Fortescue, do you? You might start by emulating her humility, for you know, dear, ambition comes to naught without it.'

'Ugh!' Angelica stamps her foot like a girl of thirteen. Mrs Chappell's company arrests her in a certain daughterish petulance, and even in the face of such advice she adopts the mantle of wounded party, and the generations-old cry, 'You *always* favoured her!' She flounces from her seat, and succeeds in screwing out a few tears as she continues, 'How I strive to please you! And it is never enough, Mother Chappell. Never!'

'None of that,' says the abbess, who over her career has raised hundreds of girls. 'She may rail against it, but Bel Fortescue owes her current fortune in no small part to having *always* acquiesced to me.'

'No, that is not so. You built her up so far, but then she went her own way. It don't signify now whether she is with you or against you.' Angelica does not have the words, but she both covets and resents what Bel has got, which is to take her own space in the world, to have come by some alignment of charms to be celebrated for her own self.

'But you are not Bel,' says Mrs Chappell. 'You are Angelica Neal. I have served you right so far, have I not?'

Angelica draws herself to her full height. '*I* think I do very well on my own. As I told you I would.'

'Oh, aye?'

'Aye. And I have met a wonderful kind man, who will take care of me.' She crosses her fingers in the folds of her skirt. 'You forget, Mrs Chappell, that I will never be a mercenary, and I will do no business of yours that don't suit me.'

Mrs Chappell has heard speeches of this sort before, and is robust enough to pay it no particular heed. 'Go, then,' she says, 'and make your own way. My door is always open to you. But dear girl, we are all mercenaries; there is no escaping it.'

'Not I!'

'Indeed you; you have need to be the most mercenary of us all. Every kindness has its price, Mrs Neal, and one so precariously set up as you would do well to know your own means.'

'There is nothing precarious about me,' returns Angelica. 'You mean only to unsettle me.'

'So hold fast, dear girl. Hold fast.'

TWO

And thus it is that Mr Hancock comes to sell his mermaid.

It has been returned to his office by Simeon's own hand, and sits on the sideboard beneath its glass dome, waiting for him to bear it home once more to Deptford. He is damping down the coals when he hears a rapping on the front door that carries all the way through the building to his private office as if somebody has taken a brass-headed cane to it. He has picked up his coat to leave, but hesitates at the sound of strange voices ushered into the outer office.

'Mr Hancock,' a man says, 'the mermaid man. Where can he be found?'

He is expecting no visitor. He puts down his overcoat and opens his door. 'Why, I am here,' he says.

In the plain outer office there is a party of four of the most splendid men. They are not dressed extravagantly, but the quality is evident: their greatcoats are of a deep rich indigo, their cravats the snowiest and gauziest white; their wigs pristine, uncrushed, unstained. And each wears a badge of a jewelled coronet on his arm, flanked with rampant gold-thread creatures.

'Gentlemen,' he says, although his mind is all a-fumble. 'What can I do for you?' He is thinking, foolishly, *are they sent by Mrs Neal? Does she summon me to her?*

'We are here on a matter of business,' they say. His clerks' quills are twitching industriously but they are alert to every word: they are not unused to visitors of some grandeur, but the organs of aristocracy – let alone equerries of the Crown – are something new in this quiet office. He notes with some disconcertion that Oliver Hay is scribbling without removing his eyes from the company.

'We can speak in my own office,' he says, and they troop past him one by one. Within, he has not an idea of what to do. The mermaid watches from the sideboard. 'Be seated,' he hazards.

'Oh, we shall not trouble you long,' says their leader, the most clean-shaven man Mr Hancock ever saw. There is hardly a shadow upon his face; he is smooth as a youth although he must be forty. 'We wish to speak to you about your mermaid, which was recently removed from the house of one Mrs Chappell.'

Mr Hancock nods towards it; the men turn too, and he notes a flicker of discomposure in their demeanour, swiftly suppressed. 'Well, please,' he says. 'Speak.'

'Do you intend to sell it?'

In matters of commerce he is rarely unprepared for such questions, and although the business with the mermaid first undid his senses entirely, he has passed into a new and absurd sharpness; an understanding that the point at which he judges his demands to be unreasonable is the point he must push beyond.

'That depends,' he says. The men are impassive. 'You must appreciate that it brings me revenue: I had expected it to turn a profit for some time longer.'

'We have money.'

'Who has sent you?' he asks, although he may judge it well enough from their jewelled badges. In the past he has arranged for such a coronet to be etched onto one hundred mother-of-pearl gaming chips.

'An interested party.'

'And it will go into a private collection? Some *Wunderkammer*? It's my belief this creature will be of scientific use.'

'It will not go anywhere that scientific men cannot find it.'

He might laugh aloud. Its little grasping hands have brought uneasiness into his small bubble; he realises he never wants it back in his sight again. 'Well, you have heard my reservations,' he says. 'Make me an offer.'

The leader takes a sheet of paper from the desk. 'May I?' He dips Mr Hancock's own pen in the inkwell, and writes with lovely fluid movements under the eyes of the dead men hanging on the walls. Mr Hancock glances up at their painted faces as if they were co-conspirators: *the strangest sale I ever did make,* he confides, *as if any of you would have believed it.*

The visitor hands him the piece of paper and Mr Hancock regards the figure in a second that feels as if all the air has been sucked from the room, so still it becomes, and so sluggishly his heart squeezes. The sum is two thousand pounds. This is above what his mermaid cost him. He looks at the number again.

'Please,' says the equerry. 'We are open to your counter-offer. Go on.'

Dare he double their proposed sum? Quadruple it, even? Eight thousand would purchase a ship the *Calliope*'s equal; would finance a new voyage entirely, if he chose. Sukie's dowry would be safely set by; his modest empire expanded by another house or two. He will sit in his office and Tysoe Jones will sail his ships, and it will be as if the mermaid never crossed his threshold at all.

Ah, what to do? Six thousand, eight thousand, ten thousand?

He thinks of himself in his counting-house, the evening before the mermaid arrived, alone and silent, surrounded by such unbearable lack.

He walks to his desk and sits down.

He takes up his pen, warm from the visitor's hand, and he adds another zero.

Thus amended, he pushes the sheet of paper back across the desk, so trepidatious it renders him almost blind.

The visitor glances at the new sum, and then says, 'Very well.'

Mr Hancock must steel his jaw to prevent it from flapping open. He had not thought it would be done so easily. He has sold Captain Jones's whim for twenty thousand pounds: enough to pay off a nobleman's debt; enough to hire a cook to run his kitchen for a century; enough to be another sort of Jonah Hancock than he has been hitherto.

'Your master,' he says to the leader of the strangers, 'whoever *he* may be . . .'

'Yes?'

'Has he – has he *seen* this specimen?'

The company, to a man, turns once again to contemplate the beast. 'He has heard excellent things about it,' says the equerry, 'and so what does it matter?'

'Its appearance is unbeautiful. It is not what people expect of a mermaid.'

The visitor is impatient. 'But it *is* a mermaid. He desired one and now he has one.'

'It is, if I may say, monstrous.'

'But it is real.' The visitor straightens the collar of his coat and looks to his men. 'It don't matter what it looks like. It is desired by everyone and yet it belongs only to him. May we now be away, Mr Hancock? Or did you have other questions?'

'Please. I am more than satisfied.' He notes that the men's eyes linger on the mermaid, and steps before it. 'You'll not take it away today. I shall wait for your payment.'

'Of course, of course.'

'Let me see you out.'

He ushers them through the office, where all his men sit up goggling. In the yard the stationer's children and their black dog are playing some sort of chasing game, and pelt across the flagstones shrieking while their pet gambols in pursuit; the visitors are obliged to stride stiffly amongst them, executing little nervous side-steps when one child or other runs too close to them. Eventually one of the smaller boys wallops into the leader of the visitors' legs, which throws him sprawling to the ground clutching his knee. It is at this point that Mr Hancock closes the door on his benefactors. When it is fast, he leans against it and tries to quiet his breathing so as not to arouse the curiosity of the clerks so nearby. He cannot decide what to think. He holds his hands up before him, and they shake.

THREE

Little boys' fingers patter against the window of Mr Hancock's counting-house. He hears the chime of their sticks dragged along the grilles in the pavement, and the high earnest wondering of their talk. If he turned from his desk he would see their figures slithering in the whorl of the glass, swimming and dispersing in its waves: he would see the light of their sunny hair and the stockings wrinkling down their legs as they break into a run, and thus vanish from each pane's vortex.

It is a Sunday, a day of exodus, and the families of Deptford are setting out upon their rare pleasures with redoubled determination, it being an unseasonably fine day, perhaps the last they see this year. The women don their gay dresses and fresh-trimmed bonnets, and the men hoist their babies onto their shoulders, and they walk out with children and dogs running about their feet, all equipped with bats and balls and nets and fans, their bread bound in clean cloth, their pennies carefully counted. Stout matrons take their husbands' arms with girlish pleasure, and suitors attend bashfully to their sweethearts, and bands of lads from the yards unbutton their shirts and uncork their first ale of the morning. Out they stride, one and all, bound by river and road for the pleasure gardens at Vauxhall or the tumbled green hill of Greenwich or the breeze of Blackheath, where the sky dances with many-coloured kites. They fill the street with the tramp of their feet, and their shouts and laughter waft across the twinkling river-water, no matter that it stinks. In the little rowing-boats the women shriek and clutch at their bonnets; the boys spring from stern to pitching prow without anxiety.

Mr Hancock remains at his desk. He is rich now, in the manner of a man long-apprenticed in handling other people's money. His wealth drives him to no feverish excess (besides the ordering in, as the weather grows colder, of spiced currant buns and new woollen underwear): he has laid money aside for Sukie's dowry and her boy cousins' apprenticeships, but for the most part his ambitions remain unaltered in their substance, merely greater in their scale. He will still build houses, oh, most certainly, but he will build not one terrace but two, and they will not be here. What man builds in Deptford, after all, who has the means to build in London?

And so there is much to be done, and so he remains at his desk.

Furthermore, who would he walk out with?

In his boyhood he scampered ahead of his sisters amongst those tramping feet, with the admonishments of Hester harsh in his ears, but their father rarely came with them and their mother was dead beyond remembrance. The girls – Grace and Dorrie, Rachel and Susan – sometimes ran too, matching their steps to his. They ran altogether like pups in a pack, so hard that their lungs ached with the joy of it, but Hester was right to call them back to her.

'Stay with me,' she hissed, a skinny girl, as tidy then as she is now. 'Walk nicely. They will say we have no order.'

'*They* run,' he said, spreading his hand at the children vanishing down the lane, the dust clouding behind them.

'*They* have mothers.'

And he and Philip (whose skin was tight as a bladder by the time he washed up in the creek all blue and fish-nibbled) and Rachel (who was spirited off to Bristol, no more to see her family), and Grace (who, delivering her first child, bled and bled, and bled away), and Dorrie and Susan and even Hester grew quiet and took one another's hands. Still they capered, but they doubted themselves, and could not skip and leap as carelessly as the other children.

Sukie has gone for the day: at morning prayers, her favourite spotted kerchief was already knotted about her shoulders, and as he intoned her feet jigged on the floorboards to run and meet her own sisters at the turnpike. She has been skittish of late, like the cat when she is out of temper, eyeing him suspiciously and saying nothing. This, he knows, is since the sale of the mermaid.

'Oh,' she had said when he told her.

'Is that all? I had thought you would be pleased.'

She shrugged, and brought her thumbnail to her mouth.

'It is a lot of money,' he explained to her as she made for the door.

Turning, she said in a most accusatory manner, 'I *helped* you.'

'Aye, you did – you are a fine little helper. And now I have done my part too.' But she is out of the door. 'It was mine to sell,' he called after her.

He hopes her day out might restore her cheer.

From somewhere in the house, Mr Hancock hears a strange twittering. He scratches on with his letter, but there is the sound again. A gurgle, fast suppressed. He puts down his pen. Venturing from his counting-house and into the hall, the gurgling becomes a giggling, and is joined by others to make a little chorus. The kitchen is dark and cold, made darker yet by the brightness of the open yard door, where Bridget leans against her broom, her back to the room. Her cot is still tumbled in the corner, its blankets thrown back to reveal the dent in the tick where she slept. There are breadcrumbs on the table, and a splash of milk, and dishes unwashed.

He crosses the room until he is only a few feet away from the yard door, and still Bridget does not notice, so deep is she in mirthful conversation with a knot of young girls who have gathered outside. They have let their good shawls drop from their elbows, guiltily enjoying the sunshine upon their forearms, and they have blacked their brows most startling. While maids they certainly are, they are also a diminutive masquerade of the town's ladies, each being dressed faithfully but imperfectly in her mistress's cast-off clothes. He recognises the blue tabby gown favoured by the doctor's late wife; the black-and-red trim of the mantua Mrs Lawlor had been so proud of until she caught its cuff on a candle; the sprigged skirt worn and discarded by all four of the Master Shipwright's daughters. Poor Bridget, he thinks, to find herself so poorly clothed. It is a wonder she has not run away.

'What's afoot?' he asks, and the giggling stops. Bridget hardly turns at his approach, but the little mummers outside crane over her shoulder at him.

'Good morning, sir,' bob the girls one, two, three. 'And a fine morning it is,' says the bravest of them.

'Aye,' he says, 'and what brings you here?'

'Come to say good day, aren't we?' says Mrs Lawlor's girl, flirting her patched mantua. 'We're off to Greenwich.'

Bridget sighs heavily.

'Back by six, sir,' says the girl in the blue tabby, which scrinches along her flanks with its imperfect adjustments.

'All of them going,' says Bridget. 'Their masters are out, and they at their liberty.' The girls nod eagerly, and she turns her eyes balefully upon him.

'Well,' he says, 'but *I* am still here. And Bridget was off all Thursday afternoon and evening, were you not?'

'My mother had need of me,' she protests. 'I was not at my *leisure*.'

'You have had your freedom for the week, 'tis not my lookout what you used it for.'

The girls fall quiet.

'But may I *not* . . . ?' Bridget gestures to the girls, the dresses, the sunlight, as if drawing his notice to what he might otherwise have overlooked.

He steps back from the door to let the girls see inside. 'Crumbs,' he says, 'on the table.' He tries to be jovial, but it takes an effort to keep the tremble from his voice. This is not his sphere: his dominion over Bridget ought to be at great remove, as God's dominion over His subjects, with many intercessors before the one is necessitated to confront the other. And yet in this house there is not one intercessor, and so he goes on. 'And her bed not touched since she left it – my dear young ladies, I trust none amongst *you* left your duties undone before you took your liberty?'

The maids are mute, Bridget too, an angry pink spot burning on each of her cheeks.

A fool, he thinks as his heart pounds, *to be afraid of a mere girl*.

But he cannot afford mutiny. And Sukie's disappointment if Bridget were to quit his service, and the trouble of finding a new maid – for he has not the privilege of the circle of Deptford ladies, who advise one another which girls are reliable and how to train those that are not – even to think of it is to sense defeat.

'Will you be sure and do your work the moment you are back?' he asks Bridget. 'And leave the kitchen as clean as Mrs Lippard would expect to discover it, were she to arrive tomorrow?'

The girls ripple their pleasure, but Bridget merely nods, already tugging her apron loose. 'Of course,' she says, and leans her broom against the wall. She retrieves from beneath the carver chair Sukie's sprigged jacket, all screwed into a ball, and shoves an arm into its sleeve.

'Well?' he says as she knots its tapes across her stays.

'Hmm?'

'You've no thank-you for my kindness?'

She looks at him then, briefly and quizzingly. 'Thank you,' she says, 'thank you, thank you, much obliged,' fading away as she steps out of the door and closes it behind her. It becomes dark in the kitchen. Without, a shriek of laughter.

He takes himself back to his desk, and is much displeased.

FOUR

Mr Rockingham has observed, of course, that the austere Mrs Frost seems to have taken a dislike to him; he needed no more evidence than the tone in her voice when – the third consecutive night he spent in Angelica's bed – she said, 'Oh. Are you are still here?' And now, a week later, he curls once more next to his lady while her erstwhile companion taps in vain at the door.

They are playing spillikins on a lacquered tray they have brought into the bed for that purpose, for as a pair their tastes lean towards the infantile and the trifling. He is resting his palm on the spot where Angelica's hip becomes her thigh, and she is making a great flirtatious show of extracting a stick from the heap on the tray – a fatuous endeavour since they slide in all directions every time she giggles – when Mrs Frost taps again.

'What is it?' calls Angelica.

'I need to speak to you.'

Angelica groans.

'Tell her to go away,' whispers George, inveigling a finger beneath her chemise.

'In a moment,' says Angelica. 'Perhaps she has something to say for herself.' She rolls over, and calls out, 'What do you *want*?'

'Come out here. I wish to speak with you.'

'Whatever you have to say, it may be said in front of Georgie.'

The door opens a crack, and a small slice of Mrs Frost's face appears at it. Angelica and her lover loll like sun-drunk seals on the shore, his hand half within her chemise. Mrs Frost fixes her eye to the wall somewhere to the left of the bed and says, 'Mrs Chappell has sent a chair for you. You're wanted at King's Place.'

Angelica pauses. 'Well! That is interesting!' She has not seen Mrs Chappell since their disagreement over the removal of the mermaid, and her pride does not permit her to recognise the conciliatory nature of the sedan. 'I shan't go,' she says briefly. She taps her index finger upon George's lower lip. 'She don't deserve me.'

'Are you certain you—'

'Go away!'

The door closes abruptly. Without, Mrs Frost waits a moment. 'The chair is *here*,' she says.

'For pity's sake.' Angelica rises and draws her wrap about her. 'Take your turn,' she says to Rockingham, nudging the tray of sticks towards him. 'I trust you to play fairly.' She pads in her bare feet out into the corridor, where Mrs Frost is waiting. 'What are you thinking?' she hisses.

'I am reminding you of your duties,' says Mrs Frost primly. Angelica seizes her elbow and fairly shoves her into the living room.

'You have no right,' she whispers furiously. 'I have told you before; if Georgie is here you send callers away. No questions.'

'Mrs Chappell may send for you as she pleases.'

'Even after she was so fearful rude to me? I should think not.'

'Do not disoblige her. She wishes to keep you in the fold, and you ought to be grateful for it. To be seen at her house – to hold your assignations there – 'tis a privilege ...'

'One I do not need,' says Angelica. 'Mr *Rockingham* is the sole recipient of my attention. Send the chair away; tell old Mother Chappell I'll not pander to her any longer.'

'And how are we to eat?' demands Mrs Frost.

'Oh, histrionics! How are we to eat! When have we ever gone hungry?'

'We may yet.'

'No, we may not. George takes care of us. And, Eliza, I know what you are about. You pretend your concern is with the money, and oh, how sensible and prudent you are, but that is not the case, is it? It is because *he* claims a greater part of me than *you* do.'

'Nothing of the sort.'

'You are *jealous*.'

'I am trying to protect you.'

'You! Protect me! *I* am the protector. I give you good clothes and a place to sleep in return for really very few demands on your time, and yet all you do is defy me. I think you forget sometimes where you would be without me.'

'You are turning away good connections,' entreats Mrs Frost.

'On the shelf,' Angelica taunts her. 'That is where you would be. On the shelf like a pawned shortgown.'

Mrs Frost will not be provoked. 'You are isolating yourself; you must stay in the favour of the world, and when you shut yourself away you—'

Angelica digs her nails into her palms. Her face is hot and her ears ring. 'What would you have me be?' she demands. 'First I am putting myself about like a common drab, in *your* opinion, and I must find myself a respectable keeper; now I am true to one gentleman and you say I ought to be less discriminating. Which is it?'

Mrs Frost does not betray much anger, but her face is notably without colour. 'How many nights this week have you gone out?'

'I was out until dawn on Wednesday.'

'With Mr Rockingham. You are never without him. You do not respond to invitations – you do not repay Mrs Chappell's kindness; you are not at home to men who might really help you, who would further you in the world.'

'I don't want furthering. I want to be happy.'

'You have chose the wrong man. This happiness is not of a sort worth having.'

'Oh, get you gone, Eliza Frost. Get you gone. As if you would know anything at all about it.'

She flounces back to her chamber, her hair bouncing down her back, wiping her face on the sleeve of her chemise. Within, Rockingham sits up in the bed.

'What is wrong, dear heart?' he asks, and she sets about weeping again, noisily and messily. 'Oh, come here, you poor creature,' and he opens his arms up to her.

She gets onto the bed on her knees, and wilts against him. 'She wants me to give you up,' she sobs.

'Is that what she said?'

'Almost in so many words!'

'And what did you tell her?'

She sits back, wiping her eyes. 'Of course I said no. Of course. What pleasure would there be in this world for me without you?'

He wipes her tears with his thumb, which is no match for them. 'Here,' he says, and mops her face with the bedsheet. 'Why don't she want me with you?'

'Oh, she is a sad, ignorant *husk* of a woman.' She sniffs hard. 'And also she is afraid about money.'

He frowns. 'With reason?'

'She thinks – well, 'tis a small thing really – she thinks that if you were not here I would see more men. And we would be – we would be better off.'

'Do you see other men?' His face shows true surprise.

Looking all askance at him, she tries to laugh it away. 'I hardly have the time! You would know, would you not, if I were entertaining others?'

'But you *would* see them.' He withdraws his hand from hers as if it were a glowing ember.

What else would I do? she thinks. *How else does he imagine I pay my way?* Aloud she says only, 'No, no. No!' With nothing to cling to, she knots the tear-damp bedsheets about her fingers. 'Not if I did not need the money.'

'I had not . . .' He gazes at her face in stupefaction. 'I did not think . . .'

'Tis always the way, she thinks. *Treat them as if they are the centre of the world, and they do not hesitate to believe it. A charmed life these men lead, if they have never needed to look beneath the surface of things.*

Knowing his next emotion will be anger, she grasps about for something to say. 'It can't be helped,' she tries. 'You must understand my circumstances. Of course I would not gain a moment's pleasure from other men's society; of *course* it would wound me horribly, and all the while my heart would break at my betrayal of you.' This is untrue. Angelica has no particular feelings about spending an evening of mutual flattery with a stranger: on the whole she finds it enjoyable. Besides, she knows that to privilege desire in one particular man's bosom is not to extinguish it from all others – there is no mutual exclusivity in attraction, and therefore it is no crime to encourage it wherever it appears – but she has come upon few men who appreciate this argument.

'And what would you do with them?' he demands. 'Would you – would you lie with them? As you do with me?'

'No!' (Perhaps.) She folds her arms across her naked bosom and says coldly, 'I am no whore, sir, no mercenary. Pray do not think me so base.'

'What, then? What do you do with them that they pay you for so handsomely?'

She shrugs. 'They have my company. That is all. I play a little music; I make conversation. They may escort me to plays and parties, if they desire it and if I am amenable to being seen about with them.'

He had thought she smiled upon nobody the way she did him. 'You might as well open your legs to them.'

She begins to weep again, having over the course of her career developed a great knack for pathos. 'Oh, how can you say it? Georgie, how *can* you? I allow them to be near me, that is all, a privilege *you* enjoy gratis.' Raising her swimming eyes to him she sees he is gazing steadfast out of the window. 'And if they bring me presents,' she continues tremulously, 'it is because they know with what *great difficulty* a woman survives in this city, and not with the expectation of any favour. *That* I only bestow upon the one man I truly love.' But her words are in vain: he rises from the bed, and she has a glimpse of his glorious buttocks before he pulls his shirt on. 'Smelly old men,' she says, ascending again into a lament, 'who fart in their sleep and talk about their years in the cavalry! Do you think I enjoy a moment of it?'

'So do not do it.' He buttons his breeches.

'I have no other way of keeping myself together.' She wipes her eyes on her wrist and adds in a scandalised whisper, 'Some of them have hair that grows from the tips of their noses.'

'What decent woman finds she must keep herself together at all?' he demands. 'The very fact that you must support yourself is a judgement on you. I am going.'

'But where?' She rises now, in true fear. 'Wait for me –' she gathers up her clothes – 'wait! I shall come with you.'

'Do not follow me. I can't bear to be seen with you.'

FIVE

In the evening, the families returning in tired straggles, the lovers still unaccounted for in the hedgerows, Jem Thorpe arrives at Mr Hancock's door. He puts his palm flat upon its frame, his other fist propped loosely upon his hip. He looks as he is: a man at the end of a day of leisure, still and smiling, as if the sunshine his skin took up now sits warmly within him.

'I came,' he says. 'Like you asked of me. I'm at liberty to build your houses, and my boys eager to start.' He reaches up and pats the belly of one of the twin cherubs flanking the lintel, put there by his grandfather and fluttering still.

'Oh,' says Mr Hancock, who in the absence of the girls from the house has been compelled to get his dinner from the pie shop, and now guiltily shakes crumbs from his cuffs, 'there will be no need.'

Mr Thorpe is as a man still awaiting an answer. He stands a moment longer, blinks, and says, 'Why's that, then?'

Mr Hancock shrugs. Above him, the cherubs are frozen in their joy, flourishing scrolled paper and compasses, ready to draft edifices as yet unthought-of.

'If you mean no longer to put up any houses,' says Mr Thorpe, 'I would strongly counsel you to change your mind.' He puffs with enthusiasm. 'Now is the time, sir. So many are in want of a genteel sort of living, and you are in a fine position to supply it.'

'Certainly I am,' says Mr Hancock, 'but I have bought a very handsome parcel of land in Mary-le-Bone where I mean to do so.'

Mr Thorpe takes his hand from the cherub and places it upon his wigged pate. 'A great distance from here,' he says.

'Quite so,' says the merchant. 'In *London*, or near as makes no difference. The countryside there is wide and pretty, and so close to the fashionable squares. Every gentleman wants a country home, and how right you are, sir: now is the time. *Now is the time.*'

Jem Thorpe clings to his notion like a drowning man. 'That is a great distance for my team to travel,' he says. 'I suppose you ...?' But the supposing, however groped for, does not come to him. 'You mean to take your business elsewhere,' he concludes flatly. 'You mean not to hire my men.'

'It would, I fear, hardly be practical.' Mr Hancock is anxious for his pigeon pie cooling on his desk, a skin puckering upon its gravy. 'A shame, but what is there to be done? Now you must allow me—'

'There is plenty to be *done*,' says Jem Thorpe. 'Were you not born here? Yes, you were; I know you, I know your family, and your father would never have treated my father in the manner you now treat me.'

Mention of his father pricks at Mr Hancock. He shuffles, defenceless, as the shipwright goes on, 'If each man born here were to do as you are doing, there would be no town left at all. Make your fortune in London, sir, nobody grudges you that, but do not spend it there too!'

'I must look to my own interests.'

'Your interests are our interests!' Mr Thorpe's eyes have a great deal of white to them. 'Or ought to be! Sir, why build there when you can build here?'

He shakes his head. *Why keep an ass when you have the means for racehorses?* 'That is where the opportunity is,' he says.

'*You* have the money –' Jem jabs his finger – 'therefore *you* make the opportunity!' He looks about himself. 'I declare, you are as bad as the Admiralty. They grudge us the work we are due, and now so do you.'

The pain these words causes Mr Hancock is startling. 'I have bought land here,' he protests, 'good growing land at Lady-well. I shall cultivate fruit and vegetables; those want jobs—'

'Fruit-picking!' spits Thorpe. 'Children's work! Old women's work! Not for my men! Unrivalled, sir, unrivalled in their capabilities. No. If we cannot build ships we ought at least to build houses.'

'My hiring you would be no more than an act of charity,' says Mr Hancock.

'An act of *unity*.' Mr Thorpe would almost place his foot at the threshold; instead he doffs hat and wig and all, and clasps them to his chest. His head is shiny back to its crown, and thence fuzzed with greying curls. 'Come, sir,' says he, 'we cannot go on without regular employment.'

'I am sorry,' says Mr Hancock.

They stand in dismay, neither one knowing what else to say. Jem Thorpe knows certainly what he *would* say, for once or twice he draws breath, and shifts upon his feet as if he were about to burst again into speech, but as for what he *should* say he is at a loss, and so remains silent.

From far down the street and beyond the lane there comes a voice, such a scrap of a call as might be made by a bird, and at such distance as to make it of no significance. Jem Thorpe, however, marks it, and tips his head. It comes again, a little nearer: 'Daddy!'

'Ah,' he says. 'My children,' and they are at the end of Union

Street, a girl in a white apron and a boy in white stockings, bending at the waist in their enthusiasm to shout his name.

'Come home!' they call, cupping their hands about their mouths. 'Mama says where be you?'

'My *children*,' he repeats. 'You do not think of them. I suppose you have no occasion to. I am coming!' He holds a hand up to them. To Mr Hancock he says, 'It is clear to me that you share none of our concerns. *None.* That is to your discredit, not to ours.'

Mr Hancock is torn quite in two. He has sought to make the best profit he can from the surprise of his mermaid; to rescue his reputation from mockery, and to raise himself some little way up in the world. He is inquisitive, in fact, as to what might come next, and refreshed by the newness of his situation: to build in a place where his forebears have not built before, and for people with whom he shares no bond of blood or society, is an appealing prospect. Why should he not build in Mary-le-Bone if he wishes?

And yet the cost of it is more than he can stomach. 'Jem,' he says as Mr Thorpe walks away. 'Jem, attend a moment.' He descends from his step and pursues the shipwright, who wavers. 'I do have work for you.'

'Aye?'

'Aye. I lost my ship.' He shuffles in the dirt. He had not yet thought what to do about the *Calliope*'s replacement; this decision comes almost viscerally, as if he made it in peril of his life. 'I shall need a new one.'

Mr Thorpe is quiet for a moment. He narrows his eyes as if Mr Hancock were a troubling calculation.

'Truly,' says Mr Hancock. 'You and any men you like; I leave that to your own judgement. I won't meddle in your methods for even one second.'

'And you'll pay us what we are worth?'

'Aye. And the sweepings, the chips, all the wood that's over – that is yours too.'

'As it should be.'

'As it should be.'

The children of Jem Thorpe caper up now, and tuck themselves one under each of his arms. Their eyes are very bright with their exertion, and their shoulders heave as they snatch at their breath. Mr Thorpe cups his palm about the back of his son's head. 'Very well,' he says. 'Time I returned to my home.'

'And you are satisfied?' asks Mr Hancock. The children watch dumbly.

'Aye,' says Jem Thorpe, and although he does not smile his brow uncreases itself, and he stands a little taller. 'That is the work I want.'

'Good. Ah, but Jem, I want one more thing.'

'What's that?'

'I've a new venture in mind – I need a ship right away. Something modest and seaworthy, for business in the North Sea only. Not much beyond, I would not have thought. Do you know of anything likely?'

Mr Thorpe squints. 'The North Sea? That is not your usual area.'

'We must always be prepared for change. That is how we survive.'

'Aye, well, I reckon I know a likely bet. The *Unicorn*, on the blocks at Mitchell's yard, although he has no buyer for it yet. You might take a look.'

'Much obliged.'

Jem Thorpe walks away with his children swinging at his arms, filling up his long strides with their leaps and skips. Mr Hancock shades his eyes against the redding horizon to see them go, and meanwhile hears – from this place and that, in streets unseen – the rising calls of women as they go to their thresholds and call home the ones they love. The bells of St Paul's and St Nicholas's begin to chime in conversation with one another, and from the back lane rises the percussion of children's running feet. Mr Hancock returns to his own doorstep, where no wife stands with her arms outstretched to him, and no children buzz with their observations of the day.

The cat, at least, emerges from some shadow or other, and remarks upon his arrival with an impertinent chirp. He bends to chaff her ears but she'll none of it, and swipes at his hand, and canters crook-backed across the floorboards with her tail puffed up.

'Please yourself,' he murmurs, and pacing alone to his cold pie is perplexingly put in mind of Angelica Neal, as if she had just sighed past him in the darkness of the hall. He thinks, *how much longer can I tie myself to this town? Heaven help me, I'll not tolerate such solitude much longer.* He thinks, what he has long known, *there is not a single woman in Deptford who will please me.*

SIX

Angelica is sick with nerves; she has never known a thing like it. For two days she walks about her rooms and weeps intermittently. Grief crouches like a demon on her chest by night; by day it hangs about her shoulders and every little thing sets her off crying again. The first evening she cannot control the panic in her breast; she writes to him, and pays for its delivery, but although she stays by the window all night and through into the next morning there is no reply. Her food is like ashes in her mouth. She cannot look at Mrs Frost, who is unable to entirely conceal her satisfaction at Mr Rockingham's departure.

'Perhaps you should try going out,' says Mrs Frost as coaxingly as she is able. 'The theatre; you like that. Shall I write to some of your acquaintances? I think one of them will have a box for you.'

'No, no. No theatre. I must wait here in case he sends word.'

'And then the pleasure gardens are busy, they say, now that Parliament is back in session.'

Tears escape Angelica's closed eyes and roll down her cheeks. 'I cannot,' she says. 'I cannot be seen in such a way. I want nothing of any of this.'

'Now, you must *try*—'

'*Why?* What is the use in it? Oh, it is all very well for you to say;

this is a triumph for you, is it not? *You* have not had your heart broken.'

'Angelica, you have not known him even two weeks.'

'Juliet knew Romeo three days.'

'And if you had paid as much attention to the play as you do the audience, you would know not an ounce of good came of it. You are being a fool.'

'You are made of stone.'

'I will summon Mrs Fortescue,' says Mrs Frost. 'She will have some sense.'

'No!' cries Angelica in a panic. 'Not Bel! I beg you, do not let Bel know of this misfortune. And besides,' she spits, 'she is *married* now. Her fine Hanover Square wedding won at such expense – she'll want none of *me* now she is elevated.'

'Well – perhaps then—'

'Leave me be! I want nothing! I want only to wait for him.' Angelica flounces into her bedroom.

She may be forgiven. If such stirrings of amorous passion came as a shock to her, being spurned by the object of her most ardent affection is quite beyond Angelica Neal's apprehension. Love grapples judgement and experience from the hands of even the wisest of souls: what hope is there for anybody else?

On the morning of the third day, he returns.

She is locked in her bedroom, her eyes raw, with blue shadows beneath. Her chemise reeks and is stained, for she has not thought to change it in days, and until this moment had barely noticed. She marks this fact with some interest: her anguish is most certainly genuine, then. Even her hair is in disarray.

When all of a sudden she hears his voice softly without, she thinks her heart must crash out of her body; she thinks the blood pounds so hard in her veins it must rupture them one by one. She can barely stand for shaking, but she stumbles to the door and hears Mrs Frost's voice: 'Greatly distressed – no time – let her be.'

Angelica throws open her door. In the living room Mr Rockingham looks as sorry as she, his hat in his hands, and his face all drawn and tired.

'Good day, sir,' she says, and it is an agony to look upon him; she does not know if he is hers; she thinks she will not bear it if he has only come to take himself away again.

He looks at her, and looks, and parts his lips helplessly. His poor bruised eyes are fixed upon her face, and he reaches out his hands. 'I have barely slept while we were parted,' he croaks.

'Huh! At the gaming table all night, I suppose,' says Mrs Frost.

'Go away, Eliza,' whispers Angelica.

'You can tell it by the stink of him,' says her friend. 'He has been carousing, not pining. Open your eyes, madam.'

Angelica is gazing steadily at her lieutenant. She swallows hard. 'I said, go away.'

They lie on their naked bellies side by side, and Mr Rockingham strokes his hand down Angelica's back. He fits his fingers into the valley of her spine; on either side her flesh swells warm and soft to her hips, her waist, her ribs. Her eyes are closed; there is a little gloss of sweat in the crook of her elbow, where she pillows her face. Her curls are bound safely but the pleats of her cap are crushed: the corner of her mouth twitches upward.

'Why do you keep that woman with you,' asks Georgie, 'when you and she are so at odds?'

She sighs, and her eyelids flutter. 'We are more often in accord,' she whispers. 'She is my most beloved friend.' She is not the first woman to confuse 'beloved' with 'necessary'.

'You are too loyal.'

'No, no.' She turns to him, pulling her knees up to her chest and blinking sweetly. 'We have known one another a long time, since I first arrived in London.' She will not tell him of the days they were maids together in a magistrate's house, for she likes to screw her history tight inside her bosom. The past is the past, and beyond helping: it strikes her as unseemly – untidy, unnecessary – to air it. Nor, therefore, will she tell him that it was Mrs Frost who first encouraged her into the Temple of Venus, and thence King's Place. When she remembers their being girls, racked with laughter at one another's hilarity, or crushed into a narrow bed as dawn broke, whispering their secrets to one another, she feels such warmth. And so she only says, 'She was kind to me when there was no other soul to remember me.'

'Hmm.'

'Perhaps she is sadder now than she once was –' she cannot have George think she chooses her friends carelessly – 'and so her good qualities are not as evident to you as they are to me. You do not know the hardships an abandoned wife must endure.'

'Abandoned!' says Rockingham. 'Stuff and nonsense. She can hardly *want* for her husband, you treat her so well.'

'If I could do more, I would,' says Angelica with pride. 'She might have gone her own way, might she not, when my protector died and I was penniless? And she did not. She found me this place and she has got me well set.' She closes her eyes again, and hooks her fingers through his. 'She has helped me in all kinds of ways. You cannot imagine.'

Still he persists. 'But she does not help you *now*.' He is stung more by her tender history with Mrs Frost than by her mention of her old lover.

'Maybe not.'

'And besides –' he presses his body to hers, dragging the sheet over their heads – 'you have me now. I am here to help you. *I* am your friend. And I mean to be your keeper too.'

These words fizz in her blood. 'Really?'

'Truly.' He takes her face in his hands. 'You need struggle no longer. You need not see other men. I shall pay for you.'

'Oh!'

'Anything, anything you need. Say the word.' He seizes her wrists and she feels him growing hard again. She is overwhelmed with him; her fingertips brush his hair; his breath is on her cheek; their noses touch, their teeth, their eyelashes. 'I shall never have you want for so much as a pin,' he says.

'You are so kind. My love, my love,' and such heat and an aching in her heart she does not know what to do with, as if she were bewitched.

'And you will be mine,' he whispers, hooking one thigh between hers so that they fall open; she draws him into her arms. 'All and entirely my own. Oh! My dear one!'

But here is Mrs Frost tapping at the door. 'Angelica,' she insists. 'Angelica, come out. You are wanted here.'

Rockingham lets out a groan and flops onto his back. 'That woman!'

'Perhaps you are right,' says Angelica. 'She is overbearing in the extreme.' She sits up. 'Shall I go to her, then?'

'No, no,' he caresses. 'Stay here with me.'

'I think I must, or she will never be easy.' Angelica rises naked from the bed and opens the door in her perfect undress. 'What now, Spindleshanks?' she demands. She has a delightful plump body, classical in its proportions – although her legs are a little too short – and while some years have passed since she caught the painterly eye of Mr Romney in King's Place, she remains testament to his good taste.

Mrs Frost will not look at her; she fixes her gaze upon the door handle. 'There is a man here to see you.'

Angelica leans against the door frame, her arm behind her head. Her breasts rise pacifically. 'There is a man already here to see me,' she says. 'I know not how else to convey to you that I am indisposed.'

'He has been here before. Again and again. You may know him – he says he is the mermaid man.'

She laughs. 'The mermaid man! Georgie, mark this! That gentleman who brought us together – the man who discovered the horrid little sea-sprite – is waiting to see me. Well, he could not tolerate me before, so I wonder what has changed.' She claps her hand to her mouth. 'Oh! Does he believe he can afford me now? What did I hear, that the thing is sold? He means to trade one curiosity in for another; Eliza, what fun! Did you bring him inside?'

'No, he is still on the street.'

'That's as well. For what am I to tell him? Do I oblige dear George, and closet myself from all men but him? Or do I take your advice, Eliza, and make myself available to any body with a few pounds in his pocket?' She passes by her friend, who flinches from her, and goes into the living room. The flesh on the backs of her thighs quivers as she moves. 'Who do I please? Or do I, perhaps, form a compromise?' She feels pleasantly giddy to be undressed in that room of her own volition; and indeed, before her lieutenant began visiting her she was rarely ever so undressed at all. A man who is pleased to collect up the pins as he strips her is a rare jewel.

She throws her shawl about her shoulders as she goes to the open window – 'I am not, after all, a peep show' – and leans out to view the street, her hands on the window ledge. The stout and shabby Mr Hancock stands below expectantly.

'Ahoy!' she cries. 'The maritime wonder!' She lets her shawl slip off one shoulder, and bolsters her bosom on her crossed arms.

'I – ah – ahoy.'

'He does not know what to do with himself!' she crows over her shoulder. To the street she calls, 'You find me otherwise engaged. What brings you to my doorstep after such an absence?'

'I wished to see you,' he says. 'You see, many things have occurred and I found myself – I mean to say, I thought – I wondered if . . .'

'You seek an audience?'

With the lightest of gestures she beckons Rockingham over, and he hovers just within the window frame to spy upon her unprepossessing suitor, who now nods vigorously. 'Yes,' Mr Hancock calls. 'That is it. Exactly so. You have hit upon it.'

She twists a strand of hair sorrowfully about her finger, catching Georgie's smirking eye before continuing, 'Oh, sir. My prices have risen since I was offered to you for nothing.'

'What do you ask? I mean only to – only to sit with you.'

'Are you a rich man, sir?'

Below, he twists the brim of his hat in his hands, and looks bashfully about himself. There are a great many people watching with interest. 'I presume to say – why, yes – yes, I believe I am.'

'So money is no object to you? Well, it don't signify, for money is not what I want.' She taps her index finger against her bottom lip. 'Let me see. I want . . . your mermaid.' Taking mastery over her amusement, she leans an inch further out from the window. 'Give me your mermaid and I'll give you an hour.'

Even from such a distance she sees his face drop.

'What?' she asks. 'You do not think me worth the price?'

Mr Hancock frets below. 'A sorry specimen of a man,' whispers the lieutenant, whose fears are now by some measure allayed. 'Surely you would not let him touch you.'

'Shh!' Angelica twitches. To her erstwhile suitor she calls again, 'Well?'

'The truth is, madam, I have sold it.'

'Sold it! Well, that is a tragedy! For, you see, mermaids are my sole currency at this moment, the economy being what it is.'

'I could offer you a great many other things,' he blunders. 'I am perfectly a match for any body else who calls on you.' At this George snorts, but Mr Hancock, unknowing, adds, 'I am speculating.' He puffs up; the vision of his building project shimmers before his eyes.

'Only a mermaid will do,' says Angelica, and he regards her with redoubled hesitancy.

'I think you are playing with me.'

'Not at all! Ask any body. I am hard to come by.'

She rocks forward, her pale shoulders emerging from the shawl, her hair spilling over the windowsill. They regard one another for some long time.

'Very well,' he says. 'You must excuse me. I have an important errand to run.' He puts his hat on and hurries away through the crowd, something he seems to be physically unused to, for he moves at a sort of duckling scoot. Angelica is seized by laughter.

'There!' she cries, turning back into the room. 'Does that satisfy you both? I have accepted the overtures of another man –' she nods at Mrs Frost – 'but the terms –' winking at Rockingham – 'are *impossible*. So, there you have it! Bring me my wrap, Eliza, I am icing over.'

'You should not treat him so,' says Mrs Frost. 'He is a decent man.'

'That's as may be,' says Angelica, threading her arms into the sleeves held out for her, 'but I have no use for him. Georgie wishes to become my sole protector, is that not wonderful?'

'Really?' Mrs Frost turns to the lieutenant. 'What are the terms of your agreement?'

'I have not thought yet,' he says.

'Well, you ought to. We can have the lawyer come this very afternoon to draft a contract.'

'. . . lawyer?' he echoes stupidly. 'I had not . . . you see, I never did . . . is it necessary?'

'Christ, no!' laughs Angelica. 'Eliza is taking everything too seriously; that is what she does, you know. I do not need any formal agreement; I know you will take care of me.' She comes to nestle again beneath his arm.

'He is either settling money on you or he is not,' says Mrs Frost. To the lieutenant she says, 'She will need an annuity; two hundred a year would be a tolerable start – but only a start – and she will want a dressing allowance additional to that sum. You cannot expect her to remain exclusive to you for anything less.'

The young man is beginning to look rather pop-eyed; he seizes Angelica's hand and clings to it more in terror than affection.

'Eliza, you are making me out a mercenary!' says Angelica. 'I *trust* him. We love one another. Can he not simply pay for what we need?'

'Certainly not,' says Mrs Frost. 'I am not creeping for *his* approval every time we want lace for our caps. He has not the first idea how a household is run; why involve him in such female things?'

'I am still here in the room, you know,' says the lieutenant. 'If I had thought this would be so troublesome I would not have suggested it. Here –' he digs in his pocket – 'take this for your housekeeping.' He hands over a fistful of crumpled notes with great carelessness. 'It makes no odds to me.' He fishes in the other pocket and comes up with a handful of loose coin. 'My takings at Almack's are excellent; if you want more you need merely apply to me.'

'There!' says Angelica as Mrs Frost smooths out the notes, which amount to one hundred and seven pounds and a French livre. 'You see? Why must you make it so unpleasant?'

'I am being prudent,' says Mrs Frost, tucking the money away in her pocket.

'You are making trouble.'

'If you would credit it, I mean to save us all trouble. None of us may know what lies ahead.'

'Peculiar, then, that you act as if *you* do.'

'And this,' says the lieutenant, ignoring her, 'is for you, my sweet.' He rummages again in his pocket and draws out a black leather box with gold tooling.

'Georgie!' coos Angelica. 'What is it?'

'Open it.'

The lid slides back on its hinge. Within is a little pin, formed in the shape of Cupid's dart, and studded all along its length with real diamonds.

'Oh, George!'

'For Eros has smote me with his arrow,' he whispers.

Mrs Frost shudders. 'Who did you win *that* from?' she asks.

But Angelica has flung herself into George's arms and is kissing him backwards into the bedroom, murmuring, 'Oh, you are so kind – so good – our first piece of jewellery – my own darling – *real diamonds*. Not paste, Eliza! Not paste.'

SEVEN

Mr Hancock makes it his business one afternoon to seek out Captain Tysoe Jones. This is very easily done, for when on shore Captain Jones is a regular patron of the Pelican at Wapping, and today is seated — as has been his habit since he was a young man – in the great bow window overlooking the river. He favours this spot for the fine view it affords of Executioner's Dock: Captain Jones is partial to all forms of public entertainment, but most especially to the jig that is enacted on this foreshore several times a year at the end of a short rope. The tide is mercifully up when Mr Hancock arrives, so that the gibbet is all but submerged, and only bloated piratical fingertips breach the surface of the water. Captain Jones himself is surrounded by watermen in gaudy green jackets, for those of his family who do not venture upon the sea still heed the call of some lesser water gods, and ply their trade upon the river: when he sees Mr Hancock, he rises in surprise.

'Oh, you are come back?' he cries. 'Come to thank me for that creature I brought you? Aye, I'll wager your mind's been changed on the profitability of mermaids since last we met!'

'Well,' says Mr Hancock as they depart the tavern and set to strolling along the waterfront, 'it served me better than expected.'

Winter is drawing in upon them; the water is flint-coloured and so is the sky, and there is a flinty coldness in the air. Captain Jones chortles, and seizes his friend's shoulder. 'Did I not tell you? No body speaks of aught else. Everywhere I go – Woolwich to Richmond – every body has seen the thing, and if they have not seen it they affect to have. I brought you a marvel, certainly I did.'

'Aye.' Mr Hancock walks a few steps in silence. 'And now I desire another.'

'Another mermaid?' asks Captain Jones in consternation.

'That's so.'

'But you did not want the first one.'

He shrugs.

'"Tysoe,"' mimics the captain. '"Oh, but what shall I do with this thing? I am no showman, Tysoe!"'

'I have changed my mind,' says Mr Hancock firmly. 'I want one.'

'Do you apprehend – surely you know that it was a chance in a million that I came upon the last one? I do not expect to see another in this life or the next.'

'If it can be done once, it can be done again.'

'No, no. I've money enough now to retire, and grow old surrounded by my children.'

'I do not see them here now,' says Mr Hancock. 'Come,' he adds, knowing indeed how little his friend enjoys staying still: the desire to go forth again is in Captain Jones, he is sure of it. It is merely a matter of steering him towards this discovery. 'I've come by a fine little ship, the *Unicorn*, all rigged and seaworthy, all set for a new adventure, and who will captain her if you do not?'

'There are other men.' Captain Jones picks up his step, and walks fast along the pavement: he is almost tempted. Mr Hancock changes tack.

'Do you not want to enjoy your final voyage? Your last run was most irregular; you did not even have the parting gift of sailing your own ship back into port. What farewell is that, to your life's employ?'

His friend grins and turns up his collar against the cold. 'My wife has designs for our future. We shall buy some land in the country- side, and build a house there to our own liking. A cow or two in the back field, and raspberry canes for the children. And I will take a part in the little ones' upbringing, and be well acquainted with their characters: a child ought to look upon his father's face every day, not at several years' interval.'

But Mr Hancock is not to be dissuaded. 'There is time for all that once my mermaid is got.'

'No, no. I cannot do it. I promised I would not go to Macao again. Another two years away, Jonah, surely you appreciate—'

'Perhaps you need not travel so far abroad,' Mr Hancock says.

'What do you mean?'

'It strikes me that you need not go to Macao for a mermaid when there is an abundance of evidence to support their inhabiting our own waters.'

They repair to the edge of the dock and ease themselves down, neither as young as he once was, to dangle their legs over the water as they pack their pipes. Captain Jones twirls the bone-white stem between finger and thumb. 'So what would you have me do?' he asks slowly. 'Gather a crew, and have us sail up and down the coast of England in search of one?' He snorts at the folly of it, but Mr Han- cock does not join him.

'Not only England; Scotland and Ireland too. As far as Greenland if it pleased you.' He pauses to assess his friend's countenance, and continues placatingly, 'Come, 'tis not so mad a notion. I have after some study compiled a list of all the villages in our isles where mermaids have lately been sighted; all it leaves you to do is travel from one to the next.' He produces his notes: 'You see, I have indicated those where mermaids are very regularly said to visit, and even come ashore. I have made it *easy* for you.'

Captain Jones is shaking his head. 'No, no. I've not travelled those waters since I was a boy.'

'So find men who are accustomed to them. Greaves has crews who traverse west, and know the North Sea and even the Atlantic, were you forced to go so distant.' He looks about himself. 'Walk into any public house in these parts and you will find ten experienced sailors eager for work. Whalers, too.'

'So ask one of them.'

Mr Hancock draws deeply on his pipe and the smoke billows about his face. 'I want you in charge, Tysoe. I know that my request is not usual; I do not trust any other man to do right by me. *You* know what you are about; you have found me one mermaid, so find me another.'

'It ain't so easy as that. You think my head is all full of dreams, but I know when a scheme is worth pursuing, and surely this one is not.'

'How do you know its worth? I can pay. Three thousand pounds, I could vouch towards this venture.'

'The Devil and his good wife! Three thousand! What has got into you?'

'I need it,' he says stubbornly, and feels a schoolboy scowl touch the muscles of his foolish face.

'Have you lost your wits?' says the sea-captain. 'Does your life so lack meaning – can you find no other way to spend your fortune but on impossible curiosities? I have heard of this before – this is a thing *gentlemen* do, *collectors*, who find satisfaction in making perfect wonders their own possessions, and hoarding them away in dusty cabinets. Is this your intention, my friend? Is this how you wear your wealth, in having other men run about the world hunting down your whims?'

'No!' Mr Hancock is stung. 'No, no; I have only practical uses for my money, which is after all what it is made for. I am speculating. I shall be landlord of half of Mary-le-Bone.'

'Then it is some other sort of madness.' Captain Jones rubs his jaw. He scrutinises Mr Hancock's face for a good long time. 'Well, it cannot be a woman.'

No answer.

'A woman?' asks Captain Jones, and his eyes as round as billiard balls. He lands Mr Hancock a clout about the shoulder blade which almost tips him into the water below. 'Well! I never thought such a thing would pass. And who is this lady? Some comely widow, I am certain; rich on her own account. An exacting woman, for you to go to such lengths, and clever to put you to them. Am I correct?'

'Exacting.' Mr Hancock tips his chin into his collar; he does not know what to say. He thinks, *I am a rich man. I have a right to rare things.*

'Good man! And what do you get in return, should you acquire the thing she wants?'

Mr Hancock shakes his head. In fact he wants nothing particularly of Mrs Neal, except to have her attention. This neuter life he leads! A man who has no effect on the world, no body to depend on him, waited on by servants and relatives, can he be blamed (he asks himself) if he desires the natural attention of a woman? All across the city, other men sit comfortably in chairs with their pipes, and their ladies at their elbow. Partnership he cannot imagine; to be yoked so equally to a prudent widow or a hard-working old maid does not excite him of late. Mrs Neal is neither prudent nor hard-working; she is something apart.

'Three thousand pounds towards this venture?'

'Aye.'

'That is a great deal of money.' Captain Jones sighs deeper. 'But to leave my family, and travel waters I am unfamiliar with . . . a great hardship for the sake of another man's whim. And the dangers involved, when I have said I am unwilling to go.'

'But think of it!' Mr Hancock is warming to this new scheme. 'You will never be more than two weeks from home.'

'Three, more likely. Four, even . . .'

'. . . you will have no responsibilities of trade, no cargo to fret over, no victuals to eke out over months.' He gestures broadly with his pipe. 'Think of it as a quest. A novelty. An undertaking never before attempted: to seek out and capture a mermaid!'

Captain Jones looks sideways at his friend. He stretches his boots out over the water, and studies his toes. He draws again on his pipe. 'I would expect adequate return,' he says.

'Name it, name it.'

Behind his eyes, the sea-captain's thoughts click rapid as a counting-frame. 'Is this what you want?' he asks.

'Truly.'

'A thousand, then. A thousand and you'll never afterwards call upon me to sail again.' Mr Hancock offers him his hand, and Captain Jones seizes it, his grip firm, his palm coarse and cool as raw leather. They shake hands. Then they sit for some long time, staring into the water beneath their hanging feet, which is gelid and glinting. Captain Jones draws on his pipe, and smiles. 'Here's a safer wager for you. That the river will freeze again this winter. It runs more sluggish than ever.' He chuckles. 'You remember the last time? When we strolled all the way to London Bridge, as if the river were our own road?'

'We were young men then.'

'Such strange magic as is in this world,' he says. 'Mermaids out yonder and horses and carriages trundling up and down this very river.' He shakes his head. 'Aye, me, what sights I've seen.'

We are the lost.

We dart minnow-quick.

Those on the shore see our faces break the waves far away, or see our dark shapes shift and disperse somewhere deep below, and they insist:

Yes, it was more than animate, it was human!

No mistaking it – not some dumb beast – nor ice nor rope nor flotsam. It called to me, they say, it waved an arm, it knew me, before it vanished into that cold void beyond, dived into such endless space as you cannot imagine.

Our breath is the heave and pull of the sea on a black night, which rocks the sparks of moonlight in its ripples. We are foment, white foam spreading and leaping; we dash against the crag and are dispersed. We are the long briny hiss of tide retreating from the land. The pebbles skip when we pass by; the stones roll over. We are the waft and spread and bloom of purple weed. We lie smooth and polished. We tug, tug, haul at strong bodies. At our gentle, endless touch, wood is softened, sharp edges licked smooth, the strongest locks corrode.

EIGHT

November 1785

The winter comes in bitterer every day, but does not trouble Angelica in the least. She is happy and lavish in the arms of her dear George: when Mrs Chappell visits, with her girls all bundled up in swansdown pelisses, she finds them sprawled together on the sopha, a snaggle of limbs, feeding one another tipsy-cake. Polly, Elinor and Kitty cannot tear their eyes away from the spectacle: Mrs Neal in her robe embroidered with palm trees, and Mr – who? – with his banyan embroidered with monkeys, sucking custard from one another's fingers and chortling. It is obscene: they stare and yet they cannot bear to see. Nobody notices the blood that heats their faces, for the fire is banked up so high that even Mrs Chappell, who certainly has no delicacy left to offend, appears flushed. Groping for Mrs Frost's arm as she is deposited in the apartment's largest and ugliest chair, Mrs Chappell exchanges a look with her – or in fact does not, for Mrs Frost mournfully lowers her eyes to mutely avow, 'Tis nothing to do with me.'

The girls dither. 'Be seated,' says the abbess, and they crush in where they may, the sopha being occupied. Rockingham takes up his newspaper, and absent-minded takes up Angelica's hand as he reads, caressing its fingers one by one.

Kitty leans so far forward her elbows balance on her knees. She clasps her hands and stares. *Stop it,* mouths Polly, but it goes unmarked.

'I've not seen you in a good long time,' observes Angelica, stroking Mr Rockingham's palm with her own even while looking deeply and frankly into Mrs Chappell's face. *Of course she has come to make amends,* she has already assured herself. 'Are you staying long?' she asks.

'Why?' asks the abbess. 'Have you another engagement?'

George looks up from his paper to meet Angelica's eye, and they both smirk. 'No.'

'We shall not keep you,' says Mrs Chappell. 'We merely came to remember ourselves to you.'

'Good of you, good of you.' Rockingham's fingers visibly tighten upon Angelica's waist but his eyes return to his paper. She is dressed exotically *à la turque*, with a scarf wrapped most becomingly about her head. The colours are ones she has never been in the habit of wearing – oxblood, mustard, jade – and Mrs Chappell thinks she cannot quite like it, what with such hectic colour in the girl's cheeks and lips, such spark in her eyes: everything about her seems brighter, sharper, fuller. *Presumptuous,* she thinks, *to make such a show of herself. Too* much. She likes her own girls in charming white gowns. Sartorial daring is for women who may choose how they are looked at.

Even now, under the abbess's scrutiny, Angelica bristles. 'Hmm?' she asks sharply.

'I merely look upon you.'

'*Merely.*' Angelica stretches out her arm to show off the drop of her sleeve, so busy with embroidered tendrils and fronds, and cupping within it a foam of white lace. Her knuckles are dazzling with jewels. 'You are always thinking something,' she says, 'I know. What do you think now?'

'Very fine, I daresay.'

226

'Georgie bought it me.'

Mrs Chappell looks at him. He is transfixed on his reading, but runs his fingertip along the edge of Angelica's ear: she shivers and squeaks.

'Oh, you did?' says Mrs C. 'And all of this –' the Turkey rugs, the coloured prints, the piles of books and ribbons and shawls and flowers – 'you pay for it?'

'She'll want for nothing,' he says without looking up.

'But I want to keep *house*, Georgie.' She thrusts out her bottom lip. 'You and I, in our *own* home.'

'Patience.' He folds the newspaper over and shakes it at Polly, although he has hitherto given no hint that he has noticed her presence in the room. 'Here,' he says, 'what do *you* make of this?'

'Of what?'

'The problem of the blacks. There are too many of them in this city; they will not work.'

'I know nothing of it.' She lowers her face.

'You've no family? They cannot be rich, or else you would not very likely be in the position you are—'

'No family,' says Polly. Elinor is trying to catch her eye, but Polly will not look at her; she feels her face burn with what exact emotion she cannot tell. She tries to feel nothing.

'Then it were well you are where you are,' he says, 'for your brothers the Lascars and the Africans can find no work here, and are begging on our streets. Look –' he flaps the newspaper towards her again – 'there is a public subscription to help them. Public subscription! Food and beds and whatever they demand this cold winter! A suit of clothes, if they asked for't. *Some* say they have earned such charity, *I* say—'

'Certainly they have,' says Elinor bravely. 'They have fought for us in the war with America, and they have sailed our ships and been all manner of use to us – we who enslaved them, and who brought them here. We grant them their liberty, but what does liberty count for when its condition is destitution?'

'A very pretty speech,' says Rockingham, 'but you cannot understand the half of it.'

'We owe them a fair living,' says Elinor.

'A great many of them are nothing more than runaways,' he says. 'We owe them nothing; in fact, they have positively *stole* from us. My uncle keeps a plantation in Jamaica and he cannot bring even his most favourite slave with him when he visits here, because what will the fellow do? He will escape at the first opportunity. And furthermore, the people here will protect him! They've no loyalty, not a grain of respect: they might be kept by a good family their whole lifetime, and educated, and clothed, and given a place in the world, and yet none of this means a thing to them when they see their chance to escape.'

'No man is a slave on English soil,' says Elinor.

Rockingham turns to Mrs Chappell. 'Is this something you encourage?' he asks. 'Her tongue is too ready; no man wants that in a wife.'

'Men keep their wives at home,' says Mrs Chappell most pleasantly. 'They do not come to us for more of the same.' To Elinor, she says, 'Do not contradict the man; he don't like it.'

'I was not addressing her anyway,' says Rockingham. He gestures again at Polly. 'I was asking *her* opinion of her people's plight.'

'I know nothing of it,' says Polly.

'Put them all on a boat and send them away where they came from, that is my solution to the matter. If they cannot earn their keep, we've no room for them here.'

'In that case we would do best to put *all* the beggars on a boat,' says Elinor triumphantly. 'The white ones too, and all the destitute mothers that we cannot keep, and the blind and the idiots and the cripples who are passed from one parish to the next until they fall down dead, and set off a new argument as to who should pay for their burial. It is not only the black poor who cause nuisance and expense.'

'Who are you,' asks Rockingham, 'to think you know anything of this? Ah! You are the favourite of an abolitionist, is that it? Does he talk fine words of emancipation as he beds you?'

This is closer to the truth than Elinor is pleased to concede, for she has taken the eye of a man who writes many letters to newspapers on the subject. 'I *read*,' she says. 'I observe the world about me,' and to her credit this is also true.

Angelica has not been paying much attention to the conversation, but when it strays to the bedding of another woman besides herself, she bridles. 'We mean to keep *house*,' she repeats, 'and we are kept from it by *absurd* circumstances, for do you know Georgie will not get all the inheritance that is due to him until he is twenty-five? It is a scandal, when you think of it, that he has been deprived of what is rightly his in such a manner, and kept on an allowance as if he were a child. You are *not* a child –' she turns scoldingly to Georgie – 'you ought not to be held back from your own fortune.'

'Perhaps those who hold the purse strings know what he would do with it,' says Mrs Chappell.

'And what do you mean by that?'

'Oh, come. When young men are so inclined to women and dissipation? They make a very wise choice.'

'I am hardly dissipated. If they only *met* me ...'

At this Mrs Chappell can only laugh, a great choking bark that leaves her breathless for some moments.

'*I* am much in favour of it,' insists Angelica. 'George has spoke to his uncle – to all of his people, in fact – of the true domestic happiness we have found, haven't you, Georgie, but they positively refuse to see me.'

'They positively refuse,' he says, acquiescing to her fingers twining through his hair while the girls make cutty eyes at him.

'And the only reason for it is the unhappy accident of my birth! Why must I suffer all my life for my father's lack of standing?'

'You should not,' says Rockingham, foolishly besotted. 'You are as refined in your intellect and your sensibility and your beauty as any heiress.'

'Thank you for your compliment,' says Mrs Chappell. 'She was a stubborn student.'

'Oh no, madam, you misunderstand. She is a true daughter of nature, where others must resort to art. Her perfection comes from within.'

Angelica preens. 'You see? He understands me. We are serious in our desire to marry, you know. Truly his uncle treats him as if he did not know his own mind, as if he were a mere boy. Well, madam, I have no hesitation in declaring that we will do it *with* or *without* that man's approval.'

A ripple passes through the girls, of appreciation or it may be horror; they hardly know.

'Well . . .' says Mr Rockingham. 'Perhaps if it were—'

Angelica claps her hand over his mouth and squeezes his cheek. 'Fussing!' she says, touching her nose to his, with only the flat of her palm to keep their lips from meeting. He looks up at her as the magi look up at the virgin. 'Fussing, fussing,' she croons to him. 'How you fret.' She turns back to her audience and continues, 'At any rate, he will be of age in only two years, and then quite beyond their control. So we shall have the last laugh. I say, Eliza! Eliza, dear, would you bring me some of those pretty biscuits we had?'

'There are no more,' says Mrs Frost wearily.

Angelica whines like a dog. 'But I want some!' She rolls over on the couch, stretching from its arm to see where her companion is at. Her gown, twisted about her legs, rides up to reveal her bare calves. 'What else have we? Any cake?'

'No. We have apples,' says Mrs Frost. 'There is a cheese on the slate. Or I can—'

'No, no, no. I must have a cake! The little chestnut ones . . . you like those, Georgie, do you not? Eliza, Georgie is hungry, will you not go out and bring us back—'

'Where is the maid?' asks Mrs Chappell sharply.

'Maria? Oh, 'tis hardly worth *having* her, the little she does.'

'I bade her come only mornings and evenings,' says Mrs Frost. Angelica is in whispered communication with her lover; behind her unseeing back, Mrs Frost rubs thumb and forefinger together meaningfully. 'So I run the errands.'

'And what if a *visitor*—'

'There are no visitors,' interjects Angelica. 'I do not take visitors any longer, do I, Georgie?' She cranes over the back of the sopha. 'Eliza? You are still here.'

Mrs Frost eyes the chilly street outside the window and reaches for her cloak.

'We shall take our leave,' says Mrs Chappell. 'Girls.' She lifts up her elbows and they haul away, their fingers digging into her arm-pits as her face bloats and her breathing accelerates to a shallow pant. When she lets out a moan of exertion Rockingham barely stifles a snigger: Angelica eyes him for a moment and then conceals a smirk prettily behind her hand.

The girls in their great pelisses fill the whole of the staircase, a rustling sighing host about Mrs Chappell, leaving behind them a fragrance of roses and lavender. Mrs Frost follows their laborious progress; at the bottom Mrs Chappell seizes the newel with both hands and clings to it, winded, as a shipwrecked mariner to a providential shore. Her breath is painful to listen to, so light and rapid, and when she speaks it is with a rattle of phlegm in the back of her throat.

'Frost,' she says, 'tell me how is that dandyprat keeping her?'

'That I cannot say,' says Mrs Frost. 'I do not trust him, madam; he says we may depend on him but he has not the first idea . . .'

'Anything set down in writing?'

Mrs Frost hesitates to report her friend's foolishness where it will be so quickly condemned. 'Some agreement *shall be*,' she says. 'She is not so stupid as that.'

'I suppose you receive a regular stipend from him. Punctual, an agreed sum on an agreed date? Monthly? Quarterly?'

Mrs Frost's muteness speaks all that is required, and Mrs Chappell groans.

''Tis all right for fancies,' Mrs Frost excuses him, 'sweetmeats, ribbons, gowns – whatever she has a whim for. He would buy her anything she asked, but you see she will not ask for pins, or stay-tapes.'

'An absurd arrangement,' commiserates Mrs Chappell. 'Indeed, 'tis no sort of arrangement at all – domestic disarray of the worst sort.'

'He cannot fathom how quickly stockings wear through,' says Mrs Frost, warming to her topic, for she has had many resentments piling up in her mind, and nobody to air them with, 'and yet she will not allow me to mend them – we must have new, Angelica says, always new and nothing darned.' Her voice rises in pitch, and her face breaks out in white-and-pink blotches as she proceeds. 'And when I ask him for more he becomes certain I am swindling him: "You have the maid sell them on," he says. "No two women could run through so many."' She raises her skirt to show the scars of neat darning in her stocking; a new hole opening up on her calf. 'And so she wears the new stockings, and I take them once she has worn them out.'

'Fie, for shame!' Mrs Chappell comforts her.

'I cannot continue to apply my requests for his approval – as if he knew better than I what this household needs!'

'He has not the first idea, of course he don't.'

'No bread but cakes,' laments Mrs Frost, and indeed now she is most thoroughly distressed, almost hiccoughing with emotion, 'no beer but sack, no pins but what have diamonds on their heads. And the bill with the collier yet to be settled although they would burn the fire day and night without cease. If they would only wear more clothes!'

'You are an excellent woman. 'Tis an affront to your work that you should be under such duress.'

'I manage as best I can,' says Mrs Frost. 'But I am so ill at ease as to the bills, and the laundry, and the maid – how shall I continue to run this household when they believe I may do so on a farthing, and mock my asking for any more?'

'What do you need?' says Mrs Chappell, swinging about the drapes of her pelisse until her pocket comes into view and she is able to seize it in her little pointed fingers.

'Pardon me?'

'You ought not to have to ask him. What sum will cover your needs for the moment? Ten pounds? Twenty?'

'Are you certain?' Mrs Frost puts her fingertips to her throat. What would Angelica say if she knew she had spoken of her finances to the abbess? And what else, if she secretly accepted money from her? '... I ...' She shakes her head. 'I cannot. To put her in your debt ... it does not seem ...'

'Nonsense. She will never know. Let this be a gift, from me to you – to ease your mind.'

'I am ashamed,' says Mrs Frost.

'No need! I know how it is. In this world, we have nobody but one another; I seek to protect Angelica, for our collective reputation.'

Within Eliza Frost's soul the pecuniary takes mastery over the honourable. 'It would reflect worse on her,' she says slowly, 'if there were *no* money. If bills were *not* paid.'

'There you have it. There is nothing so shameful as a woman who cannot keep her own house. Here, you do the right thing. She will not have to know.'

'Still I feel . . .' Mrs Frost glances aloft, as if Angelica might be peeping through the ceiling joists. She tucks her bottom lip inside the top.

'Trouble yourself no longer,' says Mrs Chappell. She takes Mrs Frost's hand and closes it around a clinking purse. 'Only pray that in time the gentleman will come to a better arrangement with his finances.'

Holding the purse, Mrs Frost is enlivened with a new spirit. Indeed, she almost giggles. 'Or melt away entirely,' she says.

'Humph. I fear *that* is inevitable.'

'Thank you.' Mrs Frost inspects the purse and presses it tightly to her bosom. She feels a prick of conscience, but relief from want is a great balm. 'Thank you, madam, I will not forget your kindness. If we can repay you—'

'Hush you! Do not consider that at this moment. Simply go on as best you can – the wheel will turn. It always does.'

NINE

She is jovial until they are out of the door, but as she is hoisted into the carriage Mrs Chappell allows herself to express some provocation. '*Wilful*,' she says to the girls who wedge themselves into the seat opposite her, their eyes blinking in the depths of their swansdown. 'They are wilful in their infatuation.'

'They are in *love*,' says Elinor, who despite her altercation with Rockingham is still a mite impressed: compared to certain of her regulars he is a veritable *homme comme-il-faut*, so handsome and so young.

'Only because they have both chose to be,' sniffs her mistress, shifting uncomfortably in her seat. 'Ay, me! I should not have drank so much tea! I shall never last until home. Stop, girls, stop – Pol, pass me the thing.'

Mrs Chappell's bourdaloue is made from fine white porcelain with dragons rampant about its rim. She has a great abundance of skirts and petticoats so that it is almost impossible to discover her legs beneath them; above her garters, Mrs Chappell's thighs are vast and dimpled as dough, and faintly mauve. 'They each went out in search of an *affaire du coeur*, and it is no accident that they found one another,' she huffs, heaving herself up so as to accommodate the vessel against her coarse and greying cauliflower. Her legs brace upon the boards and she trembles with the effort; she plucks with small fat hands at her skirts as they subside over her knees, and the sound of her pissing fills the carriage.

Elinor looks kindly out of the window, but Polly wrinkles her nose; she pulls her hood further over her face and scowls to herself. Kitty, so very lately plucked from Billingsgate, does not mind it, and sees her chance to contribute to the conversation. 'They are marvellous well suited,' she observes foolishly.

'Pish posh,' says Mrs Chappell. Her water has a mineral, creaturous smell that creeps into the nostrils; it tinkles to a cease and then spurts again. 'They are both young and handsome. What is marvellous in that? They spur one another on, that's all; they give one another licence to abandon good sense. Take this.' She passes the piss-pot to Polly, who stares at it for a long and haughty moment. 'Well?' She brandishes it with vigour, so that its amber contents leap within.

Polly drops her eyes and takes it. Its porcelain belly is hot against her palms, which on a cold day such as this is not unwelcome, but there is a great anger in her throat. 'And what am I to do with it?' she asks coldly.

'Put it out of the window,' says Elinor. 'Here, pass it me, I shall do it.'

''Pon my word!' Mrs Chappell mops between her legs with an edge of her petticoat, and rearranges her skirts to sedateness. 'You certainly shall not! On a public road, in my own carriage, for any body to observe and chatter on later? No, Pol, it is not far, keep hold of it until we are set down.'

'If only *you* had done so,' growls Polly, but very quietly.

Elinor apprehends her friend's rage. 'Only round the corner,' she comforts her, and puts a lid on the offending thing, 'then you may leave it under the seat for the servants.' Polly says nothing. Her lips are pressed tight, and although she holds the lid fast, she feels with each jolt of the carriage the abbess's piss slop and jump in its shallow vessel. A trickle escapes and tickles her finger, but she closes her eyes and will not look. Elinor returns to the conversation. 'At least the gentleman will see Mrs Neal well provided for,' she says, 'and that is all we can any of us hope for.'

'No! Did you listen at all? *He cannot afford her.* Prick up your ears, girl, people speak for other reasons than to simply exercise their jaws. What you have the privilege to overhear, you ought to have the sense to make use of.' She knits her fingers across her belly and sighs. 'And no, Nell, simply being *kept* is not enough. How long will it last? Until he tires of her, or she him? *Perpetuity*, that is what you want. *Dignity.* A certain what-shall-I-call-it – a *cachet*.'

'Love, though!' says Elinor.

'Oh, *fools* fall in love. Children, dogs, dotards. What you want, girls, if your time ever comes, is a gentleman who sees your rare value. An admirer, certainly – for what are you intended for, except to be admired? But ask yourself, *can this gentleman appreciate me?* He ought to prize you as he prizes his Sèvres, his antiquities, his best-bred hounds. You seek a gentleman who knows exactly what he has got in you; who understands the responsibility he has to you. You are ladies quite apart from the common water.'

'And does Rockingham not . . . ?' asks Kitty.

'Oh, he appreciates nothing. He is a mere boy! Any country slut has soft tits and a warm cunt; that is all *he* wants, whether or not he knows it. Mrs Neal is of no worth to him whatever, and if this affair transpires to the benefit of either party I shall be vastly surprised. You watch, girls; they will be the ruin of one another.'

They are returned, and all descend from the carriage with

237

varying degrees of ease. Polly is last to alight; Simeon the footman comes to her assistance, and the sight of him with the dogs scampering at his heels puts her into a worse temper than before.

'Here is a jar of piss,' she says, holding it out to him as the others vanish within. 'Pray dispose of it.'

He looks at it, and then at her. 'I shall send a maid,' he says.

She sniffs. 'What? Too good for it?'

''Tis not in my duties.'

''Tis not in mine, and yet Gunderguts Chappell compelled me to carry it all the way back, and here I am holding it in my hands still.' Being around him always makes her feel spiteful; it is something about the livery, how tidy he keeps it and how puffed up he is within it. And then Rockingham's words have ruffled her – 'your brothers', as if she had a single thing in common with the Africans and the slaves and the indigent poor who clutter the streets.

He apprehends her fierce expression as boding no good at all. He does not like the way she clings with such loathing to the bourdaloue. 'Pray put it down,' he says. 'I shall not report to her what you just called her. Here, let me assist you.'

But she remains crossly seated, holding the pot as if it were a weapon. 'She should not treat me thus,' she says. 'She would not give it to Elinor or Kitty to hold. As if I were lowlier than them when I know it to be true that men will pay twice for me what they will for *them.*'

Simeon has access to the date books: the men pay more, he knows, but fewer of them choose her. 'This is a good position,' he says. 'Be grateful.'

'You speak as if I were a servant,' she says.

'Not at all. You are singularly positioned to become something else entirely.' He is turning his gloved hands over one way and the other in front of his eyes, inspecting them for smuts. 'I mean only to be a friend to you,' he says.

'I would advise you to abandon that ambition.'

'Only there are not so many of us in these parts,' he says.

'Us?' Her nostrils twitch with annoyance; she shakes her head and pulls her pelisse around her as if she were about to leap from the carriage. 'No, no, sir,' she says as he darts forward to take her hand, 'you and I are not the same at all.'

She does not know why she does it. One moment she is holding the bordaloue still in her lap, the next her arms shunt back as if they were sprung, and the vessel tips forward. Its lid falls first; its contents hurtle sparkling behind it.

Simeon lets out a cry, and leaps back, but there is no avoiding it. The urine splashes off the pavement; it soaks his stockings and spatters up his breeches, and sends the dogs capering in terror back into the house, a trail of wet paw-prints behind them. Even Polly, elevated within the carriage, is not spared; it catches the edge of her pelisse and the hem of her gown. Shards of porcelain zing in all directions, like an egg dropped.

'What have you done?' cries Simeon, dancing on the spot for sheer horror, the drops flying from his calves. Seeing that his gloves are also caught he utters some inchoate disgust and shakes one hand, then the other. Fragments of the pot are scattered across the steaming flagstones. 'Mrs Chappell will have you pay for this,' he says, more in reproach than anger.

'I do not care.' Now she does jump down, and strides past him towards the house, her little slippers dancing smartly around the pool.

Simeon, alone, hooks his thumb beneath the cuff of one glove, and peels it from his hand with great fastidiousness. He lets it drop to the pavement, then flings down the other. He tuts, nudging them with his toe, but when he turns around he sees that Polly has not gone into the house. She is standing by the railings, watching him. There is a peculiar dark look about her, as if she might be about to run.

'Go on,' he says, and is relieved when she turns reluctantly again to the door. 'Go on, inside. You're not to loiter about out here – do not make it worse.'

TEN

December 1785

'I do not understand why you have to go *now*,' says Angelica, following Rockingham into the parlour. 'It is so nearly Christmas. The entire Ton is only just arrived; everybody is here. There is so much fun to be had! So many parties!' Well might she be wistful: this is the first season she has been in London for some years. There are new dances to learn, new faces to acquaint herself with; new amusements at every turn. And then she misses her old circle: the rupture between herself and Mrs Chappell is not mended, and Rockingham will not let her very near his own friends. *It is my life with the duke all over again*, she thinks crossly, and then knocks the thought from herself. It is not like that.

Now he says tersely, 'I've no choice.' He is dressed for the road, having received an unmannerly letter from his uncle summoning him in the most muscular of tones to appear before him. 'Still I cannot think who has written at such length to him about my dealings with you,' Rockingham says as he strides about in search of his watch – his handkerchief – his pocketbook. '*Somebody* has dripped poison in his ear.'

'Who could wish us harm?' says Angelica, only lately out of bed, with her curls in her cap and her wrap pulled tightly against the cold.

'You are sure not one of your old beaux? Trying to get me off the scene?'

'No, no!' She follows him, and presses into him so the folds of his travelling cloak fall about her. He smells of wool and of horses, and of the pastries and parched meats that must accompany a long journey. Outside the sky is lowering and dark, and what little light survives it is lead grey and dismal.

'Hmm.' He rests his chin on the top of her head. 'Well, 'tis a damnable nuisance. The old fool has been well and truly convinced that you are leading me astray, and yet it is I who must make it right. *Who* would write to him so?'

'It must be one of his old friends in Parliament. Brr,' she shivers, nestling closer and drawing her arms around his waist, ''tis colder than Greenland. How will I stay warm all alone in my bed?'

The thought of it inflames him; she permits him to press his hands over her waist and slide them up her ribcage to her breasts. 'Confound it!' he sighs. 'I desire to leave you as little as you desire me gone – but this is the only way. In person I can convince my uncle of anything. Perhaps this is fortuitous; I shall persuade him to increase my allowance ...'

'... and we may take our own house?'

'Yes, indeed.' He kisses the tip of her nose.

'At last!' Her three Dean Street rooms are crammed with luxury of every sort. The curtains are heavy brocade, riotously worked with birds and flowers, with a great fringed pelmet overhanging, and her cabinet has more glasses in it than she can possibly drink from, their slender stems marvellously wrought with twisted strands of white glass, fine as lace; and rummers etched with roses; and jelly-glasses crammed into every corner, stickily collecting fluff and soot. There are shawls flung on every chair as if once she has discarded one she will not wear it again; a mahogany box spills lovely painted slides which would shine upon the walls, if their radiant surfaces were not cracked and blotched; a clavichord sheds sheets of music of every sort. Views of Greece and Italy jostle the walls; flowers wilt; fans lie crushed. Mr Rockingham's love is measured out in countless trinkets and sweetmeats and scent bottles, and Angelica hoards them all, and sends out for more.

'You must be patient,' he says. 'These delicate matters take some tiptoeing around. I shall be gone a few weeks, perhaps a month, if you can bear to be without me so long?'

'A *month*? Oh, but that is . . .' She crushes herself against his chest, speechless at the prospect. 'And you would have me spend Christmas all alone.'

'We'll have fun together all the year – what's Christmas to us?'

'Why, only the best part!'

He tips her chin up to his face. 'Trust me, my angel. Endure this for me.'

'I shall miss you,' she whispers.

'And I you, poor darling. But think what it will do for us!' He steers her towards the window. 'And look, what I leave you with in my absence.' Yonder in the frosty street is a carriage painted shining almond green, and its doors have angels painted upon them. It is hitched up to two handsome greys, who stamp and shiver in the cold.

'Oh, Georgie!'

'You shall have the hire of it, if you like it.' He waves a hand imperiously and the coachman flicks his whip; the carriage moves onward. 'I could not leave you with no transport of your own, on such a cold winter. You'll travel by chair no more.'

'I never saw the like!' She rode in better when she was kept by the late duke, but there is no profit in saying so. 'Oh, how will I thank you?'

'I have conditions,' he says.

A moment in which she studies her own fingernails. Then, 'Aye, name them.'

'You may ride out all you like,' he says, 'but not to any of the pleasure gardens—'

'Ah! In midwinter?'

'Not to the Pantheon, then, smart-mouth, nor to any parties at all. I shall have you go nowhere there is drinking and gambling and dancing.'

'No dancing? Now, Georgie, allow me a *little* fun – you would not grudge me a night or two's society? And all through Christmas! All through Twelfth Night, I am to go nowhere?'

'I'll not have you catch other men's eyes. This is a licentious time of year.'

'But *my* eyes are all for you.'

He is not to be moved; she sees it from the shape of his mouth. 'I am paying for the carriage; 'tis mine really,' he says. 'So I choose where you go.'

She sighs. 'Very well. No dancing, no merrymaking. And am I allowed to be sociable at all? May I visit my female friends, go on errands?'

'As much as you like. I would have you happy.' He takes her hands in his and traces her fingers as he always has. 'Only, I remember in what circumstances I first came upon you.'

She draws down her brow, but her lips smile on. 'I remember too,' she says, and tightens the twine of her fingers about his. 'And so may *I* impose any conditions on *your* behaviour?'

He chuckles. 'You jokeous creature.' Then serious again, pulls her to him and whispers, 'Do not forget me.'

'Never!'

There is embracing, and a few tears shed by both parties, and then he must away, leaving Angelica alone in her crammed living room, clasping and unclasping her hands. She has not been left to her own devices for a great long time; the hours fairly loom before her. How can they be filled? She hardly knows what time is if it were not spent with him, or preparing to meet him, or subsiding after he has gone: now she paces a little, her old nervous habit, and puts more coal on the fire, lump by lump, and crouches to watch it begin to gleam red seams of heat. Outside, the sky is thick and greenish black, and moment by moment it seems to sink down upon the street, like a lid shut. It will not be long before the weather engulfs them entirely, and so she is relieved when Mrs Frost returns from the mysterious errands that running a house necessitate, her cheeks and nose shining pink and her hair all of a tousle under her windswept cape.

'He is gone,' Angelica says tragically, and totters as if into a swoon.

'And not a moment too soon,' says Mrs Frost, righting her briskly. 'When will we know?'

'I cannot bear it! To be without him so long! What am I to do? I think my heart will break.'

'Will he send us word of his arrangements as to money?' persists Mrs Frost, drawing close to the fire and stretching her fingers to it. 'Oh my,' she sighs, flexing them in its heat, 'there ain't a drop of blood in my hands; how they do ache.'

'You and your mercenary heart! He undertakes a great long journey to plead our case, and settle all so that we may be happy for a good long time, and all you must yap is, "When shall we know, when shall we know?" I cannot say, Eliza! For he left my house not fifteen minutes ago! Where is your gratitude that he is gone at all?'

'Gratitude don't pay our way.'

'I never said it did. He has left us twenty pounds under the fruit bowl.'

'Well, and what good is that to us?' Nevertheless, she snatches it up and presses it into her bosom. 'When he is gone who knows how long?'

'A month, merely,' says Angelica, but she quails within. 'If we are very good, and quiet, and keep to ourselves, twenty pounds will see us for twice that time. We do not pay Maria even ten pounds in a year.'

'I should like to see you live as Maria does.'

'I need nothing, if I have him. Let us show him how faithfully we wait for him, Eliza; buy me some magazines, and some books; we shall cut out a new dress if you will help me, and pay nothing to a seamstress.'

The sky is rent; the snow tumbles from it and patters now against the window. Even if they had desired it there would be no leaving the house today. 'A frightful winter,' says Mrs Frost, and she draws the curtains against it.

ELEVEN

Polly is in the little top room she shares with Elinor, which in a different house might be the maids' room. The beds are neat and narrow, and she has drawn from beneath hers the box in which she keeps her scant possessions. It holds not a coin, not so much as a single gemstone – Mrs Chappell would know at once if it did – but many items of inscrutable value. Two little novels and three broad ribbons, rolled tight and pinned, well suited for barter or bribery in her female universe. Her own box of pins, and her own scissors in their shagreen case; her spectacles and her pencil. There is also a dirty pair of kid gloves, crushed into a ball; each time she opens the box she turns them over with a cluck of irritation, but she will not throw them out. She had thought them very fine the day she arrived in the house; they are the most raw totem of her folly, and too powerful to allow out of her possession. Then there is a little prayer book wrapped in a spotted handkerchief. Although she has not opened it in some long time, it has her mother's name writ carefully inside. Her hand aspired to the easy flow and loop of a gentlewoman, but the effect is ruined by the blots where the pen has hesitated at the top of the 'L', the crooked turns of 'C' and 'Y'.

A tap on the door.

'I am busy,' she says, for it is only six, and she had hoped for some time longer before being required again.

Simeon puts his head around the door. 'A moment of your time,' he says.

'You are not allowed here.'

'Just *one* moment.'

He steps into the room, and she watches him crossly. He looks nervously to the landing; then pushes the door to, and she cannot help but shrink into herself when it clicks shut behind him.

'What do you want?' she asks, and every fibre of her being is fierce at their being alone in the room; she feels the closing of the latch as if it were a hand clamped about her wrist.

'Yesterday,' he says, all unaware of her dis-ease. 'At the carriage. When you . . .'

'The piss,' she says, and at mention of it he brushes at his livery as if filth still clung upon it. She sits up straighter. 'What of it?'

'I saw how you looked.' He drops his voice to a whisper. 'If you ever wanted to leave this place . . .'

'Why would you say that?' Her box is still on her lap; she folds her fingers around the knobbled case of her scissors. 'You are not allowed to be in here,' she persists.

'I know people,' he says, drawing from his waistcoat pocket a little piece of paper. 'Here. Addresses. If you wish to leave, they will help you.'

He holds it forth for her but she does not rise to take it. 'How dare you?' she says. 'To come in here where you have no right! To talk to me in such a way?'

He holds up his hands, the paper pinched between his fingers.

'Ever since you came here you have presumed a kinship between us that frankly, sir, insults me. And *these* people, who give aid to *slaves*, to *runaways*. Why do you think they would help me?

'They help the black poor, our brothers—'

That word again! 'I've no brothers. I am not poor.'

He looks at her, clutching her box to her chest. 'I suppose that is where you keep all your money? Come, now, ain't this enslavement of a sort? You, here, unwaged, with no prospect of leaving . . . ?'

'And Nell and Kitty and the other girls, you'd call them slaves also? Could they make use of this address?'

He shakes his head. 'I have tried my best with you.' She does not guess what effort it has been for him to come to her thus; he perceives that elsewhere in the world he is categorically her inferior, for he guessed from the first day he saw her what she is: the child of some chosen woman, picked from the fields to share her master's bed and wear the clothes that please him, and to bear infants who will be cherished despite their skin, and whose father will put gold rings in their ears and lace at their wrists and books in their hands, while lamenting that he cannot do better by them. In Carolina, Simeon himself had been a mere house slave, valued but uncherished. He tries again: 'Here in London, this is a fine place for us.'

'*Us*,' she mocks, and rolls her dark eyes, not seeing how it strains Simeon to speak on so coolly.

'The living is good; the conversation is good. I have friends who, if you were to meet them—'

'I do not wish to,' she says. 'By all means seek your own satisfaction in this life; who am I to stop you if you wish to join up with others of your race in one great mass? I do not see the advantage. I want to mix with *all* people . . .'

'. . . with the white people . . .'

'. . . and be judged only on my own merit; I wish for them to converse with me and come to know me, and accept me on my own account and nobody else's.'

'Then you will be nothing but a curiosity.'

'Better than joining a mob. 'Tis a very fine thought, sir, but one unfortunate cannot help another; if they could all we girls here would have a vastly different life.'

'We have comradeship,' rejoins he. 'It is not nothing to commune with others who understand our own experience.'

'But nobody does,' she says firmly. 'What in your life is comparable to anything in mine? If you believe the colour of our skin – or the ancestry you suppose we share – bonds us, you are stupider even than I thought.' She bends once more over her meagre effects and dons her spectacles before turning her face coolly upon him. 'Thank you, Simeon, you may go now.'

He looks her in the eye and makes sure she watches as he puts the paper down on the washstand. 'I thank you for your time,' he says.

She sits quite still while he departs. As he descends the stairs, she presses her hand to her heart, which is pounding. When she is quite sure he is gone, she gets up and locks the door fast behind him.

Ay me!

    Once I was we. Roiling in the water beyond light, we heard our sisters' calls upon us. That was how we knew we were alive. Far away, they were, an age away, but our voices swam together, our songs wrapped tight one around the other. Our every thought had its own chorus; to speak was to be agreed with, replied to; to hear was to respond. However far distant we were, we were a shoal, a one, our voices darting and swathing and weaving together for drowned mariners to hear. We enclosed everything that descended. We shoaled towards it and about it, our singing cradled the curved backs of corpses whose fingers were drawn upwards as if still reaching; and we poured into the mouths of cracked vessels, and we crept with the barnacles over prized booty.

    We investigated everything that came, and whispered to one another across the depths:

    this is a man, linen-wrapped
        this is a great ship ruptured
    this is a chain come adrift
        these are the bodies of children, flayed
    this is blood, here in the water
And we knew everything, all the doings of the water.

I find myself an I. An only. How has this come to be? I am enclosed. I cry out and my cry cannot swim, cannot speed away from me; it bounces back. It is trapped with me, and with it I explore the space I find myself in, but truly it is no space at all. I am caught in a bubble, in a box, in a vessel, and there is no expanse any more, across which my sisters' voices reach me. I do not hear them call at all, I cannot ask them, what is this? For they do not know where I am, and I am all alone.

I cry out and there is a dull nothing.

I cry out and hear my own voice back.

TWELVE

January 1786

Polly and Nell, hired to celebrate Twelfth Night in a great house at Portland Square, arrive that afternoon in as voluble and merry a mood as might be desired. Their hair has already been dressed under Mrs Chappell's own direction, and they find great hilarity in the crackle and rustle of the brown paper bound all about their persons, to protect their fine gowns against the journey. The young men – who are fourteen in number, and boisterous, and admiring of the ladies although they do not dare lay finger upon them yet – gather delightedly in the hall, in the well-mannered excitement of a pack of hunting hounds, to greet their female playmates. Elinor would by instinct plunge head first into the party; she leans from the carriage as it approaches, and halloos into the brisk cold air, but Polly places a hand on her arm and says loudly for the coachman, 'We'll not descend here in view of the street; we wish to go first to our rooms.' Mrs Chappell's instruction is clear in her mind: 'Do not go along with any amusement they demand of you; you are not their servant or their whore. Refuse them a small thing immediately: that will help train them.'

'Only allow us a little time to compose ourselves,' Elinor calls as the carriage bowls past the bloods' faces arrayed at the window, 'then you will have our undivided attention,' and they speed away to the mews beyond.

The house, where they are ushered through the back door and into the now empty hallway, is every bit as marvellous as Mrs Chappell's. 'Perhaps nicer,' Polly remarks, 'for there is no mistaking real cultivation of taste,' by which she means that the antiquities at Portland Square are cut from real marble and their members a fraction of the comparative size. The entire place smells of cloves and oranges, and roasting meats, and the resiny boughs that adorn the walls; in one of the grand front parlours the men can be heard whooping and guffawing. 'Quickly, Nell, do not let them see us so,' whispers Polly, and indeed their paper robes are not only a peculiar sight but one markedly lacking in allure.

To the consternation of the panting footmen labouring with their trunk behind, they rustle at double speed up the great staircase to the top of the house, where they find their own adjoining rooms. 'I like to have a quiet place to retire to,' says Polly, divesting herself of her papers and fluffing her hair as the footmen leave, perspiring.

'I like it *all*,' says Elinor, testing the tautness of her mattress. 'D'ye think there will be much retiring?'

'No,' and they snigger together. 'And look, Nell, we have our own bell pull.'

'What is it for? Is't really for us?'

'Of course. We are guests here. Shall I call for something?' They jig with excitement. 'Oh, I dare not! They have only just left us alone!'

'Go on!'

Polly yanks it with all her might and then skips back, her hand clapped to her mouth. 'I did it! Oh, what shall I say, what shall I say?'

'Someone comes!' cries Elinor.

'Remarkable prompt. Oh, you talk, I dare not.' The step of the servant on the stair is clearly audible. 'I shall hide!' whispers Polly. 'If I must look upon them, I think I shall die laughing.' She darts into the other room, and only a tuft of her powdered hair peeps about the door frame when the footman attends once again, somewhat discomposed from his second ascent.

'You rang for me, madam?'

'I did.' Elinor's voice quakes – how will she maintain her composure? 'Now, we are hungry and thirsty after our travelling. Would you bring us please a little Portugal wine – it must be very good, I will know at once – and a bowl of oranges? A *big* bowl.'

From behind Polly's door there comes a squeak. If Elinor's face twitches it is only for the briefest moment; she smiles most bland, and inclines her head in gratitude to the servant.

'Certainly,' he says. 'Is there anything else you would have brought up? To save your ringing again?'

'Walnuts. I should like some walnuts, and a copy of the afternoon paper.'

'Any one in particular?'

She considers. 'All of them.' There is a discernible quiver to her delivery; she must gabble quickly if she is to survive the interview. 'And a jug of hot chocolate and that will be quite everything, thank you very kindly and goodbye.' She slams the door upon him and leans upon it, weeping with hilarity; Polly staggers from the other room, scarlet in the face; she has stuffed her fist in her mouth to keep from howling, but now they lean upon one another and laugh until they cannot breathe. 'Walnuts!' gasps Polly. 'Walnuts and newspapers!'

'I *like* walnuts,' says Elinor.

There is a jovial holiday air to the afternoon: when their food has arrived – on polished trays with thick linen napkins, which they are ashamed to receive, knowing themselves so naughty – they kick off their shoes and perch carefully on Elinor's bed, spreading out their skirts and patting nervously at their hair, cracking nuts and reading aloud to one another. Seldom are they left so entirely to their own devices, and they drowse most happily for an hour.

'We are treated so nice here, Nell,' Polly sighs. 'Perhaps we should never go back,' a remark which – if she had known then what she was later to discover – Elinor might have marked as of particular significance. But having no talent for prophecy, she merely murmurs and cracks another nut.

THIRTEEN

The day of Twelfth Night. Rockingham has been gone two weeks, and Angelica is bored. She and Mrs Frost have indeed embarked upon the work of cutting out the parts of a new gown, and they have pushed the furniture to the sides of the room. The floor is spread with ivory damask, and Mrs Frost kneels there: *shrik* goes the steel of the scissors through its gleaming fibres; *shrik shrik shrik.* Outside, there is laughter on the pavement, and the smell of hot brandy and plum cakes. At night they hear merrymaking, but Angelica and her companion go obediently nowhere. Now Angelica stands up, pushing her hair out of her eyes. 'How much longer must we continue?' she asks.

'Until 'tis finished,' Mrs Frost murmurs.

'I cannot remember a time before I was making this dress! And it is no more done than it was when we began!'

'Wait until we get to the stitching.'

'*You* can do that. I am finished.'

'You desired a decent pastime. Well, here it is. Won't your George be delighted when he sees your industry?'

'Women of consequence do not make their own dresses.' She flings down her scissors. 'Oh, what can I do?'

'Read a book.'

'I have read them all.'

'Take up a magazine.'

'Their nonsense bores me. I want some *society*, Eliza!'

'Wait awhile and I will play you at knucklebones again.'

'Ah!' She shrieks with mirth that slips into horror. 'No, no, I can bear it no more! What is there to *do*?'

'He did not forbid riding in the park, did he?'

'Ugh, too cold. And I do not suppose I could go to the theatre without prevailing upon a gentleman for a box. Why has he not rented me a box for my own?'

'He'll not have you looked at. We could visit somewhere new. A menagerie, perhaps. The Academy.'

Angelica groans. 'What point would there be? All the effort and discomfort of getting there, and then we should only have to come back. It all palls without Georgie.' She crosses sadly to the window and twitches the curtains back to observe the quiet street. 'In the whole of this city the best you offer me is knucklebones.'

From below, a faint call of 'Ahoy'.

'Who's that?' Angelica looks up and down the street, and sees trotting along it Mr Jonah Hancock, cloaked in dark green, puffing frozen clouds of breath. 'The mermaid man! Well, it has been some time!' She pushes up the sash and leans out. 'Halloo! What are you doing abroad this cold day?'

Inside the room, Mrs Frost says, 'Angelica, no. What are you thinking?'

'I had business,' says Mr Hancock. 'And in passing by I thought to see how you did.'

'What business? Nobody has done a stroke of work in weeks.' She leans out further, most merry to see a friendly face. 'Where's my mermaid?'

'Angelica!' snaps Mrs Frost.

Angelica shoots a glance behind her. All within is dismal. She is conscious of the need to keep him wanting, but very likely his devotion will compensate for any lapse in her. 'What are you doing now?' she asks.

He almost hugs himself. 'Nothing – nothing at all. I am at my liberty.'

'I cannot credit you,' tuts Mrs Frost. 'You do not know what is good for you.'

'I know that I shall die of boredom if I continue thus,' Angelica hisses. Leaning again from the window, she calls, 'I am not quite prepared for company. If you return in twenty minutes I shall be better disposed. And just to talk, you understand? Come up to amuse me, and leave when I give the word.'

As she draws the window down, he bounds off proud as a crow in a gutter. A few times he has passed hopefully by here since their last encounter, but always the window was dark, or filled with the stern face of Mrs Frost, whose favour he does not dare attempt to solicit again. His contact with Mrs Neal herself is so little, in fact, that he does not know she has a keeper; it is gossiped all over town, but he, ignorant of how close their streams of commerce run, passes through taverns and coffee-houses alert to mention of this ship or that insurance, but never for the name of Angelica Neal. It does not occur to him that if he had wanted news of her he could have asked for it and had an answer from half a dozen different quarters – but no. He thinks Angelica Neal his own secret.

Any astute gentleman would have questions, but he is more now than he was when he first met her; his fortune is equal to any body's, and so, therefore, is his right to be received by her. Besides, the vision of the crescent of her naked breast rising above the window-sill intrudes yet upon his mind, and the press of her fingers upon his, and how nearly, in the mermaid's closet, they had . . .

Still, when he returns after pacing briskly around Soho Square for fifteen minutes, and is led wordlessly to Mrs Neal's door by her companion, he wavers on the threshold.

'Are you ready to receive me?' he asks.

'I am,' Angelica Neal calls from her parlour. She is in her white gown, and her hair all shining under the starchiest cap he ever saw, with the most evenly crimped frill. 'Come, sit with me,' she says.

His approach is not without hesitation. And indeed he finds this room, which he has never been in before, quite peculiar. It is very warm, and elegantly proportioned, with large windows, but it is cluttered in every corner with luxury of all sorts.

'You are well appointed here,' he says. He has noticed the ivory threads strewn here and there on the Turkey carpet, but he does not imagine that only ten minutes earlier the beginnings of a dress had been laid out here, and that down the passage in Angelica's bed-room, its components have been hastily heaped.

'*I* like it.' She looks at him expectantly. He seats himself in the chair opposite her, and folds one hand upon the other. 'Good day,' she says, and in the quiet room her voice is soft and pretty. There is a small round table at her elbow, set up with tea equipage, and she leans to pour hot water into the pot; her eyelashes brush her cheek most beguilingly.

'Why do you bring me up here?' he asks.

'I had nobody to talk to,' she says, and looks up to smile at him. 'Besides, I desired to know you better. We met so briefly; I have been much caught up with life since I returned to London.' She pours a cup and holds it out to him; he must rise to receive it, she being so distant. 'I suppose your Christmas has been very busy.'

'No,' he says. Christmas is the time he feels most like a stray dog, and each year it stretches on a little longer, an endless procession of babies to hold and exclaim over, sweethearts clutching one another under the mistletoe, spouses grown content and old together. 'I took my niece to her mother's house, which pleased her but did not much please me.'

Angelica has not spent a Christmas with any of her blood since she was a girl of thirteen; in her maturity she has gone wherever she is summoned and admired, to be herself as much a part of the festivities as the gilded gingerbread or the riotous song. Thus she continues to perceive the celebrations in many ways as a child would: a hazy whirl of frumenty, hunt the thimble, plum pie, blind man's buff and scorch-cased chestnuts: endless laughter and no anxiety; she expects to light every candle and dance beyond sunset, but not a moment of expense or resentment. And so she does not say anything.

'Oh –' he has forgot his gift; he produces a parcel of coarse little tarts, and hands them over to her – 'these are for you.'

She giggles, but he thinks not mockingly, rather in appreciation. 'Much obliged! I am always in want of small and delicious things. Here, would you fetch me a plate?' She wafts her hand towards the cabinet, and he rises gingerly to pick one out. All her dishes are beautiful in the absurd – New Hall, figured with pink roses, not Chinese but as close in quality as could be hoped for – but only imperfectly clean, with tidelines where dishwater has been allowed to dry upon them.

'By the by, I came to tell you I have ordered your mermaid,' he says more casually than he feels, as he passes her a plate, and she puts the tarts on it one by one, taking each gently between finger and thumb. Ever since Tysoe Jones left London he has thought, what are the chances? The scheme is doomed; he will never have another such creature in his lifetime. But now, sitting at last so close to this lady, in such extravagant surroundings, he feels an inclination to boast, and when she chortles he is pleased.

'I look forward to receiving it,' she says, looking to the mantelpiece. 'That's where I'll put it. I mean to have it mounted in such a way that it can easily be got down, to be passed around and remarked upon.' She stops and looks directly at him; there is that deep and simmering look in her eyes. 'I shall owe you something, I think.'

He opens his mouth to speak but she draws back as if he has reached out to her, and springs to her feet. 'Then perhaps I shall start a collection,' she continues, and paces the hearth with her sheer gown all sighing. Is she teasing him? Her eyes twinkle. 'What other curiosities can you get for me?'

'One thing at a time,' he says.

'No, no,' she says, and he sees her bosom tremble, delicate as pastry cream. 'Everything at once! That's how I want it. Elf arrows, bound in silver so they do no harm. An elephant to ride about on. A manticore, a centicore, a gryphon.'

'Oh no,' he says, 'they are not to be found in the places I send my boats.'

'Then spread your net wider, sir.' She tilts her head like a bright little bird.

'Ah, no.' Now he has begun bragging he finds he cannot stop: 'I mean to cease trading in a few years; I have an income from my investments large enough to see me at leisure to the end of my days.'

'Very fine for you.'

'Enough, in fact, that I have made a donation to a ragged school, and I mean to build almshouses.' His charity hitherto has been as vigorous as any other man loyal to his parish: his failings in the matter of progeny are not reflected in his contributions to the maintenance of Deptford's churches and widows, his Valentine's Day coins to its poor children; the generous purses he keeps ready for a journeyman carpenter whose tools have been stolen, or newlyweds whose house is burnt down.

'Oh,' says Angelica, with some interest. 'You do not keep it all to yourself?'

'Certainly not.' He cannot think what wealth would be without these gestures, which are not so much obligations of his financial improvement, but signifiers of it. From his earliest memory he never owned so much as a farthing that he did not seek to share with his neighbour, for the purpose of money is to be spread about. 'I've no children, no wife. What would I do with it all?'

She shrugs. 'There must be something you are in need of.'

'No. No, I am content.' He holds the tea bowl in the curve of his palm and swirls it gently. 'Although I've nothing so fine as this in my house.'

She drains her own. 'That is where the fun starts,' she says, and licks the moisture from her lips. 'In the purchase of fine things.'

He looks about himself: the sheer quantity of goods in the room defies inventory; there is such a clamour of textures and colours, of good taste and bad, all the parts combining to an effect that is overwhelming to the senses and yet speaks plainly to his merchant's heart: *here is wealth – for the moment.* A lady secure in her income may purchase a new tea set each season, but to buy three at once is an economy of anxiety, which seeks to anticipate every loss, every breakage, every change of whim the years might bring.

'I see you do not let your own money sit idle,' he says.

'It were best spent. You cannot ever know what tomorrow will bring; you might be ruined, and never enjoy the splendours you could have had.'

'They await us all in the next world,' he says, which thing is rather a sprite of a belief, since it seems most real when he does not look directly at it.

'I am told by those with authority in the matter that they do not await *me*.' This puts him out of his ease.

'Repentance,' he hazards, 'is always possible.'

'Aye, and how would I support myself then? Besides, a woman who makes her own wage must always be found wanting; my mother sought a blameless living and still found great shame in it.'

'Why was your mother compelled to work?'

She frowns very prettily, as if she wavered to tell him. 'My father,' she says, and then breathes, so that the two words sit alone in the room with them for a moment; then she continues, 'went to seek our fortune in the colonies.'

'And left you unsupported.'

'He was gone longer than he had thought. The sea, you know,' and he nods in sympathy which is what she desires of him. 'And so we were forced to look for genteel work – sewing and such, and when it was not enough my mother sought to teach a school. And the people in our town did not like that. "How can you use his name thus?" they asked her. "How can you so broadcast that he has left you unprovided for? Where is your loyalty?"'

Mr Hancock watches her with a stirring of new interest. She sounds all at once a breed in common with his own sisters and nieces; he had perceived her as a different sort of woman, to be weighed on other scales, but perhaps this is not so. 'He did wrong,' he says.

'Oh, he was an adventurer,' she says with a gleam of pride. 'He had concerns beyond our ken.'

'Still, good men do not forget their dependants.' She looks to him very fragile in her white gown, her face only lightly powdered and her hair falling from its bindings in natural yellow curls. And how ordinary she looks, her skin like any other woman's skin, and her eyelashes and her movements; he could imagine her on a street like his own, amongst the women of his own society. 'Where were your uncles, grandfathers? Your mother's plight should have been their responsibility.'

She shakes her head. 'Nobody.' Then stumbles on; she seems surprised by what she says but it comes with a great urgency and trouble. 'And when you are a poor woman, and unprotected, you are near as well a whore, even if you have not fallen yet. If one small thing goes awry, of course you must be tempted to it. Everybody knows that the moment will come some day; however honourable you are the taint of it is already on you. Eventually one feels one has no choice.'

The more she talks the more comprehensible to him she becomes. 'Did your father return?' he asks.

She presses her lips together and looks out of the window, the cool light turning her eyes palest grey. 'How long should I have waited to find out? I came to London, to seek *my* fortune.'

How grateful he is that his sisters are all married and his nieces protected by webs of property and connection. Sukie, out on her own, would she . . . ? She is sensible, he assures himself, her skills and education will help her – but then he has heard of the ways in which girls are duped; drugged; raped.

'Don't look so sorrowful!' she says. 'My situation is a matter of economy. What shall I be, all on my own, a poor woman who is ashamed of herself, or a rich one who is not?'

It may be another folly of his to feel such sympathy for her, but pragmatism is a quality he and his kind admire in a woman, and he nods a wondering approval. 'I daresay you have behaved with prudence. And chastity is not a woman's only virtue,' he adds generously.

'Although it is her chiefest.'

'Females have little enough of their own in the first place,' he says, weighing the thought to see whether he believes it. 'Many good women are coerced into things they are not easy with; I do believe that redemption is possible.'

'When I marry –' she offers up an enigmatic little twitch of the lip – 'perhaps it will be. Repentance is much easier when one is of comfortable means. For now –' waving her hand across her cluttered room – 'I enjoy my earthly glamours. But, sir, the hour for tea is over.'

He dons hat and coat most meekly. Then he fumbles; holds out a banknote as a token of his gentility. 'Where do I put this?' he asks.

'Back in your pocket, sir.'

'But—'

'I have asked nothing of you,' she says softly.

'No.' And in fact he has not expected any transaction, only that, if he be the quality of gentleman who may visit and sit with a celebrated courtesan, he must also be the quality that can afford it. 'A gift,' he says.

'No, no.' They stand apart a little longer. Her eyes are all downcast, and her mouth has a droop to it. 'I do not need reward for every ordinary meeting I have.'

'Permit me,' he says, and takes her hand. 'I mean you the warmest friendship.'

She sighs. 'Even the warmest friendship has conditions to it.' But as she shakes his hand she brightens. 'You may visit me again,' she says. 'I would like that.'

FOURTEEN

In the Portland Square house there is a vast basin of wassail highly spiced and bobbing with apples, and there is music from a fiddle and a pipe. More girls have been delivered from Mrs Rawson's, amongst them Miss Clark who is a whisper over four feet tall and famed for the extraordinary tininess of her feet, and a pretty black-eyed Malay maiden in a silk turban. 'Oh, we shall have a fine time of it,' says Elinor, and seizing Polly's hand draws her into the room, where the men let up a great cheer. 'A dance! A dance!' Elinor cries, and dance they do, until the room grows hot as an oven and Polly must throw herself down into the window seat, panting and laughing.

A young gentleman comes to sit by her. 'Are you tired?' he asks.

'Only hot,' she says, and indeed her brow is wet with perspiration. She takes out her handkerchief and dabs it upon herself; when she looks up she sees him watching with peculiar interest. 'What is it?' she asks sharply, but he shakes his head and looks quickly down at his shoes. She dabs again, and watches as he darts a look at the handkerchief upon her skin.

She touches her own cheek and holds her fingers up for him to see. ''Tis my skin,' she says sharply. 'It does not come off.'

He colours deeply and still will not look her in the eye. 'Only that one never sees ladies of your complexion about the town.'

'You do not go to the right places,' she rejoins.

'We were very glad to have secured you for this party,' he says, taking her hand, 'for not a one of us have ever tried it with a negro before now.'

All of a sudden her mouth is a stopped bottle ready to pop. To restrain herself, she looks about for Elinor, nods towards her. 'And why did you order Miss Bewlay?'

'The sorrel-pated one?' He leans in confidingly. 'We hear they are *most* unnatural in their appetites.'

She laughs aloud but the pressure in her head is not relieved. 'Rarities, are we? To add to your collection?'

And he grins with relief, not seeing her anger. 'Yes,' he says, 'oh yes, that is exactly it. You are a woman entirely out of the common water; we all desire to sample every sort of woman there is in the world.'

'What an education it will be,' she says, and rises.

Elinor, just seized jokeously up into the arms of young Mr Hammond, the host of the party, sees her: 'Are you going outside?' she calls. 'Wait for me, dear.'

'Let us all go,' says Mr Hammond. 'It is fiendish hot in here.'

And out onto the terrace they go, Polly casting about for a glimpse of Elinor's bright hair, but she is leaning against the parapet lost in conversation with some young blood, and does not look up. Polly, standing yet amongst the group, bethinks herself to regain her composure with a stroll, and surveys the dark garden, its paths mapped out with twinkling lights. There is a little round hut at its centre, with a weathervane atop it, and a pretty lattice up which a dark vine grows. Is it a place she might sit quietly for a little? Or too secluded? She would not like a gentleman to be inspired to follow her there. 'Is it a summer house?' she asks, and the men guffaw.

'It is the necessary!' they say. 'Is it not artfully done? You never did suspect.'

'So clever,' she says.

The young man who first spoke to her has reappeared at her side; now he seizes her wrist, a gesture she finds quite startling. Caressing her fingers with great earnestness, he says, 'Madam, may I ask you a great favour?'

'I think you are going to either way,' she says.

'What I said before – we are all in dispute amongst one another as to who will have you first.' He looks over at Mr Hammond, who is regaling Elinor Bewlay with an anecdote she finds irresistibly hilarious. 'Now, I believe *I* was the first to talk to you . . .'

'Sir,' she smiles. 'There is no first. There are no *turns*; I am not a toy to be passed about. I am an item of great value and rarity which few men are fortunate enough to ever possess. If you want me, you will earn me. Excuse me, please,' and she gestures to the little rustic necessary. 'I must avail myself of your summer house.'

She walks – and this part of her journey is clearly observed by several onlookers – down the brick path bordered by ankle-height box hedges, and circles the wall of the building until she finds its door. It is dark within, a mere snib of candle yet burning, and a draught comes up from the three apertures over the soil, which smells of nothing at all but fresh sawdust and dried lavender. Polly, whose skirts would prevent her from using them even if she needed to, rests for a moment on the edge of the bench, and ruffles her fingers in her hair, which she suspects of wilting. *Christ, the things we must tolerate.* She thinks that later she will tell Elinor about it; '"*Most* unnatural in your appetites,"' she will mimic, and surely they will laugh together, but still she cannot find much mirth.

She closes her eyes. She could sit here all night; without, the noise of the party goes on – the men are laughing immoderately at something – and she hears Elinor's high and joyful shriek. *Must I return?* she thinks. *Oh, I must.*

She sidles out quietly, hoping to peep at the company and better prepare herself to rejoin their merriment, but as she looks to her right something catches her eye. It is a door in the high wall, a plain little wooden door just wide enough for a gardener to pass through, and it stands ajar.

Beyond it – what? She does not know.

She glances again at the group, but they are playing and shouting without thought for her. Elinor has snatched something from one of the men, and as he lunges to retrieve it she skips away, and darts into the house holding it aloft.

'After her!' they cry. 'Catch the little hussy,' and several tussle, jammed in the narrow doorway in their pursuit of her. Nobody is looking back into the dark garden. Polly looks down at her white dress; if it catches their eye . . . but she knows what she will do.

She takes up her skirts in each hand and walks fast and purposeful along the path to the little door. It is no more than ten steps, and she is out, in a narrow alley flanked on either side by tall walls. Her instinct is to turn right, and thus walk in the opposite direction to the house she has escaped: she goes briskly with her head held up, but does not run. The brick paving gives out to thin gravel, and she smells it all with such gemmed clarity, the wet stone and the moss between the pebbles. Though she cannot see beyond the deep walls of her little channel, the moon rides high above her, and the slice of its radiance that falls upon her is lovelier than she ever knew before. She comes to a mews of stables and strides its length without fear, although she is terrible exposed: straw wafts beneath her feet, and horses groan and fart in their sleep; she smells the huff of their breath so brightly that it is almost as if their flanks are under her hands, silk this way, coarse the other. She continues only to walk, tugging her shawl up over her head, and pulling its warmth as far around her body as possible. It is fearful cold, the sort that gets down to the bone, and already frost has begun to spangle the ground and the walls, and the air is sharp as knives. *No matter.*

She reaches a grand paved square, and now she is afraid, but she says to herself, *I shall not think about it; I shall think about it later if I must,* and takes a breath and crosses it. Her steps ring out. Each house sits dark behind railings. The servants are fastening all the shutters, and behind the doors she hears the drawing home of many bolts, but some houses are sites of merrymaking like the one she has left; their windows flicker brightly and there are hoots and songs within. If somebody were to see her, on a festival night such as this, would they perceive immediately that something was afoot? A girl alone – a black girl, indeed – hurrying in the dark. Her dress is not that of a servant. What will she say if she is challenged? She cannot think; she shakes her head; she bustles onward as if with great purpose. Thus she goes quite unobserved through square after ordered square. A nightwatchman turns his head when he hears her footsteps, but onward she scurries, and in the rays of his lantern the frost makes a great burst of stars upon stars.

FIFTEEN

The next day, the streets being clear of snow nor so treacherously icy as they might be, Angelica determines to take her carriage out. It arrives filled with rugs, and all the seats warmed, and a great bag of feathers for her feet. She rides immediately to the home of Bel Fortescue (Countess, to acknowledge her legal due, although not many do). Arriving in such splendour she is able, almost, to close her eyes to the high concealing walls of her friend's home, the wide courtyard within, the pillared and porticoed façade where Bel awaits. It does not take a great effort to disregard the many pruned bay trees there, nor the liveried servants all in Bel's employ, for she is confidently assured that when Rockingham comes into his fortune, she too will live this way. And so it is as equals that she confides in Bel, 'Money is so tiresome, do you not find? The amount of running about Georgie has to do simply to get what is his – why, it is almost not worth having it.'

Countess Bel raises an eyebrow. 'I hope he receives it soon, for your sake.'

'I would take him if he had no income at all,' says Angelica stoutly. 'You do not know what it is *like*. You cannot imagine – that is the problem – nobody can. It is a very rare thing we have together. We are matched as souls, as Beatrice and Dante, Romeo and Juliet,

Tristan and Iseult ...' Her reading is slender; here she falters. 'I could have no other, whatever situation we were thrown into.'

'And him? Does he have any other?'

'Certainly not.'

'Well, you must make quite sure; he is not bound to you. It is different for men.'

'Not for him,' Angelica says with resolution. 'I forgive you your incredulity, for very few people are fortunate enough to understand what Georgie and I share.'

In Berkeley Square, Angelica puffs up the white muslin spilling over the lapels of her redingote, and despite the cold lets her cape hang open. She has fastened Rockingham's diamond dart at her throat, and likes to be sure it is seen. Bel, taking her arm as they stroll, persists. 'Has he settled something on you yet?'

'Everybody is always asking! That is what he has gone away for. 'Tis a shame he was obliged to leave when the town is so lively. Perhaps you recall, Bel, what a nuisance it is to be in demand, and of course the minute I am left unprotected for one second the whole world descends – they would have me if they could.'

'Is that so?' Bel's forbearance is one of her greatest strengths. Whatever she thinks, she does not betray it as Angelica goes on. 'There is a gentleman – the mermaid man, do you remember him? – he has visited me once, and insists he will come again this afternoon.'

Her friend frowns. 'You do not let him touch you, do you?'

'By no means! And he would never try.' A few days have passed, but she remains no less perplexed by the manner in which her interview with Mr Hancock ended. The money he offered would have improved her situation, and yet she had refused it without thought. If she had done so out of loyalty to Rockingham she would be congratulating herself on her own virtue: in fact, she having rejected it for her own sake, and for Mr Hancock's, she feels a certain guilty flutter. She has stooped to conversation with a man whose station is so different from her lover's, who is sympathetic to concerns *he* cannot conceive of; who compels her to remember the particular facts of her history that were better forgotten. She would like to have been born full-formed and pristine from sea-foam. To have strode such treacherous and demeaning paths to become Angelica Neal is displeasing to her. 'He knows about Georgie,' she says appeasingly, and steers them towards the confectioner's window.

'As long as he is content with a friendship,' Bel pursues. 'He did not seem to me the sort of man who understood such codes.'

Angelica gurgles with amusement. 'If he ever gets any sort of look in his eye,' she says, 'I lean right in close, like so, and tell him, "I want a mermaid." I let my breath touch his cheek and I say, "Where is my mermaid, Mr Hancock?" The poor fool has only sent a boat out to find one for me.' This scene is purely imagined, but it is well to have a response prepared for every possibility. In the face of her friend's silence, she babbles in haste, 'Come, now, Bel, there is hardly a Christian wife who has not been driven to much worse at least once in her life, and really you see it is out of *loyalty* to Georgie, for if I cared only for security I would leave him.' She leads her friend into the fragrant shop, assuring her, 'In every other particular we are as faithful to one another as a pair of turtle doves.' Her eye is already straying to the tower of millefruits on the counter, and her steps follow it forthwith. To the starched apron behind the counter, she says, 'Half a pound of those, if you please. Charge it to Rockingham's account.'

The woman has begun to scoop the biscuits into a sheet of folded tissue paper, but she stops when she hears this. 'No, ma'am,' she says. 'We give him no credit here.'

'I beg your pardon?'

'No credit. We require cash on this account.'

Angelica draws herself up to her full height. 'I suppose,' she says acidly, 'you do not know who I am.'

The woman regards her with cool pale eyes. 'Oh, I know who you are, madam. 'Tis only that your keeper's name is no good here. He's a bill a foot long to settle up.'

'For pity's sake, it is only *cakes*,' snaps Angelica. 'The miserliness of tradespeople! It is quite astonishing, do you not agree, Bel?' Those others in the shop – respectable ladies – turn to peer discreetly at the set-to, and less discreetly as it goes on.

'Cakes,' says the server sternly, 'that have gone unpaid for since November. Not to mention three jars of peaches in syrup, thirty-nine jellies – *and* their glasses, not a one returned – one fancy Savoy biscuit measuring three feet high, seven cases of macaroons, and gills of fancy liqueur numbering –' she pauses to draw breath – 'thirteen in total. The entire sum owing is fifteen pounds and eight shillings.'

'Is that all! For fifteen pounds you subject me to *this*?'

'If I allowed every body to dodge their bill in such a way, where would I be?'

Angelica sighs. 'Clearly there has been some oversight, and more likely on your part than his. Very well, then, put it in my name. I shall have my woman settle it up.'

The woman shakes her head. 'If he cannot pay his bills, I deduce he cannot pay yours. Or have you income from other pockets too?'

'How dare you!'

Bel touches her arm, her face downturned. 'Hush, Jellie,' she whispers into her stock.

'Certainly not! Did you mark what she said?' Angelica's voice is high and shrill, and resonates through every cloche and tile. The company of sweet-eaters is beyond concealing its interest;

gentlemen and women sit rapt. 'How dare *you*, madam!' Angelica repeats.

'If you do not have the coin,' says the woman, 'I cannot help you.' She places her hand on the half-filled tissue, and the paper crunches.

Angelica's pockets contain a notebook with ivory leaves; a miniature deck of cards; a tin in which to collect errant pins; a small mirror in a case; a portrait miniature of dear Georgie; a length of red ribbon and a bottle of rouge. They do not, however, contain so much as a single dusty ha'penny. She has got so out of the habit of keeping money about her that she has almost forgotten its physical form: it merely drops from her lips as a casual flow of promises. 'Why do you expect anybody to carry cash?' she demands. 'That is very revealing of your class.'

'*I* have it,' says Mrs Fortescue.

'Oh, Bel, no—'

'Comes to two shillings,' says the woman.

'For the biscuits?' asks Bel softly, opening her purse. 'No, no, I shall pay the balance.' She darts before Angelica to lay the coin on the counter. Angelica's ears look as if they have taken a dab of cochineal themselves, they are so unnaturally scarlet; a film of liquid wavers across her eyes as she watches the sugared parcel tied off with a length of red string. Then Mrs Fortescue presses it into her hands. 'A gift,' she says.

'It must be a mistake,' whispers Angelica as they leave at pace. 'Surely a mistake,' but she finds her hands are quivering and her brow cold with sweat. She remembers her wretchedness after the duke's death was reported in the papers and his credit useless in shops, the bitterness in the back of her throat and the fluttering of her heart as if her terror had become trapped in her bosom like a bird in a chimney flue. She remembers also – an accident, she does not mean to recall it – once being small for her age, and walking the high street of the town where she was born with the buildings tall about her; the counter of the butcher's shop, when she entered it, came to the height of her nose. The smell of blood and rancid fat.

Got any bones?

What's that, little miss?

Bones, for the pot. Just bones. Any ones'll do.

You Morgan's girl, ain't you? So your daddy's not come home.

He's making our fortune.

Oh, aye? And how will I make mine, if I give away all my scraps? Not good business.

I don't want much.

What have you got? Not a coin on you? Now surely you have some-thing you'd be willing to trade? No? A girl's always got something.

And the world heaves.

'Easy, dear, easy now.' Mrs Fortescue has her arm around Angel-ica's shoulders, murmuring in her ear as if she were a frightened horse. 'Take a moment; take a breath or two.'

She gasps in air; feels better for it. She keeps her chin down for the street is busy and she is afraid to be recognised while in such distress. Presently she composes herself.

'Shall we go home?' asks Mrs Fortescue. 'My house is not far.'

'No, no. This need not spoil the day.' She attempts a little laugh, which Mrs Fortescue pretends to find convincing. ''Tis one uppity shopkeeper, that is all. Let us go on.'

'But perhaps—'

'Deduce nothing from this!' Angelica blots her forehead with her handkerchief. 'Stay out with me, Bel; I never see you now-a-days. Take me to your favourite jeweller's. I want something pretty to wear for Mr Hancock – diamonds, I think, and solely for my own satisfaction. He won't know them from paste.'

'Perhaps it were better if you hired a piece,' Bel soothes her. 'Or I shall lend you something of mine.'

'No! I do not *hire* diamonds! I do not *borrow* them. As if I were some cit's wife allowed to her one masque of the season! Come, Bel, I wish to buy something lovely – Rockingham is good for it.'

But each shop they go in they meet the same response; a discreet shake of the head, a draper running his finger down his ledger and saying sadly, 'Madam, it is out of my hands.' Rockingham's name is not good in one single establishment along the length of Bond Street.

'I do not know what has happened,' Angelica says, quite numb with the shock of it, once they are back in the sealed cabin of her new carriage. 'Sincerely I do not. Perhaps somebody has a vendetta against him?'

'Somebody has simply tired of paying his bills,' says Mrs Fortescue. 'If they ever did.'

'Oh no, that can't be so. He has an allowance, you know. That is what we live on.'

'An allowance! Which comes to no more than – what? A boy like that? – five hundred a year, I'd wager, and you have a bill for a hundred at the jeweller's alone. See sense, Jellie. He has no means to pay anybody off.'

'Christ.' Angelica puts her head in her hands. 'No, no. He has the means. He has kept me most comfortable – I have nothing to fear in the world.'

Mrs Fortescue raps on the roof of the carriage and leans out. 'Twice around the park,' she calls to the groom. She closes the window tight and takes Angelica's hand. 'My dear, those are exactly the sort of things they say.'

'Not Georgie. You patronise me, Bel – no, 'tis true. Do you believe you are the only one who has a good keeper? I am at *least* as loved as you are, *at least*.'

There is a great deal of gentleness in Bel's brown eyes. 'Very well. Yes. He is a young man who has got into some financial trouble – who has not? This can be resolved.'

'How?'

'That's his trouble, not yours.'

Angelica dabs at her eyes. 'Oh, where is your feminine liberty now? I must simply resign my fate into his hands?'

'I believe you did *that* the moment you took his word as sole assurance that you need not protect your own interests. Jellie, Jellie, do not cry any more. I did not mean to upset you. But if you have made yourself a chattel, his spending is hardly *your* responsibility. Nobody blames the coach-and-four if a gentleman cannot keep up his payments on them.'

Angelica gasps. 'The carriage,' she whispers with awful urgency. 'This very carriage we now ride in! Hush, do not let our driver hear a word of this or else he will eject us onto the pavement, for I fear his wages cannot be paid.'

'Oh, now, Jellie, you do not know it is so bad,' says Mrs Fortescue. 'And besides, no hireling would throw you over so abruptly – they know a *little* discretion.'

'Hush, hush! Lower your voice, Bel.' Angelica is hugging herself with worry. 'As for discretion, they don't trouble themselves with it once the money is gone. You saw how loudly that woman denounced me in the shop. It will be the same all over. *I* know how it is –' she digs her fingers into her upper arms so tightly the knuckles whiten – 'they positively triumph at one's misfortune.' Mrs Fortescue pats and shushes her, but she frets on, and groans, 'Oh, this is grave! This is very, very grave!' For the full awfulness of the situation is creeping chill into her bones; here she is alone with his debts, and no word of when he will return. 'He cannot have expected this.' She looks appealingly at Bel.

Her friend hesitates. 'No, dear, no, he cannot.'

'Oh, if I could only speak to him! I would be so much easier if I only knew his plan. If he had left me more cash!'

'I can give you—'

'No!' Her poor cheeks flame scarlet. 'I have too many gowns; I will have Eliza pawn something for the time being.' If he were with her he would reproach her for her lack of faith. Oh, but she has been so faithful! She permitted herself for once to believe his every word! Is this where it leads one? She feels Bel's hand on her back.

'Do not think the worst. When he comes back . . .'

Angelica's handkerchief is soaked through; she fishes for another and here is Bel's pressed into her hand, embroidered with her husband's crest. She blinks, and blinks again as the tears waver across her vision, gazing upon the lovely coronet, the unfamiliar letters. Then she screws it into her hot fist and hies it to the floor. 'Foolish me,' she says, 'making such a meal of this. Why, all I need to do is write and acquaint him with my situation. He will be mortified to hear of it. I am as faithful a mate to him as he is to me – we are matched souls.'

'But in the meantime, if you need help . . .'

Angelica has now entirely left off crying. 'If you really mean to help me, you will leave off your naysaying,' she snaps. 'You have not uttered one encouraging thing throughout this entire sorry episode; you assume the worst of him at every turn.'

'I meant only to be prudent; you would not be the first lady to have her trust abused—'

'You see? You cannot simply be glad for me, not for one second.'

A certain tightness goes out of Bel's figure; her shoulders droop, and although the slump in her mien is barely detectable, slump she most certainly does. 'All the years of our friendship,' she says in a little voice. 'I rejoice at your rejoicing; when you weep, I weep with you.'

'Then why are you so at odds with me now? Rejoice! Rejoice for me! I am the best I ever have been!'

They complete their journey in silence, and at Mrs Fortescue's house Angelica will extend only the most muttered and insincere of fare-you-wells. If she had guessed that this would be the last ride of its sort – that they will not meet again under such circumstances – would she have discovered more warmth for her old friend? But she does not watch Mrs Fortescue go, and rides home without a backward glance.

SIXTEEN

Meanwhile, Mrs Chappell has rushed to the house at Portland Square, where Polly has been vanished more than twelve hours: the Christmas greenery and stars still adorn every surface, but the doors to even the smallest cupboard are all flung open, and there are men searching the attics and knocking at the walls in search of secret compartments. Mrs Chappell is crumpled and irritated and over-hot after her one-mile voyage across the city, for she hates to be harried about. She takes one look at the uproar and hurries Elinor into the library for a private interview and a glass of watered spirit. Even that closet is decked with branches of yew and mistletoe, most pathetic in light of the aborted festivities, which only heightens Elinor's state of panic.

'I helped Pol choose her stays,' she now sobs, 'and she said, "Nell, how many pairs of stockings are you taking? Well, I had best take double what you do, for I mean to dance all night." She packed twelve new pairs of stockings, madam, and they are all in our trunk still.'

'As if that signified,' snorts Mrs Chappell.

'She brought all three volumes of *Evelina*,' insists Elinor, who is struggling with the peculiar sensation that she cannot get enough air into her lungs. 'Nobody who means to leave on the first day takes all three volumes.'

'Stop crying,' says Mrs Chappell. 'You do yourself no favours.'

'But I knew nothing of it!' Elinor wails.

'I believe you,' says Mrs Chappell, a magical incantation guaranteed to start any tongue flapping. 'But you must be sure and tell me all you know. You were the last to see her.'

'I and all the gentlemen,' Elinor persists. '*All* the gentlemen. We were in company from seven o'clock until she disappeared.'

'And then what?'

'I've told you.'

'Tell me again.'

Elinor wrings her hands. 'It was about ten,' she says, and sets about pacing up and down the little room as if she must chase from one recollection to the next, 'or half after, or eleven, perhaps. And we had dined, and took a drink, and to be sure you remember what a fine clear night it was, though very cold –' and here she hesitates, doubts herself, stumbles onward more shrilly – 'at least it was fine *here*, I do not suppose the weather is much different in St James's, although I have heard before of showers in Whitechapel when it was quite dry in Threadneedle Street, so who can truly—'

Mrs Chappell clicks her fingers. 'Blathering, Nell. Pray, back to your story.'

'The men will attest that the weather was just as I recall. And they said, "Why do we not go out onto the terrace and look upon the garden?"'

'Were you drunk?'

'I, madam? *No*, madam!'

'But Polly is inclined to drink? And in her cups she becomes reckless, does she not?'

Elinor looks at her cautiously: which is the better reply? 'You think . . .' She stops but her thoughts are a burst of panicked birds wheeling in all directions, and she is short of breath as she darts to catch hold of them all. 'Well, she is no sort of drinker – but now you cannot think her actions were *calculated* – and perhaps she did not go willingly – all the wassail may have gone to her head – if Polly came to be repentant, what would you . . . ?' Her palms are wet: she clenches her apron in her fists. 'You could forgive her, surely.'

'But she has not returned,' says Mrs Chappell.

'She may be in some trouble,' says Elinor, 'that we do not know of.'

'What trouble could ever have come to her? She has been kept safe, has she not? As you all have been. She has wanted for nothing, and I have given her my protection without stint.'

'She may have been kidnapped,' says Elinor. '*Gypsies*,' she adds hopefully.

'Kidnapped for what purpose?'

'Oh, madam, such terrible things happen in this world! When a young girl with a good face disappears in such a way, six times out of seven it transpires they have been drugged and carried off by terrible old ladies who debauch them and keep them captive! And then sell their honour, and profit by it. This is a daily occurrence in this city; no girl is safe from it.'

Mrs Chappell snorts. 'You never were an observant child. Kidnapped! Cast the notion from your head. She went of her own accord.'

'But why would she simply *leave* . . . ?' She is thinking, *but why would she leave me?* She is thinking, *but I did not know we had such secrets from one another.* She is thinking, *but our lives were identical; I did nothing that she did not do. Why then was she so dissatisfied when I was not?* She begins, precipitously, to sob. 'I know nothing, madam, nothing at all of this matter.'

SEVENTEEN

'You ought never to have let him up in the first place,' says Mrs Frost, knotting the last tie of Angelica's gown.

'I do as I please.' Angelica has no intention of telling Mrs Frost anything of Georgie's financial oversights; her reaction would be beyond tolerating.

Even so it pains her when her companion demands, 'And your protector? Does he have no claim on your heart?' Mrs Frost circles her, minutely adjusting the gathers in the muslin; her disapproval does not extend to leaving them less than perfect, as very well she might.

'He has sole claim to it! He has no rivals for it! I only have the gentleman up because I am bored, criminally bored.'

'You think nothing of propriety,' says Mrs Frost. 'You must always be entertained. Sit down; there is more to be done to your hair.'

'You are forgetting I *have* no propriety.' Angelica throws herself into her chair and leans her elbows on the dressing table, knocking trinkets and boxes without care. 'I lost it long ago, and thus I am at liberty to be alone in rooms with strange gentlemen.' She sighs. 'You are no model of virtue yourself, Eliza, you know where your bread is buttered, that is all. I never saw you take Georgie's side until now, when you believe your living depends on it.'

'How dare you! I have been nothing but virtuous. Rectitude is ever my watchword; it wounds me to see *you* break your promises with such little provocation.'

'Shut up, Eliza.' For this lecture is hardly to be tolerated either.

'No! Truly! I should like to see in your behaviour some inkling of female decency, but I begin to think your appetites are baser than they ought to be. I had thought you more restrained . . .'

Angelica casts her eyes to the heavens. 'I am only taking your advice,' she says, 'remembering myself to the town; I do not closet myself away from those who might one day be of use to me.'

'Now is the time for closeting,' says Mrs Frost. 'You jeopardise our position when you—'

'Are you finished here?' Angelica rises abruptly from the table. In doing so her hair delivers a soft clout to Mrs Frost's chin, but she affects not to notice as she whisks the powdering cape from her shoulders. 'Yes, I think I look very well. You have dressed me very fine. That is what you are good for. I go now to await my visitor.' She stops before the mirror, smooths her dress. 'Oh, by the by, I would have you pawn a gown or two. My sole protector keeps us so *very* comfortable.'

'You are vexed today,' he says.

'Aye, and what if I am?' She slumps on her sopha, picking at the varnish on its scrolled woodwork, and the light from the window touches one cheek but not the other. Now and then she turns her face towards the glass, a despondent little gaze that lingers on, and ends finally with a sigh, and which puts him in mind of Sukie when her friends do not call by for her. 'There is a great deal in my life that is vexatious.'

He shrugs. 'You may be as you are. I am not so cheerfully disposed myself.' And this is so. He slept badly. Since the *Unicorn* completed its creep along the west coast and struck out past Ireland, he has had no word from Captain Tysoe Jones. It being such an unusual voyage, he cannot guess when next he might have news, but the coldness of the winter has sown dreams in his head of crooked and cured mer-children: they squawk to him from dark cradles; when he looses their swaddling, he finds their little bodies crushed to a handful of dead leaves.

'What can be wrong in *your* world?' she asks.

'Well, what is wrong in yours?'

She scowls. 'No mermaid, for one thing.'

'Patience,' he says shortly.

'A virtue I have very little of, today.' She looks again towards the window. 'Forgive me, sir, I have a great deal on my mind. I am waiting for something – it may never transpire – but my fortune depends upon events that take place far away, which I can neither know anything of nor do a single thing to alter.'

'I have lived all my life that way,' he says.

She looks at him askance, purses her lips. 'Well, *I* am not used to it. If it don't happen under my nose, or by my own hand, why ought it to affect me?'

'Providence,' he shrugs. 'We live in a great world but may only see one tiny corner of it.'

'I cannot be at ease with it.' She begins to bite her thumbnail, then takes it from her mouth guiltily, and slaps a cushion instead. 'Why nothing in the meantime?' she demands. 'Can you not acquire me some little amusement *now*? No mermaid – why not the skin of a selkie? They can be got in Scotland very easy; there is nothing to prevent you.'

'Oh no,' he says, 'I could not give you that in good faith, for then the poor lady would never return to her kin.'

'*I* don't care,' she retorts. 'It's a luxury few enough of us have in this life.' A movement from the back rooms catches her eye and she breaks off; here is Mrs Frost scuttling through, clutching several gowns to herself, their skirts hung over one arm, their jackets the other. He sees the bright chenille border of the flower-garden Angelica wore when they met first. 'You see?' says Angelica. 'There go *my* sealskins.'

'What is she doing with them?'

Mrs Neal looks away. What expression is on her face he cannot see, but some of the animation leaves her body. 'Oh,' she says, and any light that was once in her voice is fading, 'they are to be laid up in lavender.' She smiles then, as if she has solved a problem, and returns to her seat. Her arms are spread on the cushions, wrist-upward: her skin is white and her veins are lilac. 'I have so many gowns this season,' she continues, 'I cannot fit them all in here. There is simply not enough room for all the luxuries I possess. Besides –' she tips her head back so her pale throat shows – 'I tire of them.'

Mrs Frost snorts, which he does not much like, but she is already out of the door. 'I am taking them to her uncle's,' she calls mockingly over her shoulder.

'Pay her no heed,' snaps Angelica. 'She is sent to vex me; or perhaps it is vice versa, she does not like me much of late.'

'I did not know you had an uncle in this city. You said you had none.'

She grimaces. 'It is a turn of phrase.'

He stops and thinks. 'Oh, I see.' He steeples his fingers. 'Are you comfortable in your household economy, Mrs Neal? Are you amply provided for?' He knows he should not have asked; so perfectly does her face close up that he would not have been surprised if it had been accompanied by the sound of a slammed door. Her body closes up too; she buries her hands under the fold of her shawl, but he can see the nervous movement of her twisting fingers. 'Forgive me,' he says. 'It was indelicate.'

'You would not have asked that of any other lady,' she says.

'No, I believe I would not have.' But is this not Mrs Neal's very problem? Since their last meeting he has been nagged by the thought of her as an ordinary woman, and once a girl as deserving of protection as his own Sukie, or Bridget, or any daughter of strait-ened means. She is a woman out of place, this Angelica Neal, a piece fallen loose from a great machine. Her concerns are not those of other women. 'I should not have opened my mouth,' he concedes.

'Aye, assuredly you should not.' She rises, dropping her shawl onto the sopha. 'I find I have forgotten an engagement, Mr Han-cock, and am very much delayed in my preparations for it. I must ask you to take your leave of me.'

But he does not move. He dares instead to keep watching her. 'No,' he says. 'You are distressed. What is your trouble?'

She shakes her head, but her lip is quivering and her eyes one wink away from overflowing.

'Now, come,' and he drops to an ungainly knee beside her couch. But Angelica has pulled down her chin, and her shoulders are quaking.

'I do not mean to cry,' she hiccoughs. 'Do not look at me, sir, I beg you – oh, pay me no mind.'

He cannot think what to say, and there is nothing to do but decently avert his eyes from her evident embarrassment, all the while patting her arm and hazarding expressions of bland comfort. 'I know,' he says, 'I know, 'tis a hard thing to maintain oneself in this world. A very hard thing,' until she wilts altogether, her back bent and her head in her hands, and her shoulders heave with awful sobs. 'There, there,' he whispers, placing his hand more firmly upon her sleeve. And while she does not raise her head, and her tears fall afresh into her lap, her hand creeps out from beneath the tumble of her hair, and rests, trembling, upon his own.

EIGHTEEN

There is a knock and the secretary of Mr Hammond, whose house party has been so sadly spoilt, puts his head around. 'Mrs Chappell,' he says, and bows. 'What news?'

'None,' she grunts. 'And there'll be none until I have finished interviewing my girl.'

'So make haste,' he says, darting a quick look at Elinor's tear-stained face. 'You must appreciate a situation of this sort is most distressing for all involved: not the atmosphere one wants, for a celebration. Puts a bad taste in the mouth.'

'It is hardly on me,' says Mrs Chappell. 'I have lost a valuable asset.'

'Quite so, quite so. But we will be expecting our money back.'

'Money?' quavers Elinor.

'Yes, miss,' says the secretary. 'Two hundred guineas. I've a good mind to ask for the entire sum returned, for there is no coming back from this: the week is ruined.'

'Now, now, no need, no need,' says Mrs Chappell. 'It may seem so now, but I shall send another girl – this will be swiftly forgotten, I assure you, there is nothing like a little music and revelry to restore good humour to any party.'

'Two hundred guineas?' asks Elinor in stupefaction.

'Vulgar, Elinor!' snaps Mrs Chappell. 'The money is the thing of least significance.'

'A hundred up front for her, a hundred for you,' says the secretary. 'And the same sum to be paid again if the thing went off to my master's satisfaction, which of course it has not. Well, I shall leave you to decide between yourselves how this may be made good,' and he brisks away.

As the door clicks to behind him, Nell turns to Mrs Chappell for verification, wiping her eyes with her knuckles. 'I had not thought it would be so much. Were we to see any of it?'

'The cost of living is very high,' says Mrs Chappell.

'Well! But two hundred apiece, surely you—'

'And it is brought no lower when girls make off with clothes that do not belong to them,' the bawd continues. 'What dress did you say it was? The white, with spangles? That alone cost me five guineas. Then petticoats, fifteen shillings; stockings, half a crown; then stays and shoes and shawl and pockets – what was *in* her pockets, by the by? Coins, I'll wager – to say nothing of her jewellery . . . it all comes to well over ten guineas' worth of apparel she has stole from me. Twice that, perhaps.'

'Oh, come, not *stole*,' says Elinor.

'Then what? She has taken what is not hers. Those clothes were my own property. Oh, this is a beast of a situation we find ourselves in: Polly was an excellent earner, and an asset to the house. How could you have let her get away?'

'I!' Elinor trembles. 'I never would have if I had known!'

'And I shall never find her on my own.' Mrs Chappell rests her chin on her fist. 'If she has made her way into the streets she may as well be lost for ever.' Then she raises her head to meet Elinor's eye. 'But with this man Hammond's aid . . . his father knows every constable in London.'

'What are you going to do?' quails Elinor. She wants very badly to go home. *Oh, Pol, you have brought great trouble upon us.*

'Light a fire under them,' says Mrs Chappell. 'Oh, dear! Don't start so! I mean figuratively. Have him come back in; I know how to persuade him to find her.'

Nell totters to the door, rather numb, and finds the secretary helping himself to the hothouse grapes piled without. When he comes back into the room, Mrs Chappell has drawn herself very upright: only Elinor sees the way her right arm, propped on the table, trembles to support her pose.

'Here, sir,' the bawd barks, 'tell this to your master: that I hold him responsible for the loss of an excellent servant.'

'Oh, when they wish to go, they find a way.'

'She has never expressed a desire to leave before. She was always quite content; Miss Bewlay here can vouch for that.' Elinor nods weakly, and Mrs Chappell continues. 'I cannot help wondering whether something untoward happened to her here.' She raises an eyebrow. 'There is also the matter of the items of valuable clothing she fled with, which it is reasonable to expect him to replace.'

'You cannot propose this is my master's responsibility.'

'Why not? It is due to his negligence that she has vanished.'

The secretary is baffled. 'Now, madam, she is *your* employee . . .'

She holds up her hand. 'I am not done speaking! I expect from Mr Hammond the full account owing on her; by which I do not mean only the cost of the items she took with her, or the sum he agreed to pay for her, but also the debts she ran up with me. Perhaps you do not apprehend that since this young woman came into my care two years since, I have clothed her and fed her, and trained her in every one of the arts that so delighted your master. You think all that can be effected at no cost to myself? You think I do this for the fun of it? Four hundred pounds I have invested in Miss Campbell's care and education, and not a penny of it has she paid back. So how will I recoup it?' Apprehending his expression, she shrugs. 'One of your young bloods would demand no less if I had mislaid one of his racehorses. How is't different?'

They stare at one another: the severity in Mrs Chappell's face is startling, her mouth hardened to a mere crease in her face, her small eyes very bright. Elinor, daring to turn to the secretary, perceives that he is not entirely composed; he turns his face away too quickly, and makes for the door. When he reaches it, and his hand is safely on its knob, he says, 'She is a servant.' Then, growing in bravery as he swings it open and sets one foot into the hall, 'Not even that. A whore. And if she has robbed you, well, you should have expected no more of her.'

Mrs Chappell does not so much as twitch. 'The debt is your master's,' she says coolly.

'Do you risk making an enemy of him? He knows the men who wink their eye at your disorderly house ...'

'On whose authority do you threaten me?' she asks. 'I am protected. Always have been.'

'I would not be so certain,' he says.

'If you can restore her to me, I shall have nothing at all to pursue,' says Mrs Chappell. 'You tell your master that. It may yet all come to naught.'

Elinor's heart is in her mouth as he closes the door behind him. She turns to the abbess, who leans more deeply upon the table, and closes her eyes briefly. 'He was extremely displeased.'

'Pah! And what does it signify? *He* don't make the rules.' She mops her brow with her scrap of handkerchief. 'All the great men know they are bound to please me more than I am to please them; there ain't a bawd in St James's who matches the service I provide. We are safe.'

'But what if—'

'No ifs!' Mrs Chappell's joints ache, and her chest is heavy. She admits to herself that this to-do has agitated her more than it might have were she a younger woman. *Is it possible I have overshot myself?* she wonders. *I am not as nimble in my mind as once I was.* 'Polly!' she sighs. 'I would not have thought it of her. Well, she was always saucy – never as biddable as I would have liked – but to have stole from me! Stole a gown! I would not have thought that of her at all.'

'She had no other,' wheedles Elinor. 'Pray, what was she to—'

'She was to remain in the house!' thunders Mrs Chappell. 'She was not to abandon my service as if she were no better than some wilful housemaid!' Her voice vanishes to a croak, and she subsides in her chair, her hand to her breast, panting painfully. Her face is ashen, her lips blued, and Elinor takes alarm.

'Madam!' She crouches beside her. The abbess's skin is cold and dewy, but her eyelids flutter over the rheumy orbs beneath. 'Do you need your salts?'

'Water,' she croaks, and Elinor pours it with terrible trembling, so that its dropples fall to the carpet and stain her slippers. Once Mrs Chappell has sipped, coughed, sipped and gulped, she looks a little better. 'I'll have no more of your worrying, miss,' she says. 'You are to go out of this room and make those gentlemen forget they were ever disappointed.'

'But Polly!'

'Leave that in my hands,' says Mrs Chappell.

'Will she be got back?'

'You assume we shall be so fortunate as to find her. If she has gone into the rookeries we'll not see her face again – and if we did she would be welcome in my house no longer. You would do well to forget she was your friend.'

He dreams, one night, of grey seawater, its surface leaping, its depth incomparable. Beneath its surface, very far below, he sees a black shadow, vaster than any thing he can even conceive of. Its scale is not of this world, it is bigger than factories or mountains, bigger than the growing ships that tower over his little Deptford home. The shifting tugging water obscures its shape, but its largeness is such that his breath aches in his throat and his fingertips tingle. And all the time it is coming towards him.

In his dream this dark creature rises and rises up to the surface, its pace stately but gathering speed, until its shadow is all that can be seen beneath the water. It must shortly crash through the waves, scattering white wings of foam in its triumphant upsurge into his own realm, to loom into the sky and block out the sun.

But before it does so, he wakes up.

It is morning and the room is full of pale light, the dream hanging upon Mr Hancock still, a heavy sadness across his chest and shoulders. He has seen his own smallness, the futility of all of his doings. He rubs his eyes, massages his sternum to ease the knot of grief that has formed inside him. When he sits up, he sees that there by his bed stands a grave pale boy of eight years old, his dark curls lying on his shoulders.

Mr Hancock cries out. He kicks the bedclothes aside. He reaches, grasps, his heart thundering. But nobody is there.

NINETEEN

'Mr Hancock?' Mrs Neal turns restlessly, and lays her face upon her arm. 'Were you ever in love?'

He tugs at his cravat. He feels that Henry has walked beside him all the day, and many hours after waking, his mind is still so distracted that the word *love* on the lips of a beautiful woman puts him in mind of nothing that it ought, but instead lays in his arms once more the weight of his little boy, Henry, as he had cradled him that one and only morning. The child was already dead at that time, his poor blood crisping at the jag in his head that the instruments had made. 'That is scarcely a thing to complain of,' the surgeon had said (not his fault – nobody to be blamed – they had paid for the best). 'If the infant had been any faster stuck I would have been obliged to bring it forth in pieces; be glad you've something to honestly bury.' And that was something to be grateful for, was it not, for despite his wound and his lips going greyer, and his tiny shoulder strangely crushed, this long-awaited Henry looked as perfect as any living child. Mr Hancock remembers Henry's shawled body in the crook of his arm as if he carried it there still: he thinks, *it will be the last thing I feel before I die.*

But he can say nothing of this to Angelica, who knows, after all, no atom of such suffering. So he knuckles his brow and, 'Aye,

296

yes,' he says, 'I had a wife. Mary was her name. That is a long time ago.'

'And what happened to Mary?'

He says not a word.

'Forgive me,' she says. 'It ain't my business.'

He is about to nod and turn his talk to other things, but then he thinks of how she had so unwillingly wept before him, the memory of which he has been holding at arm's length since last he saw her. He never speaks of Mary, certainly never of his son, but he has seen a tender part of Angelica Neal's soul, one she would not have volunteered to him, and it is in this spirit of transaction that he offers her his own story. 'We were married four years,' he says, 'and were very content, but we had no child, although we sorely desired it. And when she at last took one, there were no two more joyful people than we.'

Mrs Neal puts her fist under her chin, listening. It is too late for him to stop: he feels as the boys who line up on the jetty on hot days, to fling themselves into the still and tepid water. He remembers well how it was to jump; the moment his feet left the boards and the time stopped to nothing, and he knew that there was no altering his trajectory. His heart quickens. He has not spoken these words often enough for them to have lost their sting, and to recount his loss even at the distance of fifteen years is to relive it.

'This story does not end happily,' he warns her. 'Mrs Hancock was brought to bed and she laboured for days, but finally she was tired and could do no more. Perhaps she was too old.' He tries to smile. 'But women a good deal older than she labour safely every day of the week. Perhaps it was her physiology.'

'Some women are ill suited,' says Mrs Neal sympathetically.

'If I had known it! I would have put all thoughts of children away from me, and been grateful for our lot.' Poor Henry, whose face was swollen and cruelly bruised, his eyes closed in a perpetual frown, keeping to himself the secret of whether they were to be blue or brown or grey – were it better that he had never been conceived at all?

'Oh no, but you cannot have foreseen. Well, what happened?'

'There is no more to say. I buried my wife and my son – I am glad they lie together.'

'I had hoped the child had perhaps lived,' says Mrs Neal.

And where would you be now, Henry Hancock? A young man, slender like his mother, Mr Hancock thinks, and most assuredly with her dark hair, for he already had it on the day he was born. *Yes, he thinks, he would have gone to the navy,* and this is a happy thought, and proud. If he had lived and grown, he would not now remain at his father's side; the pain of parting would have been delayed, but never avoided. It may be that at this moment Henry Hancock is not dead but only very far away, with the breeze of a foreign ocean stirring those brown curls. 'Some say that in such circumstances it were better the child died,' he says, 'leaving me free to start my life anew.'

'Not I,' says Angelica. 'A living child is always good fortune.' She furrows her brow and casts the full light of her blue eyes upon him. 'These are very sad things that have befallen you.'

'No worse than anybody else's lot.'

'Maybe so; that is not to say it does not cause you pain.'

'I am advised to forget,' he says, 'but if I did not have the pain, I would have no memory of them at all.'

Her face is still cupped in her hand; she sits up straighter and says, 'Shall I tell you my opinion on it?'

He is never to hear it, for at this very moment the door flies open and all the room is taken up by the gentleman in the blue coat. He is very handsome. He looks at Mr Hancock and says only:

'Get out.'

'Georgie!' cries Angelica. 'What are you about?'

Rockingham seizes Mr Hancock by the arm and pulls him to his feet. 'Leave,' he says. His face is so close Mr Hancock can see the white cap of a pimple glowing on his chin. Turning back to Mrs Neal he says, 'What am *I* about? When you have brought a man in here?'

'I am doing nothing wrong! We are only sitting, only talking.' She looks to Mr Hancock.

'That's so,' he says. 'I meant nothing by it.'

'You give them your society!' he spits. 'That is how it starts, you told me so yourself.' He turns again to Mr Hancock. 'You fool. What do you think she can do for you?'

'I am leaving.' He backs from the room, hands raised. 'I am leaving, think no more of me.'

'And what have you to say for yourself?' Mrs Neal cries. 'Sending me no word – troubles that I was by no means prepared for – *you* who abandoned *me*!' She has begun to gabble now. 'So what can you blame me? Another soul to hear my unhappiness –' she darts a glance over her shoulder to Mr Hancock on the landing – 'which cannot be borne alone. Listen to me, sir, you and I have a great deal to discuss . . .'

As Mr Hancock retreats, the door to Mrs Neal's apartment slams. On the street he looks up again: her windows show nothing, but he thinks he hears her voice, talking anxiously on.

TWENTY

'It should not have been like this,' she says, composing herself, for if she is not conciliatory all must be lost. 'I had plans to celebrate your return, Georgie, you ought to have sent me word you were coming.'

He throws himself onto the sopha and it shuttles back some six inches with his weight. 'And give you warning?' he mutters, but the retort has no spirit to it. *Something is amiss,* she thinks. This is a knowledge she has held concealed from herself for some time; there is no disowning it now.

She comes to sit beside him but he looks up at her with such a peculiar expression that she stops short. 'What is wrong?' she asks, but before he can draw breath she stumbles on, 'If it is about the bills, I already know.' She takes her place next to him, but she feels at once that the small ways in which he holds his body and responds to her movements have changed. She cannot say it, but she knows. Still she blunders, 'But it will be all right. I am not angry. It was just a horrid – a very slight – *shock*. If you had warned me, I would hardly have been upset at all . . .'

'I am giving you up,' he says.

'No,' she says.

'It is hardly your choice,' he snorts. 'If I am leaving, I am leaving. It is merely a case of my walking out of the room.'

'But I . . .' She wishes now that she had not let Mr Hancock quit the room. Then he would have had no polite opportunity to say these words, or if he had exploded it would have been for another reason swiftly explained away; all would have stayed just as it was. 'About the money,' she ventures, 'we can find a way.'

He is shaking his head, and snorting as if she were absurd. She has never known such coldness from him. 'There is no other way than this. Do not reason with me; you will look a fool.'

'But how can you leave me?' she demands. She would like to choose the safety of rage, but she needs his favour too much to show anything but the most even emotions. She takes a breath, and touches her hand to his cuff: 'I am as good as your wife.'

Her fingers tremble there for one aching second, then two. It is all the sensation she has; she is praying that it may stay there for ever. But he draws his arm away.

'No,' he says. 'You are my mistress. And you are immoderate in your spending, and intemperate in your demeanour, and in short you have ruined me. I cannot pay the debts you have run up.'

'With your permission! It is *your* recklessness as much as anything . . .'

He stands. 'I need a woman with a fortune, not one who will leech me dry.'

'Please, George.' She lowers her voice. 'Talk to me. Is this your choice or your family's? Do they wish you to marry someone else? For you know that is not insurmountable; nobody is faithful now-a-days; you need not relinquish me.' He stares ahead, impassive; he has learned from Mrs Frost that Angelica cannot tolerate being ignored. She gabbles on, 'I shall make no demands on you. I shall not be jealous. We might carry on as we did before.'

'We might,' he says. 'If I were not sick of you.'

She can say nothing to this. Inside her there spreads a great emptiness, which is better perhaps than feeling. 'Then I have no argument,' she says carefully. 'I suppose your family will pay your debts.'

'As if it is any of your business.'

'They ought also to pay mine. You promised to keep me and you bade me pass my bills to you; I had no knowledge at all that I was living on tick.'

'They're debts in your name, ain't they? *You* take care of them. Do not tell me you have forgotten how.'

She does not remember what else he says. She is at one moment entirely numb, and also in agony, as if great fists were twisting at her viscera. She knows she follows him about the apartment while he collects the last of his possessions. Mrs Frost, returning from an errand, looks on impassively. It is she who sees him out; Angelica goes to the window and watches him as he strides the length of Dean Street. The flower-girls and drapers' assistants and beribboned whores approach and lay their hands on him, or walk alongside him a little way, but he never looks back.

She watches until he is out of sight, with a blacking at the edges of her vision and a rush of cold all across her body, as if she were drowning. She might be lost at sea; there is a great cold void beneath her, and she fears she is not strong enough to avoid being sucked under. *Am I dying?* It may be so. She closes her eyes and swallows hard; then she pulls away from the window and says aloud, 'No, no. This won't do.'

And so to action. She goes at once to her dressing table, and whisks open one drawer after another, to seek within them their finest pieces: the necklace of millefiore medallions; her golden arm-let; the earrings set with rubies. She takes out her patch-box and his snuff-box; she seizes the best of the candlesticks, and the books, and ransacks her box of lace to choose which cuffs and fichus she can best do without. She sighs mightily as she does so, for every scrap she seizes up is as delightful to behold as it was the day she chose it; the beauty of each stitched flower and star and swag is enough to make her ache. She had not tired of owning them yet; the glee that they are really hers has not abated, and yet she is packing them gently into a basket to be taken away.

'Eliza,' she calls, 'help me.' When Mrs Frost comes to the doorway she hands her the basket. 'Pawn it,' she says. 'Sell it. Whatever is best. And this. And this.'

'Is this necessary?' asks Mrs Frost.

'You keep the books! You tell me.' She is rummaging through a drawer full of fans, throwing them onto the carpet one by one without looking at them. Then she starts on the linens. 'They will call in their debts if they know he has left me, and I have no way of paying. It must be hundreds that I owe – thousands. There will be bailiffs.' She wheels around, her skirts heaving: her composure flees her. 'Must they find out? Perhaps they need not know.' She paces the floor, twisting her fingers relentlessly, and her speech ascends and ascends into hectic gibberage as she continues, 'Oh, perhaps if we ask him – a few weeks' grace – to let nobody know he does not protect me – he might find it in his heart, if he understood – I shall go away for a while – the countryside? – where?'

Her agitation is such that Mrs Frost becomes almost afraid; *she will do herself a mischief,* she thinks, and, to still her, seizes her first by the shoulders and then wraps her in her arms. Her body is rigid; there is panic in its every fibre. 'I think not,' says Mrs Frost gently. 'He will not help us any more. He is gone.'

Angelica clings to her for a short while and then breaks free, shaking herself down. 'Well, then,' she says with resolve. 'If you do not want me to go to prison, you will help me.'

'Surely there is *somebody* you can appeal to,' says Mrs Frost.

'*Who*, Eliza? I have no admirers left. I have given my attention to no one else, and now I –' her voice trembles and she gasps but does not sob – 'and now I am back where I began,' she finishes. 'Only a good deal stouter. And the line on my forehead is there all the time, and not only when I frown. I know how it goes when a woman my age is abandoned. The bailiffs come, and she must needs return to the nunnery to open her legs; and the men she gets are of less and less consequence each year that she ages, until she is quite abandoned, and ruined, ruined, ruined. Oh, Eliza! That cannot be my fate! Not so soon! I feel no older than fifteen – how have I come to this?'

'It may not be as bad as you think,' says Mrs Frost with distaste. 'If I take these things away, it will be in the faithful hope that we shall have it all back a month from now.' She is glad to see Angelica brought to her knees; it makes her feel far softer towards her. She is moved again to touch her; she smooths her friend's shoulders. 'All will be well,' she says. 'You are young yet; you are beautiful.'

Angelica knuckles her forehead. 'I fear I have mis-stepped. I am twenty-seven. If I were to have peaked, should I not have done so by now? Indeed, I was on a good trajectory. To have followed the duke with *Rockingham*, to have so misplayed my hand when I was most desirable – oh, I am a fool!'

Mrs Frost, however vindicated she may feel, betrays nothing of it. 'That young whelp is no one at all; an aberration you will recover from. The whole affair will be forgotten in six months. You will climb yet, I am certain.'

Angelica tries to smile. 'Thank you. My dear friend. My truest friend.'

'I hope I shall always be so.' A thought strikes her. 'I shall send for Mrs Chappell.'

'Oh!' Angelica feels in sore need of a mother – any sort will do – but she knits her brow. 'No,' she says. 'What a stupid idea; as if I would want her to see what has befallen me.'

'Perhaps she may help?'

'Perhaps she may dance a gavotte. Certainly not. The thing to do is make as little of this episode as possible. So he has tired of me – what do I care? Let the world see it makes no great difference to me.' She begins to survey the room more coolly, and rifles its contents for value with her eyes alone. 'After all, there is no need to strip the place bare,' she says. 'I shall be in need of a certain level of splendour, for my entertaining.' Her voice again falters with a new burst of shame. 'Only take these jewels I have set aside, Eliza. They are of greatest value. Go back to the jeweller and tell them – tell them I am displeased! The quality is not what I had been promised. Demand that they return what I paid.'

'But there is nothing amiss with them.'

'Better something amiss with the jewels than with me. I need the money. That might settle whichever bills come in first. Then we shall see what steps must be taken. And oh …' She reaches up to her throat and unpins the twinkling dart from her fichu. Her hands tremble, and she cannot look Mrs Frost in the eye as she turns Rockingham's first love token over to her. 'See what you can get for this.'

Her voice cracks and gives out. Mrs Frost has the decency to take the pin without a word, and quits the room as Angelica lowers herself onto her sopha and perches trembling there as if it were already no longer hers. She traces the place on its arm where an entire glass of ratafia was upturned. *I am not ruined – never ruined,* she assures herself. *There is always a way through.*

TWENTY-ONE

The alley is not three feet wide, and within it that air peculiar to the rookeries; cold, certainly, but palpably damp, and with a vegetable-ish smell to it, as if the hand of a drowned man had been placed across one's nose and mouth. There are other smells too; first the smoky runnels of old piss; then a dark foul scent, of things rotting unknown and unseen. Polly cannot think whether she is grateful for the concealing darkness or not; were it better to not see what dreadfulness lies so close to one?

Behind her the breath of this man who has claimed her next ten minutes; she is glad not to look upon *him*, some journeyman carpenter who stared at her coldly when she asked him the questions Mrs Chappell taught her. 'Flatter a man with conversation. Engage first his intellect; it will make you all the greater a prize. Any girl can fuck; that is not what he comes to you for.'

'Here,' he says in the darkness, and no more.

'Oh, but sir, I've a room just this way – would you not prefer a bed and a glass of something? I shall sing for you . . .' she trails off.

'What, and have you rob me? I know your sort.' He presses her up against the wall, and she shrieks before she can help herself. He claps his hand over her mouth as she begins to tremble, whispers, 'No, please, do not hurt me,' and bridles away with a cowering curl of the lip which is her best attempt at a smile. 'Forgive me,' she whispers, 'forgive me.'

His breath reeks so strongly of decay it were as if his mouth were a meat-safe that some sluttish housewife had abandoned a flitch of bacon within.

'Command first of all his admiration, and second of all his appreciation. Never let him forget what a rare and valuable item you are. Display yourself to your best; you are an envoy of Venus herself, and he cannot enter the temple without your first beckoning him in.' She need not conceal her own disgust, which on the one hand is a mercy; on the other, at Mrs Chappell's she never had so much disgust to mask. For not only does this man's mouth smell but his clothes do as well, of stagnant water and sour milk, gravy splattered from the crust of a pie, and his own dreadful odour, of an animal lived too long in one small space, turning around and around in its own sweat and filth.

The wall is lichenous and wet against the back of her head. She has lost count of how many men she has taken in this way, with a sort of numbed horror, thinking each time, *this will be the last one,* but the coins are like elf money, which vanishes from her hand not hours after she has earned it, for the sake of her daily needs. Bread crusts, candle stubs, gin, and it is all gone again, and she forced back onto the street for another round. How quickly it has become routine for her! Hitching up her skirt, she thinks, *this must change.* Simeon's note remains in her pocket, although she had determined not to look at it again. *After tonight I shall go out of the city at once. I am too easy to find here.*

He is unbuckling his trousers, and she makes to guide him but he pushes her hand away and, bracing one elbow across her chest, presses himself upon her. He holds her so hard against the wall that she thinks he will do her a mischief; his arm holding her shoulders too far back, bruising, she thinks, her breastbone. When she wriggles to seek greater comfort for herself, he curses and holds her tighter. Her head knocks against the wall behind her as he fucks; she would raise an arm to cushion behind it but cannot risk his patience. *And will it not be done in a trice?* she says to herself. *And then the sixpence will be my own.* And so she remains there, the back of her head bumping the wall, wondering how this all has come to be. When she walked from Mrs Chappell's care it was as if she – all unknowing – passed through a door into a world that, although it is like London, is nothing at all like London, and its natives nothing at all like the Londoners she knew before. *Some bewitchment,* she thinks, *a glamour.* The man is pounding at her faster now; she hears his teeth click with the determination and the breath all rough in his throat. He has seen his quarry and he is closing in on it. *Or perhaps* – and this thought comes to her with some surprise – *it was my old life that was the glamour. Feather beds and courteous gentlemen; hot milk for breakfast; riches beyond riches, there for the taking. How can that have been real? How could I have credited such good fortune?*

When he is done, she walks alone up the alley. Her knees feel wobbly and her sex hot and smarting; his leavings trickle down the inside of her thigh, warm at first but cold where the air begins to touch it. She stops to mop herself with her petticoats, and stooping smells the roe-and-fungus fug of strange men's spending, all crusting in the folds of her silver-spangled gown. *Perhaps I shall hang for this,* she thinks. *The petticoats alone worth fifteen shillings. Milk for breakfast! I must have been dreaming,* and her stomach rumbles. She stops to lean against the wall, bending as if she would vomit, but she only spits, and closes her eyes against the spinning world. To comfort herself, she reaches through her skirt and into the pocket that hangs upon her bare hip, to touch once again the scrap of paper that bears Simeon's neat hand. She had not thought to make use of it, but now, brought low, the mere kindness of his intentions is a balm to her, and she draws it forth, although it is too dark to make out those small and crooked letters of his. *Does he think of me?* she wonders, pulling her scanty shawl about herself, and then, as she returns to her place on the street, shaking out her shimmering skirts, *is now the moment I go on to the place he directs me?*

Ah! How many worlds there are contained upon the earth, and how many will she pass through before she reaches the next?

TWENTY-TWO

A week later, a remarkable letter is delivered to Mr Hancock's office, which has travelled by stage all the way from Oban. He tears it open all unsuspecting, to find the flamboyant hand of Tysoe Jones unfurling like creeping ivy all over the page. It reads:

Dear Friend,

Wonder of wonders! Forgive me if I do not stand on Ceremony, but I have such Marvellous things to tell you that I cannot think how to begin this Letter. I would prefer to plunge immediately into my Story – would you not prefer this also?

I made enquiries and befriended the crew of a whaling ship far north of the Scottish isles, and on my third day out with them we came upon a true Mermaid. She had been caught up in the Nets of a fishing-boat, which mistook her at first for a school of Herring, so vast and glinting was she. They hauled her aboard all silver & shining, but no sooner had they done so, then she burst the Net and sprang out again. They catching her once more, she shrieked up and down the Bay like a Mistral, dragging the Boat behind her, and she continued in this manner all through the Night, until finally at dawn she was exhausted.

*She is very large & fine, and nothing indeed like you have ever
seen in your life, and yet there is no mistaking what she is.*
    Yours,
    Capt Tysoe Jones

He thinks for a moment that he may faint, but then he recovers
himself. He does not stop to put on his hat, or file away his letters,
or check his diary. He simply rises from his chair, pulls on his coat,
and leaves the office.

He has never walked so fast in his life. He ought to hail a hansom
but it would save no time; the roads are crammed as ever. Instead he
weaves between wagons and sedan chairs and yoked milkmaids, trotting so vigorously he fears his heart will burst. He is taken unawares
by a half-wild pigling – a lean little thing with coarse black hair –
which gallops from a yard and into his knee: its weight sends him
reeling, and he staggers at the burst of pain, but the pig goes on,
shrieking hoarsely, leaving a smear of something foul on his breeches.

At Dean Street he seeks out Angelica's door, raising his stick to
rap against it. But something is wrong. The door stands ajar, and
from within emanates some sort of commotion: the pattering, it
seems, of anxious feet; raised voices. He pushes the door open and
steps into the little panelled hall. Nobody there, not even the
sharp-faced Mrs Frost, usually so officious about what visitors make
their way up the stairs.

He stands for a moment and listens. The running noise again,
coming from overhead, and Angelica's voice, cracked and hysterical:
'Oh! What shall I do? What am I to do?'

'Calm yourself!' comes Mrs Frost's voice, quite as shrill as
Angelica's.

'But he told me he loved me! He gave me his word!'

'And you did not secure an agreement – now that was careless,' says another voice, quite calm. Mr Hancock recognises it as that of Mrs Chappell.

A flurry of sobs, and Mr Hancock can hold back no longer; he hurries up the stairs. When he enters Angelica's parlour he finds it almost empty of furniture: the sopha is gone, and the wardrobes, the writing-table, the glasses, the golden mouse-cage, all vanished away. In its newly emptied state the room has a strange quality of sound in it: a hollow ringing. Here and there are little heaps of debris – crumpled dresses, piles of books – and Mrs Frost scuttles hither and thither cramming what she may of each heap into a large sack.

In the centre of the room stands Mrs Chappell, hands on doughty hips, looking down with distaste at Mrs Angelica Neal, who kneels at her feet in pitiful supplication. Her curls are knotted and wilting, and her chintz wrap falls open to reveal merely a chemise beneath it. Mr Hancock has never seen her in her loose clothes before: he tries not to stare, but he can see the outline of her bosom and her buttocks quite plainly through the thin fabric.

'Oh, Mrs Chappell, *dear* Mrs Chappell,' Angelica weeps, 'take me back to King's Place. I'll give you everything I earn. I won't begrudge you a penny. I'll teach the girls for you, anything. Anything! Only save me from penury!'

'I have no space for you.'

Angelica embarks on a fresh bout of sobs and wraps her arms around Mrs Chappell's calves. 'Save me!' she whimpers. 'You are the closest thing I ever had to a mother—'

'Oh, spare me!' the bawd snaps, shaking her off. 'Even if I were your mother, you have exhausted my patience. No, you have let me down too often; you have been petulant and unreliable. I cannot have you in my house: every man knows you spend twice what he can lay on you. I am only here to choose what of your effects I might take for myself, which will go some way – only some way – towards recompensing me for the money I laid on you. This is the last favour I will do for you.'

'. . . the money?' asks Angelica. 'But we are all settled. The duke, he bought me out.'

'The money I donated to support you these last few months, since Mr Rockingham could not.'

'But I do not . . . Eliza?' Angelica turns to her.

'We needed it,' says Mrs Frost helplessly. 'What could I do?'

'You accepted money from her?' And Angelica is quaking, her wrists and elbows gone to jelly, so that she subsides onto the floorboards. 'Oh, Eliza, how could you have done it?'

'With remarkable few scruples,' Mrs Chappell interjects with relish. 'And you owe me a hundred and twenty-five pounds, so you will appreciate my desire for recompense.' She shuffles into the bedroom, Mrs Frost close behind her.

Angelica's shoulders heave; she lowers her face to the floor and rests her brow there as if she were a Mosselman at prayer, and indeed she whispers, 'Oh God, oh God, what is to be done?'

At last Mr Hancock ventures, 'What has happened here?'

Angelica's head whips up. Her face is damp and blotchy, her eyes very swollen.

'Sir? Mr Hancock?' she stammers, wiping her nose on the back of her wrist. She tries to smile, and gabbles, 'Mr Jonah Hancock, the mermaid man, I was not expecting you.'

'What is afoot?'

She rises to her knees, hunting about for her handkerchief. 'To be frank, sir, I believe I am ruined.' She pats her face, then ventures a laugh. Mucus is trailing from her nose; she snatches it into her fist but more runs, and then her eyes fill up again. 'I have been abandoned by a – by a *most* inconstant friend, and consequently my rent has gone unpaid, and I have creditors all over town that I knew nothing of until this week. Even Mrs Chappell –' she stops to gulp breath like a landed mackerel – 'even *she* has contributed to my penury. Even Eliza. They have hurled me into the jaws of my debtors! They offer me no assistance.'

'Oh.' He dithers in the doorway. From the bedroom can be heard those two ladies picking over what belongings remain.

'There is a better bolster than that,' comes Mrs Frost's voice. 'You see, that one has a mend to't. But let me see, I believe there is another drawer of linen that may be of use to you . . .'

'There,' scowls Angelica, wiping her nose on a fistful of her own skirts. 'What d'ye think of that? I might be dead – the vultures. They waste no time.'

'Perhaps it were better if I left,' he says.

Her raw swimming eyes are fixed on her hands, which she clasps in her lap. 'No question of it,' she sighs.

He retreats onto the landing. Within, he hears the soft slump of her collapsing back to the floorboards, and then a string of half-suppressed sobs. He wrings his hands, agonises in the unlit passage. Then he returns softly to her parlour. He crouches down beside her and presses his own handkerchief, large and coarse as a sail, into her small fist.

'But who will look after you?' he asks.

She shrugs, her face quite buried in the folds of cloth. 'I shall fare quite well,' she says. 'There will be a way.'

'You mean there is nobody?'

'Look about yourself,' she says. 'Do you see any kind helper here? No. Rats from a sinking ship, sir. Even my faithful toadeater Frost has abandoned me.'

'And what of your debts? Who pays those?'

'Who but I myself?'

'But you have no means to do so.'

'Then I shall go to prison.'

He is a pecunious man; this is what it comes down to. The very word 'debt' strikes cold fear into his bones; it is a black spot, a curse, a dreadful reckoning. No man could hold his head up after being ruined, with everybody knowing what a judgement that was on him. Only death itself could be worse, and that by a slim margin. But it is not her fault; she has fallen out of the order of things, and the network of wages and inheritance that ought to keep her safe has failed her.

'I shall pay your bills,' he says.

She blows her nose fruitily. 'You will?' She nestles up against him, resting her head on his shoulder. When he puts his arm around her he feels again the delightful softness of her body, now freed from its stays. 'My debts are very large, sir. It was hardly of my doing.'

'It don't signify. I can pay.'

She turns her wet face up to his; she is presently unlovely, it is true, but the redness about her eyes brings up the sharp blue of her irids. 'Why would you do it?' she asks.

Because it is obscene to him for a person to be ruined twice over, and if he may put right this imbalance in the world it were all to the good. 'Ah,' he says. 'I have found you a mermaid.'

'A mermaid!' she scoffs, dabbing at her eyes and hiccoughing with the last of her tears. 'You have done no such thing.'

'I have.' He pulls out the letter and she frowns to read it in haste while he rhapsodises, 'It is a sign! Two mermaids in one life-time, what do you reckon the odds to be on such a thing?'

'It sounds an utter nonsense,' she snorts. 'What is this gibber-age he has written? I expect when it arrives it is no more than a little dead monkey, like the one *she* rented from you, and which brought us to all this.'

'No, no, nothing like that . . .' Although he can barely credit it; a living mermaid, slick as a fish, strong as a whale, no grotesque mockery but the beast of London's dreams, to be delivered to him and nobody else.

'Who is this gentleman? He dupes you, that is certain. This is the language of a mountebank, make no mistake.'

'I trust him implicitly,' Mr Hancock bridles. 'This creature is genuine, there is no doubt. And it will be *yours*.'

'Why would I want it now? This affair has quite ruined my appetite for mermaids.' Angelica gazes again across her denuded apartment, but catching sight of Mr Hancock's face which is all at once utterly disconsolate, she is contrite. 'Well, I don't care.' She sniffs hard, and sets about raking her fingers through her hair, until she looks altogether more herself. Her skin has lost its patchy look, and her eyes, although red-rimmed still, are bright and lively. 'The very thing I asked of you, you have delivered to me, although I had thought it impossible.' She squeezes his hand: her fingers are damp and hot. Then her bottom lip wobbles apparently without her bidding, and she chokes out, 'Take me away from here, I beg of you.'

'Yes, indeed, you must come home with me,' he says. Then hesitates. 'Do you know that my house is not grand? It is not at all like your current situation.'

'My current situation! What do I have? What part of it was ever mine? Please, please, if you are certain you would have me, I do not care where you will take me.'

Mrs Frost and Mrs Chappell return, their arms full of goose-feather pillows. They incline their heads to Mr Hancock: Angelica shoots a glance at them but remains on her knees, clutching Mr Hancock's hand. 'I have one request,' she says, 'but it is an important one.'

'Go on.'

She shoots a glance at her erstwhile friends, who stand in perturbation and disgust. 'I need you to marry me.'

VOLUME III.

ONE

February 1786

'Not possible,' snaps Hester Lippard, who is wearing out the wheels of her carriage, she must so often fly to her brother's house. She has not so much as removed her cape upon striding through his door, and remains immovable in the hall, which in-between place strikes him as a very unsatisfactory site for a row. 'She'll not live here.'

Mr Hancock is in jovial spirits, not easily damped. 'Good afternoon, sister. How do you today?'

'Ugh! Not a grain of contrition! I never had you for a rake, sir, but you have not only taken a whore, you have brought her under this roof and now lavish her with Hancock money.' She looks about herself, seeking evidence of his debauch: an abandoned garter, perhaps, or a brimming punchbowl. 'Fresh paint, do I smell?'

'We have undertaken some improvements.'

'Oh, she has got her feet under the table! What liberty to take with a house that is not even her own.' She is such a conduit of rage it is a wonder she does not catch alight.

''Tis my house,' he says mildly.

'Our father's! Our grandfather's! What are you thinking, to bring such a serpent into the nest? I suppose you would have Sukie ruined; that matters nothing to you.'

'There will be no ruination,' he says.

'You will ruin us *all*,' she pronounces with relish.

'Sister, you are not dependent on me.'

'I cannot hold my head up in society. I cannot! You go from bad to worse – do you think Mr Lippard's clients do not mark it? "He acquires a sideshow one day; a mistress the next. What sort of family do you come from, Mrs Lippard?" That is what they ask me. Furthermore, the lady our William has been working on these last six months – at considerable personal expense – has turned very cool towards him indeed, and I cannot but suspect that this is as a direct result of *your* conduct. And you know William's troubles in catching the eye of any lady, let alone one with two hundred a year settled on her; if she does not accept him after all this, the blame will be on you.'

'So be it,' he says.

'I beg your pardon?'

'If that is how you will have it, I cannot help it.'

'Oh, you are not one bit sorry! What has got into you?'

Angelica is upstairs in the bedroom, pinning closed the bodice of her plain rust-coloured gown, Bridget having quit her to answer the door. She has been in the house only ten days, but she has already overseen the repainting of the dark bedroom panelling, and replaced the curtains and the hangings of the ancient bed with new ones of shining moreen; fine, to be sure, but not extravagant. In the shadow of growing ships she is in the midst of a sort of convalescence, sleeping early and long, and eating plain and honest foods like an invalid or a little child. Her dress is neat; her countenance natural; she lives very quiet and blameless in this sturdy ship-built house. Nothing is as grand as she has been accustomed to, but none of it can be taken from her: sometimes she walks from room to room touching the panelled walls, the heavy furniture, the whorled glass in the windows. She touches them lightly with the tips of her fingers, and thinks, *this is mine, and this, and this.* She may walk from her parlour (she has had it done in almond-green) into Mr Hancock's counting-house any time it pleases her, and see his strongbox and his ledgers and his own buff-coloured back hunched over his desk, and although he does not make her feel the way certain other men have, it is sufficient that he is pleased by her; he wishes her there; he has chosen her as part of his home. The querulous agitation of her time in London has almost fallen away from her now; she has not felt moved to write to her friends, and she is grateful to have heard nothing from them.

From two flights below, she hears the hectoring tones of a woman's voice, and is in no doubt as to whom it might belong. She has not yet met Mrs Lippard, but from Mr Hancock's description and Sukie Lippard's demeanour she has surmised precisely what sort of woman she is.

'Sukie!' Mrs Lippard barks. 'Susanna!' and Angelica hears her stir in the parlour below.

I shall go down too, she thinks to herself, *and make myself agreeable to this lady.* She fluffs her hair and ties her apron, and proceeds downstairs. Sukie is coming onto the landing, book in hand.

'Is that your mother?' Angelica asks.

'How did you guess? Will you come down to meet her?'

Angelica is not yet decided about Sukie, and principally because Sukie seems not yet decided about her. She finds she can do nothing in the girl's presence without scrutiny; whatever she gleans from watching this newcomer butter a roll or read a book, shake the dust from her cape or close the shutters, she voices none of it. There is no mistaking she has seen more than Angelica had intended to show her, and this is discomfiting.

'What have you told her about me?' she ventures now. Sukie

walks before her down the stairs; Angelica cannot see her expression.

'I? I don't tell her a thing.'

'Sukie.' Hester Lippard stands at the foot of the stairs. 'You condescend to join us.'

'I was in the parlour,' says Sukie. 'The fire is burning. Why do you not come up?'

'Oh, may I? Dare I? Is't not *her* house now?' as Angelica comes into sight. She turns back to Mr Hancock. 'This is your jade? All these years you resist the expense and trouble of bringing a wife into the house and yet you will install a mistress?'

'She is not my mistress,' says Mr Hancock. 'She is my wife.'

Angelica has never seen the blood leave a person's face with such rapidity. Mrs Lippard, in the first place less than ruddy, becomes positively green. 'You are not serious,' she whispers.

Angelica descends the last few steps with her arms outstretched. 'Good afternoon, Sister,' she cries. 'I rejoice in calling you my relation. I have heard so much about you and it seems it is all perfectly true.'

Hester is not so numb as to demur a response. 'You are not much like your picture. But then you are clothed.'

Angelica knows about women and their empire-building. She knows also that a woman in perfect control of her fate never resorts to rudeness, and this gives her a small glow of satisfaction. She clasps Mrs Lippard's hand and smiles her most honeyed of smiles. Sukie is dumbstruck; she can only snigger with shock.

'I do not know what you are laughing for,' says her mother. ''Tis your portion he is throwing away; all the fortune your grandfather spent so long building up, and we shall never see any of it once *she* is done.'

'I have made a great deal of money on my own account lately,' interjects Mr Hancock.

322

'Whatever you make, she'll spend double,' snaps Mrs Lippard, and returns at once to her interrogation. 'Married when? How can this be?'

'Three days ago. Quietly, before breakfast—'

'Oh, this is too much. A *legal* marriage?'

'Aye.'

'I don't think so. No banns were read. I'd have heard of't at once.'

'Oh,' interjects Angelica, 'we wed by licence. So much faster. And how vulgar, to have one's private business broadcast for gossip.'

'Proud, are you, to have private business not fit to be spoken of in church?' Hester returns her attention to Mr Hancock. 'So she snared you well and truly! Paying honest money to rush this wedding through; I suppose you did not pause to wonder how many husbands this whore may already have.'

'Will you stand for that?' his wife demands. 'You'll let her offend my honour so?'

All the women stare at him: Sukie quite rapt – echoed by the half of Bridget's face peeping round the kitchen door – Hester and Angelica twins of female affront. He has been afraid of Hester's wrath since infancy, but that of his new wife is yet untested. Her eyes have a virago flash to them. Her hair seems to puff itself larger; her skirts prickle.

Hester, seeing his hesitation, warms to her theme. 'Where is her bridal portion? How is she a helpmeet when she brings you only debts? And you will raise up the bastard children you get on her from your pocket alone? How will—'

He has heard quite enough. 'No, I'll not stand for it,' he snaps. 'Mrs Lippard, you dishonour my wife. It will not do.'

'Oh! I like that! *I* dishonour *her*?' Hester affects to reel in shock; Angelica claps her hands and clasps them under her chin.

'And yourself too,' says Mr Hancock, spurred on by his wife's pleasure, 'speaking so rudely of a lady who has welcomed you into her home.'

A vein in Mrs Lippard's temple is twitching. 'So be it. If you won't eject this woman from the house, I have no choice but to remove my daughter from it.'

The entire company gasps.

'Now, Hester, there is no need for that.'

'Come, Sukie,' says Mrs Lippard as if he never spoke at all, making to seize her daughter's arm, 'I am taking you home.' Sukie lets out a little shriek and, breaking free, scampers back up the staircase. Mrs Lippard turns to Mr Hancock. 'She'll stay not a minute longer. I'll have no daughter of mine in so poisonous an environment.'

'She does not want to go,' says Angelica, but Mrs Lippard sets off up the stairs in pursuit of her daughter. A great clattering and scuffling ensues as Sukie ascends further; their skirts may be seen flapping between the banisters.

'Christ –' Angelica pats about her person for her fan; finding that she has none, she wafts herself with her hands – 'I had expected a quieter life for myself.' Upstairs mother and daughter can be heard squabbling furiously. 'Well?' Mr Hancock remains where he is, frozen it seems. 'Are you going to settle this?'

'This is not for me to meddle in.'

'Meddling! You are the man, are you not? Your word will settle this.'

He looks at her helplessly. 'Let her have what she wants.'

'And what about you?'

'Hush!' He squirms in his awkwardness. 'I'd not lose Sukie for anything, but my sister is not to be reasoned with at moments such as these. Far better to give her what she wants and retrieve the child another day.'

'I do not believe that can be the solution.' Down the stairs comes Mrs Lippard and Sukie weeping beside her. 'Say something,' hisses Angelica, but her husband tugs at his stock and utters not a word.

'Sukie,' Mrs Lippard sings out, 'mark this! He has chose the whore over his own flesh and blood. 'Tis hardly to be credited, but there it is.'

Young Sukie looks crushed as a lawn cap after a day at Bartholomew Fair. She cups her hands over her face. 'Do not let her take me away,' she says. 'Oh, Uncle, tell her no.' Bridget cannot restrain herself from bursting from the kitchen and forcing herself past her master into the midst of the scene; the girls cling to one another and lament in harmony, while Hester Lippard hauls dauntlessly at her daughter's arm.

'Uncle, Uncle, do not let her!' Sukie weeps, but it is Angelica who steps forward.

'Stop,' she says in a tone of great command. 'Stop now and listen to me.'

Mrs Lippard, affronted, turns to her. Sukie's spasmodic gasps are all that can be heard. 'What do you *want?*' asks Angelica.

'Why, to preserve my daughter's virtue.'

'That ain't in question.'

'I don't believe you. Besides, it is how things *look.*'

'Aye, appearances are everything. So how can we improve hers?' Angelica glances at her husband. 'Society is wont to overlook all sorts of failings and peculiarities where money is involved.'

'What are you suggesting?' he asks sternly.

'Aye, I should like to know,' says Mrs Lippard.

'Well, what is settled on her future at the moment? Do not tell me; you have, what, six other daughters? I expect they have already had the lion's share of what even the most dedicated of parents can afford to put by.'

'Her prospects are not as good as our eldest's were,' Hester Lippard admits.

Angelica shakes her head. 'And their husbands, I suppose, deplete your fortune by asking for more investment . . .'

'How can we refuse when they have our daughters, our grand-children to support?' laments Hester. 'Young men today manage their money very ill indeed.'

'And so what will be left for your Sukie?' asks Angelica. 'The future of the youngest child is always so tenuous, so vulnerable to Fate's caprice. I cannot imagine your guilt and trepidation.'

'But my brother has always sworn he will put in for her.'

'Aye, and that he will.' Angelica smiles with beatific cheer. 'I will make sure of it, I give you my word. In fact I can vouch for—'

'Mrs Hancock,' he warns her. He is shy of Angelica's lavish bent. What might she promise on his behalf?

'. . . well, I feel sure we can come to a very satisfactory agree-ment. Come, Mrs Lippard, shall we talk this out properly upstairs? You have been on your feet so long, it is time to sit down and take some refreshment at least. Bridget —' she perks an eyebrow at the girl, whose face is still buried in Sukie's shoulder – 'biscuits, if you please. And hot water to the parlour. Sister, would you fol-low me?'

And in the almond-green-painted parlour, at the brand-new tea table with its pristine little tea bowls, these ill-matched sisters-in-law talk out every possible inch of Sukie's bridal portion and her illus-trious future, while Mr Hancock sits by with his books and his pipe, nodding to their requests or drawing his brow into a frown as he scratches out more numbers. Mrs Lippard laments her woes and Mrs Hancock soothes her.

'Oh, I know, I know – a dreadful state of affairs – how you have borne it so long – but this generation is so different – I'd never have had your patience, Mrs Lippard, certainly I would not.'

Once they are finished it is agreed that Sukie Lippard will be a great deal richer than she had ever hoped to be.

'As to her education . . .' says Angelica.

''Tis done,' says Mrs Lippard. 'Her school could do no more for her.'

'I learned nothing,' growls Sukie.

'You read every book they had.'

'If I had known there were so few, I would have read slower.'

'Well, book-learning is not very useful,' says Angelica, 'and easily faked when the effect is required. I thought more that I would engage a dance master. Her deportment, Mrs Lippard, shows promise: I feel her walking and general grace of movement could come on considerably with very little encouragement. And a singing teacher too, and let us not have her neglect her pianoforte, for that is where so many girls betray their lack of polish. One always wants a Frenchman for music lessons. Leave that to me, leave that to me, I know people.' She leans back in her chair, eyes bright. 'Is your mind any more at ease?'

Hester Lippard has begun to convince herself of the advantages to keeping Sukie in her brother's house. To be sure, the girl has plenty more to learn, and Mrs Lippard has not the time to teach it all to her. And she hates to see any child of hers underemployed, when there is work for them elsewhere; and what would she do with Sukie under her feet in Southwark; and she has not even considered yet the expense of laying another place at the table when she already has sons and daughters-in-law and apprentices and servants to feed.

'But her moral education. Her *spiritual* well-being,' she hazards. 'The child's soul . . .'

'Fortuitous we are so well placed for two churches. Not to mention our Quaker brethren, and I declare I never knew such an infestation of Noncon tub-thumpers as I find here. Her soul will be spoilt for choices.'

'And *you* . . .'

Even now Angelica does not lose her composure. She tips her head and smiles. 'I understand your concern, Mrs Lippard. But look at me.' She gestures to her plain gown, her unpowdered hair, her entire cleanliness and delicacy. 'Trust your eyes, madam, you see I am not so unlike you. And even a Magdalene can be redeemed. Say, that will be a fine lesson for her soul.'

Mrs Lippard, looking at her obediently, is filled with suspicion. But then she is suspicious also of many of the women she knows. And if Sukie were to be removed from this house, her means of intelligence would be vastly diminished.

Yes, it is better to arm oneself with knowledge. Sukie is hardly in harm's way. She is not starved or beaten; she has a room of her own and an opportunity for a comprehensive education. As for what she might see or hear in the home of a renowned harlot, well. Children are robust. When one tots it all up, it would be the crueller thing to deny her this opportunity.

Mrs Lippard concludes that her daughter has the moral integrity to withstand temptation and debauch. One might even consider it a test; if she falls, well, that is an indictment on her inborn moral weakness, from which no body could save her.

'She'll stay,' she says. 'But if I hear one thing that is not to my liking . . .'

'You will not,' Angelica assures her. 'We are a family of scrupulous morals. You will not regret this, madam, we will make a triumph of the child.'

*

Mr Hancock is somewhat surprised by his niece's subsequent demeanour towards him. He has never been so out of Sukie's books before, and is chilled by the glower she fixes upon him before retiring to her window seat, never to speak again all evening. *She thinks I did not stand up enough for her*, he frets. He tries to broach the subject with a jovial nudge in the ribs: 'Well, 'twas all to the good in the end, eh?' but she does not dignify him with any response at all.

'I wish she did not take it so hard,' he says to Angelica when they are in their bedroom. 'She acts as if I threw her out.'

'You responded very poorly indeed,' says his wife, tucking her thickly plaited hair into her nightcap. 'I was positively ashamed.' She puts her hands on her hips, but there is no anger in her strictness, and her body most inviting where her chemise strains across it. 'You are not to go on in that manner any longer. You told me, before we married, that you were determined to protect Miss Sukie, and have no misfortune befall her.'

'Aye, indeed I am.'

'You did not protect her today.'

He sighs. 'My sister is a remarkable difficult woman. If I give her her own way, that is not to say I have capitulated to her.'

'Tsk! Hark at yourself.' She climbs into bed beside him, and after a moment he turns to her admiringly.

'Indeed, Mrs Hancock, you may effect all sorts of things that I, a man, may not.'

'Huh. And think what you may do, that I may not.'

'You have a delicacy to you that I cannot emulate, and an understanding. I did not see Mrs Lippard so placid as she was today in many years. I am glad to have you here.' Indeed, he thinks, it becomes clearer by the day that he ought to have had a wife years ago. It seems to him that what they achieve together is much more than double what they might alone.

'Oh, I am accustomed to her sort,' says Angelica. 'It is easy to please her – every body wants the same thing, when it comes to it.' She bites her nail and wriggles deeper under the covers. 'But she was right on one count, sir: you did choose me over Sukie, and I wish you had not.'

'You are my wife, and she is not even my daughter. If her mother wished to remove her, what was I to do?'

'The child has been moved about according to convenience for years, I believe; she ought to have one place where she lives and is part of the household.'

'Soft-hearted! If there's work to be done in one house and she sits idle in another, where is the sense in it? Until she has a family of her own, she must make herself useful in this one.'

'But *you* are soft-hearted,' says Angelica, nudging herself beneath the crook of his arm. 'I do not think you would be without her.' She will not confide in him that she needs Sukie very much; that the girl knows a great deal about the running of a house while she herself knows nothing at all.

'But what of your promise to educate and refine her?' he scoffs.

'An investment. The cleverer she is the better she will marry. Good returns, one day.' She is yawning now, her head a weight she is less inclined to hold up. 'I shall find tutors for her.'

He hesitates. The cat creeps from beneath the bed and springs up upon it; she wades across the bedclothes at their feet. 'Not the – not the same ones as teach – as teach Mrs Chappell's charges?' he asks nervously.

The cat is turning round in circles, kneading the counterpane, and Angelica feels the spirit of Bel Fortescue rise up in her: *ain't it all to the same end?* Instead she shakes her head. 'You've nothing to fear, sir. Here –' and rolling over turns her face frankly to his – 'you did a fine thing today; you defended your household. Eventually. Is that not an auspicious beginning to our marriage?' This she means most sincerely; it is a novelty and a relief that the man who now keeps her refuses to deny her. She could not have borne another turncoat of Rockingham's sort. She clasps his hand above the covers and pats it gently; they smile at one another, the very picture of mercantile happiness. 'Let us waste no more of the candle,' she says.

TWO

March 1786

It happens that a gentleman named Mr Brierley is one day caught in flagrante with his horse-boy, or some say his horse, but either way such prurient interest in the dealings of strangers has no place in this story. It only signifies at all because after this Mr Brierley hanged himself, the extent of his debts was revealed, and his widow put his house and all its contents up for sale for a very reasonable price. This news catches the ear of Mr Hancock as he goes about his business one morning.

'I shall buy it for you,' he says to his wife at breakfast.

'Oh no,' she says. 'Not on my account. Not for me.'

She is remarkable pretty, he thinks, pink-cheeked and plump and comfortable in her sprigged white morning dress, and her habits are pretty too, for after his morning's work she has him join her in her bedroom at ten or eleven for tea and hot rolls. He sits gingerly on one of the spindly chairs she has had brought in, with his legs splayed out one on either side of the tiny round table, and holds his tea bowl between finger and thumb, while Angelica – not long out of bed – helps herself to butter and marmalade. Breakfast is a novelty for her, she rarely having risen before noon in her old life, and he likes to watch the seriousness with which she eats warm bread and cold preserves.

'I promised you better,' he says. 'I did not mean you to live in Deptford.'

'Well, I am content.'

'And for Sukie —' who has not joined them; who is still, in fact, surly about him — 'we must increase her opportunities to meet fine people and cultivate herself.' Privately, he is anxious that now her head has been turned with Angelica's promise of dancing lessons and French tutors, his niece will be satisfied with nothing less; he furthermore feels a certain guilt that he did not think to offer her such things himself. 'We can do better,' he says, 'and we ought. I am not what I was, Mrs Hancock. I am a landowner now, and a land-lord: my properties in Mary-le-bone go up at such a pace that I may soon remove myself from the business of the city entirely. 'Tis absurd,' he persists, 'for a man of my fortune to continue to live in a house like this, and more so now with a wife such as you. Every day I look at you sitting by the fire and I say to myself, a beautiful gem needs a beautiful setting.'

'Oh, go on with you. I told you, I am perfectly content.'

'Contentment is a start,' says Mr Hancock, 'but I shall make you *happy*. I shall give you everything you want.'

'There is no such thing.' She is buttering another roll. 'There is always more to want.'

He is not sure what to reply. He smiles with his mouth half-open like a big dog confused by its mistress's command: he waits amiably for her to say something more intelligible.

'And how can I believe a thing you say,' she teases, 'when you have never yet produced the mermaid you promised me?'

'You are impatient. The mermaid is impending. It is being brought home aboard the *Unicorn*.'

'And where is the *Unicorn* now?'

'Unaccounted for,' he admits. 'But this is not concerning. It was an unusual voyage for Jones. He must be on the home stretch by now.' He must be, else where could he have got to?

'Mermaids wreck ships,' she says.

'Don't say such things,' snaps Mr Hancock, rapping hard on the table. 'Even in jest.'

'Oh, don't look at me so, you great thing. So I never had my mermaid, well, I never was Queen of France either, and yet here we are doing quite well for ourselves. That ship will come safely home, and whether it has a mermaid on board or no, it hardly signifies. I have married you after all. You buy a house, sir, if you wish, and I shall come with you and be very happy in it, I am sure.'

'Sure! *I* have never been surer,' he says, perking up. 'I think you underestimate how much you will like it.'

She raises a hand to quiet him. Butter glistens on her wrist. She is frightened by strong emotion; the word *happiness* frightens her, the way *love* does. She wants nothing so volatile.

'We must live within our means,' she says.

'That ain't for you to worry about.'

'Please, Mr Hancock. Do not get into debt. I've no need for grandeur; if we are to find a new house, let it suit us just as we are.'

'You are a most sensible woman.' And what a pleasant surprise to him is their harmony. The texture of those early days with Mary, which he did not know he had forgot, comes rushing back to him of late: it is the sensation, most of all, of not being habitually alone. The absent-minded reaching of her hand to his; the quiet clearing of her throat heard from another room; the half-surfacing from sleep when she rises to piss in the night. And having a listener, to hear a joke or trouble over a problem, and always take his part. Angelica is not Mary; nothing like; but the many acts of being a husband to this second wife remember the first to him, and make her vivid in his mind again.

There is a tap on the door and Bridget puts her head round it.

'A letter here for you, missus,' she says.

'For me? Not for Mr Hancock?'

'For you.' Bridget brings it to her. 'There is a boy outside awaits your reply.'

The paper is heavy and stiff, impossible to stuff into a pocket and forget about. Angelica brings it up to her face to better inspect it. 'I do not recognise the seal.' She slides her thumb under it. 'This is unusual. Who is writing to me?'

Her heart makes a little squeeze: what if it is somebody from her past, a man, what if it is her George (*her* George! Her *George!*), what can he want with her, oh, what does he say? Bridget is hovering with idle interest; Mr Hancock is staring out of the window and tapping his teeth, but surely he must see any moment . . .

My dear Girl,

(But the writing is not his; it is rapid and neat and free of error. The creamy paper shows neither blotch nor smear. This is not young George Rockingham's work.) *Forgive me my long silence. I think of you often and fondly, and now find myself at leisure to visit you. If it be agreeable to you I shall arrive at four o'clock today for Tea.*

Your old friend,

Eliza Frost

'Mrs Frost.' The words tip out of Angelica on a great exhale. 'Mrs Frost has written to me.'

'Is that so?' says Mr Hancock.

'She puts her address as St James's, look. I think she will have very easily got herself a good position. What would you wager? That she is a housekeeper now? That is a job to suit her.

I wonder if her employers know she is using their boy for her own errands.'

Angelica now being a wife, with all the necessary equipage, she keeps a silver pencil chained to her waist. Licking the nib, she hesitates.

'What shall I say?'

'Beg pardon?'

'She wants to visit me this afternoon. What shall I tell her?'

'Well, tell her yes.'

'She never wrote to me before.'

'Perhaps she was not at liberty to do so.' Mr Hancock is not paying much attention. Angelica swallows to shift the bitter taste in the back of her throat. *Why now?* She puts her pencil down.

She has a half-feeling, a bad feeling. If she were able to pin this feeling down and regard it properly, she might see that the thought of seeing Mrs Frost makes her nervous. But Angelica's head is full of many feelings that she is unable to inspect.

She picks up her pencil again. Aloud, she says, 'I would like to see Mrs Frost again. She was my dear companion. She understood my hair.'

THREE

Mr Hancock meets with Mrs Brierley's agent on the edge of Black-heath, a wind-churned yellow plateau that drops away into the trees towards Greenwich. 'Fashionable,' remarks the agent, who has heard of Mr Hancock and believes he has identified him as a man out of his depth.

'Very fashionable,' Mr Hancock agrees, 'which will please my wife. She likes to be in society.'

'I daresay,' murmurs the agent; adding with absolute courtesy, 'The barracks are only across the heath.'

Does Mr Hancock hesitate? Perhaps his attention is only plucked away by the flight of a jay from one tree to another. For a moment his eyes track it, and then his big red face crinkles with pleasure.

'Such unspoilt countryside,' he remarks. 'Very pleasant. Very fine.' He stands for some moments looking about himself, with his fists wedged in his pockets, the wind whipping at his old stuff jacket. Then he turns his eyes mildly back to the agent. 'Let us see if this house is fit for Mrs Hancock. Lead the way, sir.'

They go through the gate and up the drive. The house Mr Hancock will buy is white and square, with five bays most regularly spaced. The agent means to open the front door with a flourish, but the lock is stiff and the hinges in want of oil, and after a struggle he manages it with more of a clatter and a heave. He ushers Mr Hancock into a large atrium with a chequerboard floor and dove-grey panelling. If he had hoped to dazzle this drab, paunchy man, he must be disappointed, for Mr Hancock goes undazzled: he follows his guide through high-ceilinged rooms, their steps loud amongst the dust sheets, and is inscrutable.

'Elegant proportions,' the agent prompts him from time to time, or, 'No expense spared. *À la mode, à la mode,*' but Mr Hancock knows this already, and at any rate is not very interested. He remembers Angelica's instruction – '*just* as we are', blotting the butter from her wrist – but he cannot help but inspect the house as he would some consignment of Macao porcelain: not as a consumer but as a gatekeeper. In such a situation, Mr Hancock's first thought is never, *do I like it?* but only, *is it correct?* And since he sees that it is indeed correct, that this house – with its library, its stables, its six fine bedrooms, not to mention the fleshy ladies painted on the music-room ceiling – is exactly the sort of house Angelica Hancock, the wife of a rich gentleman merchant, might be expected to own, this leads him to his next question: *is it quality?* He taps away at the skirting boards and gets down on his hams to inspect the parquet, and he asks tiresome questions that the agent cannot answer. 'The marble, it's Italian? What workshop made the bedroom set? Will these stains come out?'

'We might offer you a good price for Mr Brierley's horses and phaeton,' says the agent recklessly, but Mr Hancock grunts, 'Yes, yes, we shall need those,' and goes back to checking the French windows for draughts. 'I hope the kitchen is well appointed. An unhappy cook is a bad cook.' This pearl of wisdom is one of Hester's.

Finally, they process through the garden-room doors to the steps at the back of the house. It is a cool bright day but the marble has taken the sun, so that a warm haze wavers around Mr Hancock's stockings and brings out the sweat in the crooks of his knees. The lawn slopes steeply away from the house until it is swallowed up by trees, and the view towards Greenwich – of treetops and fields – is hazy and blue-tinged. On the horizon, the Thames glitters, white sails puffing across its surface as vague as angels.

'Well?' says the agent.

'It all seems in order.'

'I might direct your attention to the folly,' says the agent, pointing to a tiny Palladian temple that crouches half-concealed by the underbrush. 'Not just any folly,' he continues, 'for once inside – no, I shall show you. Come.'

The grass is soft and dense under Mr Hancock's boots. It is the correct type of grass, he observes, not prickly and faded such as animals are grazed upon, but lush as new-dyed wool. For a moment he sees it lapping a child's bare feet. 'What grass is this?' he asks. 'Where can the seeds be got?'

'Why, only grass,' says the agent in surprise. He must not know the other sort: for him, all grass is for lounging on. Nobody has tended to it for some time, and as the lawn inclines towards the folly's shaded corner the grass grows longer, closing with a velvety swish around the men's ankles, still earth-cold at its roots, so Mr Hancock's shoes come up stained with dew and mud. What he sees, in his mind's eye, is a child's feet – running feet, running under the hem of a white nightgown, running alongside him through the hissing grass. He hears a little gust of excited breath, and catches the flash of rosy toes, and thinks, although it has never occurred to him before, *this is the life I might have given my Henry.* In the other version of his life, in a garden like this one, a child is hurtling down the hill and into his arms: he feels its meagre weight thud into his chest, its hot cheeks against his face, its delicate ribs and pounding heart against his palms.

And then he realises, *it is not too late.* This ghost of a moment is not one that is lost, but one waiting to happen. He has a wife, does he not? He has a fortune, and soon he will have a fine house. Why, then, is the possibility of a child truly so unreachable? *It is all before me. It has been waiting for me here all this time.* This is what Mr Hancock is thinking as the agent leads him between slender Doric pillars and across the threshold of the folly.

It is musty inside, with the dense damp cold of a place that rarely sees sunshine. The crumbs of last year's dead leaves are accumulated in the corners and against the legs of a large stone bench. The floor-tiles are cracked and dirty, and the seashell-shaped niches that line the walls are empty, save one, where a trapped gust of wind makes the bleached vertebrae of a pigeon chatter like teeth.

'It wants a good scrub,' said Mr Hancock. 'Is this what you brought me to see?'

'Certainly not, sir. There's more.'

And indeed there is, for behind the bench is an alcove, and in the alcove – black with soot and gauzy with cobwebs – is the entrance to a tiny spiral staircase.

'Is it the coal hole?'

'No, no. This, sir, is the Curiosity.'

'The Curiosity?'

'An oddity, merely. Something to see. Go on, sir.'

The stairs, vanishing into darkness, are narrow and uneven. There is a smell of wet stone. 'You want me to go down there?' Mr Hancock asks.

'You've looked over the rest of the place thoroughly enough,' says the agent balefully. 'I thought you would want to see it. It is the *only* irregularity in the whole property.'

'Very well, very well.'

The agent rummages through his pockets with little urgency before producing, from one, a tinderbox, and from the other, a stump of tallow candle. He hunches over this equipment and huffs, his hands cupped around it as if concealing a secret. Once he gets a light he holds the candle up in his fingers, inspecting the flame. 'That will do,' he says. 'You'll not need it very long. Go down and take a look.' He puts the candle stub into Mr Hancock's hand, and propels him to the top step. 'Excuse me if I do not join you. It is not very clean.'

The extra light does not reveal much: the stairs creep steeply out of sight between walls and ceiling daubed with rough plaster, which as he descends the first few hesitant steps gives way to – what? Lumpy medallions, as if the wall were built from flint, or is it – no? – yes? – seashells. Yes, seashells indeed, caked with dirt, and when he buffs a little away he sees that they are not exotic specimens, not worth displaying, but mussel shells, cockle shells, oysters and winkles, the leavings from a thousand humble dinners. The next thing he observes is that these are not haphazardly jammed into the plaster, but carefully arranged: concentric circles of mussel and cockle and mussel again; chevrons and stripes and rosettes. The stairs are narrow and uneven, so he feels hobbled: he presses himself against the inside wall, fingers spread helplessly as he lowers his feet out into the darkness, groping for the next step if it exists, if he can trust it with his weight. Shale slithers under his feet: for a moment he loses his balance and tumbles, his heart leaping into his throat as he sees his own death rise up to meet him. He had not expected it to be so soon. He had not expected to come to it with such terror.

But then he lands again, his backside coming down hard on the edge of a step in a burst of pain: he bounces off the wall and down the flight to land on a bare stone floor. The silence is extraordinary, as complete and as elemental as darkness, but he has seldom been more painfully certain of his own corporeality. After lying flat on his back for a few seconds at the foot of the staircase, he fumbles and staggers and creaks to his feet. Nothing broken, although he can feel the cloth of his breeches flapping around his right knee, and subterranean air cold on the raw skin beneath. His knuckles, too, are smarting, and when he brings them to his mouth they are sticky and taste of iron. He has heard of the agonies of hellfire, but never an eternity of grazes. Purgatory would be the likeliest place for skinned knees, but he does not believe in purgatory. *If I were dead,* he consoles himself, *I would be more certain of it.*

The candle is no longer in his hand, and yet as he regains his bearings he finds he is able to see a little. A greenish glow illuminates the brick floor and the walls all encrusted with shells, arranged into the outlines of urns and lions, acanthus fronds and fish-tailed women. Such a peculiar light, though, like nothing he has ever seen. It emanates from somewhere to his left, maybe thirty feet away, and despite the pain sparking from his tailbone, he begins to move towards the archway from where it seems to him to leech out into the dark. He is at first afraid to leave the foot of the stairs, his route back to safety, but danger occurs when one walks into darkness, not away from it, and as he passes into the next chamber he finds it identically adorned, but lit just a little brighter. Light spills from the next archway. And so he goes on. It is startlingly silent under the ground, the sound of his footsteps not quite his own. The air is thick and heavy, but stirred by little currents of cold air. And on he goes.

There are four chambers in all, with vaulted ceilings encrusted with some queer rugged rock, and shell-encrusted walls, and each is a fraction brighter than the last. In the final chamber he comes upon the source of the light: it flickers softly up the far wall, spreads and trembles across the floor. It expands across the darkness in little semicircular flutters, which grow out of one another, expand and fade.

What can it be? It is almost beneath his feet now. The air about it is particularly cold.

'God's wounds!' comes the voice of the agent, who has finally followed him down. 'Do not fall in!'

'Fall in?'

'Fall into the pool. Don't fall into the pool. Do you not see it?'

'Oh. Of course I do. I do see the pool.'

He perceives it clearly now: a black wedge of water dug into the black floor of the grotto, rippling with a very faint light all of its own, converging into stars that sway and shiver and then disperse.

'What is this?' demands Mr Hancock.

'This is your folly,' said the agent.

'I beg your pardon?'

The agent's expression is that of a conjuror whose favourite trick has fallen flat. '*Your grotto,*' he explains. 'A shell grotto. It comes with the house.'

'This!' Mr Hancock gestures to the pool, almost wordless in his confusion. 'How is this done?'

'I cannot say, sir. I am not an engineer.'

'But ...!' His hand traces the weird flickering light up the wall. The agent shrugs.

'I do not know. It is ingenious.'

'What is it all for?'

'It is not *for* anything.'

'It has no function? There is no reason for it?'

The agent sighs. 'Mr Brierley was a person full of curiosity, and addicted to amusement and novelty,' he explains slowly. Mr Hancock's face is blank as a pudding. This ink-stained man, who demanded a yardstick so that he might measure the bedrooms, cannot perceive that sometimes a thing's beauty is in its very use-lessness; he utterly lacks the genteel instinct to own something simply for the pleasure of calling himself its owner. 'Ask your wife, sir,' says the agent. 'Your wife will understand perfectly.'

But Mr Hancock himself understands. His wife – yes, she is his. The house, aye, will shortly be so. The child he dreamed of, indeed may one day be flesh. But if this grotto is also to be his, he ought to take it as a very particular sign. A slow and wondering smile crosses his face as he realises that it has been vouchsafed for one reason and one reason alone: he is also due a mermaid.

FOUR

Deptford, at the foot of the hill and on the edge of the water, is not fresh and wind-tossed but chilly and damp, and in the Hancock house the cold lingers in the corners, seeping through the floorboards and collecting in empty rooms the way cobwebs will. Mrs Hancock has taken herself into the kitchen to keep warm, pulling a shawl around her shoulders and dragging her chair right up to the fire. She stretches her legs towards the warmth so that her honest camlet skirt rucks up around her calves; and her stockings, clean enough and only slightly darned, twitch with the contented wiggling of her toes. She is knitting a little piece of lace, nodding over her work with her lips pursed, and as she tips her head forward it might be observed that on the nape of her neck, between her plain lawn collar and her plain lawn cap, a few strands of golden hair drift in the updraught. Other than this, there is little to identify her as Dean Street's brightest diamond, except for the startlingly poor quality of her knitting.

Now, as Angelica sits by the fire she thinks, *Eliza will be pleased to see what I have made of myself.* Sensible Mrs Frost will approve of Angelica's modest clothes and quiet industry. *I am comfortable,* she imagines telling her. *I feel very much myself.* For although she is the least self-conscious she has ever been in her life, Angelica has a feeling that her errant trajectory has at last converged with its intended course. Anybody observing her at this moment would immediately apprehend that she was once a rector's daughter, or if not a rector's daughter then the child of a gentleman farmer, or the better-regarded of a flourishing town's two tailors, for while she is unwilling to cast her mind back to her origins, not one fibre of her body has forgotten them. She sits like the middling-class wife she was born to be, industrious even in repose, earnest and calm and scrubbed.

'No need to change my dress,' she says aloud to the girls, absorbed in the industry of the kitchen. 'No need to stand on ceremony.' She looks forward to leading Mrs Frost around her house: kitchen and parlour, counting-house and bedroom, over which she alone has oversight. How very neat it will all be, how Mrs Frost's face will be wreathed in smiles. *I knew you would do well, my dove. I knew you would come right.*

'Are the stairs swept?' she asks Bridget. 'Have you stoked up the fire in the parlour? I want it welcoming for our visitor. Go now! Go!'

'And what am I to do?' asks Sukie crossly. 'I am a lady of this house too. If you have a fine visitor for tea, I ought to be included in the party.'

Angelica hesitates. She is uncertain what to expect of her meeting with Mrs Frost; she does not want it overseen by Sukie's bright eyes. 'You will be bored.'

'Pah! Pshaw! Bored! *I* know what you—'

'You know nothing. I am an old lady now; I am no longer interesting. You should have met me five years ago.'

'But what shall I write to my mother? If I cannot send her an interesting bulletin soon, I think she will come here herself.'

'What notes have you so far?'

'That you did not curry the last of the duck as you should have, but fed it to the cat by hand. Which was wasteful and indulgent.

And also that when you scrubbed the linen press you did not change the papers that had lain on its shelves, but only put the old ones back after you were done—'

'That is quite enough for one missive. Do not part with all your best gossip at once; keep her hungry for the next instalment.'

'But may I not join you?'

'No.'

Sukie's face darkens. She is an amenable creature, but since she was so nearly snatched back by her mother, she has displayed a certain nervousness, and is readier to see the necessary compartmenting of their life together as a purposeful exclusion. 'Next time,' Angelica placates her, but she is already flouncing from the room.

On the threshold she turns and draws breath, but her courage confounds her and she says nothing.

'Sukie,' says Angelica, 'you *are* wanted here.'

'Not by *him*.'

'Aye, by Mr Hancock too.'

'He has *you* now.'

Angelica feels rather a pang. 'He would be very grieved to hear you say that.' She reaches out a hand. 'Here, come sit with me. We shall talk on it.'

Sukie shakes her head, and closes the door. As her steps recede up the staircase, Angelica drops her lace into her lap and turns her face to the fire. Trailing her fingers for the cat to butt up against, she feels so tired she can hardly move. She does not know yet that the brief, blunt but affectionate ministrations of her husband have put her in a particular condition. As yet, its flourishing is of no greater significance than the first shoot of club moss taking root on a stone wall, and although Angelica feels stout and sleepy and tight at the seams, it has not so far occurred to her to wonder why this might be.

First she hears Mrs Frost – a loud and insistent rapping at the front door; the scamper of Bridget on the stairs – then she smells her. A great thick floral cloud wafts all the way through to Angelica in the kitchen, as if somebody has dropped a bottle of jasmine absolute, or dumped all the deadheads of Ranelagh on the hall floor.

Perhaps it is not her. She never wore a scent. She never wore so much.

'I am here to see your mistress,' comes Mrs Frost's clipped little voice.

'Here I am,' Angelica calls, stopping to pinch her cheeks in the mirror of the kettle, 'here I am,' but when she comes into the front hall she sees that the Mrs Frost who has arrived is not the Mrs Frost of her memory. She is painted and rouged, black and scarlet and white, and her silk skirt crackles lightning bright, and her voluminous fichu quivers and froths, and her puffed-up hair wafts lavender powder every which way. It tumbles and rolls like a snowstorm. Bridget sneezes.

'Eliza,' says Angelica. 'As narrow a maypole as ever you were.' She tries to stand back.

Mrs Frost's blowsy aura makes her large; the hallway is full of her as she cries out, 'Ah! Is that little Angelica? Dear, I would not have known you.'

Do not look at me that way, Angelica wants to snap. But she is so surprised – by Mrs Frost's cold, appraising eyes, by her own sudden anger – that she says nothing.

Mrs Frost looks about the hall. 'Why is it so dark in here? Why all this brown paint?'

'It is convenient.'

'I know you, Angelica.' She speaks playfully. 'You love bright colours. You cannot be happy without a papered wall.'

'What, and then to scrub the place every day? No, thank you kindly.'

Mrs Frost stares at her as if appalled, as if she has said something indecent, which surprises Angelica for she had meant to flaunt her domestic good sense to her old friend's wonder and approval. She lifts up her chin, feeling insolent as a schoolgirl. *So I sweep my own house.*

'Bridget,' she says, 'we are going to my parlour. Boil some water for our tea. Come this way, Mrs Frost.'

At the foot of the stairs, they pass the closed door of Mr Hancock's office. Angelica no longer has any inclination to show it off to her friend, for what is there to show off? A comical old strongbox with black rivets; a jumble of papers and ribbons and broken sealing wax; the unsavoury possibility of abandoned beer bottles, reeking pipe dottle. Going up the stairs she clutches a hank of her skirt tight in each hand that she might climb faster; the wool is wadding in her damp palms, it will crease most certainly, but the fog of Mrs Frost chases behind her.

On the landing they meet Sukie, taking her book upstairs.

'And who is *this*?' asks Mrs Frost. 'You did not tell me there was a Miss Hancock, Angelica dear.' Sukie wrinkles her nose.

'My husband has no children. This is his niece, Miss Lippard.'

'Ah, but I see the resemblance.' Mrs Frost seizes Sukie's hand. 'Enchanted! And you are how old, my dear?'

'Fourteen.'

'Fourteen!' Mrs Frost repeats rapturously. 'What an age to be!' Angelica has never seen her so fawning, and yet that false ebullience is nevertheless familiar.

''Tis tolerable,' says Sukie suspiciously. Angelica tries to convey with her eyes the message, *she is not at all how I remembered her*, but it is lost in the awkward air between them. Instead she tries speech.

'We are going to take tea,' she says to Sukie. 'Will you join us?'

'Oh!' says Mrs Frost. 'That would be delightful. I wish to discover everything about you.'

Sukie regards Mrs Frost as if she were a mad dog. 'Thank you, no,' she says. 'I am not at leisure to do any such thing.'

'Of course you have a *little* time,' pleads Angelica. 'And as a lady of this house it's only right you take your place at its tea table.'

'You'll forgive me if I do not,' says Sukie, and whisks up the stairs. From a safe perch on the next landing, she stares at Mrs Frost, and mouths consternation at Angelica, who throws her a scowl in exchange and ushers their visitor into the parlour.

This room, at least, is nothing at all to be ashamed of for she oversaw its decoration herself, in elegant colours she knows to be fashionable, with a painted floorcloth certainly a notch or two finer than those in certain of their old lodgings. There is nothing offensive about the place; perhaps this is why Mrs Frost is so offended. She makes a great show of balancing herself on her chair, tussling layers of skirt and petticoat first this way and then that way. ''Tis all right for you,' she says, 'in just a little plain dress. These chairs are not designed for great gowns.'

'No,' says Angelica pleasantly, 'they are not. You are very *grand*, Eliza. I think the world is treating you well.' She is studying her friend's face. It is formidably painted – eyebrows, cheeks, lips – so there is not one vulnerable spot, not one inch of her skin left bare. *I used to share a bed with this woman*, Angelica thinks. She remembers the soft pale skin at the tops of her arms, just losing its firmness; the little creases at the corners of her mouth. The one whisker that grows from under her chin and which Angelica had to pluck for her.

'London has been kind to me,' says Mrs Frost. 'I have brought you something to remember it by.'

The parcel she hands over is tied up with red string and smells of orange blossom. Angelica presses her nose against it. Her eyes close; the corners of her lips twitch. 'Millefruits,' she whispers. She tugs the knots loose and the strings slither to the floor. Gold tissue paper crackles as it falls open: the sweetmeats inside are crisp and pale, emanating perfume and toasted sugar.

'And bane bread here too,' she squeaks, fossicking out a little golden sliver baked so hard as to almost be fired. She presses it to her lips for a second before slipping it between her strong back teeth. It cracks, sharp and clean, and she lets it soften a moment on her tongue. Crumbs of cinnamon and nutmeg melt away from shards of almond. 'I used to eat these in bed.' She is blushing with pleasure, bringing up her shoulders and wrinkling her still-pretty nose as if a lover is kissing her neck.

'When did you last taste these things?'

She wants me to say, not since my marriage. She wants me to tell her that I am sadder for it.

'You forget how carefully Mr Hancock learned my tastes.' She tries to recall her old heavy-lidded smile and fit it to her face. 'You forget I know how to ask for things.'

'You married him. He is no longer under any imperative to give you them.'

'He gives because it pleases him.' She nibbles again at her biscuit. Cinnamon and almonds between her teeth; the gust of rosewater and starch from Mrs Frost's person. The ghost-Angelica, the Angelica she used to be, is standing right at her side. If she were to shuffle just a little this way she would be back in her body again, looking out through her eyes.

Bridget comes with the hot water.

'Have you no sweet wine?' Mrs Frost holds her biscuit but does not bite into it. 'My teeth cost too much to risk in such a way.'

Angelica no longer wants to sip Madeira with her friend. 'There is only beer in the house,' she says.

'No!'

'We find tea strong enough.'

351

She waits for Bridget to leave before she takes out her bunch of keys. One key unlocks the cabinet where are kept the tea bowls and the tea caddy; another unlocks the caddy itself. Mrs Frost watches in amusement. 'What a housewife you are.'

'That is what I chose.' She knows that the tea bowls, eggshell porcelain with pink roses and the mysterious glyphs of their Chinese artists, are a match for anything in the grandest houses: they ought to be, since Mr Hancock supplies them all. She need not be ashamed of the tea either. 'This we receive direct from the quayside. Mr Hancock is intimate friends with a gentleman from the Company. What do you think of it?'

They sip in silence. A brooch sparkles at Mrs Frost's throat when she swallows, almost hidden by her necktie. The stones in it are good, not paste.

'And how is it come to be,' says Angelica, 'that you are in St James's?'

Mrs Frost brightens. 'I have a house there,' she says.

'A house? You mean you have a position in a house?'

'I have a house. 'Tis mine. I rent it.'

'An *entire* house?' Angelica says.

Mrs Frost inclines her head, just fractionally, and the light catches her brooch again. At such an angle, there is no mistaking its design. It is a perfect Cupid's arrow.

Is this a trick? A joke? Angelica cannot ask; she has too anxious a sense that this is what Mrs Frost wants. Instead she pursues her own questions: 'But what do *you* want with a whole house?'

'To keep my girls in.' Mrs Frost lets the silence spin out for a second or two. 'In fact,' she continues, 'I met one off the stagecoach this very morning.'

'A girl?'

'Fifteen years of age. A beautiful complexion. 'Tis a shame she cannot read a word, and she carries herself very poorly, but she has a fine voice and a very delicate manner, a rare quality. She will respond to training very well, once she leaves off crying.'

'Eliza, I did not expect you to resort to this.'

'I am surprised you have heard nothing of it. 'Tis a very new venture, to be sure, but it has attracted a good deal of notice.'

'I do not read those scurrilous magazines. Why would I?'

'So you will not know that my Lolly is so sought after I sold her first time for fifty guineas. Fifty guineas, Mrs Hancock.'

'You have risen so quickly.'

'I had experience enough.'

This, of course, is so. Was she not at Angelica's elbow for every moment of her life; had it not been her business to know everything of the world, and everybody in it? Angelica shakes her head. 'But this house, this fine house you say you have, after we were quite penniless. We had nothing. How did you come by the money?'

Mrs Frost does not look the slightest bit uncomfortable. 'I had a little capital.'

I had no capital, Angelica thinks. *I had nothing at all.* But she cannot say it. Her tongue feels thick in her mouth as she tries, instead, 'You were always clever with money. Cleverer than I.'

'You had your own talents.'

'You kept my books so *well*.' She spits her words out, eyes narrowing, but Mrs Frost just smiles and sips her tea. She will not own it; it is as if it has not happened. It is as if she has not come here wearing Angelica's own jewellery.

They sit.

'I believe,' says Angelica, 'that you came here with the intention of communicating certain things to me. Is there anything else you desire me to know?' *Did you scheme this all along,* she wants to demand, *or did the opportunity merely present itself?*

353

'No,' says Mrs Frost. 'I believe you perceive things just as they are. Oh – and I suppose you have not heard – our old friend, Mrs Chappell.'

'What of her?' Angelica feels a sudden chill. 'Is she well?'

'Well enough. She has been in trouble, though. The *law*.' She delivers her news with relish but Angelica wafts it away.

'The usual charges? Bless you, Frost, you have so very much to learn about this game. She'll pay the fine and that will be the end of it.'

Mrs Frost cuts her eyes nastily. 'I cannot share your confidence. She is not so much in favour as she once was.'

'Nonsense.' Angelica looks at her askance. 'Mrs Chappell will always have her protectors. Her influence is unrivalled.'

Downstairs the clock is striking six. The front door goes, and Mr Hancock is stamping and hallooing in the hall. 'Your husband is home.'

He is coming up the stairs, calling, 'Angelica! Angelica! Mrs Hancock, where be you?'

'In here,' she tries to say, but her voice falters. She feels quite overcome. He throws open the door and he is all a-fluster, his excitement hanging around him in a horsey-smelling halo of sweat. One of the knees of his breeches is torn wide open, and black blood is caked on his porky knee. He claps her on the shoulder and kisses the frill of her cap. There is a long smear of what might be soot on his cheek.

'Good news,' he cries. 'Good news, my little pigeon!'

'Mrs Frost is here,' says Angelica.

'Good evening, Mrs Frost, good evening.'

'He has been drinking,' smirks Mrs Frost. But Angelica does not care. She cannot get close enough to her husband, her foolish, honest husband. She is scooting around him, dusting him down, taking his coat from his shoulders and shaking it out.

'What have you been at? What have you done to yourself?'

'Whisht! It don't signify. I lost my footing.'

'And your knuckles!' She drops her voice to an uxorial whisper. 'Have you been brawling?'

'Nothing of the sort!'

'I must go,' says Mrs Frost. She looks delighted.

Mr Hancock remembers himself. 'I have been most improper,' he says, crestfallen. 'I have burst in on you ladies when I ought to have kept to myself.'

'Not at all,' says Mrs Frost, rising. 'It is time I left.'

'Will you stay to dine?' says Mr Hancock.

'I have an engagement. I came only to look in on your wife.'

'I shall see you out.'

'Yes, Mr Hancock, please see her out,' says Angelica. 'Goodbye, Eliza.'

Mr Hancock clatters down the stairs, taking with him the great waft of Mrs Frost. Angelica waits on the threshold of the parlour, dithering, her hand raised to her breastbone. She hears the front door close, then her husband calling:

'Angelica! My little wife. Come to me, let me tell you about your new home.'

'*What* are you about, Mr Hancock?' She trots down the dark stairs. 'Some candles want lighting down here.'

'I have bought you that house, my angel. I inspected it most carefully, and it is just so. Very grand! I wish you would excuse my bursting in. I felt my news could not wait, but I do see that it was not a gentlemanly action. It is in the countryside above Greenwich, Mrs Hancock. Exactly to your tastes. *À la mode*, my dear, *à la mode*.'

'You have truly bought a house?'

He smells of the alehouse, and there is sawdust stuck to his boots. 'Truly,' he says.

'Well, why did you not announce it while that horrid woman was here? I should have liked to see her face. Ha! That would have given her something to chew over. You are certain it is all ours? You are certain it is so grand?'

'Of course, of course. You will be astounded.' He takes off his hat and his wig, and scrubs his palms over his bristly scalp. 'Ah! Better,' he says, sliding his thumbs under the straining waistband of his breeches, 'and better yet if I had something to drink –' rapping his stick against the floor so it might be heard all over the house – 'Bridget! Where is Bridget?'

'Stop your banging. Come and sit by the fire; I shall fetch us something.'

And so the erstwhile Angelica Neal, in her caraco and her cap, trots willingly into the pantry to bring her husband small beer and cold boiled beef. She bolts the shutters and lights the candles, and comes to the dark wood table in the dining room with two pewter plates and a loaf of bread. Mr Hancock stokes up the fire and unrolls the plan of the house on the table, weighing down one corner with a candlestick and another with the mustard pot. He and his wife sit elbow to elbow, eating their beef and supping their beer.

'Here is the dining room,' says Mr Hancock, tracing a greasy paw over it, 'and here the music room, and the staircase. I had thought these rooms here for your own personal use, but you might choose different when you see them for yourself. They are very proper, my dear, not showy at all, you need not worry.'

'I do not mind a little show. Where it is tasteful.'

The candlelight and the patter of rain on the flagged yard outside are soporific: Angelica leans against her husband's shoulder, with his stout arm around her and his fingers palping at her waist. She is more certain of her feelings now. And since there is nobody else to tell, she turns to her husband and murmurs:

'I do not want to see that woman again.'

'Hmm?'

'Mrs Frost. I do not think she is a good person.'

'She was your dear friend.' He blinks his blond eyelashes but he is not arguing with her. He wants to hear what she has to say. She flops her head back against him.

'She spent ten years reminding me I ought to be other than I am. She disdained me when I was not respectable, and now that I am, she sneers at me.'

'She sneered at you in this house? In the house you are mistress of?'

'She wishes to see me as a failure. She wishes to make me ashamed. And shall I tell you one other thing?'

'Go on.' He slips his fingers under her cap and strokes the hair over her ear.

'When I was ruined. When I married you. I do now believe that I was not quite ruined.'

'What do you mean?'

'Did you not see the change in her? She is rich.'

'So she has had help from somewhere.'

'Yes, from my own purse! She kept all my accounts. She ran my house. She had not a penny of her own – she would have been on the street if I had not helped her – so how is it that when *I* became destitute *she* had a nest egg?'

'It don't mean she took it from you.'

'She was wearing my pin today. My diamond pin. Cool as cream cheese, she was, coming into my house wearing my old jewels. She never cared for me and she cares for me now even less.'

'Now, my girl.'

'She is a hypocrite,' says Angelica with finality. 'I will not speak of her again.' She folds her arms on the table and rests her chin on them. 'Tell me more about our house.'

'It has a folly,' he says. 'A summer house.'

'Oh! I shall enjoy that. I can eat ices in it.'

'And, underneath the summer house, the most curious thing.'

'What is it?'

'A shell grotto.'

She clasps her hands and opens her eyes wide. 'Grand indeed!'

'I knew you would be pleased. It even has a little pool in it, which must be fed by the spring. The agent said that the place had no function, but I know better. It is for our mermaid.'

'Our mermaid that has not yet been vouchsafed to us. Our little fakement.'

'This is a *sign*.'

'I am content with only a grotto. I shall be its nymph. If only Mrs Frost knew! *She* has no grotto. What else does this house have?'

'There is a fruit orchard. You will eat plums all summer. And there are stables, with a phaeton for me to drive you in. There are many bedrooms.'

'But I want no visitors,' she says. 'No visitors at all. I want only us.'

'Nobody else?'

'No.' Her heart is agitated. Who would come? Mrs Chappell, Bel Fortescue? To sneer?

'No children?'

He says it just too sharply. He does not mean to fix his eyes so firmly upon her, but he cannot help it. She does not know what to do with her expression. She has never been in such a position. She does not know how to have any feelings about it at all.

'Perhaps,' she says, and knows she has said something near enough to the right thing, for he clasps her hand tightly.

Inside Angelica, something is multiplying.

'What of the expense?' she demands. She likes it when he talks and she listens; she sprawls further over the table, sinking her cheek into the cradle of her own arms. His gruff voice is not musical but his words are beyond soothing to her. 'All settled,' he is saying, 'all taken care of ... paid in full ... nothing else to trouble ourselves with ... all straightforward now, I should venture.' While he talks, she reaches up to rub her knuckles fondly and firmly over his bristly jowls, and yawns, and smiles, and thinks, is it really so unlikely that she might find herself in love with him?

FIVE

He takes Angelica up to the heath. High up in the sky a kite is swooping, its beribboned tail flying out behind it, and on the tender grass beneath it, children caper and whoop. The wind catches Angelica's skirts so she is nearly a kite herself, tottering along the drive as the breeze tries to snatch her up. Her hair flies over her eyes and she puts up both arms to keep her hat on her head, but standing in front of her new home she laughs and laughs.

He sends an order with the *Eagle* for monogrammed porcelain. He sends an order with the *Angel* for good chintz. He sends Angelica and Sukie out to choose new silverware.

The spring, which began as one warm bright day – followed after a week of rain by another – has extended into a whole unbroken string of them, and there are now moments that Mr Hancock becomes agitated for the fate of Captain Tysoe Jones's venture upon the *Unicorn*. Why does it take so long to return? Sometimes he puts his hands on his desk and leans forward, out of the open window, scanning the bobbing masts of the ships beyond the Deptford rooftops and praying that all is well. At night he dreams of Javanese mermaids, teeming in the black water of his own grotto as if they spawned there. Or else he dreams of a buxom fish-tailed beauty, with sticks of coral in her swirling yellow hair and her bosom languidly rising with the movement of a warm tide. In his dreams she lies in a bathtub of mother-of-pearl, and when he lifts her out she is slippery and heavy, a cold dead weight slithering through his arms. In his dream he picks her up and staggers across a shell-shaped room with her in a kind of ungainly caper, she always dragging him to the floor while her dampness seeps through his shirt and the smell of oysters envelops them both. When she turns her cool wet face to his, it is always Angelica's that he sees.

SIX

A week before their removal to the new house, Angelica and the girls Sukie and Bridget climb up to the lumber room under the eaves at Union Street to sort through the Hancock family effects.

'There is nothing here worth keeping,' says Angelica. 'Nothing of taste or value.' She nudges a dusty wooden cradle with the toe of her slipper and sets it rocking. 'We must throw it all out.'

'My mother will not like to hear of that,' says Sukie.

'Your mother may deal with her own lumber room. This one is mine now, and I say it all must go.'

'Some good woman will make use of these things,' says Bridget thoughtfully.

'Do you think so? 'Tis all quite ugly.'

'But sturdy,' says Bridget. 'And nobody would disdain a good wool blanket like this one, or bedlinen when their own is worn through.'

'Worn through? What, right through?'

'So you can see daylight through the middle, in just the shape of the bodies that lay in 'em. In my mother's house we cut 'm down the worn part and stitched 'm back together along the opposite sides. Get twice the wear that way. But these sheets are good, madam – these will do somebody for many years yet.'

'Well! I never was so destitute as to cut my bedsheets in half. I never was.' Angelica is impressed. 'I kept body and soul together very adequate, all told.'

'Aye, and how was that?' asks Sukie. She and Bridget are both fearsomely interested in Mrs Hancock's previous occupation.

'That don't signify,' she sniffs. 'I did what I must.'

'Until Uncle rescued you.'

'Rescued me?' Angelica laughs. 'Is that what you believe?'

'Aye,' says Sukie, 'aye, rescued you, and now you may reform and be good.'

Angelica feels not entirely easy. Certainly she was desperate – certainly she was glad to have him perceive himself as her rescuer – but never in her darkest hour did she imagine that she might not make her own way through tribulation. 'A dubious hero he is—' she says lightly.

'Which is better, ma'am?' Bridget interrupts. 'Living here with us, or back in London with all the sweetmeats and the beaux?'

'Each has their privations, I daresay. It's best wherever the living is easiest. Say, Bridget, these poor people who have no bedsheets. What have they done to find themselves in such a position of want?'

'Why, nothing.'

'Quite blameless?'

'As blameless as any body can be, the world being what it is.'

'Ah. That was their mistake. Do you know where they might be found?'

'I do.'

'Very near to here?'

'Not ten minutes' walk away.'

'Well, Bridget, I trust you to identify some individuals of great want and take these things to them immediately. Sukie, you had better help her.' Angelica is loading bales of linen and wool into her step-niece's arms. 'And when you are there, find a wagon, and have it call by here, and we shall put everything else on it.'

Bridget staggers from the room, with her chin ratcheted as high as it will go above the pile of cloth in her arms, and Sukie follows her down.

'Be careful on the stairs, girls.'

Alone in the attic, Angelica smooths down her skirts. She feels pleased with herself, warmed by her own surprising beneficence. She has never given to the poor before; it is her first truly grand act. *For when I am in the big house*, she thinks, *this will be usual for me.* She imagines standing kindly on her doorstep, pressing shiny coins into the hands of a beggar boy and his blind mother. At Christmas she will send a ham to the almshouse. When she dies they will distribute mourning rings, and the orphan children will weep.

Downstairs there is a knock on the door. Perhaps it is not the first knock, for it has a frustrated, impatient sound to it.

'Confound them,' she mutters. 'I will not answer it.'

But it may be the woman who sells the buns she likes.

She thinks for a moment. Then she takes off down the stairs, tucking her hair into her cap as best she can. For a minute the knocking leaves off, but when she is on the final turn of the stairs it goes again.

'Patience!' she shouts, and throws the door open.

Mrs Frost is there, all in lilac, with the tassels of a vast parasol quivering around her head like a carousel.

'Good day,' she says, smiling. She has had a gold tooth put in.

''Tis you.'

'So it is. I was passing, and I thought – how nice it would be. My old friend.'

'You were passing? What were you passing to? The victualling yard? The tannery? Did you think to buy yourself a barge? I cannot imagine, Mrs Frost, what can have made my house convenient to you.'

Mrs Frost gives a laugh she has spent some time working up to sound bell-like. 'You are a sharp one. All right, I have come to visit you. I wish to speak with you. May I come in?' She is already stepping past her. 'Upstairs, is it? To your dear little – ah – parlour?'

'I cannot offer you tea,' Angelica says, following her up. 'I have sent my maid out. She is taking contributions to the poor. Mr Hancock and I have been blessed with far more than we need.'

'I see, I see.'

They sit down together. Mrs Frost gives Angelica a long, shrewd look, as if she were a favourite schoolmistress dealing with an unruly pupil.

'You think I have abandoned you.'

Angelica frowns.

'You believe I have profited from you and then cast you aside. Ah-ah-ah, do not speak yet, hear me out, my dear. For this is not so. My dove, *this is not so.* I have not forgotten you, not for one moment. I owe everything I have to you.'

'That part is true.'

'I freely admit it. It is all I speak of when I am in London. Everybody knows. But since I was separated from you – oh, I wept for you, I thought of how lonely you must be here, and how cruelly we had been separated.'

'You could have come too. He offered. You would not come.'

'Angelica, you had to think of your own interests. You do not need to be ashamed of that. I forgive you.'

'You would not come with me.'

'Since your fortunes turned –' Mrs Frost raises her voice a little – '*all* I have thought about is how to restore you to your previous position. You took such a fall. I have been *striving* to create a situation you might return to.'

'But I live here now.'

'Exactly. I can get you out.' She leans closer, a gust of violet pastilles and tooth decay. 'My big house, my lovely grand house – you will have everything you need. Your own apartment, a little servant of your own – an Abyssinian boy, like you always had a fancy for, and we shall get him up in livery, and you can teach him tricks. I can do that for you. And you can keep your own hours, and go to the theatre every night of the week.'

'But I am quite happy here.'

'You need not adopt such a front with me. I know you.'

'You know nothing. I do not want to come away from this place.'

'You would not credit how many of your old friends are dying to have you back. They always ask me, "That Angelica Neal, when will she return to us?"'

'And yet I have heard from none of them.'

'I can give you very good rates. Better than the little girls I am taking on, and I know you will have no trouble earning. You could buy yourself out whenever you liked.'

'You wish me to become a whore?'

'I would not say *whore*. You never were a mercenary, I know that. You would never be *obliged*.'

Angelica is stupefied. 'You wish me to become a whore in *your* establishment?'

'It is the least I could do for you. You would be absolutely free to choose. I have so many charming girls, and they will really do anything they are told, but not one of them is established. If we had a – a *figurehead*, a famous name, just to draw people *in* . . .'

'No. Oh no, no. I am finished with all that, Mrs Frost.' She stands up. 'Please leave.'

'It will always be there for you.'

'I am married.'

'What, forever?' A vein on Mrs Frost's temple begins to twitch. 'How long do you believe you can do this for? This piffling little house, that idiot man. I suppose you think you are virtuous. Well, you are not. You have merely lowered your expectations. Brown paint and oilcloth, Angelica Neal? This is not you.'

'I think you are jealous.'

'Jealous? Why? Because you are pretty? Because you are married?'

'Jealous. You arrive in my house all puffed up like a cat who has run into a terrier, and you try so very hard to persuade me that I am nothing and you are something that in the end I simply cannot credit it.'

'Do you know,' says Mrs Frost, 'how they speak of you? "That Mrs Neal," everybody says, "who stooped to marry a nobody. Who threw away all her opportunities; who could not tolerate the difficulties of this life she chose." You are a laughing-stock, my dear.'

'You have made a quite serious misjudgement. My husband has bought me my own house. Greenwich. We are rising in the world. I do not need you, or Mrs Chappell, or any body. I am free.'

'You are *helpless*. You are *kept*. You go where you find yourself best supported, as you always have; perhaps you mistake this for independence, but you are still a whore.'

Angelica slaps her, quick as a whip. 'Out. Get out. Get out of my house.'

Mrs Frost shows no agitation. She saunters across the room, Angelica's palm print blooming faintly under the crust of lead white.

'Out,' says Angelica, louder. She snatches up the broom from the landing and comes at her as if she were chasing out a black-beetle; Mrs Frost shrieks and leaps, and darts for the stairs, but Angelica

367

pursues her, beating at Mrs Frost's skirt with the broom all the way down, until by the last step the wretched bawd has completely lost her composure and yelps, 'Let me go! Let me go!' She hurls herself out of the door and onto Union Street, where the footman urinates dreamily in an alley and a stray dog urinates against the wheel of her carriage. 'James! James, get back to your post. We are leaving.'

Angelica's face is red and her eyes are gleaming; her yellow hair is bursting out from under her cap. She stands on the step, brandishing her broom, and shrieks to all around, 'This woman is a bawd! She runs a most disreputable nunnery, and she condemns me – *me!* – for my honest situation.'

Those few people walking in Union Street – and it is a fine street, home to gentlefolk – turn to stare. Mrs Frost is scrambling into her carriage, slipping and snatching in her agitation. Faces appear at windows, and a boy puts down his barrow of dung to watch.

'An old spinster getting rich off pretty girls,' continues Angelica, quite hoarse. 'She sells other women's virtue but retains her own, now tell me, do you think that is fair? Do you think it is *possible?*' The footman flicks the reins and the carriage bounces down the street. 'Go!' Angelica shrieks. 'Don't come back here! This is no place for you!'

Bridget, returned from her errand to the sheetless poor, is hurrying down the street: Sukie, some distance behind, breaks into a run, lamenting, 'Oh, no, Mrs Hancock, not in the street!'

They gather about her in breathless consternation. 'What has she done?' asks Bridget.

'Come inside, I beg you,' whispers Sukie, pulling her to the threshold, but Angelica is rigid with rage.

'I will see this woman off first!'

'Come inside,' says Bridget. 'She is gone. Madam, she is gone.'

They take Angelica by the arms and gently but firmly steer her into the house. 'Bolt the door,' she says once they are inside, her face remarkable pale and remarkable still.

'What happened?' asks Sukie, putting a shawl about her aunt's shoulders.

'She is a vile, coarse woman. This is a respectable household. My husband is a gentleman.'

'Of course. Come into the kitchen. Sit down. Let me get you a drink. I can make you a caudle.'

'I am all right. Only shaken. I saw her off, girls.' She wipes her eyes with the back of her wrist, and grins. 'She will not come back here. But I shall give you some advice, and you will both do well to heed me. *Hold on to your virtue*. Hold on to your virtue because do you know why?'

'Well, yes,' says Sukie, who has read many books on the subject, 'because—'

'I shall tell you why. Because if you do not, it is snakes like Mrs Frost who will profit by it. And that, mark my words, is if you are *fortunate*. Otherwise you will find yourself in the care of a man who goes by the name of Crusher or The Gent. And these are not good people. And you will not take any part in encouraging them.'

'No, I shall not.'

'No. Learn from me. Now I shall take that caudle.'

SEVEN

April 1786

One morning in mid-April, Angelica says to herself, *it is time I accepted that I am pregnant.*

She is in bed at the time – Mr Hancock having risen for the day – sitting up to watch the white clouds chase one another across the sky outside the window, and the thought leaps into her head very suddenly and perfectly formed. Everything becomes clear. She realises that beneath the surface of her mind she has been thinking and counting and puzzling for some time; that she knows her own symptoms perfectly well, and that the plain fact of her impending motherhood has sat unattended for quite long enough now.

She flops onto her back, resting her hand on her stomach – which has always been a plump little stomach, so there is little to discern, although she feels it well enough – and says to herself, *this is absurd.* In Dean Street she would have been more vigilant; she would have understood at once what was happening. *In Dean Street I would never have allowed this to happen,* she thinks, and feels stupid, because her instinct to obstruct this sort of development is no longer suitable for her situation. However, she cannot think how else to feel.

Angelica knows prophylaxis the way other girls know the catechism. She keeps a vinegared sponge in her cabinet and knows what to do with a cundum. She can time a gentleman's withdrawal to the most exquisite second; she will accept his spending on which-ever part of her person he most admires; in exceptional situations she will indulge in the Frenchman's vice. In the event of an oversight she might calmly draw herself a scalding bath and a quart of gin, or in a case of greater urgency call in on Mrs Chappell to acquire from her a good purgative. If further aid were required, she would not find herself abandoned; every woman she knew had a little piece of advice, or a commiseratory glass of sack, and word would be passed round until the proper expert with the proper equipment were found. It would not be pleasant – and some times less pleasant than others – but it would all be settled after one small burst of activity and anxiety; all would be well, and all concluded to her own choosing.

Now, friendless and without the first idea of how to find a mid-wife specialising in live births, Angelica is out of her element. *What shall I do?* she panics, over and over, and can only conclude, *I can do nothing. I* must *do nothing.* She can only wait for this baby to be born. It agitates her, this lack of agency; she feels itchy and restless, she flops about in bed, and then she gets up and paces the room. If such a significant thing is really to occur, why does she not have more to do?

This, she realises, is the end of Angelica Neal, and the cementing of Mrs Hancock. She had anticipated only that marriage would deliver her from her old situation; in fact it has transplanted her to another, that knits itself under her very skin and alters her every day. More has slipped from her control than she had expected, and now she sees that as the months and years pass it will only slip further. She will never be simply her own self in the world again; the cour-tesan Angelica Neal, a personality all her own, is being parcelled up and claimed by connection upon connection. She is 'wife of' and 'aunt of'; later she will be 'mother of' – perhaps some energetic young man whose achievements will never be traced back to she who birthed him. These claims upon her will only multiply – she will be mother-in-law, grandmother, widow, dependant – and accordingly her own person will be divided and divided and divided, until there is nothing left.

'Well, I have done it now,' she says.

She pulls her shawl around her and puts on her slippers, and trots down the stairs to her husband's counting-house. She taps on the door.

'Come in,' he calls.

She opens the door. He is hunched over his desk as usual, wig-less, absent-mindedly rubbing the cat under the chin. The little creature has squeezed her eyes shut in her pleasure, paws folded one over the other.

'Good morning,' says Angelica.

'Good morning.' He does not look up. He works his way around the cat's jaw with the tips of his stained fingers, and then begins to stroke her behind her ears. She purrs thunderously.

Angelica's stomach is a-flutter with nerves. 'Are you ready for breakfast?'

'Oh – ah, let me see.' He rummages through his papers with one hand, the other never leaving the cat. 'I am particularly busy today. Perhaps – perhaps I shall dine with you?' He glances up to catch her eye apologetically. 'So much to do, my dear.'

'Mr Hancock,' says Angelica more firmly. Then she realises that she does not know what to say. 'What would you . . . ?' she tries. 'I mean, if you were . . . I think that I . . .'

He turns round to look at her, his arm hooked over the back of his chair. 'Spit it out,' he says.

'I hardly know how.'

''Tis not bad news?'

'No, no. No, no, no. Good news. I venture you will like it very much.' She realises that her face is hot; she is blushing, and her cheeks have leapt into a grin. The anticipation of his joy makes her feel giddy. 'Mr Hancock,' she tries again, clasping her hands behind her back, 'Oh, sir, I am in for it!'

'Beg pardon?'

'I am in the way of increasing!'

'You are—?'

'A baby! We are going to have a baby!'

'Oh!' He rises from his seat in one movement; the cat flees and the ink bottle overturns. He takes Angelica in his arms, kissing her face and hair. 'My little pigeon. My darling. What news. So clever.'

'I am pleased,' she says tentatively. Then she says again, 'I *am* pleased,' because it is true. She has made an unremarkable middling type of man weep with the most innocent joy; this is something to be pleased about. If she is to deliver a child, it might as well be to the sort of man who will dote on it.

'When?' he says, clasping her elbows.

'In time for Christmas, I think.'

'Oh, my dear. We shall be so happy. You and I, my little wife, and a child of our own. I could not want for more.'

'Nor I,' she says.

'I told you I would make you happy. You are more than content, are you not?'

'Oh, sir.' She dabs her eyes with her handkerchief. 'Of course.'

EIGHT

That very same night, Mr Hancock sends out for sugarplums and meat pies, and for neighbours to join in his pleasure in a private, friendly gathering. He also sends for his sister Hester, who, although she strives to be cordial, cannot help hissing to him upon her arrival, 'How can you be sure 'tis yours?'

Those others in attendance are a motley group; from a nicer class of Deptford folk than those Mr Hancock has habitually gone amongst, for his star is rising. The tenants of Hancock Row are all there – or rather, the gentlemen are: the dancing master; the doctor; the fellow who has very lately opened a teawarehouse on Butt Lane itself. Jem Thorpe and the Master Shipwright are present also, frowning at the company. It used to be that there was only one sort of man in Deptford society: clever with his hands and with a mind for figures, whose living, if it did not come out of a ship, was no living at all. These land-locked leisured citizens are a breed quite apart. Where have they sprung from, and what can be made of them?

There is one thing they agree on, however: they have all, to a man, presented themselves alone without wives, sisters or children.

'Say,' says Mr Hancock, 'what's this? This company is very short of ladies.' The new friends clutch their rummers and smile nervously, murmuring their apologies. 'What?' he asks. 'Speak up, speak up! Not one of you can finish a sentence.'

Angelica, taking his elbow, steers him into a confiding huddle. 'Their wives will not be about me,' she whispers.

'No! But that is absurd.'

She shrugs. 'Perfectly sensible. I am not decent company.'

'You are my wife, are you not?'

'Aye, but . . .' she sighs. 'They will not wish to meet me. And their husbands will not wish it either,' although when she turns around she finds them all craning and staring to see her, for they have heard of her, and seen her likeness shared around. 'You may be certain that they are under the strictest instructions to remember everything they see, that they might describe it in great detail when they are home.'

'But – will they never visit? You must have female society.'

Angelica has a great wish, all of a sudden, to see dear Bel, to ask her, *how did you manage this?* Bel would have an answer; Bel would be kind. But then, Bel's cohort are all gentry, titled and landed. They are not the wives of middling provincial men; they are a breed quite apart. 'Maybe they will unbend,' she says. 'I shall endeavour to be their sort. If I make a good impression tonight they cannot take against me, I am sure.'

Sukie, setting up the clavichord, watches them whisper together; her uncle's eyes very fond upon his wife. She does not find Angelica onerous company, but she is crestfallen that Mr Hancock's attention has so quickly been transferred; she had thought herself central to his life. That he seems so quickly to have forgot her is discomfiting.

'Brandy!' cries Mr Hancock, and thus they toast the coming child, he with his arm about Mrs Hancock's waist, she blushing and pretty. Even Mrs Lippard smiles and laughs; the baby may be a mere tadpole, but it binds their union as nothing else might. There is no ousting Mrs Hancock now.

Bridget nips into the room, and tugging at Mr Hancock's sleeve informs him that there is a gentleman for him at the door.

'More visitors?' says Mr Hancock. 'What fun! Bring 'em in, bring 'em in!' but when Bridget beckons him down into the hall, he finds it is only a messenger boy. 'Are you wanting a reply?' asks Mr Hancock.

'No, sir, only to see you take receipt of the message. 'Tis important.'

'I see. I see.' Mr Hancock inspects the seal on the note: it is impressed, God be praised, with Captain Jones's anchor signet. 'Thank you. Will you have a drop of brandy?'

'Thank you, sir. No, sir. I must away.'

Once the boy has gone, Mr Hancock gazes again upon the seal. *News from my ship,* he says to himself as the muted notes of the clavichord drift down the stairs, accompanied by the laughter and hum of his assembled new friends. *Momentous, perhaps. As if I required any more moment in my life.* He thinks of the fever with which he had demanded a new mermaid; the hectic bliss when news came that one had been found. And now? *Why, it does not matter. I have everything I want; the addition of a wonder to my life will improve it not one whit.*

And if it is bad news, therefore, if the creature is lost or proved a forgery, then it matters not one whit either. Even so, he is not quite easy, and goes upstairs to fetch his wife. She is standing by the clavichord, turning the pages for Sukie; when he enters the room she turns her face to him with an expression of gentle happiness.

'What was it?' she asks quietly, so as not to interrupt Sukie's performance, but seeing the expression on her husband's face she steps away from the instrument all the same, beckoning the dancing master to take her place.

'A note. I have not opened it yet. I – I hoped perhaps you would. 'Tis from Captain Jones.'

Her eyes grow large. 'He has returned?'

'I do not know! Open it!'

She slides her finger under the seal, and unfolds the paper carefully. It is a damp and dirty sheet, its contents made out in the most ragged of scrawls. It reads as follows:

Mr Hancock,
Sir,

   The good ship Unicorn *has docked safely. I beg that you meet me at Greenland Dock tomorrow morning at seven o'clock to take receipt of its most cumbersome and unusual cargo.*

   Yours etc.,

   Captain Tysoe Jones

P. S. –

SHE IS ALIVE.

In this quiet bubble, something is growing.

It doubles and doubles and doubles again, unseen, and moment on moment on moment it begins to wake up, becomes more of itself. Slowly it will start to extend itself, to stretch out like a taproot from a tight seed, or to swell like a tadpole, limbs knotted within its body, but although it is like these things it is certainly neither of these things. It is only itself.

If it thinks, it does not know it is thinking. If it feels, it does not know it is feeling. But it strives, without knowing it is striving: it surges towards life without knowing what life might be, and although it has no understanding of attainment, to attain is its sole instinct. It has no idea of age, but it conquers seconds and minutes and hours: it lives now, and now, and now; each moment bubbles into the next, and once gone is quite forgotten. It might be the oldest thing in the world, for all it knows. It might be the very newest.

This something sleeps in the dark, a secret even to itself. People who have never seen it might credit it with fingers, eyelashes, a voice, but how can they know? Who knows what it does in its small bubble, when it does not even know itself? They will suggest it has a moral code, a motive, a divine purpose, a soul worth stealing. They assume its rules might be the same as theirs. They are wrong.

It is a seed crammed with everything it will ever need; it beds down. It swims. It flies. Blind and deaf and dumb in its sensual world, it rides on tides of dreams. It knows, or does not know, the roil and churn of fluid all about it, and the thud and rush of some eternal comforting tide. What it knows is that it is part of something bigger.

What it knows, if it knows, is that something is about to happen. It is prepared at every moment for something to happen.

Something is about to happen.

NINE

Mr Hancock has never set an alarm in his life: dawn is such a logical time to awake that he does so without complaint or difficulty. This particular morning, his eyes snap open as the bells in St Nicholas's spire sound the third of six chimes, and is in an instant as perfectly awake as if he had never been asleep.

'Mermaid,' he says in the dark, and sits up. He cannot see much, it being dark and the bed-curtains being half drawn, but he can feel Angelica, warm and sweaty, curled up next to him, and he pats what he supposes to be her shoulder. She squeaks like a kitten. 'Your mermaid has arrived,' he whispers. 'Will you come and see her with me?'

'There is no mermaid,' she mumbles, rolling over onto her belly.

'Wake up, Mrs Hancock.'

'No, sir.'

'I cannot persuade you?'

'Go and satisfy yourself it is real. I'll not make the journey for a silly toy.'

'I suppose rest is of particular importance to you,' he says, 'in your happy condition.' He opens the bed-curtains and eases himself out; she sprawls into the space he has left while he hops about with one foot in his breeches, as silently as he can manage. On the way out of the bedroom, he cracks his shin on the blanket chest and spits hoarse curses.

'Shh!' says Angelica.

'Forgive me! Forgive me!'

He tiptoes downstairs as light as a ballerina. Bridget is coming from the kitchen, carrying a full coal scuttle.

'Good morning,' he says, bursting with contentment, but she squints and scowls blearily at him, and says nothing. The shutters at least are open, and the hall is all awash with spring sunshine. 'A glorious day,' he remarks, as the cat follows him out onto the street. 'An important day. I am to be a father at last. And my ship has come in – the *Unicorn* – the most important of them all.'

The cat zigzags the road from gutter to gutter, her little snout close to the ground, her whiskers twitching. She is hungry.

'You imagine this is of no consequence to you,' said Mr Hancock, 'but this business is what keeps you in bacon rinds.'

When they reach the tall walls and slaughterhouse fug of the Admiralty Victualling Yard, Mr Hancock and the cat part ways. She darts into the shadows, her tail standing up like a mast; he strikes out across the fields, where the air swells moist and green-smelling. The birds are clamorous, and three red cows watch from under their eyelashes as he hoists himself over a stile, breeches straining. From here a long tree-lined avenue leads to Greenland Dock, and he idles happily along it, kicking up dust and screwing his eyes so the sunshine glows pink through his lids.

As he draws closer the air takes on an oily weight, which settles on the clothes and layers the nostrils with a greasy, deep-water scent. And the nearer he comes, the worse the smell becomes, until it blooms into the stench of ghastly decay: the blankets of flesh peeled from whales on the Greenland ice have lain for days and weeks upon the ships that bear them home, reeking and sweating and oozing.

On the docks, the labourers hoist them one by one from their piles, retching and leaning against one another as they unleash pockets of trapped gas and foul greasy fluid that have hitherto suppurated undisturbed. These unfortunate men have never seen a live whale, but they are experts in its parts: fat for soap and lamps, spermaceti for smokeless candles; baleen for their sweethearts' corsets.

The rendering ovens in the long brick buildings on the nearside of the dock are already roaring hot, while the labourers fill vats with spongy rashers of blubber. Mr Hancock approaches a group taking air on the quayside.

'Good morning, boys,' he says.

'Morning to you. We don't see you here so often.'

'No, indeed. I did not expect to be here today. But I have been summoned on some mysterious business. Is Captain Tysoe Jones about the place?'

One of them jerks his head back, towards the edge of the dock, and there he stands by the water, tall and narrow and all alone in the midst of this industry, his face white and immobile. He is turning his hat around and around in his hands in a constant motion, as if it were some ritual of prayer.

'He's not so good,' says one of the dockers.

'A bad voyage,' says another.

'They do get that way sometimes.' He taps his temple meaningfully. 'Crazed.'

'I see,' says Mr Hancock, who indeed has seen it before. 'He needs a rest.' He approaches his old friend, smiling and reaching out his hand, but although Captain Jones looks as if he is waiting for something, and his eyes are roving and expectant, he does not seem to see him.

'From the looks of it you have had a hard voyage,' says Mr Hancock. 'Eh, Tysoe? But you are home now.'

His friend tears away his eyes from an invisible point in the air, and fixes them with difficulty upon Mr Hancock's lapel. He is silent for a moment. A muscle in his jaw seems to be working. 'Yes,' he says, presently. 'You might say so.'

'Here, Tysoe –' Mr Hancock's jubilance bubbles up before he can suppress it – 'much has changed in my circumstances, you will not credit it. I've a wife, sir!'

Captain Jones remains impassive.

'And she has one in the basket already,' persists Mr Hancock. 'I'm to be a father. What do you say to that, hey?' But for perhaps the first time in his life, Captain Jones has nothing at all to say. He nods absently, that is all, leaving Mr Hancock to stammer and cough and then ask lamely, 'And how were your travels?'

'Strange.' His old friend's eyes will not meet his; he mumbles into his stock. Then his eyes roll off into the middle distance again.

'Do you know –' Mr Hancock hesitates, perturbed at his friend's strangeness – 'you took far longer to return than you had expected?' He longs for the gratification of a warm handshake, a clap about the shoulders; he regrets that his old friend does not rejoice in his achieving this most masculine of things. But what signifies more is that something is gravely amiss.

Captain Jones shrugs. 'What's time anyway?'

'And we are not meeting in the usual place,' prompts Mr Hancock.

'No. This is not the usual cargo. So . . .' They stand for a minute longer, silent. Then Captain Jones says, 'Come with me.'

He sets off with a little burst of energy, and moves quite rapidly in a sort of lurching shuffle: his limbs wobble like a puppet's and his feet never quite leave the ground. In this way he leads Mr Hancock along the length of the dock, where the ships jostle gently together like cattle, and towards a tumbledown warehouse beyond. When they are just a few yards away from it, his footsteps falter and cease. He stands still again, looking at the ground.

'I got you what you want,' he says. 'I found her. But I think – I think perhaps you should not have her.'

'What?'

'She will not be what you expect. She is not what *I* expected, Lord knows.'

'I expect nothing. I expected a dead one.'

'Well, I can assure you she is not dead.' He snorts mirthlessly. 'I do not know if I would call her alive, but she is not dead.'

They step into the shadowy warehouse. Squinting, Mr Hancock sees that one of the big-bellied rendering vats has been dragged from its shed, its passage across the stone floor marked by clawing lines of soot. Mr Hancock advances slowly. To his surprise, Captain Jones keeps talking:

'Every sailor is heartsick at least sometimes in his life. But this was the most melancholy voyage I ever knew.'

The water – for the vat is surely full of water, and not oil – gives a little plash, as if something very large has rolled gently over in it.

'We installed her quite comfortably in the hold. At first the crew was in good spirits. I would always catch one or other of my boys down there, just gazing at her. But after a while . . .'

The vat is as tall as Mr Hancock, and he cannot see inside. He slaps his palm against its scorched side. 'Have you any steps? I wish to look.'

'. . . well, by and by every man on that ship was overcome by grief, a sort of melancholy hollowness. As if each one of us had been gutted like a fish. Everything warm and substantial taken out and thrown away.' Captain Jones remains in the doorway, just shy of the thin shaft of sunlight that creeps in. He begins again to turn his hat around in his hands. 'How to describe it if you have never felt it?' he says softly. Perhaps he is talking to himself. But he wishes to be heard; his voice is high and urgent. 'It is like realising that one is no longer in love. The restlessness. Nobody looked anybody in the eye. Nobody spoke or sang. It was as if every soul on that ship suddenly knew that somewhere in the world there was a great love just for them, but that the world was so large they would never find it.'

'I did not know you were so poetical,' says Mr Hancock. He drags an empty keg up to the vat, climbs onto it, and peers inside.

The water stirs. In the dark it appears quite black, apart from the mica booming through it like stars. At first he thinks, *why, there is nothing here. My wife was right: I have been duped.* Then the water heaves a great sigh, rainbows glance across the copper, and he sees her. She is indistinct but there is no doubting she is there. She is like a shoal of tiny fish, all surging and flickering together, a great mass that forms and re-forms and thinks all in accord. He can make out sometimes her arms, and often her swirling hair. He sees the silvery rolling-over of her heavy tail. He hangs over the water for many minutes as she sighs and rolls.

'Oh,' he says.

'And when we disembarked last night,' continues Captain Jones, 'we all knew – we will never sail together again. We who were like brothers. I do not know where they will all go; not back to their homes for they have no homes that feel like home.' He contemplates this statement for a moment, before repeating it, turning it over as if it were a curiosity he needed to inspect. 'They have no homes that feel like home.' Then he straightens up. 'Take her away. You are fortunate we did not scuttle the ship, for we'd have done it gladly. I've a mind to return to sea again as soon as possible. What is there for me here? What good is money?'

Mr Hancock is not listening. 'I must tell Angelica,' he says, squinting into the waters once again. 'I must go at once.'

Even so, he remains leaning over the vat for many seconds longer.

385

TEN

'Urgh,' says Angelica Hancock, opening her eyes.

Something is happening.

She finds she is in a great deal of pain. 'Urgh,' she says again, and gets out of bed. Her legs will not do as she tells them; her belly is gripped by something. She drops to her knees and vomits into the chamber pot, not much.

'Urgh,' she heaves from her diaphragm. She kneels there for a moment or two, palms pressed flat to the floor, spitting saliva that glides in gobbets down threads suspended between her lips and the pot, which stretch and dangle but will not break. She waits to see if she will vomit again. No. She wipes her mouth with the back of her hand, and shunts the chamber pot back under the bed where her hair will not trail in it, but she cannot get up. She kneels, her body folded tightly, with her feet under her buttocks and her knees under her breasts, as if she were trying to parcel herself up, hold herself together. The pain in her belly is phenomenal.

'I know what this is,' she says out loud. She is almost exasperated; it is not the first time in her life. She raises herself off the floor a little, one hand pressed to her stomach, and puts the other in between her legs. It comes away bloodier than she had expected; it gleams like a beetle-back as she holds it in front of her face, splaying her fingers out. The blood stretches in mucous webs.

'Oh, dear Jesus.' There is a sob swelling in her throat. When she rolls her eyes heavenwards she catches the sheets on the bed, smeared and blotched. 'Oh, *Jesus.*' What a mess. What a state. That will not wash out.

She crouches there for a long while, hunched over her pain, as if her body only exists to contain it. Her ankles are trembling and she lets her head hang, so that all she can see is a wall of her own hair. After a while she drags the sheet off the bed and jams it between her legs. She rolls over onto her side and curls there, knees to her chest, pressing her hands to her face. The creases in her palms are sticky and smell of her own emissions.

She does not weep, though. All other things being equal she would be bawling like a hungry lamb, for she has little tolerance for pain and has rarely felt so sorry for herself, but something prevents her. She knows what is happening. And she feels a terrible sadness.

'Stay with me,' she whispers, and the tears run over the bridge of her nose, spread over her cheek, and pool on the floorboards. 'Stay with me. Oh, what will I do without you?'

There is no stopping it, of course. The only thing she can think to do is what she has been taught before, on other occasions after the usual ritual of hot baths, strenuous walks, patented tonics. 'Breathe. No, *breathe.* You'll be better for it. In. Out. In. Out. Blow it all out,' she was told. 'Blow it *all* out.' And she would blow, long and even, until all her breath was gone and it felt as if the two walls of her lungs might stick together. On those occasions there were other women around her, rubbing her back and shushing in her ears: she howled on those occasions but only with the pain. Afterwards there would be sweet wine, and a clean bed, and eventually laughter.

Now, she is alone on the floor of her marital chamber. She blows all the air out of her lungs in a long and steady stream, and in this way she is able to manage her pain, more or less, at least enough to bear witness to the passing of this thing.

Sukie must have heard her from her bedroom, for she pokes her head around the door and sees her legs knotted in the stained sheet, little bloodied fingerprints on her face.

'Mrs Hancock!'

Angelica does not uncurl herself; she does not get up from the floor. 'I think it is done,' she says. 'I think it is too late.'

'Let me help you.'

'No, no. I can't get up. Don't touch me.'

'Come on.' She hoicks her up by the armpits, carefully unlooping the sheet from her legs. Angelica cries as it falls away from her. 'Now, then. It's all right. Don't look, don't look; I'll see to that.' Somewhere in the streaked folds of the sheet might be found – if it is large enough to be seen, if it can be recognised, if it even exists in one piece – the tiny clotted froglet that Angelica carried. 'Come, into bed. I'll get things to bathe you.'

'It's too late,' Angelica repeats.

'There is nothing as could have been done. This is just what happens sometimes.'

'Oh, how would you know?'

'How would *you*?' snaps Sukie.

Angelica dissolves into tears. 'Your uncle . . .' she says. How pleased he would have been to have a living child. How delighted. And how he would have loved her for it. She cannot have it – her two-months family prised apart like an oyster shell. 'You must not tell him,' she says.

'But what shall I—'

'If he comes home this morning, tell him I am unwell. Tell Bridget so, too. There is no need for him to know anything yet. I shall sleep it off. I shall be all right. I do not wish him to see me lose my composure.'

'And if he sends for you? He will want to show you the mermaid.'

'There is no point even considering that possibility,' says Angelica, climbing into her bloodied bed. 'There is no mermaid. I do not believe there ever was one.'

ELEVEN

'Well, what is she like?' Angelica asks her husband at dinner that evening. He has stumbled in late and peculiar flat around the eyes, but she is in no state to mark this, she being only an hour out of bed herself, and less than an hour rinsed of the last traces of her loss. She feels those smears and fingerprints of blood as a mark of guilt: standing over the tub in the kitchen she scrubbed at them and clenched her teeth with sorrow. And so it is a peculiar meal, not their usual happy troughing, although she has put on her prettiest chintz and had Bridget puff the powder into her hair.

'Hmm?' he says.

'Your mermaid.'

'Oh!' He toys his fork across his plate. ''Tis hard to explain.' In truth he does not know what to make of it. He had wanted to dash back to her bed, to tell her about this thing he can make no sense of, but something had rooted him quite to the spot. Instead he found himself standing over that vat for minutes that stretched into hours, searching the water for the shifting creature within.

She does not press him. Indeed she hardly hears him; her thoughts have crept somewhere deep inside her, a little fist of pain at the centre of her body. She returns again and again to her own disbelief: that no sooner has this small thing been given to her, than it is taken away again. And could she have done differently? Has she walked too often in the evening chill? Has she been too active, or not active enough? Or was it her own thoughts that poisoned the child; did it taste her lack of fitness; did it starve for the love she had been slow to extend to it? *Oh, God, or is this a judgement on my past deeds?*

The food is ashes in her mouth; she pushes her plate away.

Her husband hardly looks at her. *Perhaps he knows, and is angry.* She tries to catch his eye, but he sees nothing in the room at all. He is thinking, in fact, of how to keep his new-found mermaid, for it is clear she cannot stay at the whaling dock for ever. What is required for her is a good-sized pool, but this answer of course breeds more questions. How long do mermaids live? This one seems hardly to be alive in the usual sense, so perhaps she cannot be presumed to die. And must the water be saline? She is, after all, from the sea.

He wishes he were a scientific man.

And yet surely this phenomenon cannot be explained by science. His mind creeps to the *feeling* he had as he leant over the vat. He thought it contained something far larger than it appeared; as if a huge void were opening up where before all was solid and dull. A strange prickling rushes over his whole body, and he thinks suddenly of Henry, of Mary, who in the midst of life were in death. *Futility creeps on us everywhere,* he thinks. *Flourishing one day, cut down the next.* And if a man may be taken from his work at any moment, the only thing that can be hoped for is that he will leave some mark of himself behind, in the footprint of a building or the pounding heart of his own child. If he leaves nothing, who can say he lived at all?

His mouth is dry. He has not felt it at all since his marriage, but all of a sudden he is fearful, and most certain that these fragile things he has will soon be snatched again from his grasp. There are words in his head that he did not put there, but he cannot quite make them out. He sighs, and reaches across the table for his wife's hand.

TWELVE

May 1786

He is absent every day. She does not know where he goes, but he is not in the bed when she wakes up, and she walks his house all day knowing she will not find him in any of its rooms. It grasps at her heart as if he has abandoned her. She tries to make ready for their removal with Bridget and Sukie, but her pace is so dull and directionless that they soon lose patience.

'Stir yourself!' Sukie says, the day Angelica stands for twenty minutes in the middle of the parlour, holding a single tea bowl in her cupped palm. ''Tis not right that *I* must do everything. The lists I write that you do not care even to read! The arrangements I have made that are surely more your business than mine. And *he* is no better.'

'I am sorry,' whispers Angelica. There are dark shadows under her eyes.

The loss of the child feels to her an omen, and the closer the day comes for them to depart, the greater her dread grows. Her husband would have her installed in a great house, the shining jewel at the centre of a finely worked setting, and she thinks, *it cannot be. I am no match for any of it; I shall fail greatly there as I failed humbly here.* The fear quite chokes her; she sits down and cannot find the life in her heavy legs, or the activity in her mind, to rise again.

The room is pale and strange, white sheets hung over every piece of furniture. Angelica, clutching a sheet to her bosom, turns to Sukie with agony in her eyes. 'Please, please, do not tell him about – about what has happened.'

'He must know soon enough.'

But her aunt hangs her head. 'Only give me a little longer. I cannot let him down so, I cannot do it.'

And Sukie, now carrying the sick anxiety of Angelica's secret, must continue with the great business of their home all alone, pattering up and down the stairs on errands without cease, with such scratching in her pocketbook as to make her mother proud. When Mr Hancock returns home in a trance, Sukie rages at him. 'Where have you been? Look to your wife! She is not well.'

'Oh?' He has spent all day standing over the mermaid's tank. His feet are pearled with chilblains from the dirt floor, and his eyes ache for searching the black surface of the water. He has not powdered his wig or visited the barber or changed his clothes for many days, but he feels that the longer he gazes upon the mermaid, the better he can hear the words she whispers. At night, lying sleepless by his sleepless wife, he fancies he hears the mermaid's voice – it must be her voice – no louder than the mutter of somebody deep in dreams. Soon he will understand what she is saying.

'Are you listening to me?' Sukie stands before him, but even as she speaks he fades away from her, as if he were slipping down into deep water. 'Your wife needs you. And yet I think that has no meaning for you.'

And no, no, it does not; for he does not go to her and he does not ask her how she goes.

It is on this day that a messenger arrives at Mr Hancock's London counting-house.

'A note for the gentleman,' he says.

'Regarding?' asks Scrimshaw.

'His use of the outbuildings at Greenland Dock.'

'He is not here.' He is there so rarely now; he has made no arrangements for another voyage and no attempt to go in on any other. The clerks fret, and pursue business as best they can. Perhaps this is what happens to a man when he attains gentility.

The messenger heaves his shoulders a little. 'My master wants this message delivered to his own hands. We have pasted up bills on the building itself but he persists in using it. What does he have in there?'

'As if that concerns you,' snaps Scrimshaw, who has positively no idea. ''Tis not for you to wonder what a gentleman does with his own property.'

'If it *were* his own. In fact, Captain Tysoe Jones has relinquished the lease on it, and left it cluttered with rotten rope and rendering drums and Lord knows what else. We are not a common tip, you know.' He thrusts the note out more vigorously. 'We are businessmen, same as you. Won't you see he acts on this information in short order?'

'You couldn't give it to him yourself? How is this practical?'

'He don't listen to a word *we* say,' says the messenger. 'He goes his own sweet way. He can't very well disregard what is written on vellum and sealed –' he puffs up his chest – 'with wax.'

'Leave it with me,' says Mr Scrimshaw. 'He'll be here by and by.'

'No. I want it took to him now.'

'So you take it to him.'

The clerks are stirring themselves, watching the conversation with some interest. 'Yes,' they murmur, '*you* take it.'

'I am paid by the letter,' says the messenger. 'They will not pay me more for a long walk. Besides,' he adds, putting the letter on Scrimshaw's lectern, ''tis *your* business.'

Scrimshaw sighs. 'Oliver?' He rolls his eyes to his youngest clerk.

Oliver looks mournfully out of the window, at the heavy sky and the first spits of rain on the glass. 'I shall take it when I go to deliver the other papers to Mr Peyton,' he says. 'I've not the time for two errands.'

Scrimshaw squints challengingly at the messenger. 'Well? That must satisfy you. We are busy men.' In the corner, Mr Jarrold puzzles over the bawdy riddle Mr Percy has doodled for him on the back on an invoice.

And so this note is crushed into the pocket of Oliver the clerk as he departs on an errand to the docks at St Catherine's. He strides swiftly with it as far as the top of London Bridge, but the sky is darkening and spits of rain are misting upon his face: on such a rough night he wishes to go no further in his errand, but take himself into a tavern and see out the weather with ale and laughter. He presses the note and a few wafered coins into the fist of a small boy sheltering in the porch of St Magnus the Martyr, and this boy scuttles onward over the bridge, wrapped about in his older brother's greatcoat, whose tattered hem drags on the ground and soaks up the puddles. His nose runs prodigiously, and he blots it once or twice upon the ink: about him the wind gets up and the river churns and leaps in its crenellated bounds, like a horse nervous before a storm.

At Greenland Dock, the rain is the least of the boy's concerns: here he is suddenly engulfed in a cloud of mood, which lies as heavy as a foot across his windpipe. Oh! What is it? It is like a mist; hangs heavy over the buildings and the ships, puts tears in the eyes and a sob in the throat. The boy, whose mother lies coughing and white in their cellar lodgings, is near-blinded by his own anguish. He wants nothing more than to run home to her, but in the rain and mist and sorrow loses his bearings, and circuits the squat dark buildings once, then twice, in the stink of murdered whales and the looming sight of tall ships. It is a labourer who seizes this boy by the shoulders and points him homeward, and who eventually delivers that crumpled paper to Mr Hancock's shack.

The merchant leans so studiously that his nose almost touches the water. The mermaid trembles and glitters within, and her largeness has become a fume that escapes from its surface and intoxicates him. Mr Hancock has himself never seen the sea, but at the mermaid's side he feels it: vast and boisterous, freezing and impassive.

When this message is brought to his elbow, he is not surprised by its contents.

Even so, 'Why was I not told of this?' he demands of the labourer who stands at his elbow.

'You were told.'

'So where am I to keep my goods?' He grips the rim of the vat in panic.

'It don't signify. But we are bound to pull down this place come Wednesday. If it does not tumble down of its own accord.' He puts his hand upon a beam, and the whole building rattles and lurches in a most satisfying demonstration of its own dereliction. A great nest of old rushes and one decayed mouse rattle to the dirt floor.

Mr Hancock begins to sweat. He gazes again into the water. What is to be done? 'I need more time,' he says.

'There is no more time.'

'I can pay you.'

'No.' The labourer twists his chafed fingers together and looks embarrassed. 'If you want the truth, we are all agreed that this place must go. 'Tis haunted; everybody feels it lately. The ghastly sadness as comes off it, and can be felt within it.'

'No, no,' says Mr Hancock in some panic.

'You must feel it. I know you do.' He clears his throat and leans nearer. 'Mr Wattle, the overseer – he lost his little girl two weeks ago. Drowned –' he jerks his head yonder – 'in the river not a hundred feet from here. Nobody's fault; she must have wandered in her play. But that sadness – such grief, we all feel it, a loss like that does tend to touch every body – has grown ever stronger since. We are all agreed; we shall burn the place. There's no price will change our minds, sir.'

Since the men of Greenland Dock have formed their own convictions as to the source of the strange miasma, Mr Hancock feels entitled to ape outrage. 'And so I must remove my stock?' he demands.

'Aye.'

'Then I need –' he thinks, rests his hand on the rim of the vat – 'I need to move this.'

The labourer snorts. ''Tis not my job.' He glances curiously at the vat of dirty water. '*That?*'

'What of it?'

'Why, 'tis just a filthy discarded thing. Why you should want it—'

'It was doing no harm here until *you* determined to pull this building down,' Mr Hancock says aggrievedly. He digs in his pockets and draws out a wad of clean notes. 'Here. How much would it cost you? I want it done at night.' He is thinking quickly. Where to move the thing? Are there other likely outbuildings? Can it be concealed somewhere about his offices? 'I need it brought to Blackheath,' he says with decision. 'To Blackheath, and then no more need be said about it.'

'I do not understand,' says the labourer.

From the vat, a gasp; a sigh; a leap of liquid into the air.

And thus it is done, very swiftly and under cover of darkness. Mr Hancock seals the rendering vat with a discarded piece of mainsail and sees it loaded onto castors and thence a raft by four bleary workmen kept from their beds to do they-know-not-what for the promise of a purse of money apiece; thus it is transported by raft along the river to Greenwich, while he sits with his back against it, rocking gently upon the black water. Thence he and the vat are taken up the hill to the heath by bullock cart. It is dark beyond darkness: not a light on the road, just empty nothing before them and the whistling of the dry grass in the wind. He is alert to footsteps, and flinches at the heard swoop of some night bird passing near, mistaking the sigh of its feathers for a blade unsheathed. Surely he is glad to see the gable of his own empty house come into view; he feels no guilt that, before his wife sleeps her first night there, he has already concealed a secret within it. The grass hisses.

'Good to be in the clean air,' says one of the men Mr Hancock's labourer friend has hired.

'Aye,' says another, tight-lipped. He is afraid of the contents of the vat; wanted nothing of it. 'You're to help,' Mr Hancock snapped at him. 'You want to see the thing gone, do you not?' He sits now hugging his own shoulders, chin tucked into his collar.

The third man hesitates. 'But the queerest thing,' he says, 'I still do feel sad.'

'Ghosts are tenacious,' squeaks the labourer.

'Aye, that's so.' His mate shrugs, shivering off a shaft of sudden chill. 'My wife's mother, God rest her, followed us to three different lodgings when first we were married. We knew she was there by the smell of burnt porridge. What fools! It took us seven years to perceive that she was attached to the hearth brush all along, and after we gave it a Christian burial she troubled us no more.'

They pass along the drive, skirting the stables, and draw the cart to a stop at the edge of the lawn. 'It is to go in the folly,' says Mr Hancock, gesturing to its shadow at the far end of the garden. 'I want no wheel-marks on the grass.'

'What, and we are to carry it down the hill?' says the labourer's mate, leaping down from his seat.

'I'll do no such thing,' says the first, backing away. 'Oh no. I'll not touch it.'

'Say, what's your trouble? Are you averse to hard work now?' But the second workman is apprehensive himself, a peculiar dread taking up the space of his heart. Something is amiss, although he cannot say what.

'Bring it down,' says Mr Hancock. 'I shall help you.'

The five men stagger with the vat through the enclosing trees. The moon being slender, there is little to be seen, but something peculiar to be heard. A tapping from within the metal, as if tiny bubbles were popping against it, a sweeping sound as if flesh brushed against it; and once a long, sonorous note of metal struck, which trembles through the vat and through again. At this the first labourer nearly bursts out weeping.

'Hush you,' says his mate, unwilling to express the perturbation he feels. 'You are entertaining demons.'

It takes some hours to manoeuvre its dead weight and fearful splosh down the staircase. The copper sides of the barrel scrape against the mussel shells and the canvas covering rucks up. Cobwebs and birds' bones spin on the surface of the water and then are gulped out of sight.

Dawn is coming in by the time they have heaved and panted the thing into the furthest chamber of the grotto. 'Thank you, gentlemen,' says Mr Hancock as he leads them back into the light. 'You have done me a great service.'

'Sir,' says the more ebullient of the labourers, most grave now, for he has had his ear pressed to the copper for hours, and heard the weird stirrings within, and felt the tug of something most unnatural, 'what did we deliver you?'

''Tis of no concern to you.'

'I judge that it is,' he retorts, but his companion gives him a jab in the ribs.

'No, no,' he whispers. 'Let us not enquire. Let us leave this place and never return.'

'Call it contraband,' says Mr Hancock. 'Call it rum, if you wish.'

'But still I should like to . . .' The labourer peers over Mr Hancock's shoulder. 'I have not had a proper look.' He moves forward, but Mr Hancock holds him at arm's length and stares him down.

'Go,' he says. The first of the men is already pacing away. From up the hill comes the peaceful sound of the oxen cropping the long black grass.

'Ah, now . . .'

But Mr Hancock shakes his head, and they are away with many backward glances. The cart creaks into darkness, and Mr Hancock stands beneath the pillars of the folly until he judges himself to be most certainly alone; then he returns to the depths of the grotto beneath. The greenish ghost-light quivers up the walls; he takes out his knife and sets about cutting the canvas from the mouth of the vat. It comes away with a sigh that echoes around the curved metal walls and out into the chamber. Beneath the vaulted ceiling, the noise of the water is magnified most peculiar, and almost vocal; a tiny groan, as if a child there were stirring from sleep.

He touches the cold belly, hears the slop of movement within.

A loss is not a void.

A loss is a presence all its own; a loss takes up space; a loss is born just as any other thing that lives.

You think your arms empty, but I shall lie in them.

I have outgrown all the room you gave me – no more swimming for me, no more flying in the deep. Gone are the days I flipped imminent head over budding heels, a nimble half-formed one, could have become many things – now I crouch, pinned in, held fast, deep underground with my limbs folded in, and my form is inescapable. You know what I am, and what I am not, but you will not look upon me.

Nevertheless my streams, like fingers, find a way. Bury me deep, I shall seep to the surface. My stirrings are as earthquakes.

In my quickening I shall stretch limbs, arch neck, test muscles. My hunched spine curves like an egg: I shall shoulder aside these foundations that pin me, in the end.

I am here; I am here; you are not alone. Here I am; I am grief, the living child of your suffering. I am the grief that sits within you; I am the grief that sits between you.

You will bury me but I shall rise up.

You will not know me, but I shall make myself known to you.

THIRTEEN

Their removal to their great new house is sombre, for neither Mr nor Mrs Hancock is much inclined to optimism. Indeed, if their souls had found a way to communicate, they would have found them twinned in their sense of futility. He thinking, *my ambitions are beyond me*; she, *it is all over. I am unmatched to the task he has set me.* Then Bridget cannot accompany them since her mother will not have her so far distant, and the cat swipes and yowls and will not be entreated into a sack to take a place on the wagon. She whisks out of the yard door before she can be caught, and is away up the pear tree and over the wall.

'She does not know we are not coming back,' says Mr Hancock. 'She has no idea that she will return here to find the doors locked and no warm fire or saucer of milk awaiting her.'

'We never fed her milk but what she stole,' says Sukie, 'so that will cause her no dismay.'

Angelica rubs his shoulder – 'there will be other cats' – but her husband does not care for other cats, only his own, who has unwittingly become a nomad, a friendless wanderer in the cold.

'I never abandoned a thing in my life,' he says.

'Cats make their own way,' Angelica tells him, but she, too, feels traitorous.

When the time comes, the women approach Blackheath by

carriage, which makes straining, creaking progress up the hill. Sukie sits bolt upright at the window, her eyes alert to everything. The houses grow sparser but handsomer, and the shady road is quiet save for a gang of red-coated young men who idle, laughing. Beyond the ditches on either side of the road is nodding, sun-touched wilderness, all figured with birdsong, and the trees tall and graceful above their bed of bluebells.

'Is this where we are to live?' asks Sukie, her palm on the glass. They rise up to the plateau: the grass is a broad sunny swish as far as the horizon, tipped with light. 'And so where are we to buy our victuals? All our everyday needs?' She has never lived but on a street before, with tailor and butcher and carpenter no more than a trot down trusty flagstones.

'As if I know,' says Angelica, who is curled on the seat with her forehead on the window. The heath looks to her as if it were reflected in the curve of a banker's glass; its expanse magnified and the houses and trees that fringe it melting away small in the distance.

'I shall make enquiries.' Sukie takes out her pocketbook. 'It may be that we must order up from Greenwich. That will be an expense.'

'Hang the expense.' Angelica closes her eyes. The carriage shakes her like a nursemaid.

And now it is that they arrive at the entrance of their home, the narrow drive that curves modestly away from the road so that only the roof of the house might be seen by those strolling on the heath.

'Oh!' says Sukie, and her nose will press no closer against her window. 'I see the expense was hanged some time back!' She stares and stares. 'And *this* is where we are to live? Oh, come now, Mrs Hancock, lift up your head. Look at it!'

'I already saw it.'

'Do not pretend this gives you no pleasure!' For the house is as delightful as ever it was, from the symmetry of its windows, to the curve of its hillock, to the pretty Dutch gables of its outbuildings. 'So well appointed! For I believe we have a dairy, look, dear! And a vegetable garden. Oh, why did you not tell me it would be so fine?'

Indoors, it is as fine as fine, its floors all a-gleaming and the fat women and infants on the ceiling puffed up with pride. And there are sixteen leather fire buckets hung up in the back hall, and copper boilers pristine in the kitchen, and down below in the cold bowels of the house, a vaulted gallery of meat-hooks. There is a room for billiards and for sewing and for reading, and in all it looms over Angelica the most sumptuous of monsters. *It will kill me*, she thinks, and cannot bear to watch Sukie dash hither and thither, near-fevered with the work before her. *Enquire as to gardener*, she scribbles in her book. *See to character of new maids; fumigate all the attics; send for wallpaper samples.*

To Angelica she cries, 'Oh! Madam! Won't this be fun?' and does not mind that she has no reply. Her aunt only stands upon the shining floor with something like dismay writ all over her face, but Sukie vibrates with the thrill of it all, for this is no longer the straitened training she has known hitherto – the trifling management of closet and cupboard – but a situation of which she might call herself mistress, by any reasonable definition of the word. She will know the proper place of everything, and furthermore have the authority to move it about; nobody but she will dictate washing and cleaning, polishing and buffing. And when it comes to feeding the house, Sukie alone will ordain how many cutlets are to be ordered; will turn the grocer's offerings over in her hands and decide their quality; will choose what fruits are enjoyed fresh and what bottled for a comfortable winter. She never was so unfettered in all her life, but at the same time she is greatly afraid. *This is an entirely new sort of place*, she observes, *for a new manner of living. I must not appear superfluous to it, or they will send me away.*

'And so we shall inspect the gardens,' she prattles on to Angelica, 'and see what grows there, and what must yet be done. It will be a great economy to have our fruits and vegetables grown here. And I would like a clutch of chickens to rear, and a—'

'Have you ever raised livestock before?' asks Angelica faintly. 'Kept a kitchen garden?'

'Details! Details! I have a book. I shall hire help in. And would you not like a little brood of speckled chicks? Think of them pecking about!'

Angelica closes her eyes. 'This is beyond me. I cannot think where to start.'

'I can! Come with me to the kitchen, and we shall make up some great lists. A list of what we have, a list of what we do not, and a list of what we must do with it all once it is got.' Sukie hops from foot to foot, her face flushed. 'So much to do, Mrs Hancock! It will keep us eternally occupied, and we may do it just as we choose, and the men can say nothing but "thank ye". I had better talk to my uncle, for you and I shall need to hire a full complement of staff to effect all the plans *I* have in mind.'

'Excuse me,' says Angelica abruptly. 'I am tired. You will permit me rest awhile.'

Upstairs she pauses on the landing, but Sukie follows behind, her face all knitted with anxiety. 'Can you not let me be?' demands Angelica.

Sukie hesitates, and steels herself. 'You need to tell him,' she says. 'If there is not to be a child, he must know.'

Angelica says nothing. She closes her eyes; she cannot think what to do. *I do not belong here,* she thinks. *If I were mistress of this house then this baby would not have been aborted.* She was afraid of her narrowing world, but now without its safe enclosure she finds she is nobody. Angelica Neal is quite gone; Angelica Hancock is already hollow as a bleached shell. She places a hand to her brow. 'He has not even noticed,' she says. 'He does not care; he asks nothing about it.' *I have lost everything.*

'Come, we are not two minutes inside the door,' says Sukie, although she is fierce afraid to see such faltering in her aunt. 'It will all change now we are here.' She takes a little step forward. '*Please.*'

But Angelica knits her brow, and shakes her head. A new wave of dejection seems to have settled upon her since arriving on the heath; now she feels most especially as if she were grasping at something quite impossible to seize upon. 'Leave me be,' she says.

Alone on the landing, she remembers that she does not know where her bedroom might be. Many doors stand before her, all closed; she tries the first, and it is a library. The second a little music room, all pearl-coloured and glowing with the window shades drawn up: her eye passes over her own clavichord to the harp and viol and flute beyond, and her stomach tightens. *He must mean me to learn to play them,* she thinks, *when I am not even equal to the task of ordering the kitchen.*

She opens doors until she discovers a bedroom – a small one, hung with yellow damask, good for a spinster visitor – and once within sits down on the bed quite numbed. She longs for the bare little kitchen at Union Street, where she could chop apples and peel carrots with innocent assiduity under the supervision of girls half her age. *What a fool,* she thinks, *to imagine I had the measure of any domestic life. And what am I to do now?* She finds herself at a peculiar impasse, the first perhaps in her life, and it is not caused by obstacles but by the lack of them.

What now? she thinks. *What now, what now?* and knots her fingers and furrows her brow.

Outside her window the heath lies flat to the horizon, its sky churning. The wind roils the clouds and the gorse bushes alike; each new day grows longer and hotter than its predecessor.

FOURTEEN

June 1786

The summer grows hot and ripe, bleaching the grass of the heath to a perfect rustling sweep of gold, where grasshoppers creak incessantly to one another, but where few walk in the heat of the day. Now ought to be the time for ventures into London, or Greenwich, or out by boat to the country homes of friends, the long bright days being so unwelcoming to footpads. The Hancocks, however, go nowhere. Sukie busies herself with hiring a coterie of servants, from cook to lady's maid to footman, who look her up and down with amused pity, and who smirk when she gives them their orders in her little thin voice. The promised dancing master comes too, and laments her slumped shoulders, her weak ankles. The French master decries her accent, the Latin master her ignorance, and in this great house she feels a coarse hick of a girl, good for nothing. Of all this she says nothing, but bites her lip, and smiles anon.

Angelica, meanwhile, robbed of the tasks of an increasing wife – no cradle to send for, no tiny caps to trim – finds that her days roll on with terrifying futility. No longer are her moments diminishing; each dawn sees her no closer to any great event. She can anticipate neither the beginning of any new life nor the end of her own: she remains in genteel suspension, her time stretching inexorably before her. As for her husband, where is he? Off about his inscrutable business in the city, or at the faraway Mary-le-Bone site of his new houses. He is never to be found about the house, unless he is lingering at one of the back windows, staring without sight at some far-distant point. More often she sees him trudging up the hill from the place where the garden gives way to wilderness.

Some assignation? she wonders, keeping her eyes closed on the blue-mooned night as he stumbles about the bedroom. *Does he go to meet a lover? Has he found a secret way to Greenwich?* but she hears no carriage on the drive, and no lantern light has crossed her window, and as he bends over the bed she detects no liquor on his breath, and no perfume on his stock. Where, then, does he take himself all night? She thinks of her other failures: the twist of Georgie's face when he said – what was it he said? – 'I am sick of you,' and the dread shame of clutching Mrs Chappell's ankles in her parlour all stripped bare. She hugs her arms about herself, and feels her body slacker and less seizable than it once was, which inspires desire in nobody who looks upon it, and cannot sustain the flickerings of any life but her own. Her closed eyelids burn with tears but she resolves to give her husband no hint that his presence has penetrated her sleep: not to flinch at the cold breeze that follows him into the room, or roll over to open her arms to him. She deepens her breathing and nestles closer into her bedclothes, but at her turned back she feels him lie still and wakeful for a good long time. She thinks, *our bad luck began when we acquired this place. We have overreached ourselves, that is certain, but is there not some horrid miasma here?* It taints her very lungs: some mornings it seems that all she breathes is grief.

'Another note,' says Sukie, 'from our neighbours.'

'We have no neighbours,' says Angelica. She licks the end of her thread and squints to press it into her needle, for they are as ever about the business of housekeeping, and in the spirit of furious industry Sukie has devised a code. Each room of the house is assigned its own symbol, spined and hooked as a skeleton key, and with scarlet thread they stitch it upon every bit of cloth that might be carried off from its designated place. The laundry house has levelling tendencies, and without proper oversight might send the fine wool blanket from the library to lie upon the cook's bed.

'Certainly we do have neighbours,' says Sukie. 'Not three hundred yards away.'

'We do not pass them in the street and they do not nuisance us through the walls,' says Angelica, 'therefore how can they be anything to us?'

'Well, we are something to *them*,' Sukie cajoles, 'and grateful we should be for it.'

'Perhaps *you* should. I daresay they have sons it will be worth your while to know, one day. But *I* . . .' Her stitching is large and ugly, her fingers fumbling. *I shall have to unpick those tonight,* thinks Sukie. She lets no criticism pass her lips, but she feels as if she were stretched tight; scampering always just before her aunt to cheer her, protect her, encourage her. '*I* am not their sort,' Angelica continues, frowning over her sorry work. 'They would not have desired to look upon me before: they would have shielded their daughters' eyes from me. And their sons'.' She runs her finger with the needle and jerks back, spitting like a cat: a bead of blood swells there.

'Not on the linen,' cries Sukie. 'We shall never get the mark out. I would rather you even blotted it on your apron.'

'I believe they come to stare.' Angelica sucks the blood away and inspects as it bubbles up again. 'I am a freak to them.'

'You are the wife of a good man, and mistress of this house the same as any.'

'They come only for curiosity. I will not have them.'

'I have already invited them here,' says Sukie. 'For tea. Tomorrow. The ladies only, of course. That is the thing to do, you know, the right thing.'

'Ugh! The ladies are worst of all! The only thing worse than the ladies would be their gentlemen.'

'Hush, hush.' Sukie suppresses her impatience. 'Remember, you are Mrs Hancock now. Once the ladies have taken a look at us, there will be other invitations. You will like that, to be back in society.'

'Not *their* society.'

To distract her from her petulance, and remind her of her position, Sukie bullies her through the messuages of which she is mistress – the dairy, the brewhouse, the laundry – and out into the orchard, where the grasshoppers buzz in the grass, and leap like popped buttons at the women's passing. The two maids hired from the village of Blackheath follow behind, hung about with baskets and coarse bags, and sharing the weight of the ladder between them as they teeter unwillingly on their pattens, picking their feet up high. The gnarled and reaching arms of the apple trees are all a-rustle, their leaves crisp and vivid and cool. Sukie stops to draw a bough down towards her and inspect the pale fruit growing there, the largest no bigger than a hen's egg.

'Look,' she says, brushing a ladybird from the curled leaves.

'T'was not for *this* I became a great lady,' Angelica grumbles.

'And when did you do that?' Sukie lets the bough go, and it hurtles upward, setting all its neighbours a-swaying.

'Nobody elevated as we have been must see to her own gardens.'

'This is exactly our duty. What, you thought you would be at your leisure because you are kept? Your work is hardly begun.'

'I had better remained where I was,' says Angelica, pulling her straw hat down over her face. Sunlight speckles through its weave; she shades her eyes.

Onward they walk to the first of the plum trees, whose perfumed boughs droop with the weight of their fruit.

'We have plums enough,' says Angelica. 'I am sick of the sight of them.'

'Well, *be* sick. They are hardly into their season, and we must preserve a good many more before winter.' The girls set the ladder up against a tree. 'Help us?' asks Sukie. 'You need not climb, dear, just pick the ones closest to hand.'

Angelica says nothing. She turns her face towards where Greenwich might be, but the basin of land beneath them is filled up still with the dawn's mist, and she does not see the spire of Alfege's, or the domes of the naval hospital, or even a single ship's mast, except through a veil of haze. The river, with its gilded barques and swift clippers, has been vanished all away, and she is alone on her hillside.

'Come.' Sukie takes her arm. She does not like the maids to see her aunt so devilled: they have a cruel way of watching. 'Collect those that have already fallen if you prefer. That's an easy task.'

'Don't it feel *worse* out here?' Angelica asks. For a tide of particular sorrow has taken her. She sighs as if she could empty her whole heart. Another breeze rushes up the hill, and she must sigh again; she feels the sorrow filling her lungs.

Sukie shakes her head. The maids lack a certain sprightliness of manner, she thinks, but then her aunt is a most subduing influence. It is hard to guard one's own happinesses against one who is so very much in denial of them. Sukie thinks, *it takes all I have even to affect happiness in her presence. She will suck it all from me; I cannot fight her much longer. Is this how it is always to be?* Aloud, she says not a word.

The plums at the trees' feet are some of them reduced to sludge, and their brandied smell is thick upon the air. 'Ugh,' says Angelica, 'they are rotted away.'

'Not all of them.' If Sukie is impatient, her voice hardly betrays it. 'See? These are good.' She nudges one with the side of her patten, and it rolls, flesh tender and true on all its faces. Flies green as opals rise peevishly. 'We must gather them up before any more go bad.'

But Angelica cannot be entreated. 'A fatuous endeavour,' she says. 'Everything is rotting.'

'Then will you go to the raspberry patch? See if the heat has ripened any,' persists Sukie, who would find true pleasure in the flourishing of her land, were she permitted. To walk out into bird-song and the damp-soil air, and discover what secret doings the plants have been about overnight . . . She feels as if she were a child who has discovered an elf-land. And yet she knows that Angelica is best appealed to through her appetite, and adds rashly, 'There may be enough to make a little tart. Or to garnish a fine duck, if Cook is disposed to roast it.'

'The more you try to please me,' says Angelica, 'the less you suc-ceed.' She starts back towards the house, the trills of a blackbird knitting about her. Behind her, the girls snort with laughter and are up the tree with a swish of branches. They pass the plums from hand to hand and lay them in their baskets as gently as eggs, watching the scene through the leaves.

'She has such queer moments,' Sukie explains, but the girls extend no friendliness to her, only roll their eyes at one another. Wishing for a friend, she seizes up her skirts and pursues Angelica up the hill through the long dry grass.

'Mrs Hancock!' she admonishes.

'Oh, leave me be.'

'You are mistress of this house; why do you give it none of your time?'

Angelica is walking fast, up the steps to the French windows, her arms clasped about herself. 'And what will you do now,' persists

Sukie, pushing her hat away from her face so it dangles on its ribbon between her shoulder blades, 'but go back to your chamber and lie on your silly bed and read your silly books, or some other nonsense thing that benefits nobody? Do you ever look beyond yourself?' She follows her into the atrium, where the marble floor gleams. 'You got what you wanted,' she says, and her voice echoes up the stairs. 'He gave you all this. And still you keep secrets from him. Still you are not happy.'

'What business is it of yours?' Angelica shakes her jacket from her shoulders and lets it fall to the floor as she storms on. She does not look back; she makes for her rooms.

'You have burdened me with it enough that it might as well be my business. This is not my own house and yet I can account for every last bolster in it, while *you*—'

Angelica's impatience erupts. 'Nebbiting, yepping thingsnitch! On and on you go, Sukie Lippard, you've tongue enough for two sets of teeth! If you wish to make such footling your life, then so be it! I am glad to say it is not *mine*, nor ever will be; trouble me with it no more.'

Sukie stands at the foot of the stairs, her hat tossed back and her hands on her hips, her mother's attitude. 'But it *is* your life,' she says. 'It must be. Or what are you?'

Upstairs, Angelica's door slams.

FIFTEEN

Mr Hancock has watched it all from the back window: the women in their straw hats and drab everyday gowns, going about their work with some animation. Could this be the same Angelica Neal he married? At this distance she is a woman as ordinary-looking as any other, not the shining and laughing ornament he had imagined keeping in his house. And that whisper again: *it can never be,* the feeling of great loss, as if the soft and lavish wife he chose has already died and it is only her shell carrying on. That distant shore he once envisaged is a mirage: what he thought were lush mountains are only churning clouds.

When she bursts into the room not moments later, he is unprepared for her storm of misery. 'Oh, I cannot bear it!' she cries. 'There will be visitors coming and I cannot think – I do not know how to speak to them at all. They will come to mock me, I am sure of it.'

'Who would mock you?' he asks. 'These are people like us. You would do well to socialise with them; they are people of a finer water, as we ourselves are now. I have chose the most splendid woman in London, and I have put her in an entirely splendid house – what can they find to laugh at?'

'Oh, as many things as there are inches of my body. *You,* sir, are *perhaps* their sort, or will shortly become so, but you have made a poor choice of wife. I can only hold you back.'

He thinks, for the first time, *is she touched by the same thing as I am myself? This fascinating melancholy that draws me back and back – perhaps its miasma has infected her too?*

She begins to weep. Her tears are fat as pearls. 'Because I am so filled with apprehension,' she says. 'I see that I shall fail you in the tasks you ask of me; I shall disappoint you in multitude ways. I cannot cook or sew or brew; I am afraid I cannot appear pleasantly to our neighbours of this class and match their manners, for I have no education in them.' She draws breath and seems to compose herself. 'I am fearful afraid, sir.'

At this he feels he might break down weeping; this is the moment he should tell her of the mermaid, whose grief and largeness seems to seize him more each day. But he is afraid what will happen if he takes the cap off such a secret. 'I am here,' he says weakly. Then he reaches through the great fog to observe at last what is true: 'I have neglected you,' he says.

'And I you.' She looks up at him with the purest expression of grief he has ever seen in his life, so that he kneels down before her and puts his chin on her knees. She takes off his wig and strokes her hands across his stubbly head, which movement both soothes her and eases him. It is something like having his hair stroked by his mother, although he little remembers her; she explores the corners of his skull as it terminates behind his ears, and kneads her fingertips over his crown. If their joy has been spoilt, it is by his bringing the creature into it. He draws breath but cannot speak it. He remains there some minutes longer, submitting to her touch which he has not known for what seems a great long time.

'I need to tell you something,' she says presently.

'What's that?'

She speaks so quietly she might as well be only moving her lips, but he catches her words: 'I lost the child.'

And ah! There it is. The feeling again of something snatched from his grip.

He feels a tickle on his cheek and looks up. A lock of her hair has slipped loose and wavers in the air between her face and his. His poor wife who has hitherto brisked about life is sad and fading already.

'I *have* neglected you,' he says.

'No. No.' The crease between her eyebrows never fades now. 'What could you have done?'

He rises so his forehead is pressed against hers. 'I could have helped you – that is something. I have been so absorbed in …' but he cannot say it. Instead he embraces his wife, breathing in her scent of apple-leaves and house-dust. He hears the sharp snatch of her breath, the shudder of grief that runs through her. 'There, there, my poor little pigeon. 'Tis all right.' He pulls away to look into her blotchy swollen face. Her lips are wet and wobbly like a child's.

'You are not angry with me?' she asks.

'No. Not at all.' How can he be? He feels nothing at all, only a dull vindication: *of course this would happen. Of course no happiness could come to us.* He cannot recall, in this moment of confirmation, the emotion of kindness, but he recalls its words and how they are used, and he reaches deeply for them now as he presses her hands in his. 'This is a small sorrow sent to try us, that is all. Am I not your husband?'

'You are. A good husband.'

'There. And so I would never be angry with you for such a sad thing.'

She smiles damply and he thinks, *she is not the woman I met.* And he thinks, *she can only get older henceforth; and the older one gets the narrower one's opportunities for happiness become.* And he thinks, *so*

416

what will be next? Will he come in one day to find her laid out dead? He squeezes her fiercely to him for a moment.

'I am relieved,' she says with some surprise. 'I do feel as if some weight has fallen from me. I could not tell you, but now that I have ...' She draws a deep quivering breath. 'Yes, 'tis better.' She stands, throws back her shoulders: she seems taller than she has in many months. 'Perhaps I am more myself.'

He stares out of the window. He feels as if he were on a ship in the middle of a great ocean, too far from home to turn about, but so distant from the strange shore ahead that his craft will be buffeted apart by the waves before it reaches it.

'Mr Hancock,' she whispers.

And he turns and sees her, golden as a beacon.

SIXTEEN

Those visiting are the ladies of the Crawford family, their fortune forged in a pin factory. Mrs Crawford, a matron with a voice so loud that Sukie, taking air at the open library window, hears it quite clearly as she watches the party arrive – '*Well*, you would think they would have had it painted, would you not, for that is the first thing *I* always do on acquiring a new home' – is accompanied by her daughter Mrs Flowerday, whose step is sprightly and whose curls bounce under her cape, and also Miss Crawford, a sister of the husband, narrow-shouldered and fidgeting. 'Mama,' says Mrs Flowerday, 'now be *kind* – not everybody has your instinct, and particularly not this lady. She is from *quite* a different world.' Miss Crawford says nothing, but then she is overburdened by some great unseasonable armful of rabbit fur and wool calamanco.

Sukie, still stung by Angelica's earlier rebuke, is inclined to closet herself for the rest of the day. *But if I have displeased her,* she frets, *she may want me here no longer. I must endeavour to do better.* And thus she steels herself to play hostess, and leaves the room in sedate haste. On the landing she taps on Angelica's door.

'They are arrived,' she says as the bell rings.

'Hmm,' from within.

'You will come down, will you not?' *Oh, do not abandon me to these strangers' scrutiny!*

'By and by.'

'They are here *now*.' A scuffle of whispers behind the door. 'Have you Catty in there with you? I've been looking for her all day.'

'She is helping me get ready,' says Angelica crossly. 'If you want me, and you want me decent, you will have to wait.'

The women's voices are loud at the door; they are on the step.

'I suppose I've no choice,' sniffs Sukie. She puts her palm flat on the door, and adds in a softer tone, 'Only do not leave me alone with them *too* long.'

The bell is jangling, and she scoots down the stairs as the footman crosses the atrium. 'Give me time,' she hisses to him. 'Send for hot water.'

In the parlour, tarts and tea bowls are laid out, just as she oversaw them. The light is poor, but it collects itself within each bowl, to beam through the porcelain like so many bottle-caught glowworms. Sukie has only a moment to arrange herself before the door opens and her visitors arrive in such a chaffing of cloth and clacking of shoes and clucking of voices that her thoughts desert her. She is kissed and inspected, and smiles most prettily, but the eyes of Mrs Crawford and her daughter are everywhere; they look from the tea bowls to the wallpaper to the bookcase with such goggling energy they risk snapping their necks.

Mrs Flowerday, a powdered young bride, takes her by the elbows to look her up and down. 'And you are *Miss* Hancock?' she says. 'Not *Mrs*.'

'I am Mr Hancock's niece,' she says. 'Miss Lippard.' Having so many elder sisters she is unused to the title, and furthermore does not know how much familiarity to extend to these women, so her own name leaves her lips as if it were a question: 'Susanna?' Her face feels hot. 'Mrs Hancock will join us by and by.'

'Ah!' Mrs Flowerday emits a gurgle of laughter. 'I thought you could not be *her* – I have heard so much about her beauty.'

Miss Crawford is still carrying her great bundle, and now she begins to remove clouts from it one by one: fur followed by dense tabby, and calamanco and finally an embroidered shawl. The women gather about.

'Oh! Little man! Are you awake?'

'Did you have a long sleep? Oh yes, you did!'

'Such a good boy to sleep so long!'

For within the bundle is a screw-faced baby, his hair awry with sweat, who blinks irritably at the company and brings his paws up to his eyes. His wrists are mere creases and he has dimples for knuckles. 'Our handsome fellow! Miss Lippard, you are honoured by Baby's first visit!'

'Oh,' says Sukie. 'Will you have some tea?'

But even once seated, they fuss about the child, whom the spinster Miss Crawford bounces upon her knee; his little head lolls back upon her bosom.

'I suppose he is your first,' says Sukie to Mrs Flowerday.

'Not only that, but my own first grandchild!' says Mrs Crawford. 'A wonder you could guess it! But do you know, when he was born I did not care for him at all. I only sought to satisfy myself that dear Caro was in no danger, for all infants are much of a muchness but there is only one Caroline. Or so I then thought.' She leans over and seizes Baby's cheek between thumb and forefinger. 'Was I wrong, was I not wrong? Are you not the dearest princeling that ever there was?' She turns back to Sukie. 'I make a dote of him now, so all is forgiven.'

A smile flickers across Miss Crawford's face. She is something about forty, and handsome in an austere, big-nosed way: she holds the infant without anxiety, her eyes elsewhere. She barely marks it when he suddenly screws up his face and lets out a squall of effort, but lets him clasp his fists around her fingers with the placidity of habit. He braces his tiny feet upon her legs and arches his back to pull himself upright, his eyes goggling with the strain and a bubble of drool glistening on his slackening lips.

'A fine strong fellow! A true Hercules! You would not guess he was only three months old,' his mother and grandmother exclaim, but Miss Crawford herself says nothing. She merely grips his fat wrists as he teeters on her lap, loose-strung as a puppet. 'And our Jane has such a way with him, eh, Miss Lippard?'

Mrs Flowerday dabs at the child's wet lips as he collapses back upon her. 'A shame she never was a mother.'

'Well now, well, *perhaps*. But if every woman had a husband and children of her own, who would be spare to help her? There must be some old maids; God makes work enough for them.'

The baby grunts in Miss Crawford's arms. 'You did not marry?' Sukie asks her. It is an idiotic question but she wishes the lady would answer in her own words.

'She was disappointed by a sailor,' says Mrs Crawford in a hoarse stage whisper.

'An officer in the East India Company,' says Miss Crawford, drawing the child back to her chest.

'Had her wait all her best years for him . . .'

'He was posted abroad . . .'

'And never returned for her . . . !'

'He drowned.'

'And so it is a comfort that we are able to supply her with occupation, although of course it cannot compare to holding one's *own* child.'

'She is so good I do not know how I shall get on without her,' says Mrs Flowerday. 'I mean to bring her back with me to Essex, and she can care for him *all* the time.'

'And that will be a relief to my husband and me,' says Mrs Crawford, 'for of course we are devoted to her but the cost of living being as it is, it were better for everybody if she were in a situation in which she truly earned her *keep*. My husband feels most tenderly for her – but that is his weakness; she was his favourite sister even in childhood – and he swears he would keep her in comfort all her life merely for the satisfaction of doing so, but we must allow dear Jane her dignity, must we not? I should not like her to feel as if she were an object of charity.'

'And so to Essex I go,' says Miss Crawford.

'We shall have such *fun*,' says Mrs Flowerday.

The infant begins to twist and whine. His face turns pink and grows pinker. His ears, in fact, are quite scarlet. He screws his face even tighter and snuffs once, twice. Miss Crawford bobs him on her knee and tots his fists about in her hands, but he will have none of it. He opens his mouth and his first cry comes in a great peal. 'Oh, hush you, hush you, little fellow,' whispers Miss Crawford, putting a finger into his mouth, but he has been duped this way before, and reels back from her. His fury bursts from him in a roar, his gums bone-hard. Miss Crawford looks up at Mrs Flowerday. 'Nothing for it,' she says.

The young mother is tugging at her stays, and fossicks beneath her fichu. 'Oh, poor Baby,' she cries over his lamentations, 'is he hungry? Hand him over, Aunt, pass him here quickly,' and he is handed across the table as if he were a plate of macaroons. Mrs Flowerday raises an eyebrow at Sukie. 'You see,' she says, 'there are *some* things that she may never do for him,' and hoists her left breast into the room. She claps the child upon it and the silence is immediate, except for her continued talking, which keeps time as she jogs him gently up and down. 'Put him out to nurse, Mama said, the very moment he was born: certainly not, says I, nobody shall feed him but I myself.'

'I put all my children out, and very happy we all were,' says Mrs Crawford, looking on fondly as the child sucks and grunts, his fingers splayed upon his mother's blue-veined bosom. 'I should have been worn to a thread if I had nursed them myself. Countrywomen are more robust.' She looks to Sukie as if she might have an opinion on it. 'You would think, to hear her, that I had told her never to see him again. But a child during its first year is more of a burden than a pleasure: why *not* put him out of the house until he can walk and talk and make himself amusing?'

'Nobody *does* that any more, Mama.'

'And what of Mr Flowerday? He cannot want his wife always so encumbered.'

'He is glad to have Baby about.' Mrs Flowerday looks down upon her child's drooping eyelids, and pauses for a moment, for her breath is taken by his feathered eyebrow and the perfect curve of his nose. 'He says he never saw such a natural mother as I.'

And it is at this happiest – or unhappiest – of moments that Angelica, Mrs Hancock, casts open the door and flounces in to meet her neighbours.

Not since she left London has she looked so magnificent. Her hair is powdered to immense height and volume – how she has effected it with only the fumbling hands of Catty, cannot be guessed – and her gown is sheer to the point of vaporous, striped organza through which the blue satin of her undergown shines. Her lacquered shoes clack on the floor, and her cheeks are a-blush and her lips soft as roses. The women cannot but flutter, for she is exactly as their imaginings wish her to be: sweat breaks out on their palms, and they feel hot and cold at the same moment, and they do not know what shapes to make with their mouths. For they apprehend that before them, pulled up to the fullest of her height, stands a true and haughty whore of the first water. And they cannot think what to do.

SEVENTEEN

Mrs Flowerday's eyes do not leave the person of Angelica Hancock even as she dumbly shifts her baby from one breast to the other. The child, feeling the nipple tugged from his mouth, lets out a little whimper, and Angelica's lips open a fraction. She looks at the little frill of his cap, and his ear so perfectly and miniaturely moulded, and the crease of fat that forms behind his frail little neck as he burrows at the breast. Even from across the room she can smell him: he is warm and dry, fragrant as if he has been baked, a malty and milky little child.

Sukie rises. She puts her hand in Angelica's; she says, 'Come, will you not sit with us? We have all been waiting for you,' but Angelica stands erect and apart. She remains for one moment longer, her chin up, surveying her audience, before she is satisfied by her opinion of them and walks with slow certainty to her seat. Her skirts hiss about her. Nobody moves until she has finished shaking them into place, so that not one fold will be crushed beneath her. Then she leans on her elbow to inspect Mrs Flowerday's son.

'I did not know you had a child,' she said. 'Sukie, you did not tell me there would be a child.' Despite herself she cannot stop staring at it, the way one stares when a man is thrown from his horse, or a litter of kittens is consumed by its mother: she would look away but she cannot.

'My husband's house – my house – is in Braintree,' gabbles Mrs Flowerday, 'and Mama attended me there, but my lying-in was so fiendish boring that as soon as I was fit to travel I brought Baby a-visiting.' The queenly Mrs Hancock does not remark upon this, so she finishes lamely, 'And here we shall stay some weeks more, I hope.'

'She missed her mama,' crows Mrs Crawford. 'She is married so short a time, dear little girl, she cannot but miss her family.'

'And Greenwich,' says Mrs Flowerday, 'for I had such society in Greenwich before I married, and my husband courted me there so prettily – I was the sensation of the season – and the countryside is rotten dull. *Blasted* dull.'

'Now, Caro,' warns Mrs Crawford, but her daughter begins to chatter again, explaining that Baby is in fact no trouble on long journeys, certainly no more than a lapdog – and in fact less trouble than a lapdog since he stays where he is put – he even seems to enjoy the rhythm of the carriage, bless his dear heart, and she must beg leave to recount an anecdote of a funny expression he once made, and to describe the extraordinary smallness of his toes, and to recount the many arguments she and Mr Flowerday engaged in while deciding if it were to be William Edward or Edward William. And all the while Angelica is staring at the back of his little capped head with awful fascination. Her heart feels small and dense, as if it were dough clenched tight in a fist. She meant her dress as a charm against fear and dismay, as it always was before: she wished to be once more Angelica Neal, who prospered and was gay, but although the gown is the same it seems the lady has altered.

Still, Angelica Hancock shares with Angelica Neal the knowledge that it is better always to be fierce than to be sad, just as it is always better to fight than to run. Therefore, when Mrs Flowerday stops to draw breath, Angelica interjects:

'Do you not find it tedious?'

Poor Mrs Flowerday's eyes widen. 'Tedious! Why no! Why, I . . . ! Perhaps when you have children of your own . . .'

'Who says I have no children?'

'If you did,' says Mrs Flowerday with triumphant finality, 'you would not say they were tedious.'

Mrs Flowerday, for all her talk, has sharp eyes. She is herself no stranger to the *Tête-à-Tête* section of *Town and Country* magazine: she is well acquainted with what affairs this splendid woman has left behind her. *And she is not so very beautiful, for all that,* she thinks to herself. *She looks tired for a woman of such notorious leisure.* She had hoped she might be coarser in her manners and speech, but Mrs Chappell's training is thorough and deep-ingrained: Angelica cannot be faulted in any respect of taste, or conversation, or appearance, although Mrs Flowerday had not thought it quite usual to dress up so for tea. But things may well be different in town; Lord knows it is long enough since Mrs Flowerday herself has had the pleasure of going there.

Most of all, as her child's muscular jaw grinds down upon her nipple, and she curls her toes in her shoes to keep from crying out with the pain of it, Caroline Flowerday is watching Angelica Hancock in order to ascertain whether this is a woman who might ever tempt a man like Mr Flowerday to forget his duties. Her lovely bosom, her translucent gown, the graceful way she moves her hands in speech and the musical prettiness of her voice: is this what he would spend his money on, if he had the opportunity? Is this the sort of woman he might keep in London (for how can she be sure he does not?), in rooms furnished from the Crawford dowry? Are the ties of desire as binding as the tie of a little shared child, and of the prosperous future promised therein?

'Surprising,' she says, 'that you and Mr H. have none yet.'

Mrs Hancock is silent for a moment. 'We have only been married half a year,' she says.

'Half a year! It did not take me nearly so long! But then you are a little *older* than me.' The baby is drifting into sleep, the movement of his lips slackening to nothing. She looks down at him proudly, and nudges his cheek, which sets him off sucking energetically again, his eyelashes brushing his cheek. 'Look at him go! The dear little pup.' She looks up. 'It was a fine wedding. We had a procession all across the heath, and all the children from hereabouts waved ribbon wands, and the horses had flowers plaited into their manes. I suppose yours was splendid.'

'In my old parish church.' Angelica remembers the cold flag-stones of St Anne's, the names of the dead carved deep on the floor of the chancel where they stepped. 'We felt no need to make a spectacle of our feelings.' She wore white kid gloves: even so she felt his hand tremble in hers. It is as slim a splinter of memory as any from her childhood; it feels nothing to do with the life she has now.

'But how peculiar nothing has *happened*,' says Mrs Flowerday. '*We* were not a minute alone before—'

'Now then, children come when they come,' says Mrs Crawford, but she has taken a practical and sociable interest in the bearing of children for close to thirty years, and sees the opportunity to dispense advice. 'I suppose this is your first marriage,' she says with matronly authority. 'You would be surprised how many young brides are inexperienced in these matters.'

'Mama,' says Mrs Flowerday warningly. 'Do you not recall our talk this morning?'

Even Sukie puts aside her anxiety and leans forward, rapt at the escalation of the conversation.

Angelica considers. Her face is serene and lovely, but it has a rigidity to it that only her niece sees. 'That's so, Mrs Crawford, no man but Mr Hancock ever called me his wife. But I cannot think that inexperience is to blame. I had more men than I can keep count of, you know. And the number of babies whose beginnings I was compelled to end – well, it cannot have done me any good.' She does not drop her face. She almost smirks as Mrs Crawford sets down her tea bowl with hands so unsteady it dances on the saucer.

'Ah,' says the old lady, fumbling with her handkerchief, and, 'Ahem.' She takes a breath, and brightens. 'But we are all ladies together now – surely it makes no odds to *me* what your past transgressions might be, since you are repentant now; and as I always say, let it be God's concern how harshly He will come to judge you, for it is not mine.'

'I had best warn you, I am a woman of great wickedness. I was a celebrated whore for ten years,' says Angelica triumphantly.

But Mrs Crawford is dogged in her piety. 'It's remarked that I am uncommon in my liberality, but those are my principles.' She clasps her hands, returning gratefully to her topic, for she is convinced she may yet discover a helpful insight into the Hancocks' childlessness. 'What of your husband's history? At his age he was surely not a bachelor!'

'A widower,' Angelica says.

'Oho! Hear that, Jenny?' Mrs Crawford nudges her sister-in-law. 'A widower! That is something for you to think on. For all the men you missed out on the first time round will be in want of a new wife before too long.' She chuckles and pats her hands together. 'A widower, Mrs Hancock, a fine choice. A good steady sort of a husband, less inflamed by romantic passions, which mark my words can be more troublesome than enjoyable. His character revealed and his fortune already made, which bypasses many of the trials one comes upon in the early years of marriage.'

'And less need of a bridal portion, which is so troublesome in broadcasting a lady's value to the world,' adds Mrs Flowerday.

'Yes, a very practical choice,' says her mother. 'I always think second wives are more of a practical necessity; the first is the true partner.'

'But this is the importance of a dowry,' says Mrs Flowerday. ''Tis what yokes man and wife equally. When my Edward has one of his foolish ideas, I tell him, sir, do you recall through whose beneficence this will be paid for? *That* gives him pause.' The child is flopping in her arms like a drunk. She passes him back to her aunt to be winded, and tucks her breast back into her gown. Thus straightened, she smiles at Angelica. 'Of course, when a gentleman is as wealthy as your Mr Hancock, there is nothing to stop him from taking any bride he chooses, however obscure or poorly thought of.' She raises an eyebrow. 'Nothing but propriety.'

'I hope you do not mind my saying so,' says Angelica kindly, 'for I am sure you mean nothing by it, but, Mrs Flowerday, your choice of conversation gives the impression of *small-mindedness*. Spiteful, some might read you. Perhaps even vulgar. Which I am sure cannot be the effect you intended.' She squeezes Mrs Flowerday's hand. 'I tell you this as a friend,' she says, 'and as a woman just a *little* older than you.'

Mrs Crawford shuffles contentedly in her seat, pleased that a lady so metropolitan would condescend with her insights. Jane Crawford, mopping a milky rime from her charge's lips, says nothing still, but for the first time a great smile springs across her lips, until she buries her face in the child's soft neck and it is hidden again.

'And now,' says Angelica, 'has Baby run through his entire repertoire or is there more? I'll gladly sit and watch him for another hour – his performance is quite equal to anything I saw Garrick do – but if there is to be a song or a tragic piece next, I may need a short interlude in which to compose myself.'

'And what would you have me do?' she asks Sukie after their guests have departed, at speed and with many lamentations. 'There is no point in my trying to be what I am not; I am a fraud and all can see it. Why would I not conduct myself as I know how?'

'You were very rude,' says Sukie.

'Pish posh! They would have me stare at a baby for two hours. What was there to be done?'

'Think of your husband, the impression that this gives . . .'

'Oh, my *husband*!' She curls her lovely lip, the most Angelica Neal expression she has shewn for a year. 'Why am I always to think of him when he never thinks of me? Miss Sukie, if he did not intend to give a certain *impression*, he ought not to have married me in the first place.'

'I've no argument to that,' says Sukie. 'You never got him under false pretences.' She feels rather excited at the prospect of real glamour residing in this house; the meek Mrs Hancock who arrived in Deptford at last restored to her splendour. 'I will look over the books,' she says, 'and find the wages for a proper hairdresser. 'Tis criminal that you are attended by nobody, and do not look as you ought.'

'Oh, Sukie, Sukie, dear heart.' Angelica kisses her face. '*You* understand me. I never felt so much myself as I did this afternoon.'

EIGHTEEN

By night-time, with her face wiped clean and her hair sheathed in its muslin cap, she feels less certain. The afternoon was as a masquerade ball: the words spoke from behind a mask may be bolder than those uttered barefaced, but this need not mean they are more honest. She stews in the bed, small and lost. By the time Mr Hancock enters it is the very dead of night, and no light whatever intrudes the room, but he has memorised his steps well. Angelica listens to him moving about; by this sound she judges he is putting his wig on its stand; by this he is removing his jacket, and then his breeches. When he comes to the bed this time, she does not pretend to be asleep. Her bravery persists; she sits up from her pillow and pins her eyes upon his shadow.

'You are awake,' he says.

'Yes.'

He nods, but says no more. His silhouetted profile shows clearly his downturned mouth, his cheeks with the grim slackness one observes in a death mask. What has happened to him, that he has grown so grave and thin? He raises his arms, and the movement of his fingers tells her he is unpinning the jabot at his throat. She bides in quiet agony at how changed he is, how all his affection seems evaporated, and when he puts on his nightcap she resolves to pursue the matter.

'Sir,' she says.

'Hmm?'

'Would it be different?' She waits. She does not like this question – she does not care to hear its answer; already the weight of truth is heavy and tight in her stomach. She is glad she cannot see him. 'If I had had the child, would things here be different?'

He pulls back in perplexion, or surprise. 'Why. Of course. Everything would be different.'

And then he gets into the bed beside her and they say no more.

Later in the night, as dawn approaches, he stirs. Angelica's slow breathing fills the room, in and out pacific as tides. *Poor child*, he thinks, but nonetheless he cannot stop thinking of the mermaid, her great voluptuous sorrow rolling over in the vat. And although his wife's tears lie heavy still on his heart, he cannot help but go from the bed.

Why do I do this? he asks himself as he makes his way through the silent house, the air of the vast staircase dancing with secrets of its own.

Why not stay with her? Because the call to leave is so beguiling. This is how a man feels at the top of a great tower; he is afraid of the abyss beneath him, but still he must look upon it, and still step towards the parapet. He passes through the dining room and out of the glass doors onto the steps. The garden is a-rustle, the lawn a dark triangle stretching down to the white smudge of the summer house, and he strides out towards it.

He pauses a moment behind the columns of the folly to let the silence settle. Satisfied, he unlocks the little rough door that leads down to the grotto, but when it creaks open he hears most distinctly a sound that makes his ears prick up, and the bristles on his neck quiver.

A door, slammed.

433

It comes from inside the house. He steps backwards into the shadows, but even so he sees one window become illuminated. The glow of light travels from one first-floor window to the next, and then vanishes again.

My wife, he thinks. Perhaps she is hungry, and goes to the kitchen to find an apple or a lump of cheese. *She will not come out here.* He hunches like a gravestone. He can hear his own breathing fearful loud, and the trembling and ringing of the vat. *Do not come out here*, he orders Angelica. *Do not, do not.*

The air is so still he hears the front door of the house open and close as if it were at his ear, and her feet moving over the gravel.

She will look at the front of the house only; she will look at the stables to see if a horse is gone. She will not come back here.

But he hears her voice, 'Mr Hancock?' and then she comes glimmering around the side of the house. She holds a lantern close to her bosom, her hand cupped about its frail flame. 'Sir?'

His blood throbs. His heart is pinned to his chest, its spasm surely audible. He holds his breath and takes another step backwards, but there is something under his foot – a dead leaf or a bird's decayed wing – that betrays him with a crunch.

She stiffens, then darts, her shawl and her nightgown and her hair flying behind her as if her movements leave a pale residue on the air. She is running down the lawn but is still some distance away; she cannot see him from his vantage point. 'Where are you?' she cries, moved suddenly to anger, and surges immediately towards the summer house, her lantern swinging high. 'I will have no more of this!'

Although she is very close she cannot quite discern where he hides, and he is able to look at her for a good long time as she stops before him, her hair standing out as if it were electrified, and her feet spread and her face furious. The dawn light makes her unfamiliar;

there are dark blooms in her eye sockets and under the shadow of her hair; her skin is luminous here, greyed there. She is panting hard; he hears her swallow with exertion or fear, he cannot tell.

'Here I am,' he says quietly.

'What are you about?' she demands. 'What are you thinking? Creeping round at all hours, never here when I seek you, and what secrets you are keeping I cannot begin to think. If you mean to drive me to madness, it is very skilfully done.' She waves her hand with such energy the lantern goes out; she drops it to the ground with no further thought. 'Enough! I demand your behaviour changes, or I will quit you. Do not imagine I will not. I do not *need you*, sir!'

'Come away,' he says, hurrying forward. He takes her wrist. 'Come indoors. We shall talk about it. Whatever you wish to say, I shall listen to you.'

She is craning to look past him. 'What have you down there?'

'Nothing.' He pushes her onward.

'Not nothing. I ought to know my outbuildings; I am mistress of them, am I not? And yet I never wondered why you kept the key to *that* one. What is it?'

'Come away. Do not raise your voice; you will wake all the household.'

She pushes him away. 'And what if I do? *I* have nothing to hide from them.' She lunges into the stairway and almost loses her footing; he hears the shale scrabbling down and then she – still not three steps in – says, 'Oh.'

'Be careful,' he says. 'The stairs are very steep; the light is not good.'

He takes up the lantern from the grass and reignites it with shaking hands. Then he approaches behind her, holding it aloft to light her way.

She is poised on the steps. She touches one mussel shell, then another. She traces their bull's-eye circles. 'What is this?'

435

'Go inside,' he says. And she advances slowly, he following behind, and her hair in the cold breeze washes back upon his hand. She descends and descends, and in the chamber exclaims.

Something has happened there in that earth-enclosed chamber. The sorrow pours from the vat as if it were steam or smoke; it is invisible but it churns in the air, and fills the lungs; there is the simultaneous sensation of being so full of grief as to choke with it, and yet an emptiness, a dreadful lonely howling void.

She seizes his hand convulsively. 'Be with me! I cannot bear it!' and turns to him, fearful. 'What *is* this?'

'I do not know,' he says. 'It came from the sea.'

'It is a trick,' she says, not too far gone to remember her suspicions. But then she turns this way and that to look at the lions, the peacocks, the fans and arches all picked out in so many thousand shells, and how the lantern light flickers over them so they seem to creep. The shine of the pool in the furthest chamber sends reflections of its ripples scurrying over the walls: in the dark, everything moves.

She thinks a great hand has seized her. The feeling is – she cannot say – longing, or grief; that thing which is called by sailors Nostalgia, whose sufferers sicken for their home and fade away still weeping for it. And if they have no home to go to, it hardly signifies: the pain is just as deep and sweet. Her footsteps are loud and cold on the flagged floor; she tips her head up and her sigh resonates off the vaulted ceiling and comes back to her own ears a hundred times. It rolls also around the belly of the great copper vat, which crouches black and unadorned.

'Is it in there?'

'Look,' he says.

He keeps a three-legged stool nearby for his nightly communions with the creature, but Angelica rejects all assistance. She hooks her fingers over the rim of the vat and hoists herself upward with all her strength. She can only remain for a short moment, before her slippers give up their grip on the copper and her arms tremble too violently to hold her. She turns to him, her fright compelling her as ever to anger.

'*Water?*' she spits.

'No, no.' He spreads his hands. The moment has come. 'That is your mermaid.'

Her poor face expresses a thousand feelings and none. She shakes her head and knots her fingers. 'I have thought for some time,' she says, 'that one of us is becoming insane. And I feel more confidently now which of us it is.' But she looks about herself. She does not believe it.

'Please. Look again. Your mermaid came. It is real.'

She twists her face. 'Real as Mrs Chappell's; real as a dead ape ever was. I am finished here, sir.'

He reaches out to her. 'You cannot pretend this creature has had no effect on you. Let me help you up, and you will see what I see.' He steps towards her with his arms outstretched, not a gesture she has known for some time, and this is why she acquiesces. Holding his shoulder to steady herself, she scrambles onto the stool. Her slippers are thin and precarious; she wobbles but she is up. She leans over the vat and frowns.

'I see nothing,' she whispers.

'I swear.'

And she is quiet. She leans forward as still as a figurehead, hair ruffled by the breeze that has played through those chambers for who knows how long, and was born nobody knows where. Her eyes are dark and downcast; her fingers dig into his shoulder, and he feels the tremble of her arm as she holds her weight steady.

'What do you see?' he asks.

'I see her.'

'And?'

'When I was a little child,' she whispers, 'I lived by the sea. On stormy days, I would to go to the wall at the edge of the harbour and look at it. I sat very still, as I am now, and I would stay there for hours.' The wind outside picks up and comes hissing down the hill, stirring the grass with its invisible fingers, and sweeping down into the grotto. Her arms break out in gooseflesh. 'It was so buoyant,' she says, 'energetic and terrible. I was so afraid of it that sometimes all I wanted was to leap into it.'

As the first streak of dawn nudges the horizon, he nods. 'Yes. You do see it.'

She does not alter her position, but her whole body trembles, for it is a cold night to be abroad in only a shawl and a cotton wrap. 'What are we to do with it?' she whispers.

NINETEEN

By the time the sun has come up, and they have quit the mermaid's lair for the house beyond, Angelica's doubts are all flown away. 'I will have it rule us not one minute longer,' she declares to her husband. They have not slept, but sat together at first simply wondering, and she asking many questions, and he shaking his head and sighing, *I cannot say. I do not know*, while she becomes increasingly giddy in her relief. 'For this is the cause of our misfortune,' she says, 'and where the cause of a trouble is plain there can be found a way to set it right.'

'I cannot find it,' he says tragically.

'Oh, can you not! Well, that is just like you.' And indeed, there is only one present in the room who has made a living of thrusting through disaster. 'It may all be set right. We are neither of us dead, are we? And all our household fine in fortune and fettle.' She rings more vigorously for the maid than she ever has hitherto in this house: 'We shall need rolls and chocolate, to eat here, yes, here in this very dining room; I shall not hide away in my rooms any longer. Hurry, hurry!'

Then, still in her night attire, she sits by him at the broad polished table by the French windows to eat. Her sleeves are rolled up, and there are crumbs on her cheek, but she appears as composed as one

439

of the old queens of legend preparing to do battle, and spreads her hands flat on the tabletop as if she stood over her campaign. 'Your judgement in concealing the creature was very poor, I think; you should have told me at once. We must devise a plan by which to deal with this creature as firmly as possible.'

'Can we not simply—'

'No!' she snaps. 'We will do nothing simply. I *outlaw* simplicity, from this moment forth.' Her muscles quiver. 'I am going to check this creature. It will pay for what it has robbed me of.' And indeed, in the face of its gusting despair she feels the most invigorating hatred; if it had been a tangible thing, a beast or a man, that had attacked her contentment so, she would have flung herself before it and fought with all the strength in her body. But there is no doing such a thing, and so she is frantic for action. How may the thing be controlled? How may she exert her will upon it? How is such a creature's power diminished?

To the maid, she says, 'Fetch me notepaper. I must write a plan.'

'A plan for what?' asks Mr Hancock.

She looks at him as if he were touched. 'A real mermaid, sir, a true curiosity, and you meant to hide it away? There is no denying the veracity of this creature, whatever it is.' She flicks her hair out of her face and looks up at him smiling imperiously. 'I shall *display it.*'

'Now, Mrs Hancock,' he says, 'I cannot think that is a good—'

She opens her eyes wide. 'Oh, why ever not? I am mistress of it, am I not? It belongs to me.'

'I *acquired* it—'

'For me!'

'For you, but certainly I had no idea—'

'I cannot imagine what else you thought I would do with it.' She reaches to him. 'I shall parade it like the beast it is. Like a tiger with its teeth pulled out, or an elephant all addled in the head. Everybody can come to stare at it, and see how powerful it is, and yet how helpless, trapped in its horrid vat, and buried under the ground, with us its masters.'

He twists his face.

'You are afraid of it,' she says.

'It is dangerous.'

'Aye, I shan't pretend not. But I am going to find a way to crush it.' She bends over her paper and then looks up again, alight with pleasure. 'And sir! Think what people will make of it! All those who cast me off! And I shall certainly invite our neighbours the Crawfords.' She feels a sharp and savage delight when she considers Mrs Frost's fright, Mrs Chappell's confusion, Bel Fortescue's quiet bafflement. They will be unsettled; they will be undone. 'Oh, I will *show them*!' She scrawls madly all the society names she can recall, the fine people of London and of Greenwich, and then indeed all the great ladies of the demi-monde, and the shipwrights of Deptford, and the niggling Crawfords and Flowerdays of Blackheath. 'Well, they will see what I am made of. Here. Lists. Invitations. Send for an engraver – the best – a stationer, somebody who can design me a very very fine card.'

'Must it be displayed? Is it not better to conceal it? It does awful harm.'

'Just for one evening, sir – I've no intention of opening a menagerie. I only want people to see what I have got.' She looks up into his face all beseeching. 'Just one party? Very exclusive. Here we are in this great house; with our great fortune; well, the time has come for me to be a lady. Besides, *I* own the beast, and since it seems to have had no compunction about exerting its powers over *us*, I see no reason why I may not do as I please with *it*.'

Still he hesitates. 'Do you really think . . . ?' he tries, but without conviction, and in fact partially to provoke her retort, which is swiftly forthcoming:

'*You* have no say. 'Tis *my* mermaid; you are *my* husband; and you must merely stand by me. Oh, they will never believe it!' Seeing her so much herself again strikes a thrill through him. 'We must proceed quickly – very quickly – before every body leaves London. I'll not wait for next season. Now, do I have your leave to spend as I see fit? You may be quite easy that there will be nothing to reproach in my decisions.'

'I leave it to your judgement,' he says, and she smiles as she has not smiled for a great long time, and settles down to her preparations.

TWENTY

Your company is desir'd
At the house of Mr and Mrs J^b Hancock
On Midsummer–Night 1786
To observe
A MERMAID

The invitation is printed on thick ivory card, and is more border than text. Angelica has had it decorated thickly with scallop shells, writhing dolphins and bare-breasted sea nymphs: the lines are so crisp and black, the ground so velvet soft, she cannot stop looking at it. It is simply the most perfect and precisely formed thing she ever saw. 'I think I shall have one framed,' she says.

Mr Hancock looks over her shoulder. 'That is not what our mermaid looks like,' he objects.

'Oh, the picture is merely there as an assurance that the thing exists; it is for them to come here and see for themselves whether 'tis true to its portrait or not. Besides, how would *you* draw it? Get away, get away, leave this to me.'

'How it will be made enticing I cannot think,' he says to himself, and he leaves hurriedly, before he can think any more on it at all.

Angelica now comes to make use of her small retiring room,

443

laying out a pile of cards on her desk and filling her inkwell for the first time. At first she only sits before them, regarding her own efficiency with great satisfaction; then she sets about her task.

The first card she writes is for Bel and she inks the title carefully, sorry that hers is not a more beautiful hand. She writes on its reverse:

Truly, dear, you must come. You will be astownded. I am sorry to have seen so little of you.

TWENTY-ONE

The former Mrs Fortescue has had a deep tiled bath built in the basement of her house at Chiswick, and here she may be found several mornings a week while she resides there; she would do it even more often if she could only shake off the suspicion that full-body immersion must present some risk to her health. There is at least no possibility of the water leaching poison through her pores, it being beautifully clean, and steaming, and steeped with sage and camomile and other herbs whose essence might very well be absorbed to her great benefit. It comes up almost to her shoulders; she propels herself with her feet on the bottom, and her shift puffs up with air and inflates about her chin. Her hair is bound up and covered, her face scrubbed clean as a little child's: she is stripped, in short, of all possible identifiers, and unashamed to drift there quite as God made her, an arresting little person with her small full mouth and long-lashed eyes and stern dark brows. Of less pleasure to her, but surely no less as God made them, are her aching back, and feet, and breasts. The child quickening in her belly is cause for rejoicing, but her discomfort is not: if God had made her with gills she would stay in the bath all day.

In come her maids, all gowned and bewigged. 'Are you ready?'

'Aye, yes.' Bel's head in the puff of her wet chemise drifts to the steps. She strips naked and the two women chafe her down with coarse linen sheets. 'What post for me?' she asks, leading the way into her resting room, which smells of roses and Castile soap and where a fire is burning and a white-draped bed made up. She always reads her messages after her bath.

'Three letters this morning,' and they each seize an arm and rub her well with lovely unguents: they are brisk and vigorous in their work and she relaxes into the squeeze-and-slacken of their hands over her elbow, ribs, the backs of her thighs, and the smart dome of her belly. Then the one woman helps her don a fresh whitework shift, still warm from its pressing, while the other measures out drams of strengthening tincture into glasses as fine as sharded ice on winter puddles. And she perches on the bed to take her doses, and at last pivots her legs up, and reclines.

There are hemispherical windows high up in the wall, and all about their frames on the other side of the glass blow filigree leaves of herb-Robert and forget-me-not. Yonder is the bluest of skies, and from time to time the feet of gardeners tramping past. She rests a hand on her stomach and reaches for her letters; shuffling the envelopes she recognises the hand of Angelica Neal, who is now Angelica Hancock and in her own great house.

Lady D—, Bel Fortescue as was, gives a great smile.

TWENTY-TWO

Sukie is at a loss as to what can be happening, except that all of a sudden Mr and Mrs Hancock are never about the house; they abandon her to her walking lessons while they do she-daren't-think-what at the far end of the garden, or vanish to London for the day, returning with mysterious crates and proceeded by endless waggoners delivering more of the same. She is dully acquiescent to being shut out of such intrigue: her loneliness and melancholy increases day upon day, until she can suppose it no less natural than the other curses of womanhood she has been rudely surprised with these last few years.

One morning, however, she awakes at her accustomed hour, and hears a sound to which she is perfectly unaccustomed: the rhythmic swish of four strong men swinging their scythes in time on the damp lawn. Peeping between the window frame and the fold of the curtain, she further observes a master gardener in wire spectacles move stoopingly behind the team with his golden shears, to snip with infinite studiousness any blade left tall.

And, furthermore, upon descending she finds the house below is suddenly fearsome busy, with footmen everywhere, and lines of hired women called up from Deptford and Greenwich to roll up their sleeves and do unguessable things to the folly on the lawn, which to her knowledge has remained firm locked since the house was bought. They file down the hill laden with buckets and brooms and brushes, and emerge some hours later weeping into their aprons.

'What's afoot?' she asks Mr Hancock, who is reading a newspaper in the library. He is hunched deep into his chair but even so there is something more expansive about him than she has detected in some time; he seems almost to smile when she comes into the room, or at least he troubles to turn up the corners of his mouth. 'Something very strange is happening,' she says.

'My wife,' he says with hesitant hope. 'She is solving all our problems – at least, she says she is.'

'Excuse me?'

'Go, go!' He wafts his paper to her. 'To the folly – you will find her busy in there. Quite extraordinary things, dear niece; she means to reverse our fortune entirely.'

Sukie squints at him. He is certainly altered. He wears an air of fragile optimism, as if he were at last recovering from an illness that has diminished him for many months, and the blood once more returning to his cheeks. 'Uncle?' she asks. 'Are you – are you *happy*?'

He reaches for his pipe and sets about packing it. 'I believe I mean to be.'

She hesitates. 'I've not seen you so in a good long time.'

At first she thinks that her observation has angered him, for he pauses in his activity for a moment, and gazes without seeing upon his pouch of tobacco. Then he reaches out his hand to her. 'Here – come.'

She lingers yet some yards away from him. To speak would be to betray her emotion.

'Do you think I have forgot you?' he asks softly, and in response she only tips her face down. 'I forgot everybody,' he says. 'But I will remember; I *am* remembering. And when I am restored to myself—'

448

'Then you will be happy with *her*.' And Sukie finds herself racked with great distress, for what is she but a spare daughter, a fortuitous pair of hands to be sent wherever life cannot be managed? She strives always for harmony, for order, for contentment – that is her usefulness – but where it is restored, her usefulness ends. *Must I live all my life in this manner?* she wonders. *For how long can this be borne?* Aloud, she says, 'I know you will send me away.'

Still he reaches to her, and observes, she knows not why, 'Perhaps it has got to you, too. Sukie, Sukie, have I not had sorrows in my life before? And were you not always my first joy?'

A secondary joy, she thinks, a compensation for those he lost. She shakes her head – 'I do not know, sir, I cannot say' – but crosses the room to him and cautiously takes his hand.

He squeezes it hard. 'You have a place here always,' he says. 'You are my family, and Mrs Hancock's too.'

She can do nothing but squeeze back, and look in the other direction, and mumble, 'Perhaps.'

'Not perhaps! Most certainly! Even when I had little else, I had you; you think I shall abandon you now?' He pats her hand and releases it. 'You are mistaken. Now, go on with you. See what my wife is about.'

She ventures into the garden with great trepidation, and steps apologetically past the gardeners, who are now wheeling in a number of white-painted classical statues to place in the wilderness behind the folly. Sukie has never spent much time at this ornamental and neglected end of the grounds; she has certainly never before noticed the little wooden door at the back of the building, which now stands wide open, the voice of Mrs Hancock clearly emanating from within.

'Higher up,' she is saying as Sukie descends the stairs. 'Just so – just so,' and she enters the darkness of the first great chamber in

449

time to see a bright apparition whisk across one of its walls. Sukie is astounded past speech: she never saw such a place, and situated under her very home! And yet, and yet, the strangest thing of all, is the vast green mermaid, fanged and terrible, that hovers upon one wall, its edges all radiant with strange light, its body knobbled and quivering. It looks so very much like the mermaid brought to Union Street that Sukie staggers, and gasps, but Angelica is laughing and clapping.

'Oh, bravo! That is how I wanted it! Lights up, now! Sukie is here.'

Some hired woman lights the sconces, and here is Angelica as finely made up as ever she was in her life; a blue sash in her heaped hair, and dolphins embroidered on the cuffs of her dress. She looks at her niece's face and clasps her hands with joy: 'Now *that* is the effect I wanted.'

'What are you doing here?'

'Enjoying my grotto. Look. I have had transparencies made up.' The gentleman who works the magic lantern holds out his work with pride. Sukie cannot but admire the glass sheets painted each with underwater creatures: here a whale, its tail flipping joyous; here a school of bubbling fish; here a terrible mermaid and here a voluptuous one with long tumbling hair. 'So lifelike, when projected. *You* were afraid. But see, see what else I have done!'

Angelica leads her forth, and indeed the changes to the grotto have been most extraordinary. A chandelier is rigged to the vaulted ceiling, and one alcove has been fitted with cool marble shelves, upon which are arrayed goblets of Bristol green, and a vast punchbowl painted with goldfish, and decanters of every sort of spirit.

'Musicians will go in here,' says Angelica, leading her through to the next chamber, whose walls are lined with elegant little chairs all painted with dolphins and putti, 'although the sound wants something. And I shall have real tanks of fish, and there will be dancing while the illuminations shine over the walls. Can you imagine what fun it will be?'

'What is this *for*?' asks Sukie. 'What has come over you?'

'Darling! Dear heart! You do not know! I have finally been brought my *own mermaid*.' Angelica shoots a vicious little glance at the furthest chamber, which flickers a strange green light. 'I *own* it. And I am going to show it to everybody.' She begins to gabble. 'Our meeting with those Crawford women set my mind right: I am a grand lady now, and I must behave so. A lavish party is the sort of thing I can do very well indeed. I have until Midsummer Day to have this perfect, so you will forgive me if I pick no fruit with you today.'

'Is it in there?' asks Sukie. She has grown bolder, but there is something about the space that troubles her – she feels here a great and peculiar lostness, one she remembers from the day she was taken from school; and again when Bridget would not accompany them from Deptford; and again when Angelica Hancock touched her toe to the fallen plums and pronounced them all rotten.

'Aye,' but Angelica's pride is evaporating a little.

'I want to see,' says Sukie, and would march straight in if, from the darkness within, a great and awful sob had not just rung out. Sukie backs into the arms of her aunt, and a hired girl rushes blindly from the chamber, racked with tears and beating her breast as if she were bereaved of somebody precious. She careers from the grotto before they can stop her, slipping and scrambling upon its steps, and groping at its walls for the blindness of her tears. '*What* is she about?' Sukie cries. 'Is she so afraid of a magic lantern?' She steps forth to call after her, 'It is only a painting, you know! Only a bit of trickery!'

All in a moment, the jubilance has leeched from Angelica. She tugs at her finger joints, her old vulgar habit.

'Silly girl,' says Sukie, and heedless of her aunt's altered mood advances again on the chamber.

Angelica swoops towards her and seizes her arm. 'No, no,' she says.

'Allow me in,' Sukie argues. The room breathes something mesmeric; she cannot help but peer within, and pull towards it. 'I want to see.'

'Come, dear,' says Angelica, all of a-flutter. 'I think – perhaps you should not see it until the place is quite done. It is not as I would *like.* You know how particular I feel about these things.' She has, for the first time, a misgiving; she thinks, *no, I cannot wish this thing upon an innocent girl.* 'Let us go above.'

'But what sort of creature is it *really?*'

'It is a mermaid.' She is pleasant and even as she walks her niece to the steps, but her heart is uneasy; she feels as if she shepherds her away from a great danger. *Do not turn back,* she wills her. *Do not go in there.* She finds that she is shivering, and recognises the strength of will she has exerted in order to remain composed in that chamber. She thinks of the hollowness in her husband's eyes, and what vast grief rolled over her when first she contemplated the mermaid in its tub. And she feels again the urge to cast herself between the creature and the one she loves; her fists in fact are clenched, her teeth gritted, as she locks the door behind them. She will not have this creature touch her niece, no, not for one second.

As she moves up the lawn, Sukie appears to regain some sunshine, and her questions become more prattle than impulse. 'No, but what?' she asks. 'Is it alive?'

'You must wait and see.'

'And you are to have a party?'

'Tis my intention.' Angelica puts her arms about the girl's narrow shoulders and squeezes her briefly as they stroll together up the hill. 'But don't you look until I say you may. *I* am mistress of this house. Do you remember? Now come, come, back to the house.'

And once they are within she is gripped with a terrible relief.

TWENTY-THREE

The invitation delivered to Mrs Eliza Frost's nunnery finds quite a different scene. A gentleman has lately complained of a certain heat and tingling in his organ such as very often betokens the growing displeasure of Venus. 'He has visited no place but this,' she says, striding before her girls who have been all gathered together in the parlour for an interrogation, 'and so *one of you* must be the source of his affliction.'

The girls are at their most innocent at eleven o'clock in the morning, which is their time for sewing and French conversation. They stare at her but none dares open her mouth, for they are all mightily afraid of the whip they have seen propped in the corner of her chamber. 'Speak up,' she says, and her shoes click as she paces from one to the next, inspecting their faces for signs of guilt or lesion. 'Which of you is it? Stomach ache, pains, foul secretions? *One* of you knows what I am speaking of. At *least* one of you.'

They shake their heads, most honestly, since none of them suffers a thing.

'If you do not volunteer yourself, it will be the worse for you. If you have gave it to one gentleman you will give it to another, and word will spread, and then who suffers?'

None of them can say.

'*I* suffer!' she bellows. '*My* name is besmirched. Not yours; you who were never any better than you ought to be. Nobody will be surprised that a whore is dirty, but *I* am a businesswoman, and it is *my* reputation you destroy.' She stalks back to her spot in front of them all. Spittle glistens at the corner of her mouth. 'Would you have us closed down? Hmm? And you all thrown out on the street?'

They shake their heads.

'No, it is not pleasant out there. Not for a girl all alone. And yet that is the danger one of you has chose to put all your sisters in.' She looks from girl to girl. 'It pains me that one of our number would be so disloyal as to bring us all so close to penury.' She pauses to study the effect of her words. The girls are agitated; they do not move about but they fret where they stand, for everywhere is the tremble of embroidery and the flutter of books, and the girls who have nothing in their hands suddenly feel a great desire to touch their faces or to put their hands to their own throats. Mrs Frost narrows her eyes. 'Can you guess what else I have deduced from this?' she asks. 'No? One of you –' she points from face to face – 'at least one – has broken a rule. What is our first rule?'

At last a question they can confidently answer. All, to a woman, intone, 'Sheath up!'

'Sheath up!' She claps her hands. 'Sheath up, indeed. If you all made use of the armour provided at a *very* reasonable rate, we would not have mishaps like this.' She brings her voice to a sing-song nursery-rhyme bounce, as if she were talking to infants or idiots: '*A gen-tle-man has caught the clap*. And it is to my great embarrassment that this occurs immediately after he – having a great deal of influence in the running of this city – has undertaken a great favour to me. *He* protects us and *you* have infected him.'

A footman appears with a silver tray, on which are piled a number of wax-sealed letters. 'Put it on the table for the present,' says

455

Mrs Frost, gesturing to the heart-wood bureau at the far end of the room. 'I shall read them when I have dealt with this trouble.'

It is a large room, with a hard polished floor, and the footman sets out upon it, his feet tap-tap-tapping while the girls watch him in dumb desperation. Tap-tap-tap he goes, and at last lays his tray down with a muted clunk. Then tap-tap-tap on his expedition back to the safety of the landing, and a row of female faces follows his progress like a field of sunflowers. Once he has retreated, one of the longest-serving girls clears her throat. She has been a streetwalker since she was thirteen, and is loath to stir up trouble, but her senior experience outstrips (although she does not think of it) even Mrs Frost, who has had a single lover in her whole life, and he of little enthusiasm. This girl clears her throat again, and speaks up: 'Not all men can be easily persuaded to wear a sheath, madam.'

'Oh? Is that the case?' The girls nod in agreement, and burble amongst themselves: 'Fuss,' they say; 'Angry,'; 'Don't dare . . .'

Mrs Frost rubs her chin as if deep in thought. 'So perhaps I see how it might have been. I know what men can be like, once they are thoroughly provoked. You asked the gentleman to protect himself, but he said, *no, I don't care for that*, or, *I'll have none of the expense* . . . Perhaps you did not dare ask him at all, you being a little nothing of a girl and he being a gentleman of some years and standing. Is that how it was? Do I come close?'

At this one of the very youngest girls lets out a small hiccough. All faces turn to her; her eyes are large with guilt.

'Sarah? Is this what happened to *you*?' Mrs Frost demands.

The child nods meekly. 'He did it all of a sudden, madam,' she says. 'I did not have a moment to—'

'*You* are the one who has imperilled this entire establishment?'

'I—'

'Listen to me! Each and every one of you!' She claps her hands again, once, for emphasis. 'If a gentleman wishes to go without, you say *no*. And I shall always support you in this matter, you may depend on that; if he will not comply, you need simply pull the bell, and the bullies will come, and that man will be removed. A visitor who cannot keep to our rules is no longer welcome, whoever he is. Do you all understand?'

They nod, and murmur.

'Very well.' She smiles. 'We are all here to protect one another. You were brave and good to tell the truth,' she says to young Sarah.

Those Cyprian comrades standing nearest to the afflicted girl gather about and touch her briefly here and there; Sarah herself smiles very faint. Mrs Frost catches the eye of the footmen who hover just on the staircase, and nods. 'Take her to the attic.'

They surge forth and seize the girl by each arm, which action is unnecessary since she is very tiny and gives every impression of going quietly. She gasps, though, and stumbles between them as they frogmarch her out of the room.

'That is five guineas docked from her, and a beating to add to my list of duties,' says Mrs Frost. 'She has put me to a deal of trouble.' She turns back to the remaining girls. 'Our Sarah is going to the attic for her good and ours,' she says, 'and there she will stay until she is recovered. And fortunate she is that she has not been immediately ejected. She spreads her filth about the place, and yet I shall pay for her physician and keep her fed and watered even as she does *nothing* to earn her keep. When I add up the money she has already lost me, it far surpasses anything I could dock from her. You are fortunate girls,' she says. 'You are by no means disposable; I have trained you and I mean to keep you. We are a family now. All right, back to your work. You have an hour until it is time to dress for the afternoon.'

She sweeps away, stopping to inspect the letters that have come for her. 'An invitation,' she observes. 'I do not receive many of those.'

457

TWENTY-FOUR

And so to King's Place, where Mrs Chappell, comfortably bailed for some months, is summoned to be sentenced on charges of running a house of ill repute. The pack of little dogs greets the constables' arrival with clamorous excitement, but Mrs Chappell is less pleased.

'Oh, for the love of Christ,' she exclaims, caught as she is in her green-papered parlour, with a mound of kedgeree just placed before her, and having mere moments ago found the position in which her bandaged foot can be balanced on its stool with only a modicum of agony. 'Is that today? I wish you had set a more convenient date; we are all but ready to quit the city. My girls need their sea air, same as anybody. And these –' she gestures to the dogs who busy themselves about the visitors, sniffing and yepping and waving their tails high, their claws all a-clatter on the parquet – 'are in sore need of a good run.'

'I am sorry, Bet,' says the constable, Mr Trevithick, who has had cause to visit her house for both business and pleasure going back some twenty years. 'But what's to be done? Today is the day.'

'I do not know why I cannot send a proxy,' she says. 'You know how it will go. I have paid out more in bail than whatever trifle I shall be charged today. 'Tis easy money for you, that is all. Why do you not spend the time dealing with *real* criminals?'

'When we receive a report, we must—'

'I do not know when it was that your people began paying any attention to *reports* concerning me,' she sighs, and reaches for Mrs Hancock's handsome invitation. 'Now, look, we have so many engagements – a party in two days' time that I am loath to miss – d'ye remember this girl of mine, Mrs Neal as was? Now *her* life took a peculiar turn. I am most anxious to know how she has made out; if this nonsense of yours holds me up I shall be most vexed. A mermaid party, now what do you think that can be? Her husband has a mania for them; I wonder what sort of freakish beast they have acquired this time. It cannot be that mummified waif they touted about before, for I hear Prinny threw that on the fire.'

'These reports—' ventures Mr Trevithick.

'It was stuffed with sawdust all along, you know,' muses Mrs Chappell. 'But then so is Mrs Fitzherbert's head, and it has not put him off *her*.'

'Madam, the things that are being said of you—'

'Oh, you will never prove a thing,' she says, reading the invitation again with a smile of pride. Mr Trevithick steps aside to draw her attention to the flagellation machine which sits in the corner awaiting its weekly polish. 'That signifies nothing,' she says.

'And the numerous women and very likely several men we shall find running about upstairs in a state of undress.'

'Hardly ever in the morning,' she says. 'You ought to have come after six on a Tuesday if you had wanted a compelling argument for moral correction.'

'There ain't a drawer in the house that hasn't a cundum in't,' he says. Upstairs his men can be heard marching from room to room, punctuated by cries of irritation from the disturbed girls. 'Now, Bet,' he says half jestingly, 'I warn you it may be serious this time.'

'I do not believe you,' she chuckles, turning back to her breakfast. 'I have friends who will never allow that to happen.'

He shakes his head, and is very truly sorry. 'You must have angered somebody.'

'Angered? Never! They are all faithful visitors.' She still chuckles, but her countenance assumes the colour and humidity of cold pease pottage. 'But – we have always had an agreement.'

'The wheel turns . . . That ugliness at Twelfth Night when the girl of yours ran away – and you would give no compensation.'

'Well, why should I have? She was under their care when she went missing. If there were any justice in the world, 'twould have been *them* compensating *me*. She was one of my best,' she says with some regret. 'Could truly have been something – an exotic of her kind does not appear more than once in a blue moon. Not that she would have been taken up by anybody so very important – not that any aristocracy would pledge his troth to a lady of *her* complexion – but she was a valuable asset nonetheless, Mr Trevithick.'

'Well, that's as maybe, but it don't do to get on the wrong side of people of that sort.'

Mrs Chappell is shaking her head in wonder. 'I cannot credit it,' she says. 'Thirty years I have been at this address. We are a beloved institution.' She turns in her chair, as best she can without disturbing her foot. 'What is become of this city?'

'Ah, it's not what it was.' He tuts and lights his pipe. 'Have a bite to eat, Bet, you might as well.'

Aloft, a shriek, a crash and a bellow, followed by sounds of pursuit. Young Kitty is shortly borne into the room, swiping and squirming in a manner perfectly commensurate with her feline name, by a warden whose wig has been knocked off and who sports on his brow a bleeding gash. 'She hit me!' he cries. 'Brought a clothes rail down on my head, so she did!'

'Kitty!'

The girl brings her lips back in a snarl. 'I'll not let them hurt you.'

460

When she is set down she darts to Mrs Chappell's side and clings fiercely to her hand.

'There, there. You are a good girl.' Above there are sounds of further struggle; thuds and scampering, and the curses of the men. 'Saints alive, they'll do somebody a mischief. Call them off, call them off,' she says to Mr Trevithick. 'Tell them I demand it.' She gives Kitty's shoulder an affectionate shake. 'They are bound to be upset; they love the seaside.'

He ventures upstairs and the furore first escalates, then abates. When he descends again with his men, they drive before them four of Mrs Chappell's girls in various stages of sullen undress, their gowns ripped, their hair tousled, and their bosoms heaving with the exertion of their fight. 'That's the lot of them,' says one of the officers with considerable pride, 'along with a gentleman wearing only a pair of stays. Ought we to bring him in?'

'What are you about?' asks Mrs Chappell, jabbing her fork at the girls. 'Fighting so!'

'Biting, screaming, throwing chairs . . .' chips in Mr Trevithick.

'Oh, but they left off soon enough. Twenty years ago they would have torn a man limb from limb by now. You're *soft*,' she says to her girls.

'When Lucy Fletcher coshed the gentleman with a rolling pin!' Mr Trevithick recalls fondly, and Mrs Chappell rocks in her seat, wheezing her appreciation.

'I shall never forget it. And the night the ladies of Mrs Scott's set fire to the whole place rather than let it be taken.' She glances at the girls. 'Now that is a course of action I do *not* advise.'

'The quality's not what it was,' agrees Mr Trevithick. 'The young ladies now got no spirit in them.'

'Well, that's the fault of the gentlemen. They demand good manners. Refinement. How would I sustain a cohort of screaming hell-bitches if nobody'd ever pay me for 'em?'

461

'Ah, 'tis a sorry time for whoring. Not like our youth.'

'We'll not see those days again. But I've kept you long enough,' says Mrs Chappell. 'I suppose you'll be wanting to do your job.' She offers her wrists and Mr Trevithick manacles them very gently before her, with so much slack as to curtail her movements very little indeed.

'Not too tight? No? Not rubbing?'

'Very comfortable. I'm much obliged to you. Come, girls, help me.' One of her white-clad mob stoops to lift her bad leg gently from its stool; another comes to her chair to help her rise. Mr Trevithick offers his arm and Mrs Chappell seizes it with both hands and hauls herself up, all the blood in her face so that her eyes fairly pop.

'Is he taking you away?' asks Kitty, most afraid.

'Oh, do not take alarm. The gentleman is only doing his duty, and once justice is served we should go unmolested by it for a good long time. Confound it; I hate to be in court, all the mob crowding in to look upon one, throwing their orange peels and making up their dreadful ditties. If I had aspired to entertain so I should have taken to the boards. Well, if I am to be looked at, I shall need my rouge. Fetch it, Kitty.'

'Anything for your comfort?' asks Mr Trevithick. 'It may be a long day.'

'Aye, of course. My cushion too, Kitty, and my pills, and my book. There's a good girl.' She squeezes the child's hand with her little shackled claw. 'I shall be out within the day, you may depend on it.'

As Mr Trevithick guides her out of the breakfast room he says, ''Tis a shame, Bet, that it's come to this. I hope you are not detained too long.'

'Ah, I shall be out again in a twinkling,' she says. 'And I am glad it was you who came for me; I have not seen you in a great long time. Tell me, how does Mrs Trevithick?'

I have been borne a great distance. This dull thud of nothing encloses me yet, but somewhere above the water is the burble and twitch of animal life. I am crushed here in this egg – I long to expand, and to rush, and to leap, oh! I strain – and I listen. And I am still. And I turn over, the better to feel their voices and movements quiver upon my being.

Out there, souls flicker. And I would call out to them, if they can hear me: come hither, come hither. Touch me again with your speaking. The hectic crowded feeling of being: I would drink it all in. Brimming with things that swell, and make me flip over on myself: elation and jealousy and spasms of love. The sensation I know is the one from the sea, when I jostled among and beside and through and about a chorus of knowings that were all my own. The drowned ones who slipped down through the water breathed out globes of grief and rage, which flew up towards the air; we shivered at their passing.

There is the thud of a heart that attracts me especially. A young one – I know this sort – all wondering like the dark-eyed calves that totter into streams; an ebullient soul which might expand vastly if it were not constrained. I like this young and joyful voice upon me, smooth as milk. Come here, I call, come here, come closer.

TWENTY-FIVE

'Pilloried!' repeats Mrs Chappell, clinging to Mr Trevithick's arm. 'I cannot credit it – sincerely I cannot. What have I done to deserve this?'

The constable shakes his head. 'A very usual punishment, Bet.'

'Aye, for some! Lady so-and-so, with her gambling den – *she* did not get the pillory. *She* is too good for it, and yet *I* am not?'

'Judges now-a-days – no sense, Bet.'

'And younger than they used to be! Did you mark that?' She shakes her head as they descend the steps of the court with agonising slowness. 'Why was the fine not enough for them?'

'They want to make an example of you. Keep the others in check. You must own that it is your turn. I have done what I can, and rushed it through – if we go now there will be no time for a crowd to gather. And then you are at liberty to go to your party.'

'As if I shall still be inclined to.' At the foot of the stairs Mrs Chappell must pause to regain her breath. 'A shame,' she wheezes at length, 'to make such a spectacle of an old woman! To mock her!' She allows herself to be led to Mr Trevithick's carriage, and expounds breathlessly as he and his men heave her in. 'Aye, that is what crowds like – to pelt a poor chained-up old woman with filth. What will my girls say? 'Twill break their hearts in two.'

'Now, it may not be so bad,' says Trevithick, taking his seat beside her. 'You don't know; you may have a kind crowd.'

Mrs Chappell curls her lip. 'Not these days. They're a nasty mob, this generation. Look at America. We are all brutes deep down, they say; well, some folk seem to have given up hiding it.'

'Do not fret. Go with dignity – do your time – 'twill all be over.'

The carriage doors are closed and it moves off. It is not the smooth ride Mrs Chappell is accustomed to; she wobbles on the seat and winces at her many pains. Her little hands scrabble at Mr Trevithick's cuff. 'I cannot do it,' she whispers. 'I cannot stand all those hours, locked up like they must have me,' and he nods sadly, knowing this to be the truth.

'Well, you need not,' he says. 'You may lie down for it. Can you manage that? To lie down for the three hours?'

She expels a juddering lungful of air. 'I am loath to. But I can.'

'There's your spirit. There's your dignity.' Mrs Chappell is to be pilloried at Charing Cross; as the carriage inches along the crush of Swallow Street, more passers-by turn to stare, and indeed the traffic is so slow that one man, on foot, keeps alongside them for some time without breaking into a jog; he scowls through the window at Mrs Chappell and mouths words that, to judge by his expression, are not complimentary.

'We should have travelled more discreetly,' says the abbess. 'This was bound to happen.'

'I had not thought any body would know you,' says Mr Trevithick, and he pulls the blind down.

'If you know me, they know me,' she snaps. 'Besides, any woman they see escorted to the pillory, they will draw their own conclusions. Hypocrites!' she exclaims. 'Who let their own daughters starve almost to death, or put them in cruel marriages, or slake their lust upon them most unnaturally. To think *I* do any worse by them. 'Tis an insult! The girls that come to me – and, mark me, their own parents bring them often enough – suffer worse abuses in their own homes than they ever will with me.'

'Now, but not all parents are bad parents! You must understand their outrage . . .'

A muted thump without; somebody has brought their fist upon the window, but provoked more by opportunity than strong principle. The groom calls, 'Hi, no more of that! My horses will take fright.' And there are apologies, diminishing as the vehicle moves onward. Mrs Chappell groans.

'At moments such as this I feel my years,' she says. 'Had I the money I'd retire tomorrow.'

Mr Trevithick laughs. 'I think you've enough, dear lady!'

'Enough for *today*. One can never be certain of the future – and who have I to depend on but my own self?' The road widens and the carriage passes beneath the blind eyes of some dead king, mounted for ever on his horse. A great hammering on the body of the carriage makes them both leap from their skins. 'Heavens! How dare they!'

Mr Trevithick raises the blind an inch and, having peeped out, immediately reels back.

'What is it?'

He mops his brow. 'There are a great many of them out there,' he says faintly. The whisper has spread that a monstrous bawd has been apprehended, aye, that squelch-gutted sow who in her youth turned the heads of half of London and who, in her vile dotage, pimps the virginity of decent girls to fill her own coffers. Not only that, but this superannuated harridan, no good now for rutting or for childbearing and thus superfluous to society, has the sympathetic ear of politicians (and even more sensitive parts of them besides), and an establishment where gadabout princes fritter away the allowances paid from the pocket of John Bull himself.

466

'Well, what's to be done?'

'Nothing, madam, nothing – they will tire, I am sure.'

'A disproportionate response,' says Mrs Chappell. 'As if there were a man among them who had not paid for it once in his life, or a woman who has not taken money.'

But a thundering breaks out on either side of the carriage, and all about it, and it shudders and rocks this way until it is fairly fit to overbalance. Men's hands slam against the window glass, and their voices are loud and harsh: 'Bitch! *Bitch!* We know what you are.'

'Can we not drive on?' Mrs Chappell has drawn her manacled hands up to her face, clinging at her shawl.

'We are blocked in,' he says. 'There is nowhere to go.' But because he is more heroic, or less wise, than he looks, he opens his door and leans forth. 'Gentlemen!' he cries. 'Gentlemen, please! I see that you are angry.'

'Give us the woman!' shouts one man.

'Give us the bawd! She wants setting to rights.'

'Now, gentlemen, I – I – I – do you see that she is being at this very moment brought to justice? Get back – get back – let us pass—'

But a great howling and jeering and booing rises up. The men's faces are purple with rage, and they are men of every sort – not only toothless and scabbed beggars but journeymen in decent clean shirts, and clerks, and fathers with their children on their shoulders, shaking their fists and shrieking along. 'No justice! A fine – a moment's glimpse on the pillory – what's that to her?'

'You protect her!'

'Who protects our daughters?'

'Please! I must assure you—'

'Let's hear no more of this,' says a young man standing nearest, and he knocks Mr Trevithick down into the dirt. Then all the mob crushes about the open door of the carriage, a hydra of snarling spitting yellow-teethed faces that burst in upon Mrs Chappell, and their hands seize upon her.

At first she does not move much, for her great weight keeps her pinned to the seat. Merely, as they drag at her, her clothes are superficially rent. 'Off!' She slaps at their hands. 'Begone!' But first their force is such that she topples sideways onto the seat, and then it is a small matter of seizing at her wherever she can be seized – her elbow, her upper arm, in the finger-hold ribs of her stays – and although she struggles, she is hauled out into the street.

She falls immediately to her knees, her hand palm down in the warm shit of some lately herded creature; struggling to her feet she cannot put weight on the swollen one; she grimaces but does not make a sound. There are razor blades in her ankle, she feels, pins riven deep into the joint of her toe, and every part of her body has men's hands on it, who shove and drag and pinch.

'To the pillory with this fat bitch,' somebody cries, and it is with their cruel assistance that she rises; she stumps and totters like a captured bear, swinging her head first this way, then that. 'Move!' and somebody slaps her about the head. 'Faster!' but her thighs obstruct one another, her lungs burn, she cannot breathe. Somebody boxes her ears, and off comes her wig, to the roar of the crowd. Her scalp gleams through meagre wisps of grey hair.

'Have mercy,' she mumbles, 'have pity. I have done nothing.'

But they are a great glee of noise; they pummel and shove her off the road and into the square. More and more are following now, women too, with their babies on their breasts, cheering and whooping.

'We are taking her to the pillory! Come, come, see her punishment.' A rotten plum is flung; it bursts upon her temple into a tawny sludge, and its vinegared juice drips down into her eye.

Somewhere far away Mr Trevithick is shouting, 'No, no! I

468

demand you cease this at once!' but it is to no avail. The first thing being flung signals for a veritable hail of objects: apples clout her, an egg explodes into shards upon her shoulder; there are pebbles, and her blood is gummed upon her. A flower-girl's rush basket pounds her temple; it smells of violets but sends her staggering, and she is afraid. She cannot control the momentum of her own feet; her limbs untrained in flight are heavy and weak, and will not do as she bids them. All about her is a rage of laughter, and darkness intrudes on the corners of her vision; there are white sparks dancing before her eyes; her chest is rent by sawing breaths which seem to bring her no air at all. And her foot, oh, her foot, the fire in it is white hot, and it will find no purchase and support none of her weight. She stumbles, slips, is face down, eye to eye with the toes of many shoes. She has ceased to think, only to do; her blood is composed of pure panic.

But being old, and fat, and sick, she moves slowly, like a snail when it is trapped by a child, which casts its head about stupidly to taste the air or see an escape, and rears its heavy body up. She rises from her knees, hands out, groping, but somebody kicks her in the flank and she falls down again, slack cheek grating in the dirt. By some miracle of effort she rises again, to her feet this time, and totters blindly through the crowd, as if there were any escape to be found.

'Look, fellows! Watch me!' A boy of about thirteen lifts his tricorn from his head and sprints towards her. The crowd parts about him; two yards away from where she staggers, he leaps gracefully into the air, hat held aloft, toes pointed. He comes down with all his weight upon her; his foot connects with her head and she is down again, he leaping and tripping clear of her all a-burst with hilarity, and his friends running to join him with their mouths wide. She is moving yet, though all the intelligence be gone from her eyes, her small hands with their tapered fingers fretting in the dirt, reaching and flexing as the hands of a newborn.

This is when Mr Trevithick's officers catch up with him. He has turned his back on the scene and is packing his pipe. 'Come on,' he says. 'Let's away. There's nothing to be done.'

'Should we not intervene?'

'Are you mad, man? With only three of us? No, no. If we take her from them now they will never forget it. Let them have her, let them have her. They will be quieter after this.'

As they turn away, a second boy makes his run-up, and flies both feet first, arms whirling behind him, to crunch into her ribs. How can it be that after each fresh blow she manages once again to rise? It must be by the energy of her will alone, for she has taken such a pummelling, and is so very old and weak, it cannot be her body that propels her. She utters not a sound; her face shows no expression; she is a machine, it seems, set only on survival, so that each time she falls she turns her face mutely again and again to the edge of the crowd, and compels herself towards it, although her mouth hangs, and there is a fluid dripping from her nose.

The boys and men about her are equally determined that she will not get away; they jostle one another jokeously, and laugh, but their eyes are very firm upon her, and whenever she looks to be making too rapid a progress, another of them launches from the group as arrow from bow, to knock her down again. Each time she rises more slowly than the last, each time takes fewer steps before subsiding to the ground once more. The last time she hauls herself to her knees, something on the outskirts of the crowd seems to catch her eye, crusted as it is with blood and dirt, and she lifts one arm – through which exertion she trembles, as if it were made of stone – to stretch her fingers towards a flash of white. If anybody in the crowd had turned, they might have observed a dusky-skinned girl in a broad straw hat, holding her starched white gown clear of the ground. Mrs Chappell is alert to the last to a remarkable face or a fine form, but it is this girl's singular poise that now arrests her attention. She moves like a dancer or a duchess, her back quite straight, as if movement were for her a long-studied art, or an expression of intellectual delicacy. At the edge of the square she pauses, and, seeing Mrs Chappell collapse once more, presses her hand to her mouth. Then she bows her head and hurries onward, and does not look back.

Mr Trevithick and his men, now hastening down an alley, hear a roar from the crowd. 'Poor Bet,' he says. 'We'll not see her like again.'

TWENTY-SIX

The night before the party, Angelica wakes at some small hour. Something feels awry. She reaches across the bed, but Mr Hancock is there at her side, snoring gently. She lies for some time, frowning up into the dark as she listens to the noises of the night-time. An owl's hollow call; the rattle of tree branches; a clank, perhaps, of a carriage passing somewhere on the heath. Nothing that might cause alarm. She rolls onto her side, but cannot settle; she rises at last from her bed, and not knowing why, crosses to the window and puts her head through the curtains, where the glass is cool.

At first she sees nothing beyond. Even at this witching hour, the sky is not yet dark: it is almost midsummer after all, and the place where the hill descends into the trees glows yet, whether with the vestiges of dusk or the first rays of dawn it is hard to say. The clipped lawn is black and still; the white statues seem to waver upon it, their limbs not quite discernible, not positioned quite as she remembered. But this is a deceit on the part of her eyes; she blinks hard and peers again, although she shivers there on the wrong side of the curtain from bed and hearth. And now she sees it; one of those white figures, vague about its borders, striding across the grass. She swallows her own breath, trembling as she watches its fixed and purposeful progress through the wilderness and across the lawn to the folly. There it stops.

'Mr Hancock,' she whispers. 'Mr Hancock, wake up.'

The white figure attempts the door, but it is locked. It rattles once again, and utters a phantasmic moan. Then it paces the building's circumference, as if it sought entry another way.

'Mr Hancock!' Angelica is loath to leave the window, but presently she feels him at her side.

'What is wrong?' he asks, still blinking with sleep.

'Out there!' she hisses. 'Look!'

He leans beside her, and together, their cheeks brushing one another, they stare out.

'Oh,' he says. 'That is Sukie.'

And so it is. She wears her thin chemise, and moves about the folly slowly and carefully, her hands trailing against the wall. She goes again to the door at the back, and they hear a great thud as she kicks the panels. She kicks again and again, and puts her shoulder to it.

'She will break it!'

A thin cry of real grief rises to them on the wind as Sukie pounds upon the door. The Hancocks do not hesitate. They hasten from the room and down the great stairs; Angelica slips on an unexpected step, and almost wrenches her arm from its socket as she stumbles, clinging to the banister, but she barely feels it; she is up and running across the hall in her bare feet without a thought. The pair rattle at the French windows that lead from the dining room onto the stone steps to the lawn, and spill into the dark, calling out, 'Sukie! Sukie!'

At first they do not see her, and run down the lawn beside one another, an exertion neither is well prepared for, their lungs protesting mightily. Angelica's gown flies about her as she cries out, 'Where are you? Sukie, go no closer!' while her husband stumbles ahead, wheezing, to get a sight of her. He vanishes into the shadows at the back of the folly and cries out. There is crouched Sukie Lippard, her chemise soaked in dew, keening with the truest grief. Her knuckles are skinned from pounding at the door; her bare feet bruised, their nails torn and bleeding where she has kicked and kicked for entry. Mr Hancock lumbers to his knees beside her and draws her into his chest; she quivers with cold, and with the sobs gathering still in her throat. Her skin is terribly cold, but when he seeks to lift her up, she shrieks, 'No! Do not take me away! No, no, I need to go in! I must go inside!'

He is not accustomed to lifting heavy burdens, and particularly not those that writhe and flail, and claw at his face, and kick his gut with bony feet when he attempts to hoist them over his shoulder, but he struggles back up the hill nevertheless, grunting with the effort of it, until a vein throbs in his temple and his face is quite scarlet. Angelica runs alongside as Sukie strains her arms towards the folly, howling as if she were being snatched from her own parent.

'Hush,' she comforts her. 'All will be well.'

'No! Let me go back!'

'You will be better when we are away from it.'

But Sukie sets about weeping anew. 'I will never be better! The only peace I can find is there. Please, oh, please, let me go.'

'Get her inside,' says Angelica, and Mr Hancock bears her up the steps and into the house. In her bedroom, with the candles lit, she is a dreadful sight, with her lips blue and her skin mottled grey; her fingernails are quite purple with cold, more as if she had been half drowned by a North Sea squall than merely wandering abroad one dewy summer night. She is bruised all over, and streaked with her own blood, and even once Angelica has stripped her of her drenched gown and wrapped her in blankets, she slumps shivering like a mouse released from a cat's jaws, her eyes quite glazed, her mouth slack. She is more than subdued; she is dejected. All the vivacity is drained from her. When Mr Hancock tries to speak to her, or coax a little caudle between her lips, she turns her face away in perfect exhaustion, and closes her eyes.

'Oh God –' Angelica hunches at her bedside, chafing her cold fingers in her hand – 'oh God, did I do this?'

Mr Hancock squeezes her shoulder. 'I did,' he croaks.

'Oh no – no. You only brought me what I asked for.'

'I should never have brought it here.'

'I should have proceeded differently when I discovered it. Oh, sir, do you think she will die of it? She is so awful still.'

But the doctor who comes just before dawn, and takes her faint pulse, and inspects her broken nails and bloodied knuckles, only raises an eyebrow. 'A nervous complaint,' he pronounces tersely. 'The night wandering – the rages – the lack of care for her own person. One sees it often enough in girls her age, although what they have to weigh so heavy on their minds I am sure *I* cannot guess.'

'What can be done for her?' Angelica sniffs.

'I shall give her a draught to help her sleep. But you must train her better. It is evident she has been indulged; you are making a rod for your own back if you do not take her into hand. Strong passions are troublesome in a girl, but intolerable in a woman: check her now, Mrs Hancock, before she gains a reputation.'

'We shall do no such thing,' Angelica storms, and the doctor meets her husband's eye with pity as he departs.

With Sukie at last sleeping, Angelica folds her arms. 'We must put an end to this,' she says. 'Immediately. Come with me.'

They lay another blanket over Sukie, and take the precaution of locking her door before descending to the hall and through the servants' door to the back of the house, where hangs the row of leather fire buckets. 'Fetch some down,' says Angelica, who is too short to reach them herself. 'Quick, quick. I am meant to be *your* helpmeet, not you mine.' Together they bear two buckets each out onto the lawn. The sky has taken on a greenish dawn tinge, fading into cobalt and bright white, and then the most blushing orange of a ripe apricot. Down the hill, the mist sits on the river. In the garden of their house, morning is flourishing: daisies unclench before the sun and bees hum amongst the overgrown roses. 'A strange wedding gift you gave me,' she muses as they reach the folly. 'A real creature too sorrowful to display. A thing that tells us what we really want is out of reach. Give me your key.'

'What are you about?' he asks, looking askance at her, but he puts his buckets down and takes the key from his chain.

The staircase descending is swept and newly mortared, fine and regular so as to trip nobody up. And down within, the vaults are musty no more, but fragrant, and scrubbed, and camphor-smelling from the rugs laid on each brick floor. There have been many sconces fitted to the walls, and Angelica parades around, lighting the candles in each one.

'You see?' she says. 'As if there were need for a mermaid in this place. It would only distract.'

She darts into the last room, lined with chairs. The vat, in the centre of the room where it was left, is large and ugly, soot-blackened and – he sees now – much dented. Its canvas cover is lashed on with a rope that is unravelling back into flax, and Angelica wrenches it off at once.

'What are you doing?' he demands, and now a sense of real panic seizes him.

'I do not want this. I cannot bear this. To be content as best we can must be enough for us.' She fetches one of the elegant little chairs that line the walls, drags it to the vat, and scrambles up on it. 'Look,' she says, 'it will be easier than you think. For she is not a solid creature.' She plunges her arm into the vat and makes a fist. He thinks he will faint. She remains there for a moment, her eyes fixed

476

intently upon his. 'See? See?' and then brings out her empty hand, dripping. She swoops again, seizing at nothing. 'I believe we can take her apart in buckets, as if it were only water we were moving.'

Outside, the dawn chorus stirs and crescendos.

Angelica climbs up to fill her buckets, and each one seems to her to let out a little 'oh', an echo of water on metal. 'Take these,' she says.

He stands immobile. 'No, no. I cannot.' *My mermaid. All I worked for . . .* 'Our party,' he protests.

'Never mind that. This thing must go.' She hauls the buckets aloft, and drips hit the brick floor with soft little cracks. He steps forward, takes them from her. 'Take them over there –' she points to the pool – 'we are going to give this beast its freedom.'

'Is that what you want?'

'I want it gone away from my family.' She has a sibyl-ish look about her, her hair awry and her white shawl draped over her shoulder. 'We have detained it too long. If it is angry, it is because of our ill-treatment of it. What trapped creature does not strike out? Now, here. Help me.'

'Oh,' the buckets drip as Mr Hancock carries them, dizzy with fear, to the rock-lined edge of the pool. And, 'Oh,' they sigh as he empties them, two by two, whole buckets of sorrow pouring into the dark water.

He thinks he sees her there, in the well's queer phosphorescence; she dances like stars and then plunges downward. Far beneath the surface, she swings in netty lengths, rediscovering her atomised self. Then he goes back to switch his empty buckets for full ones. Standing by her chair, he reaches only Angelica's bosom. She stoops to kiss him. 'You see? This is the right thing to do.'

He goes back and forth more times than he cares to count, and his arms ache and his feet become chilled. His wife's lips are the only warm thing in the cavern, and he returns to them with each visit to the vat.

Presently, Angelica finds she has emptied so much that she can no longer reach the surface of the water still contained within it. She is not afraid. 'Nothing for it,' she says, and hitching her wrap up above her knees, she climbs in. The water comes up to her shins, and is not as cold as she had expected; it is at least not the gripping cold she felt the night she swam around Mrs Chappell's fountain. She crouches down to fill a bucket. The water swirls about her, almost loving, and she feels its soft sorrow tickle her skin as if a great many little fish nibbled her.

'Take care,' says her husband.

'Oh, we are all right.' She crouches to stir the water again, the way children squat on the foreshore and study the drifting grains of sand. 'We are all right, are we not?' she croons to the water where the mermaid was. Then she passes up a bucket. 'These are the last two,' she says. 'One for you and one for me.'

He helps her scramble from the empty vat; her wrap is wet and clings to her calves and thighs: even her hair is wet, and clings to her shoulders. She seizes it and twists it like a rope; dropples fall to the floor and she laughs.

'Are you ready?' he asks, and she follows him to the pool, each leaning a little to accommodate the weight of their bucket. He realises that he is tired; his bones drag as if they have been turned to stone, but this priestish moving of the water is nearly at an end. Even the vaulted cells of the grotto seem a little brighter than when the transportation began. Angelica draws close to his side as he empties his bucket into the pool, with a swirl and a gulp. Then she steps forward herself, her pail raised above her head. With her hair loose and her white wrap clinging, she might be fourteen years old and dancing as an acolyte of Venus once again. She balances the bucket on her shoulder, tips it gently, and pours it out in a long unbroken stream, so that at the end the water closes in a perfect 'O', and one single drop leaps up into the air.

'And so it is done,' she says.

First I sink,

Then I trickle,

Then I rush.

I am here; and here; and here. I touch this surface and also that.

I mingle, I quiver with a thousand new voices, and all these voices my own. I am a great tumble of motion which torrents all in unison.

And learning and knowing are the same, and I am a mite, and we are all the space allowed to us.

And if I am made of grief, well! Here is joy, and if I am made of fury, here is peace.

Rush, rush, we rush, a sparkling stream through rock and moss, deep in the cold stone of the earth. No daylight here, no dying breaths to catch up. We rush young and bright, and ever widening, and these bitter atoms are lost in new-minted freshness.

We hasten, hasten, onward to the boundless sea.

EPILOGUE

The midsummer party – the first held by Mr and Mrs Jonah Hancock of Blackheath – is an immense success. Mrs Hancock is a hostess both affable and beautiful, resplendent in a mermaid-blue satin gown which trails gauzy sea-foam lace; her marriage has been the subject of much gossip, but as she hangs on the arm of her bluff husband, her face bright with laughter, certain minds are changed. Their niece Miss Lippard is additionally much admired. Very properly considering her age, she is permitted to appear on the garden steps for only a few minutes, a pale and elegant girl with a most arresting expression in her eye, who speaks not a word. She returns shortly to her own apartments, but on the strength of this brief sighting several local mamas add her to their personal lists of Girls With Suitable Qualities, and determine to monopolise her before she comes out. The house and gardens are declared faultless, and guests strolling the lawn praise its superlative aspect over Greenwich and the river.

Then there is the delightful surprise of the grotto, its shells gleaming in the candlelight, and illuminations of ghastly sea creatures beyond imagining flickering over it to cries of delight and wonder. The guests are enraptured. They dance beneath the chandeliers; they trample crystal wine glasses into the brick floor of the vaults. They marvel at the scientific system of periscopes that lights up the peculiar green pool in the very furthest chamber. Most of all, they are impressed by its very particular atmosphere. For this underground wonder, as chilly as it may be, is all suffused with a character of its own: a quiet ebullience that must be thanks to the genius of their hostess, or how could a small space have so much feeling to it? Friends embrace; strangers delight in new acquaintances; husbands draw their wives into dark corners.

The food is light and delicate, the sort girls eat so that they might have the strength to dance all night: syllabubs on cold slates; liqueur-flavoured jellies, and strawberries and melons and mille-fruits; and a great heaped centrepiece of butter-yellow pineapples, whose flesh both fresh and roasted perfumes the room and draws a crowd eccentric in its composition. Even its members are surprised by one another, having reasonably expected that a careful hostess takes pains to segregate her guests for the sake of delicacy, but they concede without a word spoken that this is really no different from any night at the pleasure gardens, where those of all walks of life are thrown together and yet succeed in speaking to nobody outside their own sort. Besides! This is a mermaid party – a most amphibious thing – who amongst them does not have the right to witness such a marvel? In fact it might be observed that the grotto becomes a very menagerie, a *Wunderkammer* of all the classifications of human, who pace warily together, and watch with interest as each curiosity reveals its own habits as to feeding, and dancing, and drinking, and conversation. Shipwrights hold forth beneath the gleaming white statues and fill their pockets with thin-sliced beef sandwiches; Greenwich's most rakish young couples are there, men and women equally adorned in flounced stocks and wafting ostrich feathers. Newly landed gentlemen whose money comes from ships or coal or cloth fall speechless in the presence of ladies whose faces once graced print-shop windows, and a needle-slim governess of a woman leads six white-clad beauties soberly amongst the trees, their little plumed dogs trotting behind. Mrs Hancock, low-born, the plaything of aristocracy and wife of a gentleman merchant, has run wantonly riot with her own address book and drawn all to her in the name of Curiosity.

There is even a rumour that the Countess of D— herself has been there – aye, truly! – in a gown much more voluminous than is her usual taste. So few attested to having seen her, and so briefly, that it can hardly be credited as fact – and yet what other small dark lady can it have been who walked slowly with Mrs Hancock down the lawn to the most secluded part of the garden, their arms around one another's waists, their heads nodding together in sincere and private conversation?

Another visitor, nobody sees at all. There is a young man in a deep blue lieutenant's jacket, a perfect *homme-comme-il-faut*, who comes on foot across the heath with his hat in his hand the better for the breeze to cool his black curls. Perhaps he hears the music, or sees the lights bobbing in the trees, but he stops at the top of the Hancocks' drive, and looks to where it curves towards the trees. He stands there for a long time, but ventures no further, and presently he replaces his hat on his head and turns away.

But what of the promised mermaid? Well!! There is the great joke. For nobody could forget that celebrated, hideous Hancock mermaid that so dominated the early part of the season; who amongst them had not gathered about the crooked-limbed sharp-toothed little form, or gazed upon its likeness in pamphlets and papers and posters? And who amongst them had not shuddered at it? Clever Mrs Hancock knows that the beauty of truth has only a limited appeal, and that repulsion's special frisson is best left to the freak show. Instead she has given her guests the mermaid that they most desire: it is there in the lustrous glim of her mussel-shell grotto and the illuminations that writhe and flicker across its walls, in its dancing fish-tanks and fizzing wine and the strange phosphorescent sparks that swirl in the green-lit pool. The vulgar quotidian is given no quarter here: all is beautiful and hazed as a dream.

The shortest night of the year never passed more quickly. And that summer's morning, as the last carriage straggles away across the heath, Mr and Mrs Hancock lock the door of their grotto with a sigh.

'It could not have gone better,' says Mr Hancock.

'No, indeed.' Angelica's hair is awry and her face smudged. 'I can scarce believe that I managed such a thing.'

'*I* can believe it,' says her husband stoutly, closing his eyes to the milky morning breeze. 'You and I, together – we succeed at what we please. And yet,' he frowns, 'after I have spent a fortune getting mermaids, the people were most pleased by no mermaid at all.'

'Huh,' she nudges him and takes his hand, 'they'd not have liked the real one much, would they? A grotto – a light show – strings of pearls – if that don't amount to a true marvel I do not know what does. We live in a modern age, sir: the things that are wrought may be quite as extraordinary as those that are *found.*'

Mr Hancock turns his face to the house, its stucco lit pink by the dawn. 'Are you ready for breakfast?' he asks, and they walk hand in hand up the hill, the ghosts running happy about them.

ACKNOWLEDGEMENTS

This novel was coaxed into the world by Rebecca Stott and Henry Sutton, who in the face of all my qualms insisted it must exist. Richard Beard and Katy Darby, educators after the Jean Brodie school, led me out.

I was lucky to start writing *The Mermaid and Mrs Hancock* in the company of wonderful first readers in my Novel History cohort, as well as Sarah Young whose patience and kindness were second to none, and Sophia Veltfort, who first commanded the mermaid to speak. Charlotte Bearn, Robyn Drummond, and Adam Rowles all bore me up with their enthusiasm as early readers of the full manuscript, and Dani Redd combed over it with a keen yet sympathetic eye I never deserved. Paula Cocozza's advice and camaraderie were real gifts as I prepared to send it into the world, and Rose Tomaszewska was generous with her friendship, trade secrets and cheerleading from beginning to end.

I have had the startling good fortune to be encouraged and supported by truly wonderful institutions. My MA was made possible by the Malcolm Bradbury Memorial Prize scholarship: the team behind the MsLexia First Novel Prize bolstered my confidence, and I will never forget the immense joy and privilege of attending the inaugural Deborah Rogers Foundation Writers' Award. That accolade made everything feel possible, and I am proud to be a part of Deborah's legacy. Every writer knows what a fight it can be to make the act of writing possible. I couldn't have done it without Jan Sutton, a wonderful employer and sounding-board while I began this novel; Sue Hill, who created work for me when I had none; Penny Freeman and Peter Hudson who lent me their cottage one blissful summer; and Nicky, Eve, Lene, Niall, Rachinta, Holly and Séamus, in whose box room I wrote eighty thousand words.

I wish I could give individual thanks to every historian I read during my research. If I lived and breathed the eighteenth century, it was only because you made it possible: your work gave me treasures every day, rewarded my enquiry and encouraged my empathy. However, I must particularly thank Dr Margaret R Hunt who took time to answer my pretty rookie questions, and Fiona Sinclair, who unfailingly filled me with knowledge, enthusiasm, and cake.

Thank you Karolina Sutton, a dauntless agent and wonderful companion on this adventure; and my editor Liz Foley for her patience, insight, and rock-solid support. I could not have chosen better in either case: thank you, thank you, for always seeing the book I wanted this to be.

If my parents had not made me a reader, I'd be no sort of writer at all. I must furthermore thank my mother for instilling in me these unorthodox tastes, and my father for making me proud to be a smart girl. Mandy Lee Jandrell always took me seriously as a maker, which meant the world. Thank you Oscar for every now and then – entirely unbidden – assuring me I was a good writer. You are a good brother. Agnes, my love: books will take you everywhere.

Thank you to Jamie for all the times my writing came before our relationship. If you thought that was the wrong order, you never let on. I can't tell you how proud I am to have made such a match: my heart is full.

Finally, to Simon and Maddi. They had faith in me before I had any in myself, and I am delighted to dedicate this novel to them.

A NOTE ON THE TYPE

This book is set in Caslon, a typeface named after William Caslon (1692–1766). The first of a famous English family of type designers and founders, he was originally an apprentice to an engraver of gun-locks and gun barrels in London. In 1716 he opened his own shop, for silver chasing and making bookbinders' stamps. The printers John Watts and William Bowyer, admirers of his skill in cutting ornaments and letters, advanced him money to equip himself for typefounding, which he began in 1720. The fonts he cut in 1722 for Bowyer's sumptuous folio edition of John Selden, published in 1726, excited great interest. A specimen sheet of typefaces, issued in 1734, established Caslon's superiority to all other letter cutters of the time, English or Dutch, and soon his types, or types modelled on his style, were being used by most English printers, supplanting the Dutch types that had formerly prevailed. Caslon was a reversion to earlier type styles. Its characteristics are remarkable regularity and symmetry, and beauty in the shape and proportion of the letters; its general effect is clear and open but not weak or delicate. For uniformity, clearness and readability it has perhaps never been sur-passed. After Caslon's death his eldest son, also named William (1720–1778), carried on the business successfully. A period of neglect followed which lasted almost fifty years. In 1843 Caslon type was revived by the firm Caslon for William Pickering and has since been one of the most widely used of all type designs in English and American printing.